HEIRS OF ASH · BOOK 1

VOYAGE OF THE MOURNING DAWN

RICH WULF

VOYAGE OF THE MOURNING DAWN
The Heirs of Ash

©2006 Wizards of the Coast, Inc.

All characters in this book are fictitious. Any resemblance to actual persons, living or dead, is purely coincidental.

This book is protected under the copyright laws of the United States of America. Any reproduction or unauthorized use of the material or artwork contained herein is prohibited without the express written permission of Wizards of the Coast, Inc.

Published by Wizards of the Coast, Inc. Eberron, Wizards of the Coast, and their respective logos are trademarks of Wizards of the Coast, Inc., in the U.S.A. and other countries.

Printed in the U.S.A.

The sale of this book without its cover has not been authorized by the publisher. If you purchased this book without a cover, you should be aware that neither the author nor the publisher has received payment for this "stripped book."

Cover art by Thomas Thiemeyer
Map by Rob Lazzaretti
First Printing: June 2006
Library of Congress Catalog Card Number: 2005935538

9 8 7 6 5 4 3 2 1

ISBN-10: 0-7869-4006-9
ISBN-13: 978-0-7869-4006-6
620-95537740-001-EN

U.S., CANADA,	EUROPEAN HEADQUARTERS
ASIA, PACIFIC, & LATIN AMERICA	Hasbro UK Ltd
Wizards of the Coast, Inc.	Caswell Way
P.O. Box 707	Newport, Gwent NP9 0YH
Renton, WA 98057-0707	GREAT BRITAIN
+1-800-324-6496	Save this address for your records.

Visit our web site at www.wizards.com

To win a battle, a man must be prepared to sacrifice his life. To win peace, a man must be prepared to sacrifice much more.
—Ashrem d'Cannith

Ashrem d'Cannith was one of the most brilliant minds of his generation, a man whose inventions went unsurpassed. But at the height of the War, he forsook the ways of violence and vowed to bring an end to the decades of conflict. Such was the purpose of his greatest invention, his Legacy.

But on the Day of Mourning, when the nation of Cyre died in the greatest cataclysm the world had ever seen, Ashrem d'Cannith disappeared, his invention lost.

Until now . . .

Seren, a young thief trying to stay alive in the streets of Wroat, has stumbled upon a clue that may lead to Ashrem's Legacy. What begins as a routine burglary has the authorities out to arrest her, ruthless spies out to kill her, and one of the heirs of Ashrem trying to save her.

Seren just wants to stay alive, but to do so she will have to find Ashrem's Legacy before her pursuers do. For if she loses his game, all of Eberron may be plunged into another century of war.

THE HEIRS OF ASH
BY RICH WULF

Voyage of the Mouring Dawn

Flight of the Dying Sun
(2007)

Rise of the Seventh Moon
(2007)

Dedication

This one goes out to Shawn,
a good friend and perhaps the finest human being
I have ever known.
Thanks for everything.

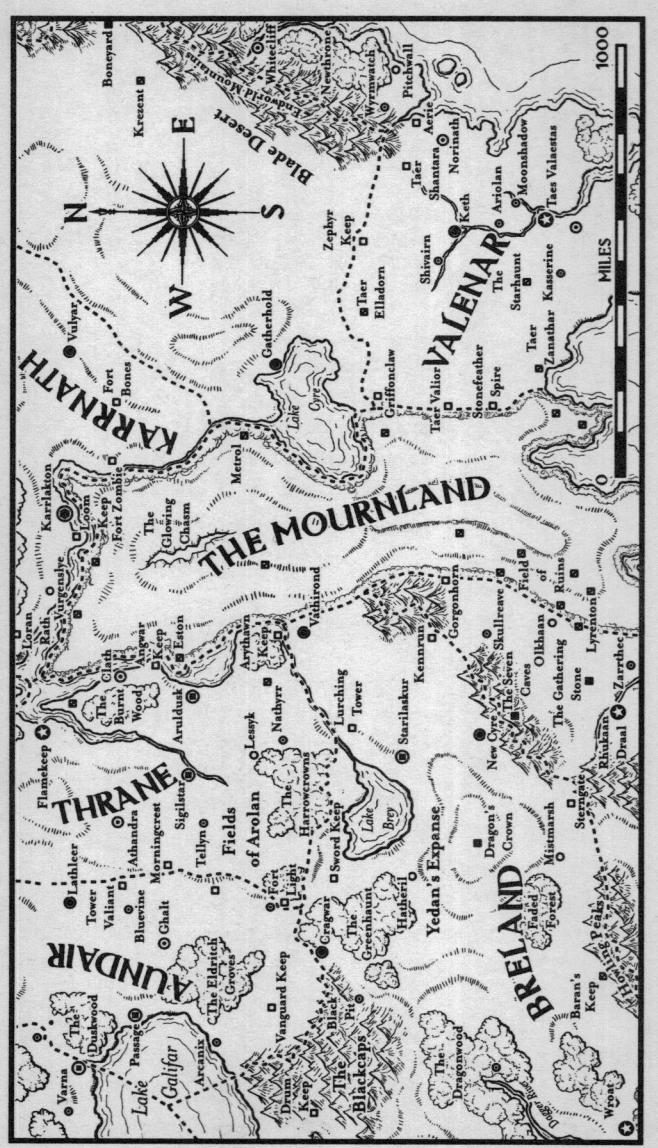

Prologue

The final days of the Last War, in the City of Wroat

It was a thing of beauty.

Tristam Xain carefully held the small glass sphere between two fingers and stared into its depths. Within the sphere floated a tiny model of a silver airship, a sleek vehicle surrounded by a metal ring. Tristam tapped the side of the glass with one finger and spoke the ship's name.

"Kenshi Zhann," he whispered.

Small particles of shimmering blue snow began to swirl within the sphere. The metal ring ignited a brilliant purple, like the pure elemental fire that surrounded a true airship. The overall image resembled a ship flying through a winter storm, a tiny replica of the same ship where Tristam dwelled. The light from the sphere suffused the smoky air in Tristam's improvised laboratory, casting the small cabin in a soft blue glow.

"Remarkable," Omax said. The warforged stood at the door of Tristam's tiny cabin. The enormous metal warrior looked down at the fragile trinket. His pale blue eyes shone in their adamantine mask, illuminated by the same magic that fluttered through the sphere.

"A gift for my teacher," Tristam said. "Do you think he'll like it, Omax?"

"A teacher can receive no greater gift than evidence of his

student's brilliance," Omax said. "I think Ash will be pleased."

"Do you think it will be enough to make him reconsider?" Tristam asked, looking at his friend.

"Perhaps," Omax said. "A simple reminder that magic can still be used to make things of beauty might grant him some peace of mind."

"I hope so," Tristam said, sounding unconvinced. The young artificer tapped the glass again. The whirling snow faded away, and the light died. "He's been in a dark mood."

Tristam tucked the sphere into his pocket and rose to leave. He stopped short, catching sight of his own face in the mirror that hung beside the door. He smoothed a hand through his unkempt hair, removed his thin spectacles, and wiped most of the soot and grime from his face with a handkerchief. His chin was rough and unshaven, but there wasn't much he could do for that on such short notice.

"Do I look presentable?" he asked.

"As presentable as anyone who knows you should expect," Omax said, patting some soot off of his friend's lapel.

Tristam shot the warforged an irritated look, but Omax had directed his attention toward a flask on the low table. Straightening his jacket, Tristam stepped out of the cabin and made his way to the upper deck, ignoring the warforged's chuckle as he departed.

Kenshi Zhann was a grand ship. In the Aereneal language her name meant *"Seventh Moon,"* though there was little about her construction or performance that could inspire regret in her creators. Tristam was still young, but he had seen a great deal of the world from the deck of this ship. He had never seen another vessel to match her, though Ashrem's other two airships were close. He was proud to serve aboard such a vessel, and proud to study at the foot of her master even if said master had been distant and moody in recent months.

VOYAGE OF THE MOURNING DAWN

Not that Ashrem d'Cannith's depression was unexpected or surprising. The old artificer had committed himself to an impossible task. Peace. He had sworn to end the war that had consumed the Five Nations for the last century. Every three months his three crews would rendezvous to share their progress, as they did now. Meeting with friends and colleagues generally improved old Ashrem's mood, even if they had little to report.

Tristam hoped for the best.

Omax fell into step beside Tristam as he made his way through the ship. The massive warforged made surprisingly little noise for a being constructed of dense metal and wood. Tristam glanced back to find Omax scanning the halls as they walked. He smiled.

"I think we're safe, Omax," Tristam said with a chuckle.

Omax looked forward quickly. Though his metal face lacked expression, he seemed to radiate embarrassment. "Old habits," he said. "To realize that I have no enemies has been a difficult adjustment."

"The war isn't over yet," Tristam answered. "You may get your chance for more excitement."

"I do not know if I want that," Omax said. "Having sampled peace, I prefer it."

"You sound like Ashrem," Tristam said.

"I take that as a compliment," Omax said. "Ashrem is a wise man."

Footsteps approached from the stairs above. A familiar pot-bellied man in a dark silken suit of exquisite cut strode down toward them. This was Dalan d'Cannith, Ashrem's nephew, local guildmaster of House Cannith. *Moon* had put in at Wroat so that Ashrem might visit Dalan during the rendezvous. Dalan's expression was bored and mildly annoyed, though it softened into a pleased smile when he recognized Tristam.

Tristam gave a small wave, hoping to move past Dalan and find his master.

"Ah, the promising young student and his bodyguard," Dalan said, upsetting Tristam's expectations. He shook Tristam's hand warmly and then nodded at Omax. "It has been some time, Tristam. How have the two of you been?"

"Fine," Tristam said. "You look well, Dalan."

"I am well, my boy. Business is growing. I was hoping that I might convince Uncle Ash to take on a few side contracts, but he insists on discussing it with his fellows first. I don't expect much. He's as stubborn as he has always been."

"You know Ashrem doesn't make weapons anymore, Dalan," Tristam said.

"Oh, I am well aware. I respect that." Dalan nodded, setting his jowls in motion. "I would not expect him to set aside the ethics he holds so strongly, even if I do not agree with them. These contracts were of a neutral nature. Enchantments to aid in the preservation of rations and medicine for Aundairian troops. Aiding the war effort without harming anyone directly. You understand. Even so, he was reluctant and has reserved his decision until he can discuss the matter with his associates. The priest seems to want to help, but I fear he will be unable to convince my uncle otherwise. Ash is a difficult man to sway once his mind is set. By the look he gave me, I think I picked a poor time to negotiate." Dalan's expression became sad, wistful.

"He's been occupied," Tristam said.

"And with the training of his apprentice, I hope?" Dalan said. "I expect great things of you, Tristam. I mentioned the light-emitting wands you crafted in my report to Baron Zorlan just last week. They've been of extraordinary utility to our miners, providing cheap magical illumination without the danger of a lantern. Exquisite craftsmanship, as well."

"You really thought so?" Tristam said, awed by the praise.

"Indubitably," Dalan said. "I am surprised Ashrem has not sponsored you for guild membership yet."

"You and I both," Tristam said, smiling weakly. "That's what I had hoped to talk to him about, actually, since there's a guild house here in Wroat and all."

"Ah." Dalan smiled. "Then let me take no more of your time. When Ash puts your name on the list, you can trust that your membership won't be delayed for long. I shall expedite the process personally." Dalan winked and chuckled.

"Thank you, Master Dalan," Tristam said, "but I wouldn't want to be put ahead of someone more deserving."

"False modesty!" Dalan retorted, walking past them as he made his way toward the galley. "My uncle is a genius. Who could be more deserving than his heir?"

Tristam looked up at Omax with a grin. The warforged nodded in encouragement, and they moved on. The ship was mostly abandoned. Most of the crew had taken advantage of the moment and scattered to the city's taverns. Tristam stepped into the large chamber at the heart of the ship. The walls were lined with brass runes and shimmering crystals. They shone and hummed, though they were mostly decoration with no true purpose. Tristam's eyes were on the column of dull black metal that stood in the center of the room. His fingers brushed its surface, sensing the magic that pulsed within. This was the ship's heart, the chamber that housed the crystals that bound the *Kenshi Zhann*'s elemental to this reality. It was a wonder of artifice, the living heart of the ship. No matter how many times Tristam saw it, he could not help but be awed by its power and simplicity.

Beyond the core, the floor opened on a large pane of thick glass. This normally offered a breathtaking view of the open sky. It currently displayed the busy street below, darkened by the airship's shadow. At the far end of the chamber, the hatch to

Ashrem's cabin was closed. Tristam looked around for a place to sit and wait when a shout from within the room drew his attention. Looking at Omax in concern, Tristam moved closer to listen.

"I can scarcely believe this hypocrisy, Ash," snapped a harsh voice. Tristam recognized the speaker as Brother Llaine Grove. Llaine was an old friend of his teacher, a priest of Boldrei who had served with Ashrem in their youth. "Many of those soldiers are near starvation. In the last five years, infection and disease have claimed more Aundairian lives than Cyre and Breland's forces combined. You would do nothing to stop this?"

"Consider what you are saying before casting the label of hypocrite, Llaine," Ashrem said in his cool, even voice. "Aundair's troops suffer because their leadership is too aggressive. Do you think any aid we offer would lessen their burden? The powers that command them would only push harder. We may save a few innocents, but countless more would suffer. Such misguided efforts only pollute our greater work."

"Greater work?" Llaine scoffed. "I go along with your plans only because no more sensible strategy has been presented. Your work is a dream, Ash. This is a reality. The war will continue no matter what we do, but perhaps we can save these soldiers' lives."

"Are you certain that your loyalties have not clouded?" Ashrem asked. "You are Aundairian. Perhaps patriotism has narrowed your vision?"

"I serve Boldrei first," Llaine said. "She values mercy foremost, and I cannot bear to hear of such suffering, countrymen or not. How can I look an Aundairian mother in her eyes and admit I allowed her son to starve or succumb to disease when it was within my power to aid him? Such an act is unconscionable."

"But necessary," said Kiris Overwood, Ashrem's consort and closest advisor. "Our artificers and wizards work toward a nobler goal, Llaine."

"Not all of them," the priest said. "This is a simple enough task. I am certain Tristam Xain could handle such a task quite admirably by himself, leaving the rest of us free to continue our work."

Tristam was impressed. Llaine was a harsh man, with few kind words for anyone. He hadn't thought the priest respected him at all. Omax gently clapped his friend on the shoulder.

"Tristam is still a child," answered the husky voice of Norra Cais. Of all his master's apprentices, Tristam knew the least about her. She was a prodigy, a graduate of Morgrave University who had only recently joined Ashrem's alliance. "He may possess the skills necessary, but he has neither the wisdom nor responsibility to understand the full import of such a task."

"Child?" Tristam whispered to Omax. "She's a year older than me."

The warforged shrugged.

"Norra is correct," Ashrem said. "Tristam was not ready to aid us in our work on the Legacy, and he is not ready for this. His progress has not been quite as impressive as you may believe, Llaine. On a relative scale, he is a mere novice."

Tristam's heart sank. He slumped against the wall, feeling as if someone had cut the cords that held him upright. Ashrem had expressed no disapproval, at least not to him. If he had been progressing so poorly, why did his master keep him here? Pity?

"Tristam is your student, Dalan," Llaine said. "I will respect your judgment. Regardless, there is power and talent enough at this table that we could easily fulfill Dalan's contract, help those soldiers, and use the money Dalan pays us to further our research on the Legacy."

"I will not use the spoils of war to purchase peace," Ashrem said. "Such deeds would corrupt everything we have done and hope to do."

The sound of approaching boots snapped Tristam back to

himself. He rose and moved away from the hatch, attempting to appear nonchalant as he loitered near the viewing window. Omax watched him impassively, standing near the ship's core.

A tall, thin man dressed in deep red entered the chamber. His blond hair was tied back in a loose tail. He favored Tristam with a quirky grin. This was Orren Thardis, captain of the *Albena Tors*, sister ship to this one.

"Evening, Captain," Tristam said, nodding to the man.

"Hello, Tristam," Orren said with a broad grin. "Omax. Are they still at it in there?"

"I suppose," Tristam said.

"Suppose?" Orren said, obviously feigning surprise. "You aren't taking the chance to eavesdrop? I would."

Tristam laughed despite himself. It was hard to take a man like Orren Thardis seriously. Orren never took anything seriously. Maybe that was why, of Ashrem's colleagues, he was among the easiest to get along with.

"You're late for the meeting again, Captain," Tristam said.

"Not late enough," Orren said, looking at the hatch in distaste. "I was hoping to speak to old Ash without all those other busybodies poking in."

Tristam nodded. "I'm waiting for him as well."

"Waiting is a fine way to waste your life, Tristam," Orren said, stepping to the glass floor and looking down at the dimly lit street. "Opportunity won't wait for you. Don't bother to wait for it."

"I think opportunity has already passed me, Captain," Tristam said.

Orren shrugged. "Then find another," he said.

Tristam thought on it a moment. Preservative reagents for rations and medicine weren't difficult to make. If Ashrem turned down Dalan's contract, he would need someone else to fulfill it. Tristam could do it easily. Ashrem would be enraged if he knew that Tristam had defied him, but he wouldn't have to know. Dalan was the sort who would keep such a favor a secret, and even sponsor Tristam for membership himself if Ashrem continued to deny him.

And if Ashrem found out, did it really matter? Was losing the respect of a master who didn't appreciate him such a bad thing?

"Thank you, Captain," Tristam said to Orren. "That's good advice,"

"Don't mention it," Orren said.

Tristam and Omax walked back to the stairs, making their way toward the galley. In Tristam's pocket, the tiny glass sphere and its miniature airship were forgotten.

CHAPTER ONE

Four Years Later

As far as Seren Morisse was concerned, Wroat wasn't the sort of place people lived on purpose. It was just where you ended up. There you were, living a normal life, minding your own business, and one day you found yourself in Wroat. Didn't matter if you were rich or poor, Wroat just sort of snuck up on you. You came here thinking it might be a good idea to visit for a time, maybe make money or contacts before moving on to somewhere better, but the city found a way of sinking its hooks into you. Wroat made you need it. It made it easier to stay than to leave, and every day you stayed, the city got a little less pretty. The flaws became a little more apparent. The stink became a little more cloying. The people showed you who they really were, and by then it was too late.

Wroat became a part of you, and you were a part of Wroat.

The King of Breland lived in Wroat. As Seren hauled herself onto the rough stone ledge, she looked at the towering spires of the palace and wondered if the King ever felt the same way. He probably did, maybe even more so than anybody. After all, who had less say in his own future than a king? Maybe she wasn't that different from old Boranel. Let him enjoy his prison of silk, jewels, and fine food. At least Seren had her freedom . . . precariously huddled on a loosely tiled ledge on the second floor of the Cannith guild house with rain pouring down around her.

Seren sighed deeply.

No, on second thought, she would most certainly trade him.

Seren peered over one shoulder, around the edge of the window. Within, she saw a richly appointed study, illuminated by a roaring fireplace and a single lamp. A large wooden desk stood near the window, buried under heaps of unfurled scrolls and books, left lying open and stacked in heaps. The walls were lined with shelves stuffed with even more volumes. The number of books was somewhat surprising considering the inhabitant's reputation; he didn't seem the scholarly type. A few plates of half-eaten food and glass tumblers, some still half-filled with wine, sat heaped on the desk and even scattered on the floor. Small models of airships, lightning rail engines, and even the adamantine faceplate of a warforged decorated the walls and shelves in a random, haphazard manner. The decorations were covered with dust, but the books were clean and well maintained.

Seren knew this house had plenty of servants—she had watched them enter and leave the house for the past four days to learn their routine—but they obviously had not touched this room in some time. Perhaps the things kept here were too valuable to trust in the presence of servants. If so, this was exactly what she was looking for. If not, then this was as good a place as any to start. Seren reached for the window, but she drew back as the door within opened. She huddled back against a nearby gargoyle, wrapping her arms around her knees to stay warm in the chilling rain. She tried once again to console herself with the fact that she was so much better off than King Boranel.

How did it happen? How did she end up here? Good question. Seren's answer was easy. Stupidity. Her father had been a soldier. The end of the War had been a good thing for a great many families—but not for Seren's. Other fathers returned to joyous reunions with loving families. Seren's family received only a black envelope delivered by an apologetic young messenger in a travel-stained uniform. Seren remembered her mother dropping the envelope and bursting into tears. She remembered how the messenger hurried away—he had many more messages to deliver that day.

The army had provided a small stipend to support the families of veterans who had died in the war—but it wasn't much, just enough to get a family back on its feet or support a single widow. Seren's mother never complained, but with each day that passed the worried lines around her eyes grew a little deeper. Finally, one night, Seren decided to set out and find her own fate. Her mother would miss her, that was certain, but she knew if she stopped to say good-bye she would lose her nerve, and the two of them would starve together.

In any case, running off to the city seemed a romantic enough notion. How could she fail?

Oh, she had heard all the stories, all the warnings. Her mother had always told her how it was dangerous for a young girl to find a life on her own. Her father, when he was home, always warned her how runaways ended up doing the most terrible things to survive. It wasn't that she didn't listen or didn't believe them. Quite the opposite, she believed that sort of fate was exactly what could befall a foolish person, and she was not a foolish person. She ran away from Ringbriar to find a dazzling future somewhere, maybe as an artist or a diplomat. The fact that she had no talents in either art or politics was irrelevant. Those kinds of things weren't hard. It was all a matter of finding the right opportunity.

A tile slid under Seren's feet and she wobbled dangerously. Her hand squished something unpleasant as she clutched the edge of the gutter. She grimaced but didn't risk letting go. She watched the tile spiral downward, wincing as she waited for the shattering report on the street below. The sky flashed overhead, and a riotous peal of thunder filled the night. Seren finally breathed. No one would have heard the falling tile. She whispered a brief prayer of thanks to Kol Korran and, while she was praying, added a polite request that whichever member of the Host was in charge of the lightning this evening, please keep it in the sky until she was safely off this ledge.

In hindsight, she realized she'd been every bit as foolish as the girls in those stories. Seren was young and pretty, if in a tomboyish sort of way. She soon found quite a number of gentlemen (and one rather curious lady) with many helpful suggestions as to how she could earn her keep, but the prospect of earning a living on her back was not very appealing.

It wasn't until a particularly fat and odious fish merchant propositioned her at the Steaming Ferret that Seren learned her true calling. Seren enjoyed several drinks with the man, only sipping from her own cup as he threw back mug after mug. She entertained his suggestions with vaguely noncommittal flirtation and then excused herself to use the lavatory. While the drunken merchant sat heaped on his stool, waiting for her to return, Seren snuck out the back door with his belt pouch tucked in her skirt.

She was no artist or diplomat, but she had proven to be quite a talented thief.

Seren peered carefully through the window again. She now saw the back of a short, thick-bodied man dressed in a rich lavender suit and a peaked green cap. She couldn't see his face but recognized his build and clothing as that of the house's owner. The man sat at his desk, leaning back in his worn leather chair, holding a small frosted cake in one hand and chewing intently as he balanced a thick book upon his knee. Thunder cracked overhead again, and the rain came down even harder. Seren's long black hair was now plastered to her face and down her back. She scowled through the window, trying to compel the man to finish his reading and leave through sheer force of will. Not surprisingly, it didn't work. Seren settled back against the gargoyle, trying to find some shelter or warmth against its bulk. The statue stared blankly down at the street, showing no sympathy whatsoever.

Waiting was the most difficult part of being a thief, by far. The threat of punishment didn't frighten her. The excitement of a job well done balanced that. The danger made the job worthwhile. But this? She muffled a sneeze with one hand, her damp hair slapping forward and covering her face. Waiting was miserable. Where was Jamus? He was late, and she was going to kill him—if she didn't slide off the ledge or perish of pneumonia. Rain streamed down her back and shoulders. Seren wished that she had dressed a bit more warmly. Her short cotton breeches and leather vest offered mobility for climbing but little protection from the elements. The weather had been fair when she started climbing. It wasn't until halfway up the building that the clouds rolled in and the rain started. She should have climbed back down and put off the job until tomorrow, but Seren was a stubborn sort of person.

Carefully holding the gutter with one hand and the gargoyle's stone claw with the other, she leaned out and peered down. She couldn't give up, even if she wanted to. The climb back down would be far too dangerous in the rain. The only way out of here was through the house, and her distraction was taking an inordinate amount of time to arrive.

Almost on cue, a heavy banging sounded in the street below. Seren sat back against the wall again, peering carefully in the window to see the inhabitant's reaction. The fat man merely sat in his chair, chewing on his cake and reading his book, ignoring the commotion.

More banging followed, this time accompanied with a quavering voice calling out, "Hello? Master d'Cannith? Is anyone there?"

The man inside set his cake down and sighed. He drummed his fingers on the desk, as if waiting for his visitor to go away.

Another round of heavy banging. "Master d'Cannith, my business is most urgent! If you are occupied, I understand, and shall take my business to Master d'Phiarlan. I had hoped to offer your guild this honor first, but such is life!"

Dalan closed his book with a snap, tossed it onto a nearby couch, and stalked out the study door. After several moments, she heard the iron squeal of old hinges below.

"What?" snapped a terse voice below.

"Ah, greetings and good evening to you, Master d'Cannith."

She heard the reply, though she could not see either speaker beneath the sloping overhang.

"I bring you greetings on behalf of the Lost Children of Wroat. Surely being a member of a household whose humanitarian actions during the Last War are so renowned, you would be eager to aid this prestigious charity? I ask only whatever you can spare to help us purchase food, medicine, perhaps even new toys to brighten what would otherwise be a bleak and hopeless . . ."

Seren could not help a smile. Jamus hadn't shared the full details of how he intended to distract their target, but she had trusted the old thief to be creative. She unhooked the metal sphere from her belt, cracking it open to reveal the glowing stone within. Such magic was expensive, but light without a spark was a useful investment in her line of work. She frowned as she studied the window, finding no lock. Holding the stone up to the window, she began tracing the edges of the sill with one finger.

"Orphans?" the other voice said below. "You roused me from my leisure to beg for charity?"

"Not just any charity, Master d'Cannith, the Lost Children of Wroat, a proud and well respected—"

The sound of a slamming door connecting with the toe of a boot interrupted his monologue.

"Ahem. A proud and respected charity with, as I am sure one of your impressive social connections is aware, a sterling reputation for—"

"I have never heard of you and I can assure you I give quite generously to several *legitimate* charities. Now get your foot out of my door."

"I can understand your reluctance, Master d'Cannith, for there are many opportunistic souls who seek to twist the generosity of those touched by the War," Jamus said, accompanied by the rhythmic sound of a door repeatedly hitting a foot. "I assure you, however, that we are legitimate. Look only to these beautiful glass marbles, painted by the children—"

"Leave before I call the Watch."

"Please, Master, look at these marbles," Jamus continued, "each hand-painted in exquisite detail by the very innocents whom your money will support."

"I am not interested. Return when it is daylight and take up your begging with my servants if you must."

"But please, good master, just examine one and see the simple beauty—"

A wracking cough resounded from below, followed by the sound of a bag of glass marbles striking a wooden floor and scattering its contents.

"Oh, drat," Jamus said.

This was followed by the other voice swearing urgently in several languages.

"I apologize, good master. This chill rain has left me with trembling hands."

"Just pick them up and go!"

VOYAGE OF THE MOURNING DAWN

There, Seren found what she sought. What appeared to be a flaw in the grain was actually a mark, painted in dark brown ink, in the upper corner of the window. It formed a figure eight pattern between the sill and the wood. She didn't recognize the rune. Perhaps it simply held the window sealed unless the proper word was spoken. Perhaps it would raise an alarm, or worse, explode and hurl Seren into the street. The Canniths were artificers and magewrights, and though the man who lived here reputedly possessed no magical training, it was no surprise to find his home was protected. Seren rose from her crouch as much as she dared, studying the ward further.

In a city as large as Wroat, magic was fairly common. The city drew wizards as surely as it drew everyone else. Seren avoided stealing from wizards or magewrights, not out of any fear of magic but simply because they were more trouble than they were worth. Jamus taught her that magic was no different from any other form of power—worthy of respect, but no more frightening than the flawed men and women who used it. Even if you couldn't learn to use magic, you could learn to deal with it. Seren couldn't build a lock, but she could pick one with a bent wire. Magic was the same. There was always an answer.

Seren drew a small tin and brush from her belt pouch. Shielding the tin from the rain, she opened its lid and wrinkled her nose at the harsh smell of its contents. Carefully, she brushed the thick, clear paste over one of the glass panes, coating it entirely, then closed the tin and put it back in her pouch. She drew out several strips of thick felt and pressed them against the glass, then bound another around her right hand. Taking a deep breath, she punched the glass as hard as she could where she had glued the felt over its surface. She heard only a muffled crack in reply. She peeled the felt away in a single piece, removing the broken pane in one neat sheet, which she carefully folded and stuffed into the gargoyle's open beak.

Next she produced a small mirror with a sharp pin on one side and a long stick of charcoal. Careful to avoid the bits broken glass that clung to the window's frame, she reached through and pinned the mirror to the sill inside, facing her. She adjusted it until she could see the rune pattern on the inside and then carefully began work on the rune with her charcoal. It was the same sort of pigment most mages used to complete such wards, and if she was careful enough she could isolate the pattern on each side and disable the ward, at least for a short time. Finishing the pattern on the inside, she paused only long enough to sharpen her charcoal on a shard of broken glass, then do the same on the exterior. Tucking the tools back in her pouch, she looked at her work cautiously. There was only one real way to tell if it worked. She closed her eyes, took a deep breath, and opened the window with a quick heave.

Seren opened her eyes to discover, quite happily, that the window was open, there was no alarm, and she was still alive. She could still hear voices downstairs, one swearing in a rage and the other apologizing obsequiously as he continued to clumsily lose his marbles. With no sign that she had been discovered, Seren plucked up her mirror, nimbly hopped into the study, and closed the window behind her.

The thick smell of incense and woodsmoke hung heavily in the air, barely covering the more cloying scent of old sweat. This was clearly one man's private refuge, and she would be glad to be out of it. She looked down with a start as something wet touched her shin. A squat, shaggy black hound, its fur shot through with gray, looked up at her mournfully. Its tail thumped the side of the desk when she looked at it.

"Some watchdog you are," she whispered.

The old dog's ears perked up. It glanced up at the desk, then back at her. A low whine began to rise in the dog's chest, and it opened its mouth as if to bark. Seren quickly snatched Dalan's half-finished cake from the desk and tossed it to the dog. The animal caught the cake in midair and flopped on the floor, consuming the sweet bribe contentedly.

Seren stepped past the dog, eager to find what she sought and leave before the dog reconsidered its treachery. She drew a scrap of paper from her pocket and glanced at the illustration as she scanned the shelves. The paper bore an illustration of a small journal with a black cover, emblazoned with the House Cannith gorgon crest above the image of an albatross in flight. Seren scowled in irritation as she looked at the countless books that lined the shelves. The house's owner had a reputation for being indolent and lazy; he was not known as a scholar. She had thought one book would be easy to find in his house. Now she realized she might search all night and never find the right one. She tested the nearest bookcase, hoping against hope that they were the false vanity books that many nobility favored. They were genuine enough, unfortunately, and focused on a variety of eclectic subjects from magic to history to music and even exotic cooking. All looked well read. She would never find the book she wanted before the guildmaster returned to find his broken window, missing cake, and the small river of rainwater she'd leaked on his floor.

As she stepped back to give the bookcases a better look, Seren stumbled over a book discarded on the floor. She glanced down to see the gorgon and albatross looking back at her impassively. Seren blinked in disbelief. She looked back at the dog. It only watched her with soulful black eyes, nose buried between furry paws, mourning the untimely demise of the cake. Rather than dwell upon her uncanny luck, Seren snatched the book and tucked it into the sack at her belt.

The study door no doubt bore wards like the window, but fortunately it had been left open. Seren hurried out and down the stairs, tiptoeing with a silent grace. To her right, she could see the two men. Jamus stood near the door, playing the part of the lost and confused old man as he apologized repeatedly, stroking his long white beard with one hand. The guildmaster, apparently tired of the crazed beggar's floundering, had snatched the marble bag and was now picking up the marbles himself.

"Here, take the accursed things, and do not drop them again or you shall return to the orphans without them."

"Are you certain you found them all?" Jamus asked, blinking foolishly. "I think I saw one roll under the clock in the corner . . ."

"Then here!" The man snapped. He rummaged in his pocket and held out a handful of silver. "To pay for your lost marbles."

Jamus opened his mouth to demur again, but his sharp eyes focused squarely upon Seren in the shadows of the stair. He gave a slight nod and reached for the bag and coins, clasping the guildmaster's hands with both of his own in a gesture of exaggerated gratitude. Seren made her way to the back door and quietly unlocked the latch.

"I thank you, Master d'Cannith," Jamus said, bowing repeatedly as he clasped the man's hands. "The orphans thank you as well."

"Yes, the orphans," she heard the other man growl as she slipped out into the alley. "Give them my regards. Now go!"

Closing the door gently, Seren broke into a sprint. Darting between the puddles and strewn garbage of the alleys, she stopped at a particular abandoned house after several minutes of running. Looking back to make certain she wasn't followed, she pulled a loose board aside and stepped through the wall. The interior was lit by a single candle. An older gentleman dressed in a sleek black jacket and trousers reclined on a tattered couch. A long white beard lay discarded on the floor. He toyed with a pair of painted glass marbles, rolling them between his fingers idly.

"Did you find the book?" he asked, looking up at her with a faint grin.

She stared at Jamus. "How did you get here first?"

"I should ask why it took you so long," he said, though his smile took the barb off his words. He fell to a fit of coughing for several seconds and then looked up at her with a forced grin. "So. Find the book?"

Seren nodded, patting the bag at her hip. She picked up her cloak from where she had left it folded on the floor earlier in the evening and began using it as an improvised towel, drying herself as best she could.

"May I see it?" Jamus asked.

"After you tell me why you left me up on that ledge in the rain for so long."

"Because I didn't think you'd be foolish enough to keep climbing when the storm began," Jamus said. "I thought you would come back down and we'd try another day."

She shrugged. "Can't turn back once you start or you'll never finish," she said.

"Of course," he said. "I underestimated your stubbornness, as always. It is your second most endearing and maddening trait."

"Second?" she said. "What is the first?"

"Your infuriating willingness to speak your mind," he said. "You remind me a great deal of my daughter. I suppose before you give me the book I shall be subject to another lecture on my questionable wisdom of undertaking this mission."

Seren folded her arms across her chest and frowned. "I did the job, Jamus, but my opinion stands," she said. "I don't think it's smart to cross the dragonmarked houses. I don't care what the pay is. It's going to be trouble."

"Afraid of magic, Seren?" he asked. Jamus rose from his couch and walked toward her. "I thought I taught you better than that."

"You taught me to respect power," Seren said. "The Canniths are powerful. If they find out what we've done . . ."

"They simply won't care," Jamus said. He rested one hand on her shoulder, looking down at her with the expression of a parent soothing a frightened child. "Dalan d'Cannith has a checkered past. He may be a local guildmaster, but he is not particularly liked or respected among his family. His power is limited outside of Wroat. Our payment for this job will place us far beyond his grasp."

Seren's eyes widened. "We're leaving Wroat?" she asked, excited. "You never told me that."

Jamus nodded, though he glanced away as another fit of coughing shook his spare figure. "I didn't want to distract you before the job," he said. "Our employer guaranteed future opportunities beyond the city when she gave me our advance."

"There's an advance?" she asked with a small grin. Jamus hadn't mentioned that either. "Where's my share?"

The old thief smiled. "Right here," he said, tossing her the bag of marbles. She caught it in one hand and favored him with a sour look. "No worries, Seren, you'll be paid when we deliver. Only the most difficult part remains."

"The most difficult part?" she said, bewildered. "What can be more difficult than what we've just done?"

"Don't ask that question," Jamus said with a chuckle. "Never ask that question, lest it be answered sooner than you'd like."

"I'm serious, Jamus," she said. "What else is left? We already have the book. All we need to do is deliver it. Are you afraid the Watch will find us, or do you not trust our employer?"

"I *never* trust my employer," Jamus said. "Anyone who enters our line of work, as a client or a professional, is untrustworthy by definition."

"But we trust each other," she said. "Don't we?"

He leaned forward and kissed her forehead, then made his way toward the door. "Only because we both have something to gain," he said. "Ours is a relationship of mutual benefit, teacher and student. Trust is born from mutual benefit. We trust our employer because we are offered payment in return for our services . . . mutual benefit—but we do not trust foolishly."

"So what do we do if our employer decides there's greater benefit in not paying us?" she asked. "What then?"

"In this case such a betrayal would be foolish," Jamus answered. He pushed the loose board aside, studying the street to make certain no one was outside. "I have a reputation in this city. Were I to disappear, questions would be asked, and I have arranged for answers. I have written speaker posts addressed to certain allies, describing the details of our work here. If I do not arrive to cancel the deliveries, the Sivis messengers will whisper into their speaking stones and the truth will fly upon the winds of Khorvaire. Within hours, friends as far away as Fairhaven will know the truth."

"That doesn't make me feel much better," Seren said. "If we die, we're still dead, no matter who knows what happened."

"Then ignore the negative and focus on your goals, Seren, dear," he said, stepping out into the street. "Think about leaving this place far behind, and it will be. Until then, be safe. Stay out of sight. The town guards will be suspicious of anyone on the streets on a terrible night like tonight. I will meet you back at the house."

The old thief slid the board back into place behind him. She could hear his wet footsteps and quiet cough recede into the distance. Dalan d'Cannith would have summoned the Watch by now, searching for the thief and his beggar accomplice. It was safer to wait, to move separately.

Seren would have preferred Jamus carry the book, at least. It was his idea to steal it, after all. She took the book out of the sack and studied its cover. She recognized the Cannith crest; she had seen it in the city often enough. Beneath a small hammer and anvil design, the snarling metal bull's head of a gorgon glared up at her. The relatively indifferent albatross beneath it was not typically part of the crest. It must be some sort of personal seal. Seren opened the book and flipped through the pages cautiously. She told herself she was merely checking to make sure that the book hadn't been damaged by the rain. In reality she wanted to know what was so important about it. Diagrams covered the pages within, depicting airships, clockwork mechanisms, and other artifacts whose purpose Seren could not comprehend. The writing was in a strange, arcane cipher. It told her nothing, nothing that would explain why it was important enough to make enemies of House Cannith.

The Canniths were one of the twelve dragonmarked houses, powerful organizations ruled by individuals born marked by hereditary arcane symbols. Seren didn't really understand what the Prophecy was, nor did she really care. All she knew was that the Prophecy gave incredible powers to those marked by it. Each of the dragonmarked houses boasted magical abilities and had used those abilities to cultivate great wealth and political influence. Each house was as powerful as a country, the services they offered so valuable that their power transcended international boundaries.

House Cannith bore the Mark of Making, which granted the ability to repair what had been broken or to create new things. They were engineers, artificers, and weaponsmiths. Many of the most incredible inventions in all of Eberron—the lightning rails, the airships, and even the mysterious warforged soldiers—bore a Cannith artisan's seal. Many of the most ferocious battles in the Last War had been fought with Cannith weapons, and Breland was not the only nation that still owed them a great debt. If this book was as valuable as Jamus claimed and the Canniths realized who had stolen it from them . . . well, making two thieves in the slums of Wroat disappear wouldn't be such a difficult task for a house that commanded the loyalty of kings.

Seren pushed the book back into the sack and pushed such thoughts away with it. Her own words returned to her—can't turn back once you start or you'll never finish. There was no option now but to see the job through and try to make a profit. If this really got her out of Wroat, then maybe it was worth it.

But she hated waiting the most.

CHAPTER TWO

Seren slipped back into the streets, avoiding the main roads as best she could. She cursed the rain again as it instantly soaked her cloak and clung to her bare legs. No one was in the streets at this time of night, no crowd to fade into. Anyone outside at this time of night would look suspicious. Though she was a fairly talented thief, her face was not unknown to the City Watch. Recognition was inevitable, Jamus had said. Just as even the finest tailor sometimes stuck himself with a needle; all the finest thieves got caught. Even Seren had visited the city's prison.

All things considered, her brief stay in the dungeon had been comfortable. The cells weren't the dank, shadowed affairs she expected but were in fact surprisingly clean and dry. Her cellmate was a quiet old woman who kept to herself. Seren never even knew why she was there and hadn't wanted to pry. Warden Thomas was a polite and courteous young man. He had seemed a bit taken with Seren, so she flirted innocently to pass the time. The more she flirted back, the more the quality of her food improved. It would have been a rather pleasant stay overall if it hadn't been, well, prison.

After a few weeks as a guest of the King (as Jamus called it), Seren had been turned out on the streets. As large a city as Wroat was, its prisons were extremely crowded with all manner of serious criminals. There simply was no room for a minor offender like Seren, so it was not unusual to be set free after such a short time if you knew better than to make trouble for the guards. Yet forgiveness did not imply forgetfulness. The Wroat City Watch was annoyingly vigilant. They kept a list of known thieves, and hardly a week went by that she was not harassed on suspicion of one crime or another, usually a matter in which she had no involvement.

Ironically it was her innocence that had earned her something of a reputation with the city watchmen. Seren sometimes found it difficult to control her temper, and more than one guard had been on the receiving end of a scathing verbal assault when she knew she had a solid alibi. One such event had even led to her being thrown into the prisons again after making a particularly brutal comment about a high-ranking watchman's parentage. It had only been for a night, and it was nice to see Warden Thomas again, but Seren had tried to control her temper and avoid the Watch since then—especially on nights like tonight, when she actually *had* been up to no good and was still carrying the fruits of her illicit labor in a burlap sack on her hip.

The sound of heavy boots approached from around the corner. Seren fell into a crouch and ducked behind a rain barrel. She could hear the creak of armor and the metal clank of swords as they slapped against armored legs. A cold chill spread down her back; a stream of water spilled from a leak in the gutter directly onto her shoulders, soaking through her cloak and adding to her general misery. She grimaced and stayed where she was. She feared that if she shifted position the new sound of water striking cobblestones might alert the guards.

The footsteps drew closer, stopping near the barrels. Seren peered up to see the backs of two watchmen, standing uncomfortably close to her. They didn't seem interested in much besides stepping out of the rain, but she quieted her breathing and hunched lower anyway.

"Damn this weather," one of the guards grumbled. "First night I have patrol in a week and it rains like this. Can't believe they expect us to walk the streets on a night like this."

If the guards hated walking in it, Seren thought to herself, maybe they should try climbing in it. Preferably now, somewhere far away from here, so she could get out from under the leak and leave.

"Typical," the other watchman answered. "Someone up there doesn't like us I guess, Rolf."

Someone down here doesn't like you much either. Leave!

"Well it's not as if anything is even going on tonight, Shain," the watchman who apparently was named Rolf countered. "Nobody in their right mind would be out on a night like tonight."

Seren had no argument.

"Mmm-hm," came the other guard's agreement. She heard the dry hiss of a match striking stone, followed by the faint smell of burning herb.

"No thanks, trying to quit," Rolf said to some unspoken offer. "Wife can't stand washing the smoke smell out of my armor."

"You sure?" said the other. "Karrnathi cigars. They're the best."

"Aren't those expensive?"

"Host, yes," Officer Shain said. "This pack cost me a week's pay, but they're worth it. Finest smoke in Eberron."

"Doris would kill you if she knew you spent that kind of money on cigars."

"That's why I offered you one," Shain said. "So you don't tell her."

A long pause. Thunder cracked overhead, and the stream of rain on Seren's back came down a bit more forcefully. "Very well, then," Rolf said. "May as well enjoy ourselves and wait for this rain to die down."

Seren gritted her teeth and clutched her knees with both arms, trying to preserve what warmth she could. She suspected she had never hated two people as much in her entire life as she did these two watchmen. She shivered uncontrollably. She would have to risk moving out from under the leak and hope they were too stupid to notice. If she stayed here any longer they would hear her teeth chatter anyway. She crawled slowly, looking up at the guards as the water fell gently on the street. Seren scowled. Somehow it irritated her that they didn't even notice the sound after she'd suffered so much not to draw any attention. Shaking her head, she began to crawl deeper into the alley.

A sudden shudder passed through her and, despite her best efforts to control herself, she sneezed. Seren slapped herself in the face.

"Who goes there?" Rolf shouted, holding up his lantern and flooding the alley with light.

"Show yourself!" said Shain.

Seren peered back and tried her best to look innocent, which she found a somewhat difficult prospect crawling on her hands and knees in a garbage strewn alley at night during a thunderstorm. She held out her hands so that they could see she held no weapons and slowly rose, turning to face them. She made sure to keep her hood's shadows over her face but held her cloak open so they could see the rest of her. Watchmen, especially young watchmen, tended to be a bit more easily distracted when they saw she was a girl. Sure enough, Officer Shain stopped wrestling with his crossbow strap and left the weapon hanging at his belt.

"Who are you?" Rolf demanded. "Why are you hiding?"

"There's a simple explanation," Seren said, keeping a charming lilt in her voice despite her chattering teeth.

Rolf lowered his lantern a bit and looked at her warily. "What is it?"

Seren pretended to sneeze to buy time. She couldn't think of anything they'd be likely to believe, but at least she had stalled long enough to stand up and get a good look at them. Both guards were somewhat overweight and wore the cumbersome chain mail that was part of their typical uniform. They still hadn't seen her face. Seren doubled over in a fake sneezing fit, then heaved the rain barrel at their legs and ran off through the alleys.

"Get her!" Rolf cried, jumping back as the heavy barrel rolled past. The clang of a loud bell followed as he did everything he could to summon his fellow watchmen.

Seren wove and ducked as she ran, trying to present a small and random target. She didn't expect the guards to shoot their crossbows, but she wasn't willing to risk it. Lightning crashed overhead, throwing the alleys into a flash of daylight brilliance. In that moment of clarity she saw a mounted watchman in the intersection ahead, looking toward the clamor. Not willing to attempt outrunning a horse, Seren stopped abruptly and ran back to an unmarked door she had passed.

Well, that was what she intended to do, at least. In reality she tried to turn and found the rain slicked alley unwilling to cooperate. Her feet slipped out from under her and she skidded through the mud and garbage to stop near the horseman. She looked up at the point of a hastily drawn sword and tried to smile demurely. Given that she was flat on her back and covered with filth, the guard was unimpressed.

"Stop her!" Rolf cried, running up behind her.

"She's stopped herself, Officer Rolf," the horseman said.

Seren scowled and staggered to her feet. This time, the three watchmen surrounded her. Officer Shain had his crossbow drawn. Rolf still held his lantern and bell. He leaned heavily against a wall, struggling to catch his breath. Ironically, it was at that point that the storm faded into a drizzle, ending as quickly as it had begun.

"What's this all about?" the mounted guard asked, looking at Rolf curiously.

"She was acting suspicious, Sergeant Narem," Rolf said. "She rolled a barrel at us. Probably a thief."

"Search her," Narem commanded.

Well used to the ritual, Seren sighed and held her arms up, away from her body. At least in her current filthy state, perhaps the guard would enjoy this as little as she did. Officer Shain put his crossbow away and began to pat her down. Seren grimaced. The way he pressed against her, she realized the dirt wasn't doing a great deal to dissuade him.

"Can I at least have a cigar so I enjoy this too?" she asked.

"Quiet, you," Sergeant Narem said. "Shain, go easy or I'm telling Doris," he added in a gentler voice.

The other watchman looked embarrassed and mumbled an apology.

"Hello, what's this?" said a bright voice with an elegant Lhazaarite accent. "A little midnight justice? What drama unfolds in the weary, rain-soaked roadways of Wroat?"

The watchmen looked to the sound of the voice. Seren peered over her shoulder as well, though she kept her hands raised. A young man stepped out of the shadows of an awning, greeting them with a broad smile. He was dressed in a long blue coat and fine black cloak. His sandy brown hair was tied back by a think leather cord, and a thin pair of spectacles sat perched upon his nose. He wore a sword at his belt in the manner of a gentleman, though he kept his hand away from the hilt so as not to upset the guards.

"My, this is more dangerous than I first suspected," the man said, eyes widening as his gaze met Seren's. "Three watchmen band together to arrest a fifteen-year-old girl?"

"Nineteen," Seren said tersely.

"My apologies, my lady, but one day I think you will treasure such underestimations," the man said. He looked back to the guards. "But clearly this is even worse than I suspected. Four years more experience than I thought—all the more reason for caution. Are you certain you three can handle her? I am no citizen of your fair city, but I would be pleased to offer you my modest sword arm for the cause of justice, if deputies are required. I would be proud to participate in such a heroic confrontation."

"You're not funny," Rolf growled. "Move on, stranger."

"What's in this bag?" Officer Shain asked, tugging at the sack at her hip.

"Book," Seren said. She looked straight ahead and kept her voice and posture bored, hoping this would soon be over. She had no doubt that if they saw the seal on that book's cover, it certainly would be.

"A scholar!" the man interrupted again. "She is obviously a student of some local university. Is this how Wroat's watchmen encourage Breland's youth? No wonder this neighborhood is in such a sorry state."

Even Seren glanced back at that, fixing the stranger with a bewildered scowl. She hoped this odd person wasn't trying to pick a fight with the Watch. One man against three guards was bound to go badly for him, and she didn't want to be in the middle of that. The man noticed Seren looking at him. He winked. What was he doing?

"Go take your advice somewhere else, pirate, before we search you too," Narem said. "Chances are a Lhazaarite has something in his pockets that doesn't belong there."

"Your prejudice does not surprise me, though it saddens me," he said. "I am Tristam Xain, citizen of Zilargo and an honored guest in this city." He sighed. His shoulders slumped. "I am wounded."

"Keep it up and you will be," Narem said. He looked up at the horseman. "Rolf, detain this man."

Rolf drew his sword, moving purposefully toward the well-dressed stranger.

"Put your weapon on the ground and back away from it, please," Rolf said.

"Now this is just going too far," Tristam answered, removing his spectacles and tucking them into his jacket pocket. "I am a protected guest of the city with powerful friends. I have papers granting me immunity from such action as this. Omax, show them my papers."

The shadows behind Tristam moved. A bulk that Seren had previously thought to be a large stack of barrels rose and resolved itself into a monstrous figure. It was a foot taller than a man, with shining black wood and gleaming blue metal in place of flesh. Its face was a smooth metal plate, split only by an expressionless line for a mouth and two hollow eyes, glowing with an unnerving blue light. It wore only loose brown trousers and a soft woolen hat. It stepped out of the darkness with movement surprisingly lithe and graceful for a creature of its size. The watchmen each took a step back, and even Narem's horse whinnied nervously. Seren had seen creatures such as this before.

"Good evening, officers," Omax said, his cool voice echoing in its metallic chest. "Is there a problem?"

This was a warforged, one of the automatons created by House Cannith to fight in the Last War. Seren's annoyance was quickly replaced by fear and suspicion. She realized belatedly that the guards had not been looking for her, when by all rights Dalan d'Cannith should have roused the City Watch to investigate the theft. Perhaps he had not wanted the Watch to become involved. Perhaps he wanted to send his own agents to retrieve what Seren had stolen.

Now they were here.

Sergeant Narem climbed out of his saddle, drawing his sword and standing beside Rolf as they watched Tristam and Omax cautiously.

Seren watched the warforged with undisguised fear. She knew the dragonmarked houses could be ruthless, but she wondered if the Canniths were ruthless enough to kill three watchmen just to take back what she had stolen. She didn't intend to find out. She scampered into the horse's empty saddle. Rolf charged toward her, but she scattered Jamus's bag of marbles on the rain-slicked cobbles. The watchman squawked in comical surprise and fell forward on his teeth. Seren seized the horse's reins, kicked its flanks, and galloped off.

"Stop!" came the cry, followed by the sound of boots falling on cobblestones.

Seren ducked as low in the saddle as she could, hoping that the guards would be unwilling to loose arrows at their own horse. Rolf's bell clanged again. She saw lights flare in the windows along the road as the locals peered out to see what the trouble was, but she saw no more guards. She kept riding till the Watch, the Lhazaarite stranger, and the warforged were out of sight. Seren was not foolish enough to ride through Wroat on a stolen horse wearing City Watch colors, so she slowed just enough to leap out of the saddle and slap the animal's flanks. With a frenzied whinny it continued galloping without her. She darted into the nearest alley. In three years she had come to know the back streets of Wroat well. This was hardly the first time she had used this twisted network of alleys, tunnels, and abandoned buildings to escape pursuit.

Seren kept running for ten minutes before slowing to catch her breath. She stopped for a moment in a leatherworker's shack, using a rag left hanging on a post to wipe the grime from her face, arms, and legs. By all rights she should hurry back to rendezvous with Jamus, but she was tired, cold, and frustrated. She needed a moment to compose herself.

So Seren sat on a stool, took a cigar out of the box she had taken from Officer Shain's pocket during his energetic search, and enjoyed the finest smoke in all of Eberron.

CHAPTER
THREE

Seren waited an hour, just to make sure she wasn't followed, and then headed to the rendezvous point. As she made her way to her destination, the streets became softer beneath her feet. Manicured cobblestones gave way to bare ground, paved only by a random covering of occasional wooden planks. Even these did little to make the path more hospitable, as the rain had turned the streets into mud. The streets sucked at Seren's shoes until she finally tired of struggling and took them off with a sigh, slinging the muddy things over one shoulder by their laces.

The fishermen's district was crowded even at this late hour. It was always crowded. People moved quickly through the streets in tight groups, moving urgently toward whatever clandestine business had brought them here. Few spared Seren any more than a suspicious glance. She minded her own path and ignored them; they were content to do the same. She arrived at the meeting place soon enough.

The Friendly Buzzard was an abandoned inn. In the three years she had come here to train with Jamus Roland, it had never been anything but a ruin. Jamus lived here and sometimes met clients here to fence stolen goods. She wasn't entirely sure whether he owned the place or had simply taken up residence since no one else wanted it. A painted sign still hung above the doors, depicting a comical, grinning buzzard clutching a mug of ale and a loaf of bread in its talons. The wooden stairs squealed noisily as Seren climbed up to the door. The effect wasn't entirely accidental; Jamus had replaced several of the boards in this place to make it difficult for someone to approach unheard. She tiptoed as she walked inside, setting the sign overhead swinging with a gentle slap as she always did.

The interior of the inn was dimly lit. Seren knew the way and easily navigated the darkness to the stairwell in the back. On the second floor, a long hallway led to a series of what had once been private dining rooms. She continued to the end of the hall, the floor creaking beneath her feet, and opened the last door. Within was a small room featuring a table and three chairs. Only a single candle provided light. Jamus sat with his back to the far wall. His arms were folded tightly and his chin was tucked against his chest. He seemed to be dozing.

Seren frowned. He had been growing tired more often of late, sometimes even dozing off at important times like now. Much like his cough, his exhaustion was something he never spoke of. His silence on the matter was what worried her the most. Jamus Roland could be a manipulative cad and a demanding teacher, but he was all that passed for a friend in this large, uncaring city. Without him, where would she be? The old thief's body jerked as he was taken by a violent snore. Seren closed the door solidly behind her. Jamus glanced up in surprise, now wide awake.

"Seren," he said. He flushed with embarrassment. "I'm glad to see you had no trouble getting here."

"A little trouble," she corrected him, sitting down across the table. "A few watchmen," she said. She dropped the muddy sack containing the book on the table between them.

"But you lost them," Jamus said. There was no questioning tone in his statement, only a surety that Seren would not have been foolish enough to come here otherwise. He reached for the bag.

"I lost them," she said, leaning back precariously on her chair and propping her muddy feet on the table. "Some warforged distracted them while I ran off."

Jamus paused in the act of opening the bag's drawstrings, then offered an uneasy smile. "Ah, warforged," he said with a light chuckle. "Such curious creatures. Some were built to protect humans, you know. Perhaps he saw a young girl in danger and felt motivated to intervene."

"Jamus, don't lie to me," Seren said in a low voice. "We're hired to break into a Cannith guildmaster's house to steal one particular book out of a whole library. I steal the book, make a mess of his office, and he doesn't even report it to the Watch? And then some Lhazaarite mercenary and a warforged thug coincidentally show up to 'rescue' me from a wandering patrol? What's really going on here? What is this book? Who are we meeting here tonight?"

"The less you know the better, Seren," Jamus said, his voice surprisingly clear and even. His previous sleepy frown was now replaced with an alert, intense stare.

"I warned you it was a bad idea to steal from Dalan d'Cannith, Jamus," Seren said.

"And perhaps you were right," the old thief answered. "Now it's probably best if you left. Go home. I'll meet you in the morning, and we can leave this city behind."

"You don't actually expect me to do that," she said.

Jamus sighed and ran one hand through his thinning white locks.

"At least tell me who we're working for," she said.

"Well, make up your mind," he said with a sudden, irritated tone. "Do you want to know who we're working for or who we're meeting here?"

Seren gave him a long, angry stare.

"It's complicated," he said evasively. "Our employer's identity is a confidence I am not at liberty to betray, even to you, but she can be trusted."

Seren wanted to slap the old man off his chair. She restrained herself, holding one wrist tightly with the other hand behind her back. "Jamus, you know I trust you," she said, struggling to keep her voice even and patient. "I assumed you wouldn't suggest a job like this unless you were sure it was safe. Now you're telling me you can't tell me who we're working for? I'm risking my life. Can't you give me that much?"

"I told you, Seren, it's complicated," he said. "Suffice it to say the Canniths are the least of our worries. We have powerful allies. If Dalan d'Cannith moves against us, we'll be protected. Why do you think they offered to move us out of Wroat? Our protection was always part of the deal."

"The fact that a group as powerful as the House of Making is the least of our worries doesn't make me feel much better, Jamus," Seren said. "What are we involved in?"

Jamus folded his hands on the table before him, staring silently at his long, gnarled fingers. He looked much older than he normally did, much more exhausted.

"Have I ever told you about this place?" he said. "About what it once was?"

"This inn?" Seren asked, confused by the sudden change of subject. "You've told me a little about it, but what does that have to do with anything?"

"Be patient, Seren," Jamus said, looking at her with a crooked smile. "I have taught you many things in the time we've known one another, but I suspect this is the most important thing I have to teach."

Seren frowned, but did not argue.

"Years ago this building was home to a den of smugglers,"

Jamus said. "They were war profiteers. Scum. They stored weapons, supplies, sometimes even the occasional spy here. They used to meet their clients here. After the King's soldiers discovered what was going on, the place was cleaned out. The smugglers were executed for treason, and the building was left empty for twenty years. It was a Cyran woman, Fiona Keenig, who purchased it next. Exiled from her home, she did her best to turn it into a welcoming, comfortable sort of place. She said that she felt like a scavenger, snapping up this old husk of a building, so she named it the Friendly Buzzard."

"You've told me about Keenig," Seren said. "You said she was a friend of yours."

Jamus nodded. "Something of an understatement, but yes," he said. "The Last War drove a deep wedge between Breland and Cyre. They were indifferent neighbors at best, bitter enemies at worst, depending on which way the War had turned that week. Fiona wasn't welcome here at first, but she persevered. This was the only place in all of Wroat where you could find genuine Cyran cuisine and hospitality. Fiona's brothers still lived in Cyre that time, and did what they could to send her the spices and ingredients that weren't available here." Jamus grinned. "In a city as crowded as Wroat, it pays to be unique. People started noticing the Buzzard."

Seren stared at her teacher in silence. She wanted to demand answers, to demand Jamus stop stalling, but when she saw the sad, distant look in his eyes she could not bring herself to interrupt. There was something deeper here. This was important.

"But rumors bred, as they always do," Jamus said. "Mistress Keenig was accused of being a Cyran spy. The King's inquisitives conducted a public investigation, and Keenig's business ground to a halt. A few of the locals, people who knew her, braved the stigma of coming here. It wasn't much business, but it was enough to keep her afloat."

"Was she a spy?" Seren asked.

Jamus shrugged noncommittally. "After two years, the investigators found nothing," he said. "King Boranel offered no apology, of course, because a king cannot apologize. However, he and his retinue did dine here. Boranel gave the Buzzard his highest possible recommendation, and business turned around overnight. The wealthiest members of the nobility lined up to dine at the Buzzard, even braving the wretched streets of the fishermen's district to emulate their beloved king." Jamus smiled silently for several moments, remembering. "To her credit, Fiona did not allow the sudden fame to overwhelm her. She did not forget those who had remained her friends. The upper floor became dedicated to her wealthier clientele, private rooms and tables available only by reservation at astronomical prices. Her new customers were happy to pay. The bottom floor remained open to the common man, offering an alternate menu that was mostly the same thing being served upstairs . . . but at one-tenth the price."

"Bold," Seren said. "What if the nobles had discovered she was overcharging them?"

Jamus gave a wry smile. "Fiona was a clever woman. She knew her clientele," he answered. "The nobles expected a high price. After all, had not the king himself dined here? They were paying for the privilege of sharing in his glory. What they were eating certainly didn't matter, and they most assuredly were not going to share the details of their dinner with the scum downstairs. The nobles believed that Fiona only allowed the locals to dine here so that the Buzzard would have an authentic, earthy charm."

"She lied to them," Seren said.

"She gave them what they wanted," Jamus said. "The sheltered rich will pay a fair sum for authenticity, as long as that authenticity is kept safely at arm's length."

"Some people have too much money," Seren said.

"A simple, profound wisdom that has driven my entire career," Jamus said with a nod. "It was a similar thought that first drew me to the Buzzard in the hopes that I might relieve a noble of his excess wealth, and that is how I met Fiona. She caught me sneaking out the back door with a stolen purse in hand."

"She caught you?" Seren said, impressed.

Jamus smirked. "I could rationalize the matter and say that I was young and inexperienced," he said, "but that's not entirely true. Every man has his match, Seren. I underestimated Fiona Keenig. She took the pouch back and promised not to press charges if I snuck back into the private room and listened in on the conversation there. So I did. More jobs followed, spying on her clients or reporting the information to her other contacts."

"So she was a spy after all?" Seren asked.

"Of course," Jamus said, "but she wasn't a Cyran spy. She was King Boranel's agent, counter-intelligence, charged with defending the city against foreign infiltrators. The entire investigation had been a ruse. My life became a great deal more interesting after I met Fiona. I worked for her for over twenty years. It was only a few months before you came here that this place closed for good."

"What happened?" Seren asked.

"The Day of Mourning happened," Jamus said. "A wave of smoke and flame wiped out the nation of Cyre in a single night. Fiona loved Breland and was loyal to the king, but she had family in Cyre. The day she learned what happened, she closed the Buzzard and set out to find her brothers. That was four years ago, and no one has seen her since. This place has a great deal of memories for me . . ." Jamus looked around wistfully and laughed. "Also several emergency exits, built by the original smugglers who lived here. The perfect den for a spy. The perfect rendezvous point for a thief. No one else seemed to want the Buzzard, so I guess I've sort of adopted it."

Seren was silent a long moment. "What does any of this have to do with our meeting tonight?" Seren asked.

"There weren't many people who knew I worked for Fiona," Jamus said. "So when she vanished, I returned to being the two-bit thief the city always believed I was. A few weeks ago, I was given a better offer by someone who knows about my past. I've been offered—*we've* been offered—a chance to do something worthwhile again. The payment and escape from this damned city is just a bonus."

"So we're spies now?" Seren asked. It came out a bit more shrilly than she intended, and she saw Jamus flinch at her outburst.

"Seren, you left home to become something more than you were," he said patiently. "You can't tell me that you can look at your life now and say you have no complaints?"

Seren did not answer.

"I thought as much," Jamus said. "You're a talented girl, Seren, but you are not a normal person. Normal people do not climb on rooftops and pilfer other people's pockets. There are, however, ways to put those talents to use. Ways to help people. We've been given that chance."

"By whom?" Seren asked. "Why won't you tell me who we work for?"

"Knowledge and security are very rare companions in this line of work, Seren," Jamus said. "I can't tell you, for your own good and for our employer's. You just have to trust me, Seren."

"You say trust is born from mutual benefit," Seren said. "I have mercenaries following me through the streets already. How does this benefit me, Jamus?"

"Seren," Jamus said plaintively, but before he could say anything more he was interrupted by the protesting squeals of the wooden steps. He looked past Seren, his expression sharp and focused.

"They're early," Seren whispered.

Jamus remained silent, his expression worried.

"That's good, isn't it?" she asked.

"No, it's not," Jamus said, rising from his chair. "Early is never good."

"So let's get out of here," Seren said. She knelt and flipped a recessed latch on the floor. A small trap door in the floor led to a series of crawlspaces through which they could access any of the other rooms in the inn and make their way back to the street.

"Wait," Jamus said.

Seren looked up at him curiously.

"There's more to this, Seren, a great deal more," he said, settling back into his seat and watching the door. "Remember when I said the most difficult part still remained? Well, this is it. Run if you must, Seren. I'll understand, but I would prefer if you stood with me."

The doorknob turned. Seren stood quickly, but left the trap door unlatched. Two gruff-looking soldiers in light armor stepped inside. One held a lantern high, eyes searching the room for any sign of a hidden ambush. Seren could see the crest on his breastplate, a golden crown on a field of green. The soldier's eyes fixed on Seren for a brief instant, then moved on, disregarding her as a threat. Downstairs, she could hear more heavy footsteps. Who were they?

Seren stood, slipping her shoes back on and moving to the edge of the shadows behind Jamus. One hand moved into her cloak, resting easily on the hilt of the dagger tucked in the back of her belt. Jamus was as uneasy as she had ever seen him, though she doubted a stranger would see the signs, a faint uneasiness around the eyes. To see her normally unflappable teacher so nervous gave Seren an incredible sense of dread. Yet she said nothing, only stood beside her teacher. If they hadn't attacked yet, then this was to be a negotiation. A focused front was required for all negotiations. Disagreement would make a client nervous. Doubt would convince them they had the advantage. Confidence was everything.

"Clear," the man grumbled. "Only two of them, Captain."

"Just as promised," said an elegantly deep voice. "You are a man of your word, Jamus Roland. At least thus far."

A tall, whisper-thin man slid through the door. A cloak, so deep purple it was almost black, hung from his shoulders so that he seemed little more than a shroud topped by a floating head. His hair and eyes were ghostly white. His face was smooth, pale gray, nearly featureless save for the raw pink burn scars that covered his left cheek. Seren flinched when she saw him.

"Does my appearance upset your associate?" the man asked, looking at Seren with a crooked smile.

"Seren means no offense, Captain Marth," Jamus said.

"I understand," he said. "No doubt she simply has never seen a changeling honest enough to wear his true face? A lie may put her more at ease." The man's features blurred. His face was now lean and handsome, with rich black hair spilling out of his hood around his shoulders. "Is this more pleasing, Seren?"

Seren nodded politely. Marth ignored her and moved to the table, cloak parting to produce a pale white hand with long, almost skeletal fingers. His fingertips brushed the table near the muddy sack. "This is what I seek?"

"It is, Captain," Jamus said.

"Excellent," Marth said, gesturing at one of his soldiers.

The man produced a thick pouch and spilled its contents on the table. The white gleam of five platinum coins, each stamped with the image of a dragon, reflected the candlelight. Seren's eyes widened. She had never dreamed of seeing so much money in one place.

"Is that enough?" Marth asked.

"The money isn't the part of the reward that interests me,"

Jamus answered. He pushed the muddy bag back across the table.

Marth smiled and reached out again. His eyes met Seren's, and she was taken aback by the strange intensity of his milky white eyes. He smiled, only faintly, and then slid the book from its container. His other hand appeared, producing a strange jeweled hand lens of frosted purple glass. Marth held it over one eye as he scanned through the pages.

After nearly a minute of study, his shoulders slumped and he released a deep sigh. He opened the book carefully on the table, tucking the lens into his pocket. Before Seren could even react, one of the soldiers lunged forward and seized her arm, twisting it behind her back painfully, away from her weapon. She cried out and stomped hard on the man's foot with her heel. The bodyguard did not react, but only drew a short sword and held it to her waist. Jamus rose halfway from his seat, but Marth held out a cautioning hand.

"Please, Master Roland, there have been enough mistakes here tonight," Marth said in a calm, almost friendly voice. "A stomach wound is not a misery I would gladly inflict on one so young, but I will illustrate my sincerity if I must."

Jamus sat back down, though he turned so that he could watch Marth and his bodyguard simultaneously. Marth took the seat across from Jamus and regarded him quietly. The other soldier stepped forward and started scooping the coins off the table with a bored expression.

"You have failed, Master Roland," Marth said. "What I wish to know now is—did you intentionally seek to offer me a forgery, or is Dalan d'Cannith responsible for this? If the latter was the case, I would not hold you at fault. I would even offer you half the agreed pay for your discretion, though naturally our professional relationship would be permanently concluded. But the former . . ." He trailed off and was silent a long time.

He drummed his long fingers on the book. "I fear I know too much of magic. I know enough to realize that there is no certain way to find truth. Deceit is a powerful force. There is always a way to lie. I cannot think of a way to judge with any degree of certainty that you have not betrayed me, Master Roland. What I am sure you will find even more unfortunate is that I also cannot imagine any particularly dire consequences for me if I were to err on the side of caution."

Jamus opened his mouth to reply, but Marth held up a silencing hand with a vague smile.

"Before you seek to lecture me on honor between thieves, contractual obligations, a warning that you have powerful friends, or other such foolishness, consider this. I am no fool. I suspected that this lead might come to nothing. That is why I hired an expendable freelancer rather than risk one of my own loyal servants. However, know that I take no joy in the prospect of killing you. If you must speak, make it a convincing plea of your innocence—nothing more."

The sound of a pained shout and a heavy object smashing into something wooden sounded outside. Marth glanced at his guards in annoyance. Jamus stood, moving with the fluid speed of a man one-third his age. He flipped the table over in Marth's face and drew two daggers from his sleeves, hurling one over his shoulder at the man that held Seren. Seren's eyes widened and she twisted aside, but the knife's path was true. The weapon lodged in her captor's throat.

The other soldier charged Jamus, but the old thief slashed the air at eye level. The man shrieked and staggered away, bloody hands clutched over his face. Jamus held the weapon high and leapt at the changeling. Marth rolled aside deftly, drawing a twisted amethyst wand from his cloak and aiming it at Jamus. It vomited an explosive cone of green fire, consuming Jamus and painting the ceiling in flame. The fire vanished in an instant, leaving only the smell of charred meat behind. Jamus Roland's unrecognizable corpse collapsed with a sickly thud.

It happened so fast Seren had no time to even move. Marth pointed the wand at her and smiled as she stood.

She froze, waiting for the opportunity to act. The Cannith book now lay on the floor at her feet.

"Poor girl," Marth whispered. "He told you nothing, I imagine. Another pawn in these games, no doubt. How did you come to this life? An orphan of war, I'd wager. Do you have any idea what is happening here?"

She only scowled and waited.

"Do not hate me for what I have done to your teacher, Seren," Marth whispered. "One day you will appreciate the burden of deceit I have removed from your life. Perhaps I may yet offer opportunities for you, if you are wise enough to embrace them."

The doors burst open and three armored soldiers charged in.

"Captain, are you hurt?" one said. The guard looked down at Jamus's charred husk with no apparent surprise.

"No," he said, still watching Seren. "Nothing unexpected. What is happening outside?"

"Some lunatic and a warforged are loose in the inn," the soldier said.

"A warforged?" Marth looked at the man sharply.

Seren reacted instantly to Marth's distraction. She fell into a roll, shoved Marth aside, grabbed the book, and rolled onto the trapdoor. It flipped under her weight, depositing her in the dank crawlspace. She locked the door behind her and ran. Seconds later she heard a riotous explosion and felt a wave of heat wash over her. Marth had turned his magic to removing the trap door. She didn't have long to make her escape. She pushed open another door and dropped through the ceiling of the kitchen. The angry shouts of Marth's guards sounded from the hall outside. The chaos apparently had little to do with her—the Lhazaarite was busy piling furniture against the kitchen door while the warforged braced his shoulder against the door.

"What in Khyber?" the Lhazaarite swore, looking up in surprise as he wedged another chair into the heap. "Where did she come from?"

The warforged looked at Seren, pointed at the ceiling, and returned his attention to the door.

They were, of course, the same pair she had encountered earlier in the street—Omax and Tristam Xain. Seren's dagger was immediately in hand. She clutched the book to her chest and backed away from them.

"Don't try to stop me," she warned.

Tristam blinked. He glanced at Omax, then back at her.

"You're not getting the book back," Seren said. She continued backing away, moving toward the corner.

"Keep it," Omax said, turning his eerie blue stare upon her. "Do you know another way out of here? Please."

"Omax, she's a thief," Tristam said. "We can't trust her."

"Please," Omax repeated calmly, ignoring his comrade. "If you know a way, we could use your help."

Seren hesitated. She stood only a foot away from a sliding panel in the wall. She knew she could step through and seal it behind her before either of them could react, but she hesitated. There was something in the warforged's plain, direct demeanor that gave her pause, and Tristam seemed far too harried and confused to be threatening. In either case, if she escaped, Omax could likely just tear the wall away and follow her.

She already had enough new enemies. What did she really have to lose by helping them?

"This way," she said, sliding open the panel.

Tristam looked up at the ceiling, then at the passage with a look of astonishment. "Another secret passage?" he asked.

"This place has an interesting history," Seren said, stepping into the darkness.

Omax followed, with Tristam bringing up the rear. The tunnel was narrow, passing through the walls between the ground floor rooms. Seren passed through with ease, but grimaced at the scraping clamor Omax produced as he squeezed his thick metal body through the passage. Fortunately Marth's guards were producing too much noise to notice. The smell of smoke drifted from above.

"The top floor is on fire," Tristam whispered. "Who are these people?"

"You don't know either?" Seren shot back.

The warforged gave her a curious look. "Why else would we—"

"Later, Omax," Tristam said, his voice a low hiss. "Let's just get out of here."

Seren pushed another hidden door aside. A cool rush of air and the smell of fresh rain washed over her. She stepped into the garbage-strewn alley behind the Buzzard and looked back at the top floor. Behind the upper windows she saw flames, and a plume of thick black smoke spiraled into the sky. Seren felt a bit of hope drain from her. The Buzzard had always been a safe place, with a dozen ways to escape, a hundred places to hide. It had been a refuge from the dangers of her life, and when she saw it burn, she truly realized that her teacher was dead.

She looked down again with a glum, distracted expression, only to see Omax emerge from the darkened tunnel at a full charge, eyes burning with violent blue fire. Seren's hand darted for her knife, but she knew it would be too late. The warforged was too fast, and her weapon would likely do little harm regardless.

The massive creature charged past Seren, its heavy fist colliding with something behind her. She turned to see one of Marth's guards slump against the wall, sword tumbling from his hand. She had not even noticed his approach. The warforged had likely just saved her life. Five more guards rounded the corner, shouting for help as they advanced. Seren drew her knife.

"Get behind me!" Tristam shouted, darting forward with his sword in hand.

"I can defend myself," Seren retorted, but a heavy metal hand seized her shoulder from behind.

"Trust him," the warforged said, drawing back behind his comrade.

The soldiers moved to surround Tristam. He held his sword low to one side in one hand and flicked his left wrist. A slender ivory wand appeared between his fingertips and for an instant Seren saw a look of terror in the soldiers' eyes. Tristam shouted an unintelligible word, and a wave of sparkling white energy exploded into their scattering formation. Three fell among the garbage and did not rise, but another charged through the fire with sword held high. Tristam lifted his blade to defend himself, but his movements were slow, clumsy. Seren rolled between the guard and Tristam, slicing at the man's left knee with her blade. He stumbled and his stroke flew wide, allowing Tristam to easily parry. The guard fell to one knee and Tristam swung a second time, dropping the man beside his fellows.

The other two soldiers had rallied by now, but Omax was already among them. He bore no weapons but lumbered forward with his thick, three-fingered hands outstretched. He seized the first attacker by his chest plate; the metal creaked as it bent around his fingers. The soldier screamed and hacked at Omax's shoulder with his blade, leaving only light dents in his metal skin. He caught the other man's blade in his free hand and twisted, wrenching the sword from his grip. With a savage heave he lifted the first soldier into the air and hurled him at his fellow, crushing a rain barrel as they tumbled in a heap.

One soldier slumped unconscious, but the other scrambled to his knees, clutching his dented chest plate in pain. He glared at the warforged and searched about for his lost sword. Omax advanced a single thunderous step, squared his shoulders, and released a fierce, reverberating roar. The man kicked up a small cloud of refuse as he fell on his rear and scurried away, whimpering in terror.

Omax looked back at them, his blue eyes casting about for any other threats. The metal plates in his torso still vibrated from the fury of his roar. "We must go now," he said in his usual calm voice.

Tristam nodded, offering a hand to help Seren to her feet. She ignored him and stood on her own. The trio hurried through the alleys, away from Marth and his men. Alarm bells and panicked shouts came from every direction.

"At least this is a stroke of luck," Tristam said, looking back at the fire. "The Watch and the fire brigade should be here soon. If your mysterious visitors are wise, they won't remain here too long."

"Luck?" Seren snapped, glaring at him. "They killed my friend."

"Well," Tristam said, stopping to look back at her. His mouth hung open lamely. He smoothed one hand nervously over his grime-streaked coat but could find nothing to say. "I mean at least we're all safe. That's what matters, right? You have my sympathies. To lose a friend and a home . . ."

"My home?" she said sharply. "You think I live in an abandoned inn?"

"I . . . er . . ." Tristam glanced back at the burning Buzzard and shrugged, obviously at a loss.

"This conversation is intriguing," Omax said, still scanning methodically for any enemies as he paused beside them. "But this is not the time to have it."

Seren flushed slightly in shame for allowing herself to lose her head in such a crisis. They began to move again.

"I never caught your name," Tristam said, looking back at her with an apologetic smile.

Seren pushed past him and kept running. They emerged onto an unusually crowded street for this time of night, gawkers gathered to watch the fire from a safe distance. Seren ran out of the alley, directly toward them.

Tristam grabbed her arm. She gave him an icy look.

"Shouldn't we be keeping a low profile?" he asked.

"A crowd is the best place to hide right now," she retorted.

"I am somewhat conspicuous," Omax said.

"Then find your own way out of this," she said.

Tristam's face burned red. He seemed to be struggling to find something to say.

"You are right," Omax said, and that surprised her. "We will find our own way from here, but one more thing before we go."

Seren looked up at him suspiciously. "Everyone always wants one more thing," she said. "What is it?"

"Thank you for saving our lives," the construct answered.

Seren blinked.

Tristam gave a quick nod. "Thank you, my lady," he added. "Whatever your name is."

"Seren," she said softly. "Seren Morisse. And I'm not much of a lady."

"Thank you, Seren," Omax repeated.

"Whatever," she said, though she her tone was light and drew a smile from Tristam. She turned to vanish into the crowd, but hesitated. She looked back just as the pair were leaving. "What were you two doing there tonight, anyway?"

"Looking for answers," Tristam said.

"Answers to what?" she asked.

"I'm not sure," Tristam said. "Come to the docks tomorrow morning. Find *Karia Naille,* and maybe we can figure it out."

"I've had a terrible night," Seren said. "Quite frankly, I have no reason to trust you."

Tristam laughed. "Trust us?" he asked. "We're trusting you, Seren." He glanced at the thick journal tucked under her arm. "Enjoy the book."

The Lhazaarite peered back the way they had come for sign of pursuit, then hurried off down the street. Omax followed, pausing only long enough to bow his head respectfully. She watched the strange duo for several moments, and then slipped into the crowd before the City Watch arrived.

Chapter
Four

It was only after Seren had returned to her shabby apartment and cleaned off the mud and grime of the evening that the adrenalin of her escape faded. The reality of her situation began to sink in. In a single evening the city of Wroat had become a much darker, stranger, and lonelier place. She had known that Jamus was sick for a long time now, and though he never shared the details she had suspected it was serious. She had wondered how she might survive in the city without him. As much as Seren liked to think of herself as cool, capable, and independent, the truth was that she had come to depend upon him. Now he was gone, and she was alone.

It wasn't as if she was helpless. In three years she had cultivated her own contacts throughout the city, but Jamus was the only one she really trusted. Maybe that was because of all the people she had met here, he was the only one who honestly admitted he was using her. For a pair of thieves, they had always been remarkably honest with one another, ever since the beginning.

They had first met shortly after Seren's arrival in the city, only three days after she had realized that her future lay in crime. Seren had spent four hours shadowing a pretty young noblewoman out slumming in the fishermen's district with her two bodyguards. Seren had been watching the girl carefully. When she paid for her drink, Seren noted that she kept her coin purse tucked carefully in her sleeve. She noted the sharp blades on the guards' belts but also noted the bored expressions on their faces. The tavern keeper and patrons treated her with exaggerated courtesy, but called her "Lady Senthea," not "my lady." This was obviously not the first time she had come here. Her guards clearly expected no trouble; their presence at this point was a mere formality. If Seren were to sit beside this Senthea, perhaps brush against her arm as they reached for the same drink, none would notice that her purse had been stolen.

It was a good plan, and it would have worked if Jamus hadn't stopped her. Just as Seren was making her way across the tavern, the old man rose from a nearby table and seized her wrist. She had seen the old thief around the neighborhood, knew him by name and reputation, but had avoided him as she avoided most people. Seren tried to slip away, but the old man's grip was surprisingly strong and she didn't wish to make the struggle so obvious. Instead she merely drew a short knife from her belt, displaying it to him within the shadows of her coat.

"I'm not worth the trouble I'd give you, old man," she said.

"Neither is she," Jamus whispered with a wry grin. "You have no idea who she is, do you?"

Seren looked at him with suspicious curiosity.

"The esteemed Professor Senthea Montain is on leave from Morgrave University," Jamus said. "She is no one to trifle with."

"Morgrave University?" Seren said, not familiar with the name.

"An academy with a reputation for aggressive research," Jamus answered with a smile. "Lady Senthea's particular field of expertise is enchantment."

"She doesn't look like a wizard to me," Seren said, trying

to glance surreptitiously at Lady Senthea while still hiding her struggle with the old man.

"Of course she doesn't." Jamus cackled softly. "You can tell by the smell, though. Strawberries and just a hint of ammonia. Wizards always smell a bit off. They can never really get the smell of all those reagents out of their clothes."

"You can tell she's a wizard because she smells funny?" Seren asked with a dubious chuckle.

"No, that's how *you* should be able to tell," he answered. "I know because I talked to her at length the first night I saw her here. She was even more obvious then. I advised her that the jewels she wore were a bit ostentatious, and that she might have better luck if she used less obvious bait. She was quite grateful for my professional expertise, if a bit disappointed her disguise was pierced so easily."

"Bait?" Seren asked.

"She's a scholar doing a study on the criminal mind," Jamus said. He released her arm now, and Seren did not step away. "Exploring the use of magic in their rehabilitation. That coin purse you've had your eye on is warded. She'll sense its absence the moment it's removed and find it wherever it goes. She's left a trail of disappointed thieves in her wake, all now permanently charmed to be perfectly law-abiding citizens. Well, except for Markham. Fool got a bit violent when he learned the truth and is now exploring an exciting new life as a frog. I suppose that's a form of rehabilitation, isn't it?"

Seren looked past Jamus, eyes wide. Lady Senthea was now watching them. She eyed Jamus with the bored, disappointed expression of a cat that has just watched a bird fly away.

Seren tucked the dagger back into its sheath at the small of her back, though her hand still rested on its hilt. She looked at the old thief seriously. "Why are you helping me?" she asked.

"Honestly?" Jamus ask as he returned to his seat. "Because

I know this city. Senthea means well, but without theft as a viable means of income, what would happen to a young girl like you?"

Seren's face flushed. She looked away. "Thank you," she mumbled.

"You never needed me to save you," Jamus said. "You saw the signs just like I did. The only mistake you made was not listening to your instinct. Of course, one mistake is generally more than enough for people like us." The old thief leaned back in the chair, clasping his hands behind his head.

He was right. The smell of spell reagents was only one clue. Seren had thought it somewhat odd that the guards were so bored in such a dangerous part of town. The bartender and other servants recognized Senthea by the way she was acting. She wouldn't have survived an excursion into this part of town without some means of defending herself. Seren had convinced herself she was just lucky. She might have found a more reliable target, but this just seemed too good to be true. She had chalked it up to a well-deserved instance of good fortune. Her hand fell limply from her dagger. She slumped into the chair across from Jamus and stared at the table.

"As old as I am, I have never seen a real wolf," Jamus said, rocking idly on the back legs of his chair. "I spend too much time in cities. But I have read books about wolves. I am reminded of the lesson of the wolf."

Seren glared at the old thief. "What?" she said. Her tone was perhaps a bit more irritable than she intended, but she was not in a pleasant mood and had no patience for nonsense.

Jamus did not appear to take offense. "Though many creatures of magic and legend roam the wilds, the simple wolf is still among the most feared," Jamus answered. "The Valenar respect the wolf greatly, for it is a creature of great cunning as well as ferocity. The lesson of the wolf is twofold. The first lesson is patience. The wolf must choose its prey carefully, for if the hunt fails it will not have the strength to hunt again. A poorly chosen hunt can kill a wolf."

"I think I know that feeling," Seren said, her voice much softer now. She tried without success to ignore the gnawing feeling in her belly. Seren had counted on a quick pull to earn enough coin to eat, and had almost paid the price.

"I'm glad you understand," Jamus said. "The second lesson of the wolf is more important. Loyalty."

Seren studied Jamus's weathered face thoughtfully. There was a keen, excited look in his eye. "We had wolves out by my father's farm," she said. "Father always said that the wolf you saw was never the wolf that killed you."

"Exactly," Jamus said, snapping his fingers. "Strength in numbers. Loyalty born of mutual benefit. Each member of the pack offers strengths the others lack. Each one watches the other's back. Youth and energy are strengths. As are wisdom and experience. With these combined, there is little that the pack cannot accomplish."

"I see," Seren said. "You want me to join your pack, then?"

Jamus nodded.

"And how many are in your pack?" she asked.

"One," he said with a laugh. "This old wolf has lost his pack, and he is too old to hunt alone. What say you, Seren Morisse? Are you interested in learning what I have to teach?"

"How do you know my name?" she asked, folding her arms and leaning back in her chair the same way he did.

Jamus smiled.

Seren wiped her face with the back of one hand. She had not even noticed the tears when they came. She huddled on the tattered pallet in the corner of her apartment, rocking gently as memories of her mentor flooded through her mind. He was gone now. She was alone in the city, but that was not the worst part.

What had happened tonight? Why had Jamus agreed to take a job from a man like Marth? Why had he hidden the truth from her? They had always been honest with one another, at least professionally. Now, she knew that Jamus had not merely been a thief before they met. He had been a spy. His old "pack" had been Fiona Keenig's intelligence network, washed away when the innkeeper vanished after the Day of Mourning.

There were no answers.

She still had a little money saved up. It might be enough to buy passage on a coach out of town. She could go back to Ringbriar, back to her mother. Whatever troubles Jamus had stirred up in Wroat would never find her there. She would still have to find a way to scrape out a living without relying on her impoverished mother, but she would be relatively safe. No more stealing. No more strangers following her through the streets or threatening to disembowel her. She might starve, but at least she would see it coming.

Then she saw the seal of the gorgon and albatross looking up at her from the Cannith journal. The eyes of the gorgon glared up at her relentlessly. The albatross looked only to its flight, ignoring her completely. Seren wiped the tears from her cheeks again.

Loyalty.

If she didn't find out who Marth was and why he killed Jamus Roland, who else would ever care? Jamus had been a spy and a thief. He had taken her under his wing because he was too old to scale walls and pick pockets himself. He was no hero. Even to say he was a good man would have been a stretch.

But he was her friend. He was her teacher. He had accepted her unconditionally when no one else would. Even if he had hidden things from her, Seren owed it to Jamus to find the truth.

She cradled the thick book to her chest as she lay back on her bed, quite literally clinging to the only clue she had. She would find the truth, she told herself as she pulled the thin sheets over her shoulders.

But not tonight.

Seren lay in the dark for several hours, and the tears continued to come. Eventually, somehow, sleep found her.

CHAPTER
FIVE

The next morning, Seren set out to find *Karia Naille*. If Tristam and Omax had been truly sincere in their offer for help, then she would need to share information with them. The possibility that this might be some sort of trap flickered only briefly through her consideration. What would they have to gain? If the warforged had wanted to kill her, capture her, or take the book away from her, they could have done so easily last night.

Of course that was no reason to walk into a situation unprepared. She rose and dressed conservatively in a long linen dress and cloak, so as not to draw attention. She stuffed the Cannith journal in a clean woolen bag and then stuffed a blanket in as well. Carrying around an expensive journal bearing the seal of a dragonmarked house might draw a question or two, but carrying a sack of laundry to the river was normal enough. Plucking her coin purse from the broken wooden crate that served as a dressing table, she counted her remaining funds. It would have to do for now. Tucking her knife into the folds of her dress at the waist, Seren set out for the landing.

Seren soon arrived at the docks and carefully inspected each ship from a distance. She couldn't find one named *Karia Naille*. She began discreetly asking dockworkers and other passersby if they had heard of such a ship; most seemed to know nothing.

VOYAGE OF THE MOURNING DAWN

She felt frustrated and confused. Why ask her to meet them at a ship that didn't exist? It didn't make sense, but then again, most of this didn't make sense. Perhaps she was simply asking in the wrong place. Wroat was a large city, after all, and whatever Tristam and his associates were up to, they would likely keep to themselves. Even so, it wouldn't matter how discreet they wished to be, a ship couldn't dock in Wroat and not announce itself to the Watch. However, that meant talking to the Watch. For a known thief like Seren, that was a tricky sort of undertaking.

Luckily she soon found a watchman whose face she didn't recognize. "Pardon me," she said in as meek a voice as she could muster. "Do you know where I might find a ship called *Karia Naille?*"

The guard looked at her with a bored expression then pointed past her with his spear. She looked that way only to see an empty area of the docks. Then she looked up. It was amazing, sometimes, what the eye could miss when it was simply unprepared to see it. The city of Wroat sprawled on both sides of the Howling River, and on the opposite side of the river, a series of six short towers faced the docks, each capped by a short bridge that ended in open air. Seren had always wondered what purpose the strange towers served, for she had never seen them in use. Now a long, sleek vessel hovered in the air beside one of the towers.

Karia Naille was an airship.

Airships were a relatively rare sight to begin with, at least in the poorer parts of Wroat. Only the phenomenally wealthy could afford such vehicles, and only expert artificers could maintain them.

"Do you know who owns that ship?" Seren asked, looking back at the guard. He had already continued his patrol and didn't hear. Seren let him go. After last night, she reasoned she was better off not leaving a lasting impression on the Watch.

She crossed a nearby bridge and made her way to the tower's base. Seren felt one final pang of paranoia, a fear that she was walking into danger. She looked up at the ship. Seren didn't believe that Omax and Tristam planned to harm her. Her real fear was that, after this, there would be no turning back. Whatever Jamus, Marth, Dalan d'Cannith, and the others were involved in, it didn't really involve her yet. She didn't know enough to be a threat to any of them, and only Tristam and Omax even knew her last name. She could easily step away now, leave the city with the handful of coins she had left, and face whatever bleak and uncertain fate awaited her.

Was this why Jamus had told her nothing? To give her an easy way out in case he died? It would be just like him, she thought with a scowl. Jamus always underestimated her stubbornness. Seren pushed open the door of the sky tower and stepped inside.

She was surprised to find no crewmen inside the tower, no one on watch. She climbed the spiraling staircase and stepped out onto the top of the tower. There were no outer parapets, not even a rail to protect a person from falling off the gangplank. A cargo crane mounted on the bridge creaked and wobbled in the wind. Seren felt a sense of vertigo but didn't stumble; she had no fear of heights.

This close to the ship, Seren could hear the crackling, rhythmic hum emanate from the faint ring of blue fire that surrounded the vessel. The flames hovered around *Karia Naille*, roughly twenty feet from the top of the deck and only a few feet from the bottom of the hull. A sleek elegant wooden strut rose from the top and bottom of the vessel, grasping the fire in a pair of crystalline hooks. The ring's color shifted by the moment, flickering from blue to white to lavender. Seren had heard that airships were powered by elementals, strange creatures summoned from a world of harsh primal fire and bound into service. She had always found the stories somewhat sad. In her more indulgent moments, she even sympathized with them, forced to serve in a world they didn't want to live in. If the burning ring sensed her sympathy it did not seem to care.

Bringing herself back to the matter at hand, Seren scanned her surroundings and again found no crewmen guarding the bridge between the tower and ship. The vessel was relatively small, with a door at each end of the deck leading to a cabin and presumably below decks. She saw no one on deck at all. The only sign of life she could detect was the rather curious odor of freshly baked pastry. She peered around uneasily, certain she must have missed something. Seren had never been on an airship before, but she knew they were very valuable. Why would this one be unguarded? Shouldn't there at least be a crew? It seemed unlikely that there wouldn't be someone around. This certainly wasn't the best neighborhood to leave a valuable ship unguarded.

She stepped cautiously across the bridge, ignoring the howling winds that sliced at the high tower. Seren felt a sudden sense of unease as she prepared to step onto the deck. A wave of dizziness washed over her. The winds increased, whipping past her and raising a keening wail from the burning elemental ring. She stepped away and reached out to steady herself on the docking crane. Seren felt suddenly as if someone were watching her, someone not altogether pleased by her arrival.

"Hello?" she called out over the wind. There was no answer at first. "Is anyone here?"

There was a sudden sound of rushing air and Seren felt something heavy strike the bridge behind her. She turned around to see a reptilian beast the size of a small pony crouched on the top of the tower. Its flesh was a motley pattern of dark greens, with a pale blue underbelly. It held its long beak open just enough for her to see rows of sharp teeth and glared at her with dull black eyes. Most surprising of all was that it wore a leather harness on its back. The creature lowered its thin body and narrowed its eyes at Seren, releasing a birdlike shriek.

"He wants to know why you're here," said a voice from above her.

Seren looked up. A child dressed in wildly colorful outfit of leather and silk now crouched on top of the crane, pointing a small crossbow at her. No, not a child, a halfling. He regarded her with a confident mix of mischief and silent menace as he waited for her answer.

"My name is Seren Morisse," she said calmly, trying not to let the halfling's sudden appearance unnerve her. "I was invited here by Tristam Xain and Omax. This is *Karia Naille*, right?"

"Oh, so you're not a thief, then," the little man said, lowering his crossbow. He chuckled. "Or at least you're a thief on our side?"

Seren could not help but smirk. "I'm not on anyone's side," she said. "I only came here for answers."

"Funny place to look for them," the halfling answered, hooking his weapon on his belt. "Glad to meet you, Seren. I'm Gerith. You've already met Blizzard."

With that, the halfling flipped backward, off the crane and into the wind. Seren's jaw dropped in surprise at the suicidal act, but in the same instant Blizzard shrieked and leapt off the tower as well. With a leathery snap it unfurled wide, batlike wings and dove down, past the bridge. A moment later it soared back up in a spiral. Gerith now clung to the harness on its back. The halfling laughed as the creature flew in a loop around the burning ring and landed gracefully on the ship's railing. Gerith looked back at her eagerly, taking obvious joy at the surprise on her face. He flashed a wide smile, showing off the wide gap where he was missing some of his front teeth. Seren stood with her hands on her hips for a thoughtful moment then clapped politely, drawing more laughter from the halfling.

"Welcome to *Karia Naille*, Seren," Gerith said, hopping from the saddle with a flourish as she stepped onto the deck. "I'll tell everyone that you're here. I know you said you wanted answers, but perhaps in the meantime, you'd settle for pie? Pie is usually better than answers. Pie doesn't disappoint." He winked.

Seren had been about to refuse, then realized how hungry she was. "Pie sounds good, Gerith," she said.

The halfling nodded eagerly. "My chicken pie is the best," he said, patting Blizzard on the beak before heading off toward the nearest hatch. "Back in the Plains, it's said that great chefs make the best lovers, you know. That's a very pretty dress, Seren."

Seren looked at the halfling incredulously.

Gerith looked back at her, winked again, and vanished below deck.

Seren looked at Blizzard, but the creature was busy preening his wing. His master's antics were clearly something that no longer concerned the creature, and since Gerith had approved of her presence, she was no longer a concern.

Seren heard the opposite hatch open behind her, accompanied by footsteps too heavy to be a halfling's. "Pay no mind to Gerith Snowshale," said a familiar voice. "He's a good translator and the best scout I've ever known, but he is too eager to impress the fairer sex. Whether they are the proper age, social class, or race is rarely a concern for him."

Seren turned to face the new arrival. Her expression became grim when she recognized his face.

"Is there a problem?" Dalan d'Cannith asked with a small smile. "Did you not wish to see me?"

"I didn't expect to see you here," she said. "Usually a dragon-marked ship is a little more obvious."

"The ship bears no obvious marks of ownership for good reason, I assure you of that."

"Are you the captain?" she asked.

"I own *Karia Naille*, if that is what you truly meant to ask, but I am not the captain," he said. "I prefer to leave such matters in the hands of more qualified associates. What business do you have here?"

"I'm Seren Morisse," she said. "I came to see Tristam Xain and Omax."

"Both are in my employ," Dalan said. "Tristam and Omax are currently in the city, gathering supplies for our departure. Perhaps I can be of assistance? You may as well address your concerns to me, as it is likely they would have referred you to me in any case. Or perhaps I have misjudged your arrival. Perhaps you simply returned to see if I had anything else worth stealing?"

"I think I made a mistake," Seren said, backing toward the bridge. Dalan continued to watch her with a smug expression.

"Why am I not surprised?" Dalan said with a sigh. "A thief claims to seek answers, but when confronted with the most brutal truths, she scurries back to the safety of ignorance. Would you rather I lied to you, Seren? Would you rather I pretend not to know that you are a thief? I had assumed honesty would be our best starting point. If you change your mind, I will be waiting to discuss this. Enjoy the pie." He turned and slipped back into his cabin, closing the hatch behind him.

The other hatch opened, and Gerith appeared. He held a wooden plate heaped with a thick slice of pie and a crystal goblet of milk. His cheerful expression faded when he saw Seren standing on the bridge.

"Leaving already?" he asked, crestfallen.

"Not yet," she said, stopping and looking back toward Dalan's cabin. "I need to talk to Dalan."

"Ask him if he'd like some pie," Gerith offered cheerfully.

Dalan looked up with a frown as Seren entered his cabin. Much like his private study, it was packed with books and scrolls. The small chamber was only as tidy as it needed to be for its owner to navigate the room unharmed. A small bed in one corner was the only gesture toward comfort. The shaggy old dog lay half-asleep on it now, though its tail thumped the pillows when it recognized Seren, the beloved giver of cake.

"We knock before we enter a cabin on this ship," Dalan said, setting his quill down and placing whatever he had been writing out of sight.

Seren did not answer his barb, only dug out the journal and dropped it heavily onto the desk. Dalan reached out quickly to steady his wine glass. The volume landed so that the gorgon seal was facing Dalan.

"My partner and I stole that book last night," Seren said.

"Yes, I know," Dalan said, dusting off the cover with one hand. "Not only did you make a mess of my home, but Gunther was up all night with indigestion. Old dogs are not meant to have sweets."

"Why didn't you report the theft to the Watch?" she demanded.

"It was not the Watch's affair," Dalan said.

"The man who hired us killed my partner when he learned that book was a fake,"

Dalan looked up at her frankly. "Then perhaps *you* should go to the Watch and report his death."

Seren only looked at Dalan.

"Of course that is not an option for a person in your profession," Dalan said. "As it is not an option for me. We are not so different, Seren."

"Why did our client want that book so badly? My partner didn't tell me much before he died."

"Why do you wish to know?" Dalan asked. "If you think you might ransom it back, you are mistaken."

"No," Seren snapped. "I just want to know why my friend died to steal a fake copy of . . . whatever this is."

Dalan took a slow sip from his wine before he answered. "The book is not a fake, Seren," he said. "It merely isn't what your employer believed it to be. It is one of many mundane journals crafted by an author notable for several more significant works. Ironically, we might have more answers had you not so cleverly recovered it."

"Explain," Seren said.

"Tristam placed upon enchantments upon the book so that we could track it," Dalan said. He looked at her intently. "So you really had no idea what your client believed this book to be?"

"No," Seren said, unable to keep the edge from her voice. She pushed a pile of books from a chair across from Dalan and sat, eliciting an annoyed wince from him as the pile hit the floor. "Jamus knew more, but he didn't tell me. Marth sure didn't give anything away."

"Marth," Dalan said, weighing the name carefully. "So why did you bother to take the book with you when you escaped?"

"I thought it might hold some answers," she said. "I guess it's useless."

"Not entirely," Dalan said, leafing through the book's pages. "It was necessary to use a compelling decoy, and thus it does bear some modest sentimental value. I appreciate its return. Had you not been the sort of person who would make the effort to return my property, for whatever reason, I most likely would not be tolerating your presence on my ship. Now, let us see if we can find some answers. Please tell me as much of your client, the man that killed your partner, as you can. His name was Marth, was it?"

"Tell me why you set a trap with an enchanted book first," Seren demanded.

"A trap?" Dalan said. He laughed, steepling his fingers over the book. "The paranoid always overestimate their own importance. I did not trap you. I do not care about you. A man makes contingencies for his own protection, and you see it as some contrived plot against you. Realize where you stand. You and your partner chose the lives you did, and this Marth used you to get to me. You knew the risks, and when you failed to deliver genuine merchandise, you paid the price. If you cannot hold yourself to blame for being a thief who will offer her services to a murderer, then the depths of your denial are truly without measure. Keep in mind what your intent was yesterday evening—to steal another man's property for money, on behalf of an employer you neither knew nor trusted. Do not pretend that you are somehow the injured party in this affair. You were simply not as clever as you imagined, and your friend Jamus died. Perhaps rather than curse me for some imagined entrapment, you might thank me for sending Tristam and Omax to save you."

"I saved *their* lives, actually," Seren said.

Dalan was silent a long moment, then chuckled. "The details of that encounter varied slightly with Tristam's telling of the tale," he said. "I suppose I should have known well enough to ask Omax what happened. He may be a construct, but he's far more reliable than the boy. Now, please, let us set aside our respective motivations and concentrate on facts. You thought yourself the clever thief set to receive a legendary reward. I thought myself a keen manipulator, setting an inescapable trap to catch those who conspired against me. We were both wrong. Now tell me what you know and let us help one another."

Seren folded her arms and leaned back in the chair with a frown. "I'm afraid I don't know much," she said. "We met a changeling named Marth, who called himself a captain."

"A changeling?" Dalan asked. "He showed his true face to you and admitted he was a changeling?"

Seren nodded.

"Strange," he said. "They are a misunderstood and often hated race. Their ability to control their appearance makes them difficult to trust. It's very rare for one to reveal himself in such a manner, except to another whom he trusts implicitly."

"Or maybe he planned to kill us all along so it didn't matter if we knew what he was," Seren said.

"A possibility," Dalan admitted.

"His guards were well armed and trained," Seren said. "They were equipped like professional soldiers. I never saw the crest they wore before, but then I've never seen any soldiers other than Brelish ones."

"Omax recognized their uniforms, and so did I when he described them to me," Dalan said. "They were Cyran."

"Cyre?" Seren said. "I didn't think Cyre had an army. Or much of anything else."

Dalan shrugged. "Many Cyran soldiers survived the Day of Mourning because they were in enemy lands. The armor and uniforms Omax described were those of the Eighty-Seventh Legion, a unit that was in Karrnath when the tragedy occurred. They became mercenaries after the Day of Mourning. Such a fate is unsurprising. Imagine what that must be like, Seren. To be a warrior, fighting for the future of your homeland in strange and distant country, only to discover that you now have no homeland. All that you've fought for, all that you've lived for, is now gone. You are now irrelevant. Yet the desire to fight remains, the desire to shed blood for a cause endures even though there is no cause at all, except perhaps vengeance. What life would beckon such a lost soul other than that of a mercenary? Those who fought for king and country now fight for gold and silver. It saddens me, to see my own countrymen fall to such a fate."

VOYAGE OF THE MOURNING DAWN

"You're Cyran?" she asked. Gunther hobbled out of his bed and sniffed Seren curiously for any sign of food. Finding none, the dog rested his head on her lap and waited to be petted.

"Many members of my House are Cyran," Dalan said. "Fortunately, unlike the soldiers you met, most of my friends lived outside Cyre. My service to my house gives me continued purpose. But we are wandering far from the meat of this discourse. What else do you know of this Captain Marth?"

"Not much," Seren said, scratching the dog's ears absently. "Jamus wouldn't tell me much about who we were working for. I think he wanted to protect me. He said that he had arranged for speaker posts to be sent to his allies, and he mentioned Fairhaven, but I don't know anyone from there."

"A bluff, most likely," Dalan said. "Pity that you survived and he did not. His insight would no doubt be more illuminating than your own. No offense." Dalan smiled insincerely. "Cheer up, little thief. I am certain you are better off without a master who would hitch your wagon to a killer. Indeed, if he truly wished to protect you, he should have avoided taking a job from someone so untrustworthy."

"Are you done judging the dead, d'Cannith?" Seren asked.

"For now," Dalan said. "I do tend to go on, a trait I inherited from my mother. A wonderful woman. Pray continue, Seren. Tell me whatever you can remember, no matter how insignificant."

"Well, like I said, Jamus didn't tell me much about our employer," she answered. "I'm not even sure if we were working directly for Marth. I thought our employer was a woman, at least from the way Jamus spoke. Jamus was surprised when Marth arrived so early."

"Interesting," Dalan said, thumbing through the journal as he listened to Seren's information. "Is there anything else?"

"He killed Jamus and set the inn on fire using magic," she said. "Some sort of amethyst wand."

Dalan's eyes narrowed in thought. "That makes a great deal of sense," he said. "I have suspected that our competitor was a student of artifice."

"Competitor?" Seren asked.

"What I am about to say is quite delicate," Dalan said. "It would be in your best interests, once you leave my ship, to forget what I tell you—not for my sake but your own. My troubles are a heavy thing, and could easily crush one as small as yourself. I am loath to even speak of them, but my associates promised you an exchange of information. As foolish as they may have been to make such an arrangement with a thief, I am a man of my word. Do you understand?"

Seren nodded.

"I reiterate the seriousness of this," he said. "I am about to share perhaps more than Tristam's arrangement requires because I feel sympathy, if not responsibility, for your friend's death—but do not mistake sympathy for forgiveness or trust. You stole from me, Seren, and I do not abide thieves. However, I am not a monster, so I will offer you answers to lessen your pain. But realize that what I say to you will be entirely useless to you."

"Useless?"

"Because the answers will have no true use to you," he said. "If you betray my confidence, few will believe an insignificant thief. Those who might believe you would likely kill you, suspecting you know more than you do. You seem relatively intelligent, thus I am certain you will remain silent to avoid dangerous scrutiny. But if you do not, your death will trouble me little. Is that understood?"

"Yes," Seren said.

"Then I will tell you what I can," Dalan said. "I am currently engaged in a project that has consumed a great deal of my time for the past two years. I have certain competitors in this endeavor, and as much as I despise to admit it, this is not a race I am currently winning. Further, these competitors do not share my regard for law, honor, or human mercy. Various clues, not to mention their previous owners, have vanished or perished before I had a chance to investigate. I have long feared that my competitors might seek to derail my own meager progress, so I set this book aside as a trap. Though it greatly resembles other significant pieces of research written by its author, it is, as you know, not genuine. Tristam placed certain enchantments upon this volume that would allow him to follow it if it was stolen, as long as it remained within a certain range."

"So that was why he interfered when the Watch stopped me," Seren said. "He didn't want me to get caught."

"Not before we found out who you were working for," Dalan answered with a small smile. "Unfortunately your escape from the Watch was a bit more dramatic than Tristam expected. It took him some time to untangle himself and, by the time he was able to triangulate the book's location again, the inn was already surrounded by Marth's henchmen. Being the impulsive individual he is, Tristam resolved to fight his way to rescue you rather than waiting to summon help. Omax is a more practical soul, but his single fault is that he invariably follows Tristam's lead. Thus they became embroiled in the conflict before they realized how hopelessly outnumbered they were. You have already noted that I do not hesitate to condemn you for your previous actions, but neither will I balk at praising you for a job well done. I thank you for saving their lives. Tristam and Omax have many flaws, but their services are irreplaceable. I have precious few trustworthy allies."

"I know the feeling," Seren said.

"Imagine my surprise," Dalan said dryly. "Unfortunately, Tristam's foolishness lost us much and gained little." He sighed. "Other than your confirmation that this Captain Marth uses magic, happens to be a changeling, and bears a connection to the fallen nation of Cyre, we still know nothing about our enemy's true identity. Knowing a changeling's name means very little. They collect names as other men might collect interesting coins. They often hide behind other identities, live lives as humans or elves so that others will not distrust them for what they are. What truly bothers me is not his identity, but his efficiency. How does he learn so much while we learn so little? How can he command so many minions yet leave no trail?"

"It may not mean much," Seren said, "but he tried to recruit me."

Dalan's eyebrows raised. "Recruit you?"

"He offered to spare my life if I joined him," she said. "He thought I was an orphan of war."

"Very interesting," Dalan said. "The import is unclear, but interesting nonetheless."

"So what comes next?" Seren asked.

Dalan scowled. "I suspect after this failed theft, Marth will make a more dramatic and violent move against me," he said. "I have already gathered what I need so that I can leave Wroat, but I regret the damage he will do in my wake."

"What does he want?" Seren asked. "What's so important that it's worth killing for? What's so important that you would gamble with people's lives?"

"I am no gambler, Seren," Dalan said, looking at her intently. "A gambler is a man who risks what otherwise would not be lost. I gamble nothing, for many lives are already at risk."

"That's no answer."

"Fools always believe a simple answer will wipe trouble away," Dalan said with a sneer. "Simple answers are the opiate of simple minds; I prefer things complex. But so be it, Miss Morisse. Let the burden of enlightenment be on your head. My uncle Ashrem d'Cannith was a brilliant scholar, but his primary area of expertise was artifice—magical engineering. Though I doubt you would have heard of him, you know his symbol already." Dalan gestured at the crest on the book she had stolen. She realized many more of the books in this room bore the same crest.

"Ashrem made his career in the Last War," Dalan continued, "fashioning all manner of devices. His skill and innovation are unsurpassed even to this day. You now sit in an example of his brilliance. This airship is one of three he once possessed, and it features many of his own innovations. It was his genius that helped bring about the warforged, as well as countless other creations. Sadly my uncle's political acumen did not match his ingenuity, and thus he made his share of enemies in our house. These enemies turned their ire to me when he passed; a rather dubious inheritance. That, and this, of course . . ."

Dalan took a scrap of paper from his desk, rolled it into a tube, and held it over the small candle on his desk. Seren watched as it burned into ashes on his desk. Dalan concentrated a moment and, with a wave of his hand, rendered the page whole and undamaged again.

"Impressive," she said.

"A dragonmark trick," he said. "Those who bear the Mark of Making can repair what has been destroyed, but such tricks are the extent of my magical talents. My uncle was a true genius. My minor talents are quite literally nothing compared to his, and to those of many others in my house. My lack of magical talent, combined with the political situation he left behind, made progress in my house difficult for me. The most I could manage was to maintain my position as guildmaster here, though such a prestigious title amounted ultimately to a clerk's duties. I was to be discarded and forgotten in Wroat."

"The city has a way of collecting unwanted things," Seren said.

"Indeed. A few years ago, while sorting through my inheritance, I discovered a passage in one of my uncle's journals. It made veiled references to other unfinished works, hidden works, in particular an artifact he called the Legacy. It is my belief that the Legacy would have been the most fantastic of my uncle's creations. It is my duty to reclaim it in his name, and to do so before men like Marth can do the same."

"How noble," Seren said. "I'm sure the possibility that you'd win back your House's favor never entered your mind."

Dalan smiled. "Naturally my motivations are complex. I hardly find that unusual. A soldier may fight with all his strength and win a battle—in the end justice prevails and the king reigns for another day. Does it matter in the end that, during the battle, the soldier only wished to survive? I think we all do noble things for selfish reasons. I often find that only those who think they are truly selfless—those who act on behalf of abstract ideals or beliefs with no thought for the moment—are those who generally bring the most harm. They lose sight of what truly matters. In any case, I can assure you that my modest political aspirations are far more innocent than whatever this Captain Marth's intent may be for my uncle's work. All of Ashrem d'Cannith's closest colleagues and students have either perished or vanished since his death. Don't you find that unusual?"

"What does the Legacy do?" Seren asked.

"What indeed?" Dalan said. "I am not at liberty to discuss the specifics, but suffice it to say it is incredibly powerful."

"As a weapon?" she asked.

Dalan paused. "All things can be used as weapons," he said in a subdued tone. "My uncle would not wish his discoveries to be used in such a way. He was a man of peace."

"Then maybe your Legacy is better off undiscovered," Seren answered.

"A conclusion I have not dismissed," Dalan said, "but knowledge is not a thing that can be caged or extinguished.

Whatever the truth of my uncle's discovery, one day it *will* be found, by Marth or others like him. It falls to me to ensure that it is discovered by those who will use the knowledge responsibly."

"And you believe House Cannith will use it responsibly," Seren said.

"In fact I do," he said, his tone mildly offended. "Do not misunderstand me, Seren. I comprehend the mercantile motivations that drive my house. I understand them better than most. The lure of wealth and power are strong, and to be certain many Canniths would be seduced by the notion of exploiting my uncle's work. Yet remember that we have been the custodians of magical knowledge for over three millennia. If there are any with whom my uncle's secrets can be trusted, then who else but his own house?"

"Then why didn't he leave the knowledge to you, as he left his ship?" she asked.

Dalan did not answer immediately. "To be honest, I do not know," he said in a sober voice. "The answer to that question is one of many mysteries he left behind." He drummed his fingers on the desk for a long moment, then looked at her with a frown. "If there is nothing else, Miss Morisse, then I believe our business is concluded." He reached into his pocket, scattering a few gold coins on the table. "Take this for your trouble, and take my advice as well. Leave Wroat and do not involve yourself in this further. I can handle it from here."

Seren looked at the coins as they shone in the lamplight. It was more money than she had seen in some time, but she made no move to reach for them.

"I want to help," she said.

"You?" Dalan retorted. "Why?"

"Because you need help," she said. "You already trusted me enough to tell me what you're after."

"I told you very little." Dalan laughed. "I told you enough to satiate my own meager guilt over your friend's death, and no more. I do not need you, Seren Morisse. Return to your filthy hovel. I wish you a long, prosperous life of digging through other people's pockets. When you meet your final knife in the dark, may you bleed out painlessly."

"Marth killed my friend; I want to help stop him," Seren answered, her voice growing heated from Dalan's insults. "Maybe you can't trust me, but you know I have nowhere else to go. You admitted you need allies. What do you have to lose?"

"This ship operates with a surprisingly small crew," Dalan said, "so I do not require another deckhand. What use would I have with a thief?"

"Well," Seren said, "you claim that you've studied some of the same clues as Marth, but that he learns more than you do?"

Dalan nodded. "I possess many copies of my uncle's works, but I believe there is a code, a pattern that I do not yet understand. Marth must have broken this cipher already. It seems he is much more skilled in his craft than Tristam."

"Or he has resources you don't know about," Seren said. "Marth knew the journal was worthless when he studied it with this." She reached into her dress and took out a purple frosted lens, setting it on Dalan's desk with a clink.

Dalan d'Cannith's eyes widened as he picked up the glass and looked into its depths. "Interesting," he said. "Where did you find this?"

"I took it from Marth's pocket before I ran away," she said. She plucked it from Dalan's fingers and returned it to her pocket. "But you obviously don't have any use for a thief." She smiled at him primly.

A wide, dangerous grin spread across Dalan d'Cannith's features. "You are a shrewd negotiator, Seren Morisse," he said, leaning back in his seat. "There may be room for you on *Karia Naille* after all." He sniffed the air tentatively. Seren detected the faint aroma of cooking—Gerith's, probably. "You may remain among us, for the time being. Now let us discuss the details of your employment over lunch."

Chapter
Six

Captain Marth stood in the middle of Dalan d'Cannith's study, his expression one of disappointment and irritation. He ran one hand along a nearby shelf as he examined the titles of the books.

"Captain," called one of his guards from the doorway.

Marth looked up, his hood falling back upon his shoulders. He wore his natural face again, smooth and white except for the unsightly pink burns that crawled across his cheek.

"Speak," he commanded, beckoning to the guard.

"We discovered very little of interest in the rest of the house, Captain," the guard reported. "Only a few guild logs detailing Cannith operations in the city. Many items were hastily removed, including much of the clothing in Master d'Cannith's wardrobe and the food in his larder. Even the servant's quarters are empty."

Marth nodded. The servants would know nothing. Dalan would have already fled. While Dalan obviously bore interest in his uncle's work, the guildmaster had discovered nothing of true value. It came as no surprise. The Canniths were meddlers by nature, but ultimately harmless. They never understood Ashrem's work. Marth's fingers rested for a moment on the binding of one of many volumes bearing the House Cannith gorgon seal, and he remembered.

He had stood in a house much like this one, the modestly appointed home of a wealthy noble. The smell of smoke hung in the air, along with the shrieks of terrified children and servants. The fires blazed all around him, but Marth cared little. He wore the face of a Cyran soldier as he advanced on his former commanding officer, sword in one hand and wand in the other. Bright red blood shone on the steel blade.

"Cargul, what is the meaning of this?" Lieutenant Keiran demanded. Sweat and soot streaked the old soldier's face. He held his broadsword unsteadily in one hand, the other hand pressed up against his bleeding side as he backed fearfully away, trying to distance himself from both his attacker and the fires.

"I'm not Sergeant Cargul," Marth corrected. His face became smooth and gray. He was younger in those days, his natural face unscarred. "You remember me, sir." It was not a question, only a statement awaiting confirmation.

"You." Keiran hissed. "The changeling spy! By Khyber, if you've harmed my wife . . ."

"She is safe, sir," Marth answered calmly. "I showed your family greater mercy than you offered mine."

Keiran sneered and charged Marth with his sword held high. The changeling pointed his amethyst wand at the floor, summoning a wall of green fire between them.

"Face me without your magic, changeling!" Keiran demanded. "Face me with your sword, coward!"

"This is not a matter of courage, nor a demonstration of strength," Marth said. "This is revenge. Burn, as they did."

Green fire blazed within the purple crystal again, and the room filled with intense heat. Lieutenant Keiran screamed, vanishing within the blaze. Marth stood where he was, unharmed by the smoke and fire, and listened until the screams faded. Then, slowly, he made his way through the burning house and outside again. Huddled men and women gathered on the grass outside. Their clothing was seared and blackened with soot. They held their children close as they watched Marth with undisguised terror. He ignored them, walking past the crowd to the one man who stood apart from the rest. Marth looked up, his soot-blackened face marked now by trails of tears.

"You didn't stop me, Ashrem," Marth said to the old man.

Ashrem d'Cannith looked back sadly. The old man's crystal blue eyes reflected only sympathy. "Perhaps I did not want to," he whispered. "But it ends now, Marth."

"What happens now?" the changeling asked.

"Come with me, and face justice for what you have done," Ashrem said.

"Justice?" Marth repeated with a bitter laugh.

"If you come with me, I will stand by you, and defend you to the last," Ashrem said. "If you refuse, you will be hunted. I cannot stop them, Marth, not after what you have done."

"Why not just kill me, Ashrem?" Marth asked, dropping his sword and wand in the grass. "Why not end it here? I have my vengeance. I have nothing left and would rather die at your hands than a stranger's."

"I have hope for you, Marth," Ashrem said. "You are a good man, no matter what this war has forced you to become. The world is not done with you yet."

"You were right, d'Cannith," Marth whispered, returning to the present.

The changeling hurled the books from the shelf with a savage sweep of his arm. Reaching into one of the many pouches at his belt, he drew out a handful of pink crystalline powder and sifted it over the fallen books. He clapped the remaining dust from his gloved hands and reached into another pouch, drawing out another handful of chalky black dust. The chemical burned his skin as it mixed with the remaining pink residue, even through his silken gloves. Marth stood where he was for a long moment and studied the scattered volumes, offering no reaction even when a robed figure entered the room behind him.

"I have dispatched several of the men to determine where Dalan d'Cannith has fled," the newcomer said. He was a small, portly man garbed in flowing silken garments of burnished copper. His head was shaved in the manner of a monk, and he wore a long beard woven into a thin braid. "Doubtless he has covered his trail well, but someone might have seen something." He looked at Marth's hand, still holding the corrosive powder over the books. "Why do you hesitate?" he asked.

"Destroying knowledge does not sit well with me, Brother Zamiel," Marth said. With a sigh, he scattered the black dust over the scattered books. Where it touched the pink powder, paper, leather, and even the wooden floor began to smoke.

"An admirable sentiment, but a necessary evil," Zamiel answered. "Dalan d'Cannith is an enemy. We do not have the time to search his home properly, thus we must destroy whatever he might still hide here. We cannot afford to leave him any advantage, any security."

"Dalan is like his uncle," Marth said, stepping away from the smoke. "He is no fool. He would not have left behind anything we can use. This is a pointless, destructive gesture."

"An enemy who cannot be destroyed must be intimidated," Zamiel said. "Consider this a message—a warning to a respected rival. Dalan will look upon the ruins of his home. He will witness the destruction of so many beloved possessions. He will recognize that he should have left well enough alone. D'Cannith is no warrior. He is a bureaucrat, an academic, a coward. If he is wise, he will withdraw from this race and be content that he has only lost his home."

"Unlikely," Marth said with a frown. "I think we will face Dalan again before this is done."

"Then he will die," Brother Zamiel said.

Marth did not reply. His smooth face was thoughtful as he watched the first tongues of flame emerge from the fallen books. He turned and made his way down the stairs. Three of his soldiers stood at the door, postures tense, hands on their weapons. One peered cautiously out the window just beside the back door. He looked back at Marth with an uncomfortable expression.

"Captain Marth, there is a problem," the soldier said.

Marth moved to the window. The soldier quickly stepped aside. The first light of morning had only just begun to paint the street outside in pale, pastel colors. The rains had started again but now fell only in a meager drizzle. Few dared the muddy streets at this early hour, but Marth picked out a handful of armored men gathering in the shadows of an alley behind the house. Their eyes were on the Cannith home.

"The City Watch," Marth said with a sigh. He pushed the curtain back over the window, his gaze losing focus as he became lost in thought.

"We cannot afford to be seen here, Captain," Zamiel said as he descended the stairs. "For Dalan d'Cannith to know we oppose him is one thing. For King Boranel's soldiers to learn of our presence is quite another matter."

"Captain, perhaps we might be able to escape through the front door," a soldier offered.

"The building will be surrounded," Marth answered. "I will handle this. Perhaps their arrival might give us an opportunity for distraction."

As Marth reached for the door, his facial features shifted, becoming a young man's thin face framed by sandy brown hair. He stepped out into the street, arms folded in his sleeves.

The instant he did so, four watchmen emerged to surround him.

"Halt and identify yourself," the sergeant commanded. He kept his crossbow trained on Marth's chest.

"My name is Tristam Xain," Marth said calmly, continuing his approach. "Is there a problem, officer?"

"Hands out and to your sides!" the man said. "I said stop!"

The watchman loosed a crossbow bolt. It struck Marth in the shoulder and fell with a shower of sparks. Unharmed, Marth drew his hands from his sleeves with a flourish, releasing a cloud of sparkling dust toward the watchmen. They fell into fits of hideous coughing. All but one staggered and fell helpless to the earth. The fourth recovered enough to unsheathe his sword, only to see that Marth had drawn his twisted amethyst wand. Its length shone with green fire. The watchman ran. Marth's soldiers emerged from the house, flanking out to surround their leader. One drew his own crossbow, aiming it at the back of the retreating soldier.

"No," Marth said, pushing the weapon down and smiling with Tristam's face. "Let one escape. Let him tell others who he has seen here."

A pained coughing drew Marth's attention. He looked down at the remaining three watchmen, writhing on the earth as the toxins robbed them of their strength. With a slow, deliberate movement, Marth drew his sword and buried it in the chest of the nearest guard. A Cyran soldier drew his blade and advanced toward one of the others, but Marth waved him away.

"This blood is on my hands alone," he said. "Return to the ship."

The soldiers complied, hurrying through the darkened alleys. Marth finished the other two watchmen and moved on as well. He had not gone far before Zamiel appeared at his side, like a shadow as he walked.

"Why do you brood, my friend?" the prophet asked. "Surely by now you recognize the necessity of what we do. Do you regret the deaths of those soldiers?"

"No," Marth said. "They earned their fate when they stood against me, just as Jamus Roland did. Do not worry, Zamiel. Your killer has not grown a conscience yet."

"Then what concerns you so?" he asked.

"I fear we were too cautious," he said. "I know the man who was with that warforged last night. I recognized him from the soldiers' descriptions."

"The man whose face you wear," Zamiel said, his face darkening. "I remember him. I also remember your insistence that he would not be a problem."

"Clearly things have changed," Marth said. "Hopefully the City Watch will cause some trouble for him, at least. It will be difficult for him to return to Wroat without explaining the deaths of three watchmen."

"This only reaffirms what I have cautioned from the start," Zamiel said. "We should have confronted d'Cannith directly instead of relying on untested subordinates. We should have killed Dalan and all who stood beside him. If that lens falls into Xain's hands, it will not take long before they determine how to use it and gain ground."

"Perhaps," Marth said. "But think not on what we have lost. Think instead upon what we have gained. Tristam is brilliant, but also foolhardy. He may find clues that you and I would miss, but inevitably he will stumble and we will find his trail. Then we can harvest the fruits of his discoveries and our own search will grow much easier."

Zamiel was silent for a long time.

"You do not agree," Marth said.

"Xain should die," Zamiel said. "We do not need the complication he represents."

"You have always told me that I was destined to succeed, prophet," Marth said. "Is my destiny so frail that one foolish tinker could undermine it?"

"You misunderstand me," the prophet said. "I do not take destiny lightly, but neither should you. The Prophecy is a living thing. That which it foretells is certain, inevitable, but rarely predictable." He looked at Marth seriously. "I have no time for those who play games with their own destiny. You claim you wish to use Xain to our advantage, but your words stink of mercy. Mercy is a luxury that a conqueror cannot afford."

"That sounds almost like a threat, Zamiel," Marth said.

"Not a threat, a warning," Zamiel said in a tired voice. "You have spent only a few years helping me to fulfill this passage of the Prophecy. I have spent most of my life. Weigh this truth: You are not unique. There were others before you who seemed to be the conqueror I have foreseen. The Prophecy is a powerful force. Weak men who stand before it are ground into dust. Do not allow your enemies to gain ground, Marth. Show them no mercy, or all will be lost."

The changeling folded his arms in silent thought, pondering the prophet's words. "Very well," he said. "I will keep your words in mind."

"Good," Zamiel said. "That is all I ask. All that I say, all that I have ever done for you was intended only as guidance. Do not follow me blindly. Your decisions must ultimately be your own, or you will never become what you must be."

"I will remember that," Marth said.

"See that you do," the prophet said.

With a sudden shift in the shadows, Zamiel vanished, leaving Marth to find his way to the ship alone. He pushed all thoughts of Ashrem d'Cannith and Tristam Xain out of his mind. The past was a burden, a weight that sought to drag him back down into the miserable mire that had consumed him before. Brother Zamiel had offered him the chance to fulfill a greater destiny, to embrace his talents and forge a better future for all of Eberron. Better to concentrate on that future, he thought, as he looked into a standing puddle and saw Tristam Xain's face staring back at him.

Such a brilliant, glorious future.

Chapter
Seven

Seren sat on the railing of *Karia Naille*. She crouched beside the ship's figurehead, overlooking the city. Though much of the deck was shielded from the elements, sitting on the rail offered no such protection. The wind rushed past her, whipping her long hair back in a fury. She paid little mind as she ate her lunch. She had no real fear of heights, and with one foot hooked behind the rail, she was balanced well enough. The old dog, Gunther, lay on the deck behind her. He kept his head nestled between his paws, watching intently for any fallen crumbs. Seren ignored the dog, her thoughts consumed with more urgent matters. She hadn't found the answers she was looking for, but she was off to a good start. If nothing else, she had decent food, a steady wage, and would soon be leaving the city. That, at least, was an improvement.

Seren enjoyed the view from up here, but she found herself returning her attention to the figurehead. It was an impressive piece of sculpture, depicting a slender elf woman with arms folded across her breasts. Her eyes were closed, head thrown back with long hair that spilled over her shoulders. The statue was unpainted, carved from rich, dark wood and highly polished. Something about the statue resonated with Seren, made her feel more at peace here. It seemed so free and untamed, even bound permanently to the hull of the ship.

Other than the rush of the wind, the ship was strangely silent. Gerith was busy scrubbing the deck, singing a soft tune in a tongue Seren did not recognize. Blizzard perched on the rail nearby, regarding his master solemnly. Occasionally Gerith would halt the song for a moment and the animal would produce a high-pitched note in reply, singing along.

"What are you singing?" she asked, looking back at him.

Gerith looked up with a crooked smile. "Just an old song."

"What is it about?" she asked.

Gerith paused in his scrubbing and tilted his head. "I don't think you're old enough," he said with a chuckle. "Let's just say it's a song from my homeland, the song of an explorer, er, yearning for the comforts of home. We'll leave it at that."

"Fair enough," Seren said. "So where is the rest of the crew?"

"Rest?" Gerith asked, peering up at her again. "Well, you've met Dalan, though he isn't really crew, since he really doesn't do anything to help keep the ship going other than pay the bills. Then there's the captain, Tristam, Omax, me, and . . . and, well that's pretty much it."

"Doesn't a ship this size need a bigger crew than four people?" Seren asked.

"Usually, yes," Gerith said. "Throw magic in the mix and things get a bit odd, and airships are things of magic. Think of it this way: The wizards and artificers are already there binding the elemental and enchanting the ship so that she'll take to the wind. They may as well add in a few extra spells so that the ship can function a bit more efficiently, right? *Karia Naille* has it better than most. One of the finest ships it's been my pleasure to crew on. She has a few special features."

"Like what?" she asked.

"I'm not giving away her secrets," Gerith said with a laugh. "Wait till you're with us for a bit. Maybe you'll find out."

VOYAGE OF THE MOURNING DAWN

Seren nodded and let the subject slide, though the idea of more secrets didn't sit well with her. She looked past Gerith, at the creature perched behind him. "What sort of animal is that? I've never seen a lizard so big before."

The creature glared at her with angry black eyes. The leathery crest behind his cheeks flared.

"Careful," Gerith said. "Blizzard's sensitive. He's not a lizard. He's a glidewing with a proud pedigree. Only the finest warriors in my tribe can ride them. They're the most glorious creatures in all of the Talenta Plains, the rulers of the sky. And he's my friend. The two of us have seen the whole world together."

Blizzard gave an irritated flap of his leathery wings and let out a quick shriek.

"And he gets irritated when we do not finish our song," Gerith explained, turning and flicking his towel at the creature. The glidewing blinked, snorted, and shook off the soapy water. Preening one wing, he huddled on its perch and waited patiently for Gerith to continue.

The cabin hatch beside Dalan's opened just as the halfling resumed his song. A tiny old man, only slightly taller than the diminutive Gerith, strode out onto the deck. He was dressed in an immaculately pressed black uniform, a tight leather cap, and a pair of frosted goggles. Seren recognized him as a gnome, though she had met only a handful of them during her time in Wroat. Jamus had always instructed her to avoid gnomes. Not only did their sharp, inquisitive nature make them difficult to rob, but you generally didn't want to know what they had in their pockets.

"Good afternoon," the little man said, bowing toward Seren.

"Hello," she said.

"You are Miss Morisse, the thief Master d'Cannith invited onto my ship?" he asked in a pert voice.

"I am Seren Morisse," she said, taken aback by the abrupt greeting.

"Excellent!" the gnome said. "I am Captain Pherris Gerriman, of the Zilargo Gerrimans, of whom I am almost entirely certain you've never heard and likely couldn't care less. That makes us even, for the details that would lead Master d'Cannith to invite a known thief onboard my vessel would most likely only raise my lather and induce another in the chain of many headaches that have plagued my days of late. Therefore I prefer my ignorance. More importantly, now you are acquainted with me and I am acquainted with you. *Most* importantly, I see that you are now acquainted with the rail, and that pleases me a great deal."

"Why is that?" Seren asked.

"Because if you steal anything on my ship, Miss Morisse, or if you steal and draw trouble back to my ship because of it, then you will be going over that rail," the gnome said in the same cheerful tone. "Until then, we have no problems with one another, and I will show you the same loyalty I show all my crew. Your past means nothing to me so long as you obey my orders. You are one of us now. Agreed?"

"Agreed," she said, somewhat stunned.

The gnome clicked his boots pertly and turned away from her. "Master Snowshale! Where in Khyber are my artificer and his bodyguard?"

"Tristam and Omax are still in the city, I suppose," Gerith said, not looking up from his scrubbing.

"Blast," Pherris said. Grumbling under his breath, the gnome climbed onto the railing beside Seren and stared at the skyline. "I should have sent the dog for supplies. At least he always comes back for dinner. We should have left Wroat hours ago."

"Do you want me to look for them?" Seren offered. "I know the city."

"Excellent idea, Miss Morisse," Pherris said, rolling his eyes. "There's nothing I'd like better than to waste time looking for you as well. No, my dear, that shan't be necessary. Master Xain is a magnet for trouble, but I've no doubt he'll find an opportunity to . . . ah." The captain pointed at the southern skyline. "There. That's their signal."

Seren looked in that direction to see a streak of red light dropping from the sky, leaving a trail of thick purple smoke.

Pherris stomped back to the middle of the deck, climbing a short ladder to reach the ship's helm. Sensing what was to come, Gunther rose, trotted across the deck, and pawed impatiently at his master's hatch. "Prepare for takeoff, Master Snowshale," Pherris said in a grim voice.

"Aye, Captain," the halfling said, already hopping to his feet. "Seren, lend a hand."

"What do I do?" she asked.

"Just follow me and do what I do," the halfling said, busily beginning to untie the mooring ropes that secured the ship to the tower. Seren helped as best she could, though the halfling's deft fingers undid the knots more quickly than she could.

"Is there trouble, Captain?" Dalan asked, opening his cabin hatch and peering out. Gunther shoved past his master and disappeared into the shadows beyond, obviously eager to flee the deck before takeoff.

"Tristam and Omax have been gone too long," the gnome said. "They sent up a flare." He pointed in the relevant direction, though he did not take his eyes from the ship's controls.

"Those fools had best not be drawing attention," Dalan said angrily. "They've caused enough trouble."

"Time enough to cast blame when they're back onboard, Master d'Cannith," the captain said. "Ready for launch!"

Dalan stepped back with a sigh and closed his cabin hatch. Gerith nudged Seren. She looked down to see he was now holding a thick rope, one of many tied securely to the rail at regular intervals. She seized one as well, and Gerith gave a whistle. Pherris nodded and spun the wheel with both hands. Above the deck, the glowing blue ring seethed with red energy and sang with a steady, high-pitched hum. A vibration passed through the deck and the ship lurched away from the tower. Blizzard released a sharp cry and dropped off the rail, only to appear again on the other side of the ship, wings spread wide to catch the wind. Captain Gerriman pulled sharply at a lever beside the wheel and the ship righted herself, falling even and roaring off over the river. Seren saw the streets of Wroat pull away beneath them, people dwindling into dots and buildings shrinking. It was an odd, detached feeling, as if she were falling away from the world. It was strangely thrilling.

"First flight?" Gerith asked with a wide grin.

She nodded, unable to find any words.

"I envy you," he said. "Wait till you fly through your first cloud."

"Master Snowshale, I would appreciate it if you would scout ahead!" Pherris shouted over the hum of the elemental.

"Aye," the halfling said. He gave another sharp whistle, and Blizzard appeared once more, soaring beyond the ship's flaming ring. Gerith signaled to the glidewing, and it dove just as he leapt over the rail. Seren watched in astonishment as the halfling caught his steed's leather harness in midair and pulled himself into the saddle just as Blizzard leveled out and soared away over the city.

"Showboating lunatic," the captain said. "He'll miss one of these days, and I'll never see the money he owes me."

"What do you want me to do now?" Seren said, shouting over the howling winds.

"Just hold on, Miss Morisse," Pherris said. "Though I've no doubt those two will need a hand when . . . Khyber." The gnome continued swearing under his breath and concentrated more intently on the small crystal mounted on the ship's wheel. The ring of fire flashed green and the ship surged forward with a burst of speed.

Seren looked ahead and saw a plume of black smoke rising from the city. She saw the black silhouette of Blizzard rise up from the buildings, circle the plume, and then turn back toward *Karia Naille*. The glidewing banked sharply and landed on the ship. Gerith cartwheeled out of his harness and landed beside the captain, grasping Pherris's shoulder for balance.

"They're alive!" Gerith announced in a bright tone. "Though we should probably hurry before they die in the fire."

"Why have they set the city on fire, Master Snowshale?" Pherris asked with exaggerated calm.

"It's just one building, to be fair, Captain," Gerith said. "I think they intended to distract the Watch, but then they got trapped on the roof."

The captain cursed again, in a variety of languages. "Guide me to them, Master Snowshale."

"Easy enough, Captain," the halfling said as he climbed back into his saddle. "Just head for the fire."

Blizzard took to the air again, his broad wingspan barely clearing the elemental ring around the deck. The glidewing soared down toward the city in a dizzying circle and *Karia Naille* followed, falling into a controlled dive. The city grew beneath them. Wroat looked so strange from above; though Seren knew her way around these streets, nothing was arranged quite how she thought it would be. The crowds that gathered in the streets to look at the rising smoke now stopped and pointed up at the airship in awe.

The plume of smoke rose just ahead, to the ship's port side. It rose from a dilapidated four-story building. The airship fell level with the streets, soaring between the city's taller structures. Seren could see a large contingent of City Watch galloping down the street beneath them, as well as a brigade of citizens carrying buckets of water from the Howling River. The airship rose gradually, banking to port as she circled the burning building. Blizzard dove and landed on the roof farthest from the smoke, where Tristam and Omax waited. The ship pulled as close as she could, the elemental flames that surrounded her preventing her from getting too close lest more damage be done.

"Throw that cable to them, Miss Morisse, and pull the lever when they are secure," Pherris said, nodding to a nearby coil lashed to the deck.

Seren quickly complied, hurling the heavy cable over the rail. Omax caught it in one hand, passing the slack to Tristam, who gave a quick salute. She pulled the lever and a winch began to turn below the deck, hauling them both up toward *Karia Naille*. Omax crawled over first, carrying a body over one shoulder. He dumped it unceremoniously onto the deck.

The captain looked down at the limp bundle with a sour expression. "Omax, why did you bring me a dead watchman?" he asked, looking back to the wheel.

"It was Tristam's idea," Omax said.

"He's not dead!" Tristam added as he climbed over the side. "He passed out in the smoke."

Pherris pulled a lever and the ship banked upward again. "Then we are merely kidnappers and arsonists, not murderers. That's good news. Don't you agree, Miss Morisse?"

The sound of a metallic thunk sounded from the deck beneath them, followed by another.

"What was that?" Seren asked.

"Crossbows," Gerith said, alighting on the deck nearby. "I'll be forever working those bolts out of the hull. Tristam, what in Khyber did you do?"

"Not now, Master Snowshale," Pherris said in a warning tone, concentrating on the ship's control. The airship pulled smoothly to a halt above a low building and Pherris looked back at the warforged. "Omax, please return to Wroat what is Wroat's."

Omax nodded and, picking up the watchman, rappelled over the rail again. He laid the man carefully on the roof and then began scaling his way back up the cable. The flaming circle flared green and the ship started off again even before Omax had cleared the rail.

"Secure yourselves," Pherris said as Omax climbed onto the deck. "Miss Morisse, say your good-byes to your home. Aeven, please give us a boost before the King's soldiers discover their own airships."

The captain did not remove his hands from the wheel, but the ship lurched heavily. Seren fell to the deck, clinging to the nearest secure rope with both hands. Tristam also fell nearby, though when he saw Seren's eyes watching him his own terrified expression became a grin of false confidence. Even Gerith scrambled for the ropes, securing himself and Blizzard to the deck. Only Omax seemed unaffected, standing in the middle of the deck with feet splayed and shoulders squared against the ship's sudden momentum.

Karia Naille's bow fell forward, and the elemental ring burned white with an incredible burst of speed. The city melted away beneath them, dwindling to the size of a toy and eventually becoming nothing more than a distant black dot beside the blue ribbon of the Howling River. The deck boards shuddered against one another, and sweat streamed down Pherris's face as he gripped the wheel with white knuckles. After several minutes of such frantic speed, the flaming ring burned blue again. The ship fell into a calm cruise far above the Breland plains. Seren wobbled to her feet, holding the railing for support. The ground was now far beneath them. Wisps of white clouds streaked past on each side, some far below. It was unlike anything she'd ever seen. It was like entering a new world, a sea of calm far removed from the chaotic land below. Out of the corner of her eye, she saw Gerith look at her with a knowing grin.

Dalan d'Cannith's cabin opened and the fat guildmaster strode out onto the deck. He looked calm and unruffled by their rapid escape. Gunther peered warily around the corner of the door, then retreated rapidly back inside.

"What happened in the city, Tristam?" Dalan asked. He folded his arms behind his back as he looked down at the prone artificer. "You started a fire and attacked a watchman?"

Tristam scrambled awkwardly to his feet and tried to dust the soot off his jacket with one hand.

"I'm sorry, Dalan, I dunno what happened," he explained. "Omax found a wanted poster with my face on it, so we tried to investigate . . ."

"If the Watch was looking for you, then wouldn't it make more sense to return and let Gerith and Omax investigate?" Dalan asked interrupting Tristam's explanation.

"They think I killed city guards and burned down your house, Dalan! I'd hoped I could set the record straight."

"And making their arson charges a reality and nearly justifying a murder charge in so doing is how you set things straight?" Dalan asked. "What a unique approach."

"The building was empty," Tristam said. "The Watch was already chasing us. That was a distraction, to throw them off while we ran back to the ship."

"I understand that," Dalan said. "Why did you choose to create such an elaborate distraction and then trap yourself on top of it?"

Tristam's shoulders slumped. "We meant to run," he said. "But Omax saw that stupid guard run inside. I guess he thought someone might be trapped inside. We had to help him." Omax stood beside Tristam, looking impassively at Dalan with his strange blue eyes.

"We could not let him die, Master d'Cannith," Omax said.

Pherris looked back from the wheel, giving the young artificer an appraising look. Dalan only chewed his lip thoughtfully. "We can scarcely afford such reckless heroism, Tristam," Dalan finally said, though his voice was softer now. "You know how much is at stake here."

Tristam nodded.

"Our apologies, Master d'Cannith," Omax added.

"No harm done," Dalan replied. "Our Captain Marth is a changeling. No doubt he assumed your identity and framed you for his own crimes. Now at least one watchman in Wroat might not be so quick to believe you are a killer. Not that it matters in the end; I doubt we'll soon be returning to Wroat. Miss Morisse has provided us with a most intriguing lead in exchange for a position among our crew."

Tristam looked back at Seren in surprise, then back at Dalan. "So she's coming with us?" he asked, not sounding entirely pleased with the news.

"What did you find, Seren?" Omax asked in a more pleasant voice.

"An enchanted hand lens," she said. "Marth used it to study the book I stole. Whatever he was looking for with it, he didn't find it."

"Some sort of magical cipher," Tristam said, scratching his chin. "Ashrem was a prolific writer. He could have easily hidden his work on the Legacy in his many books, written invisibly, and used something like that to read them. May I see the lens, Dalan?"

"Of course," Dalan said.

Dalan reached in his vest pocket and produced the small chunk of frosted glass. Tristam grabbed it eagerly, hurrying past Dalan into the cabin. Seren followed, watching Tristam curiously. He picked up one of the many volumes marked with

Ashrem d'Cannith's seal and flipped through its pages, holding the lens to one eye.

"There's definitely something there I haven't seen before, but I can't understand the text," he said. He pushed the book aside and quickly seized another, flipping through that one and setting it aside as well. He reached for a third, but stopped as Dalan interrupted with a heavy sigh.

"Encoded as well as hidden," Dalan d'Cannith said, circling Tristam and seating himself at the desk again. "And if it is one of Ashrem's codes, then all your skills will not unravel it. That is why we are going to Black Pit."

"Black Pit?" Tristam said, incredulous. "We don't need his help, Dalan. He already turned his back on us once."

"I hope that you are correct," d'Cannith said. "Yet surely you agree if this truly is some sort of magical code, then his talents are better suited to this matter than yours. Until then, I will retain the lens."

"You aren't even going to give me a chance to crack this myself?" Tristam asked.

"If I cannot read it, I doubt you can," Dalan said. "I cannot afford to see an item so valuable lost or broken, Tristam." He held out his hand.

Tristam dropped the piece of glass onto Dalan's palm and turned with a scowl, nearly tripping over Seren as he stormed out of Dalan's cabin. Tristam coughed an embarrassed apology and circled around her, headed to the far end of the deck. Omax sat down cross-legged by his friend's side in a posture of deep contemplation, the glow in his blue eyes dimming.

"Black Pit," Gerith said with a whistle, appearing beside Seren again.

"What's in Black Pit?" she asked. "For that matter, what *is* Black Pit?"

"It's a hole in Eberron," Gerith said.

"Like Wroat?" she asked.

"No, I mean literally a hole," he said. "It's a crack in the ground that leads right into Khyber itself. There's a village right near the edge, and it names itself after the pit. That can be a bit confusing, having two places with the same name, but then humans have always been a confusing sort of people. The village built up near the end of the Last War. It's not even on most maps; the folks there prefer it that way. It's a place for deserters, smugglers, mercenaries, criminals. It's also the backbone of Breland's thriving black market. Very interesting place, with all kinds of interesting people."

"Why are we going there?" Seren asked, looking down at the halfling with a worried expression.

"Like I said, all kinds of interesting people," Gerith answered. "Zed Arthen is one of them. He's an inquisitive."

"Inquisitive?" she said. "An investigator?"

"An inquisitive is a bit more than that," Gerith said. "Sort of like a glidewing is a little more than a lizard. An inquisitive answers questions that nobody wants to have answered, questions that folks generally figure can't be answered. You'd like him, I think."

"Why would Arthen be in a place like Black Pit?" Seren asked.

Gerith grinned a broad gap-toothed grin. "Maybe because in a place like that a person like him always has something to do. Maybe because in a place like *that*, he hopes that people like *us* will leave him alone."

CHAPTER EIGHT

It was all so frustrating. She should have known better than to listen to Jamus.

Eraina d'Deneith watched the strange airship leave a trail of flame across the northern sky, taking her answers with it. Around her, watchmen and civilian volunteers formed frenzied bucket chains, passing water from the river to the burning building. She ignored them, steering her steed directly toward the building where she had seen the airship pause. Dropping from the saddle and pushing the door open, she strode inside. An elderly couple had been watching the fire from a nearby window, and looked at her with alarm.

"What is the meaning of this?" the old man demanded, voice shaking as he looked at Eraina's polished armor, spear, and the shortsword that hung from her belt. "Get out of our house!"

Eraina drew a thin metal case from her pocket and snapped it open for the couple to see the identification documents inside. Within was a small packet of papers fixed with an official seal, featuring a small illustration of the dark-haired woman that held the case.

"I am a Sentinel Marshal conducting an official investigation. I have business on your roof and won't be more than a moment."

The man glanced at the papers in Eraina's hand but stayed

well out of reach of her sword arm, holding his wife fearfully. Eraina had hoped for as much; though she had not lied to them, she would prefer not to have her name remembered. She snapped the case shut and continued toward the stairs. She climbed up onto the roof and looked around, holding her short spear in her left hand, right hand resting on the hilt of her blade. Her hand fell away when she saw the limp form lying on the roof. She leaned her spear beside the door and knelt, pulling off one mailed gauntlet to press two fingers to the man's throat. He was alive. His armor was blackened with soot but he did not seem to be badly burned.

"Get up," she said, standing and rolling the man onto his back with one steel-toed boot.

The man lay where he was, unconscious. Eraina knelt again and laid her hand on the man's chest. Her other hand grasped the amulet about her throat and she whispered a brief prayer. For an instant, her hand glowed with a white light. The glowing energy drained from her fingers into the man's body. A spasm shook him and he stirred, his eyes snapping open at the sky.

"What is your name, watchman?" she asked. She held one finger out before his face, watching as his eyes focused upon it.

"Watchman Markus," the man said, still a bit dazed.

"Get up, Markus," she repeated with an impatient gesture. She rose and began to pace beside him.

The watchman sat up with a groan, pulling off his helmet and rubbing his head. Blinking in astonishment, he patted himself down with both hands for any sign of injuries. He looked about in confusion, his gaze eventually resting on the dying plume of smoke rising from the building to the south.

"How did I get up here?" he said in a bewildered voice.

"You were dropped out of a fleeing airship," she said. "Do you remember that?"

He stood up unsteadily, staring at the three-headed chimera

crest on her tabard with some amazement. "A Sentinel Marshal?" he said. "What's going on here?"

Eraina sighed. "Boldrei's teachings advocate patience for those who have suffered," she said, replacing her gauntlet and stretching her fingers within it. "However, as a Sentinel Marshal I am required to seek the truth efficiently. I called the Hearthmother's blessings upon you to heal you, Watchman Markus. Thus I would appreciate it if you finished gather your senses swiftly." She fixed him with a stern expression.

"My apologies, Marshal," the man said, flustered. "What would you like to know?"

"As much as you can remember before you awakened here," she said, folding her arms across her chest.

The guardsman nodded. "I can't remember much, to be honest," he said. "We were pursuing a Lhazaarite who burned the Cannith estate and killed three watchmen last night. When the fire started I ran inside looking for anyone that might have been trapped."

"What was this man's name?" she asked.

The guardsman shrugged. "No name, only a description."

Markus took a folded scrap of parchment from his pocket and offered it to Eraina. She unfolded it and studied it for a long moment. It was a hastily printed wanted poster, and the man in the illustration was unfamiliar.

"He was the last thing I saw," the watchman said. "He and his warforged friend ran into the fire to rescue me."

"The killer rescued you?" Eraina asked.

The man nodded, though he looked rather confused. "Seeing as how I'm here, Marshal, he must have."

Eraina sighed. Somehow, after all that had happened, she had hoped that the clues would begin to fall together. She was not truly surprised; she had enough experience to know that the truth rarely fit together in a convenient way as it did in stories.

VOYAGE OF THE MOURNING DAWN

More often, even after a crime was solved, she never knew the full truth. Sometimes she just wished that a mystery would come together cleanly, if only for variety.

When she spoke again, her voice was a great deal softer. "Thank you for your help, Watchman Markus." She folded the poster and tucked it in one pocket. "I have nothing further. No doubt your superior officer will be eager to discover you are still alive."

"Thank you again, Marshal . . ." he said, letting the end of the sentence hang as he hoped to catch her name.

Eraina merely gave a brief salute and turned, taking up her spear and heading back down the stairs. The elderly couple was just as she had left them, still huddled by the window in terror. Eraina stopped with her hand on the door.

She moved to the window beside them, looking out at the smoking building. They moved away as much as they dared.

"Were you at this window the entire time?" she asked, studying the skyline.

"Y-yes," the old man answered.

"Did you see the airship?" she asked. "Did you see the direction it came from?"

"Downriver," the old man said, pointing out the window to the south.

"Boldrei walk beside you," she said, bowing thankfully and stepping back outside.

Eraina's horse waited patiently where she had left it. She climbed back into the saddle and rode toward the river. The crowd, slowly realizing that the fire was under control and there were unlikely to be any more airships swooping over the neighborhood, had begun to disperse, making passage a great deal easier. The farther south she went, the poorer the neighborhoods became. This was near the place that Jamus Roland had called home. Eraina scowled, pushing away thoughts of the old thief.

She had hoped for a better life for him, but now there was no chance of that. He was a good man, despite his flaws. He had deserved better.

She would never forgive herself.

The sight of six towers looming above the fishermen's district quickly drew her attention to the task at hand. The towers were four stories tall, double the size of the average surrounding buildings. Each tower had a swooping bridge at its height, leading to nothing, with a large wooden crane mounted on the end. They were airship towers, though they looked to be poorly maintained. It was hardly surprising to see the docking towers unused. The Last War had ground most nonmilitary travel to a standstill. The few privately airships that remained would surely seek to dock in safer areas of Wroat. The thugs, smugglers, and ruffians who frequented this part of town would find greater profits traveling by boat or by road. On the other hand, someone seeking to slip an airship in and out of the city relatively unnoticed could do so quite easily here. Few locals would pry too deeply if the ship was well guarded.

Eraina stopped, her brow furrowing as she saw two horses gathered outside one of the towers. She galloped in that direction, drawing a muttered curse from a drunken sailor as he stumbled out of the way. She vaulted to the ground, took her spear from the saddle, and ran toward the tower. A tall, blond man in armor and a tabard matching Eraina's stepped out to greet her with a grim smile. A smaller, dark-haired man stepped out beside him, watching her without expression.

"Marshal Eraina," the blond man said with a brief nod.

"Marshal Galas," she said, striding toward him. "Marshal Killian." She nodded to the other man.

"Fortuitous timing, Eraina," Galas said. "I see the clues have led us to the same place. Let me spare you a great deal of wasted time. There is nothing here."

"Are you certain?" she asked, looking past him into the tower. "I believe the airship containing the suspect came from one of these towers."

"She did," Galas said, tightening his gauntlets as he prepared to mount his steed. "Killian questioned what passes for a harbor master here. We drew him from his cups long enough to learn that an airship docked here last night, shortly before the debacle at the Friendly Buzzard. There were no symbols of ownership on the vessel. No crew wandered out to hit the taverns. No guards watched the tower door. A few nondescript figures boarded, followed by a girl who visited this morning. She matched the description of your friend Roland's partner."

Eraina looked at Galas. "Seren Morisse?" she asked.

"Whoever," Galas said, looking at her with a frown. "Obviously the thief was not as reliable as Jamus believed and was somehow complicit in his death. It doesn't matter, Eraina. Your friend failed. We are done here."

"Done? How can we be done? This is the first real lead we've had!"

Galas turned to face her, placing one hand on her shoulder. His frown softened into a sympathetic smile. "Eraina, I understand your feelings on the matter," he said. "It is always hard for a Marshal to lose one under her protection, and it must be harder still for you, with Roland having been involved. I have served House Deneith as a Marshal for twenty years, so understand that what I say next is not said out of callousness, but out of practicality. While it is important for a Marshal to have passion, it is also necessary to have clarity. We have made a mistake here. Best to let it go rather than compound the danger, Eraina. We should return to Korth to plan our next move."

"Best to let it go?" Eraina said. "We have a duty to uphold, Galas!"

Galas sighed. "You have an admirable thirst for justice, and I won't deny that injustice has been done here, but remember that your first duty is to House Deneith. Consider the facts. Dalan d'Cannith is rumored to have discovered a lost journal penned by his famous uncle, the very same sort of prize our quarry seeks. We hurry here, believing that the killer may strike again. You discover your old friend, Jamus, has already been contacted about acquiring the volume for an anonymous client. Upon your urging, he takes the contract, hoping to draw the client out so we may learn more. Somewhere the deal goes bad. Dalan d'Cannith's house burns down. Jamus Roland dies. Roland's partner flees in an unidentified airship, pausing only long enough to hover over a burning building and load a wanted killer aboard before fleeing to Khyber knows where. Pardon my swearing."

Eraina frowned at him.

"You can't deny how it looks, Eraina," he said. "We've become entangled in something that is no longer our affair."

"None of our affair? We came seeking a killer, and we found one! The trail is still warm. Llaine Grove died for what he knew about Ashrem d'Cannith's work. This is obviously the same suspect. Why would we return to Korth now that things are only beginning to make sense?"

"Because nothing makes sense, Eraina!" Galas snapped, gesturing wildly as he turned away from her. "Your desperate need for vengeance is forming patterns where there are none. If you wish to hunt random murderers, we could spend the rest of our lives in Wroat and find our fill of them, but I've seen nothing to prove that this is the suspect we seek. Perhaps your friend Jamus discovered the book wasn't what we wanted, tried to fence it, and died when the deal went bad. Perhaps his partner turned on him. Perhaps d'Cannith killed Roland himself and burned his own house down to cover his tracks. We could speculate forever, Eraina, but it's all too random. You dealt with a thief, and things went poorly. Roland's death was regrettable, but it is not our concern."

"Jamus Roland was not just a thief. He deserves better than to be abandoned by us."

"Jamus Roland," Galas said, "was not our client. We owe him *nothing*. Baron d'Deneith will be upset enough that we became involved with the Canniths without his knowledge. Best that we cut our losses, withdraw before our involvement is detected, and wait for another opportunity for justice."

"An opportunity which may never come," Eraina said. "I cannot believe after two years that you would give up so easily. Do you forget your vows so easily, Marshal? Or does your fear that we will fail again cripple you from any decisive action?"

Galas turned to face Eraina again. His mouth opened, then closed with a click. His face grew dark red as his temper began to build.

"Perhaps a compromise is not out of the question," Killian said, stepping between them.

"What?" Galas demanded, too filled with rage to say anything else.

"You have already determined that this investigation has struck an impasse," Killian answered. "We are to return to Korth and continue our research into the case. In the meantime, with no other leads, what harm could it do to allow Eraina to investigate her friend's murder? If, by chance, she should be correct and it somehow bears connection to our investigation, then we can only benefit. If there is no connection, we can at least foster good relations with Wroat for aiding them in resolving what must appear to be a truly baffling crime."

"A Sentinel Marshal does not take leave to conduct independent investigations," Galas said.

"Why?" Eraina demanded. "Is justice our cause only so long as there is profit?"

"Guard your tongue, Eraina," Galas said. "Simply because you bear the Deneith name, do not assume I will not report such insubordination to our superiors."

"Galas, Eraina, please!" Killian said, holding restraining hands toward them both. "We are friends! Comrades in arms. Such arguments accomplish nothing. Galas, I realize our duties to House Deneith are your primary concern, but recognize Eraina's position as well. She is a Spear of Boldrei. You cannot possibly expect that she would leave a comrade's murder to the City Watch when she has it within her power to put things right."

Galas closed his eyes and did not speak for a long moment. When he regained his composure, he looked at Eraina sternly. "Eraina, I cannot spare the resources to aid you," he said. "I do not intend to send you into such a dangerous investigation alone. You . . . are worth too much to us."

"I am never alone, Galas," she said, one hand moving to the amulet about her throat.

"Stubborn paladins," Galas said. He grumbled a chain of curses under his breath. "So be it! I hope you give the Hearthmother as many headaches as you've given me."

Eraina smiled wryly. "Thank you," she said.

"Thank Killian," he answered, climbing into his saddle. Galas looked pointedly away from her, studying the road north intently.

Eraina bowed to Killian. The soft-spoken marshal returned the gesture silently and mounted beside his commanding officer.

"We'll be expecting regular reports, Eraina," Galas said, still looking at the road. "Weekly ciphered speaker posts."

"Yes, sir," she said.

"Come back to us alive, Eraina," he said softly, still looking away. "May your goddess take good care of you."

"And you as well, sir," she answered.

Galas gave a final sharp salute and rode away. Killian did

the same, though he shared an apologetic smile before he left. Eraina watched them go in silence. Then, with a heavy sigh, she returned to the matter at hand. She looked back at the looming airship tower and ran through the facts in her mind.

Jamus Roland was no saint, but he was a man of his word and he knew better than to lie to a paladin. He had promised Eraina that he would help her trap the killer she had been following. He would not betray her. Of Jamus's partner, Seren, she knew little. It was possible that Seren might have betrayed Jamus and fled with the book.

But why burn Dalan d'Cannith's home? Why did the Lhazaarite stranger murder three guards and let another escape? It was obviously sloppy and hardly seemed to fit the pattern she and her fellow Marshals had been following thus far. Either Galas was right and this entire messy affair was entirely unrelated to their quarry, or all of this was a distraction. She frowned as she turned over the details. It wasn't entirely inconceivable that Roland would have invited a potential killer into his tutelage. The old thief had always been a rather spotty judge of character, especially where pretty young girls were concerned.

Such thoughts began to draw back memories, and with memories came undesired emotion. Eraina cast such distractions aside. She needed answers. She stepped into the tower, seeking focus as she searched for clues. She saw little other than dust. The stairs were well-traveled; she counted several sets of footprints beside those of Galas and Killian. The rest of the tower had fallen into disrepair. She moved to the top of the winding spiral staircase, the butt of her short spear thumping the stairs ahead of her. Her right hand rested on the hilt of her sword out of habit, though she was fairly certain the other two Marshals would have left no threats behind. She stepped out onto the bridge atop the tower, wind whipping around her with a low, keening whistle. Eraina extended one hand to steady herself as she looked down at the river. She wobbled on her feet and prayed to Boldrei for strength. Paladins were said to be without fear. For the most part that was true, but heights made her a little nervous.

Eraina stepped out farther onto the bridge. The cargo crane hung at an odd angle, and upon closer inspection she saw that it was long broken. Whoever came here had not been smuggling or taking on supplies, at least not in any great volume. They came specifically for their passengers and left just as quickly. She stepped back toward the safety of the doorway and pondered. Far below, she saw her steed had shied away from the door. The animal tossed its head and shifted weight from foot to foot. Eraina frowned at the horse's odd behavior. She cocked her head, listening more closely. A faint wooden creak sounded on the stairs below.

Eraina drew her sword and whispered a brief prayer to Boldrei. A sensation of quiet strength issued through her arm and into her spear. She slid her mailed sleeve up over her left forearm, revealing the swirling dragonmark pattern that extended from her wrist to elbow. She concentrated and felt its power flare as well, surrounding her body with a shimmering protective aura that quickly faded from view. Thus strengthened by her goddess and protected by her House, Eraina d'Deneith stepped into the stairwell.

"Who goes there?" she demanded, holding out her spear and shortsword. Brilliant light shone from the spear's head, filling the stairs below.

The twang of three crossbows issued in reply. Eraina did not flinch. The bolts struck her chest harmlessly and fell on the stairs with a clatter. Three gruff-looking men stood on the stairs beneath, staring up at her in awe. Each now held an unloaded crossbow.

"Khyber," one swore and reached for the knife at his belt.

VOYAGE OF THE MOURNING DAWN

Eraina did not hesitate. Planting her spear against the stairs for balance, she lunged forward and planted her foot in the nearest man's chest. He yelped and rolled backward, seizing the railing in time but sending his friend tumbling into the void. He landed on the ground floor with a crack. The third man leapt over his fallen friend and charged Eraina with a stout pipe, rushing inside her reach before she could swing. She punched him sharply in the throat with the hilt of her sword and he fell backward. She swung her spear in a deadly arc, leaving a trail of red across his chest. He fell backward, screaming, down the stairs. The surviving thief clung to the railing as his dead friend rolled past. He held his knife in his free hand, looking up at Eraina in terror.

"Stay back," he said, though he could barely force the words out for his terror.

Eraina sneered and struck out with her sword, viciously slapping the man's wrist with the flat of the blade and sending his dagger flying into the depths. She sheathed her blade and seized his collar in a twisting grip, dragging him to his feet. She held the point of her broad-bladed spear an inch from his eye.

"Who sent you?" she demanded.

The man looked up at her, terrified. "Nobody sent us!" he said. "Three against one seemed like an easy mark is all! Please don't kill me!"

"I walk a path of compassion," Eraina said. "I kill only to defend myself or my charge. You are no threat to me."

"Thank the Host," the man whimpered.

"You should," Eraina said. "Boldrei has given you mercy, but I have no time to spare you kindness." She leaned her spear against the wall and punched him hard in the temple with a mailed fist. Taking her spear back, she left him lying in an unconscious heap on the stairs. She frowned uncomfortably at the two corpses as she reached the bottom of the stairs. As usual, the rush of combat took all certainty with it. Now that the battle was over, her doubts returned, little by little. These men had been wicked, but could there have been another way? Was redemption beyond them? Now there was no chance for them and she was to blame—again. She could not bring herself to pray for forgiveness; she suspected she deserved none.

But doubt could wait till later. Eraina peered out of the tower, wary of any more accomplices that might lay in wait. Either there were none or they had wisely fled when the screams began. As the excitement of the battle faded, something stuck in Eraina's mind. She looked back at the tower door. It hung wide open. The doorknob and lock were missing, probably scavenged by some enterprising local decades ago. Eraina frowned.

An airship was a highly valuable piece of property. Only a fool would land one unguarded in a neighborhood such as this, yet Galas said that there were no guards or obvious crew. It had taken only a matter of minutes for a band of thugs to follow her in here. An airship would not have survived docked to an unlocked tower without incident, not even for one night, unless other precautions were taken.

Eraina stepped back inside the tower and looked at the door frame. There, where the door's lock used to be, she saw a strange pattern etched into the wood. She prayed to her goddess, drawing upon Boldrei's wisdom to grant her insight. The pattern glowed blue to her eyes, displaying an intricate pattern of magical energy. It was a ward, intended to seal the door against outside entry until the proper command was given. It was inactive now, but that was not what truly interested Eraina. Like any form of art, magic was given to particular styles. To the trained eye such things quickly became recognizable. She noticed a looping curve in the runes here, a signature flare there, and the particular pigment of the ink was also noteworthy.

This ward was made by a Cannith, or someone who had been trained by them.

VOYAGE OF THE MOURNING DAWN

Many possibilities ran through Eraina's mind. Could one of Cannith's underlings have made plans with Seren to obtain the book, kill Jamus, and burn his master's house to conceal the crime? Other than Dalan, there were no members of House Cannith in Wroat who were wealthy enough to possess such an airship, and any who had such holdings would probably be so highly ranked in their house they could have simply demanded that Dalan surrender the book. That left only Dalan d'Cannith. Could he still be alive? Why would Seren betray and kill Jamus only to turn the book over to the man she had stolen it from? Who had burned Dalan's home? Who was the mysterious Lhazaarite who had murdered the guards, and why was Dalan consorting with him?

Too many questions, but at least this was a beginning. Now Eraina knew what to do. Once she had alerted the Watch to the thief and two corpses she had left behind, she could pursue the matter in earnest.

Marshal Eraina d'Deneith climbed into her saddle and galloped away through the streets of Wroat.

Chapter Nine

Seren woke with a pounding headache and a knifelike pain in her back. All about her was darkness. She sat up awkwardly, feeling around for some sense of her environment. She did not remember this room, nor how she came to be here. She felt a pang of alarm when she realized the knife at her belt was gone. Had she been wrong to trust d'Cannith's strange crew? Had they decided not to trust her after all and locked her in the brig? A thousand paranoid theories burned through Seren's mind.

Fear swallowed all rational thought as two pale blue lights suddenly shone in the darkness. The dim light was followed a moment later by a small lantern flaring to life, held by the warforged, Omax. Seren lay on a narrow cot in a cramped chamber. The warforged knelt in the center of the room, holding the lantern in one hand. A small table stood beside the cot. Seren's dagger lay atop it, still sheathed. She quickly snatched the weapon and huddled in the corner, as far away from the construct as she could. The weapon would do her little good if Omax was hostile, but some chance was better than nothing.

"Hello, Seren," Omax said in his deep, measured voice. "Are you feeling better?"

"What am I doing here?" she asked. "What are you doing here?"

VOYAGE OF THE MOURNING DAWN

"The captain felt it best if one of us remained to watch over you," Omax said. "Sky sickness can leave one confused and disoriented. We did not wish to see you come to harm. I apologize if I frightened you."

As the initial terror passed, Seren began to remember the events of the previous day. The ship had continued her steady pace over the Brelish landscape. Seren had spent the better part of the first day helping Gerith and Omax tend to the ship, keeping the decks clean and preparing the meals. While helping scrub the aft deck, she had begun to feel unusually ill and could not remember anything after that.

"Sky sickness?" she asked, tucking the dagger into her belt. She felt rather foolish for her paranoia but saw little need to apologize to the construct.

Omax nodded. "The enchantments that keep a ship like this afloat also provide some modicum of comfort, but they are not perfect," he said. "The air is much thinner and colder than you are used to. The movements of the ship itself can be disorienting. A human not accustomed to the conditions can easily be overcome with exhaustion without any warning."

"I see," she said. Seren climbed off her pallet. Her thighs felt rubbery and sore, and for a moment her legs threatened not to support her. Omax held out a metal hand and she seized it for support. She pulled away just as quickly, unnerved by the construct's thick metal fingers. She had expected them to be cold, but Omax was warm, like a living creature.

The warforged lowered his gaze. When he spoke again, his voice was subdued. "I will leave you to your privacy, Seren," he said. "If you require me for anything, I shall be meditating in the forward cargo bay."

Seren did not reply. Omax rose, gave a strangely formal bow, and departed. She waited where she was, listening to the sound of the construct's heavy metal footfalls receding through the ship. When she was fairly sure the warforged was gone, she opened her cabin door and tentatively stepped out into the hall. She was on the lower deck of the airship and could hear the steady hum of the ship's elemental ring pulsing beneath her feet.

Small doors lined the narrow hallway on either side. This part of the ship's lower deck was filled with these small cabins. As she continued forward, Seren heard movement inside the cabin closest to her own. She smelled a pungent, chemical smell from beyond the door, accompanied by a faint bubbling. She leaned closer to listen, and the bubbling grew more intense, followed by the sound of breaking glass and Tristam Xain swearing violently.

Seren moved on, climbing the ladder that separated the cabins and cargo bay, emerging on the main deck. She felt a chill as the wind rushed over her bare arms and cut through her thin breeches. Looking out over the rail it was difficult to tell how high the ship flew. All around was a vast sea of clouds, showing only a rare hint of green beneath. In the distance, she saw Gerith's glidewing diving in and out of the clouds. She felt a detached sense of peace and safety. The flight of an airship was so calming, despite everything that had happened. She had no idea what lay ahead or what truly motivated Dalan d'Cannith and his strange crew, but somehow standing on the deck of *Karia Naille* she felt safer than she had since leaving Ringbriar so long ago.

"Good morning," Captain Gerriman said blandly from the ship's wheel. He peered pointedly at the sun, fixed precisely overhead in the noonday sky. "Glad to see your first day on board was such a productive one."

"No one warned me about sky sickness, Captain," Seren said.

The gnome looked at her, stroking his bushy white moustache with one hand. "I think you misunderstand me, Miss Morisse," he said. "I meant what I said. A crewman willing to work herself to a stupor on the first day is exactly the sort of person who leaves a lasting positive impression on me. Just don't do it again. I respect determination, but I am not a great admirer of stupidity." He returned his attention to the ship's controls, turning the wheel idly with one hand.

"Well," Seren said with a small laugh, "then I should get back to work." She looked around at the deck. "What needs to be done?"

"Nothing, really," Pherris said with a shrug. "Gerith can be a little obsessive, always finding something to clean or polish, but she takes care of herself just fine most of the time. Sit and rest for a bit. If you plan to stay on my ship, I'd appreciate coming to know you better."

"I thought you said you preferred ignorance," Seren said.

"About how you came to know Dalan, yes," he said. "But what sort of person you are and what sort of things you've done, while not entirely unrelated, are separate affairs. It is the former that interests me."

"It isn't much of a story," she said. She climbed to the upper deck and sat cross-legged in the bow of the ship. "I come from a little village called Ringbriar. After the end of the war, I just thought I'd be better off somewhere else."

"Ah," Pherris said. "Did you lose your family, then? Parents dead in the war?"

"My father died in the war," she said. "My mother was alive, the last time I saw her."

"You don't know for sure if your mother is alive?" he asked, incredulous.

"I haven't seen her in years," Seren said. "She's better off without me."

"Hrm," Pherris said. He studied the clouds off to the left. His thoughts were elsewhere.

"You seem much different today, Captain," Seren finally said, breaking the uncomfortable silence. "A lot calmer than you were when we first met."

Pherris wrinkled face twisted in a grin. "When you met me, I had just been commanded to fly my ship unauthorized into the Brelish capital in the dead of night to rescue my employer from unknown enemies. Today I have the luxury of patience. My patience is not an infinite commodity, and I find it is expended more often than not in Master d'Cannith's service."

Seren glanced quickly toward the door of Dalan's cabin, then back at the captain.

"Oh, trust me, Miss Morisse, he is well aware of my opinion of him," Pherris said. "I am a gnome who speaks his mind, and he knows the ship would fall apart without me."

"If you think so little of him, why do you work for him?" she asked.

"Because *Karia Naille* once belonged to Dalan's uncle, a good and honorable man," Pherris said.

"Ashrem d'Cannith built this ship?" Seren asked.

Pherris looked extremely shocked. "Built her?" he said, scoffing. "Ashrem didn't build *Karia Naille*. He improved her, certainly, and he understood what drives her better than most humans. I'll argue none of that, but *Karia Naille* and her sister ships are products of gnomish ingenuity. The Canniths would have you believe they build everything, but I assure you that is not the case!"

"I didn't mean any offense," Seren said. "I don't know much about airships."

"Ah," Pherris said, his tone softening somewhat. "Well, if you ever wish to know more, I am at your disposal. But to answer your original question, Ashrem once had three airships, *Karia Naille*, the *Kenshi Zhann*, and the *Albena Tors*—or, translated, the *Mourning Dawn*, the *Seventh Moon*, and the *Dying Sun*.

VOYAGE OF THE MOURNING DAWN

If you ask me, this one is the finest of the three, fastest at a sprint and prettiest by far. Ashrem had her built for Kiris—the young wizard who stole his heart. Of course Kiris spent most of her time with Ashrem on the *Kenshi Zhann* and left the ship under my able command. When she shared Ashrem's fate, the *Mourning Dawn* passed to Dalan. I can't imagine why Ashrem would bequeath such ship to his nephew—the two were not particularly close—but he did. I offered Dalan my services on the day the will was read. I could not envision *Karia Naille* in the hands of another captain. Master d'Cannith knew better than to refuse. We have our differences, but on professional matters we recognize one another's talents. He leaves the ship in my hands. I leave the rest to him."

"And what of the others?" she asked. "Gerith, Tristam, Omax. How did they end up here?"

"Gerith's tale is simple enough," Pherris said. "He was looking for work, and I'd flown with him a few times before. His experience as a scout, explorer, and translator speaks for itself. He's lived half as long as I have and seen twice as much of the world. I was afraid he might get bored and leave again until we hit Wroat. Now we're moving again, so he's interested, and I'm sure a pretty young human girl joining the crew didn't hurt. Tristam and Omax are a bit more complicated."

"Complicated?" she asked.

Pherris looked back at the door of Dalan's cabin, then back at Seren. His voice became much softer, as if concerned he would be overheard. "It all goes back to Dalan," he said, "and his uncle, of course."

"How?"

"You ask a great deal of questions, Miss Morisse," Pherris said shrewdly. "You are quite fortunate that gossip is the Zilargo national pastime."

Seren laughed.

"Dalan is obsessed with his uncle's work, and rightly so," the captain said, answering her question.

"The Legacy is some sort of ticket to promotion to him with his house," Seren said.

"Well, it would be ironic, wouldn't it?" Pherris said. "It was Ashrem's work that crippled Dalan's career."

"Crippled?"

Pherris sighed. He cast another look toward Dalan's cabin, but this time his gray eyes shone with sympathy. "It's a sticky sort of story, all blood and politics," he said. "Let's just say that old Ash earned his share of enemies in House Cannith right before the end. He was such a genius that few would ever really oppose him, but when he vanished, his rivals shifted their resentment onto Dalan."

"Dalan said Ashrem disappeared?" Seren asked. "I was told he died."

"Died, vanished, it's all the same," Pherris said. "Near the end of the war, Ashrem packed up his flagship, the *Dying Sun*, and left Zilargo for Metrol, the capital of Cyre. Kiris went with him. She told me that Ash intended to make peace with his family, to make peace with everyone—whatever that meant. That was two days before the Day of Mourning. Ashrem's ship hasn't been seen since, but House Cannith proclaimed him dead. That was bad news for Dalan, as it meant all of Ashrem's enemies had to find someone new to focus their hatred on. Dalan isn't exactly popular in his House these days."

"Hard to believe," she said wryly. "He's such a charmer."

Pherris's bushy brows furrowed. "You'd be surprised," he answered. "Dalan is coarse when he has to be, but he has a way of getting what he wants out of people. It's to his credit that despite all his enemies, he managed to remain the Tinkers' Guildmaster in Wroat."

VOYAGE OF THE MOURNING DAWN

Seren cocked her head at the gnome, surprised by the words of praise.

"Oh, don't get me wrong," the captain said quickly. "I don't like Dalan much, but even I won't deny his talents. Dalan is clever; he knows how people think. He knows how to *make* them think. He knows what you're about to say before you say it. He knows how to make you change your mind, and you'll believe it was your own idea. But for a Cannith, even that gets you only so far. Wordplay and manipulation have a place, but the Makers want results. Other than a few dragonmark tricks, Dalan has no magical talent. He knew if he wanted to earn a place in his House it would be through his uncle's accomplishments, but he had no chance to understand Ashrem's work alone. So he sought out Ashrem's apprentice."

"Dalan said that Ashrem's colleagues and students were missing or dead," Seren said.

"Oh, not all of them," Pherris said. "Just the most important ones. Kiris vanished with Ashrem. Orren Thardis disappeared not long after. Bishop Llaine Grove and Emil Harek were murdered last year. Norra Cais has been missing for months. Those five were the ones who helped Ashrem with his most critical research. Tristam was just an apprentice, and he left Ashrem two months before the Day of Mourning." Pherris frowned at Seren. "Ashrem refused to sponsor Tristam for membership in House Cannith, and Tristam resigned in outrage. The boy came to work in my shipyard after that, and Omax followed him like he always does. Just on about a year ago, Dalan came to us with his grand quest. Tristam was eager for a chance to prove himself, to reclaim his master's work and earn a place in the House of Making." Pherris sighed. "Poor Tristam. He's a bright lad, but he's such an idiot."

"I've had somewhat the same impression of him," she said.

"You don't know the half of it," Pherris said. "So much potential ruined by so much doubt. Makes me want to toss him over the rail and be done with him some days. But he has his moments. Omax is proof of that."

"Did Tristam build the warforged?" Seren asked.

Pherris laughed. "No, no, no," he said, then paused. "Well, actually, yes, I suppose he did but only in a sense. Nobody builds warforged anymore, not since the end of the war. No, Tristam saved Omax's life, gave him purpose when he had none. Beyond that, I'm not at liberty to say."

"More secrets," Seren said ruefully.

"Not my secret to share," Pherris said. "Some of us prefer to leave the past where it is. Omax follows Tristam because the boy gave him a chance to become something better. Omax is not what he used to be. He's some sort of holy man now, calls himself a seeker on a path of enlightenment. If you want to know more, you'll have to ask them yourself."

"Tristam doesn't seem an inspiring sort," she said.

"Well, like I said, he has his moments," Pherris countered. "Everyone on this ship has their moments. I suppose you do, too."

Seren stood up languidly and frowned at the gnome. "How do you know for sure?"

He only laughed and nodded at the figurehead. "Because she likes you," he said.

Seren looked at the gnome for a long moment. He only smiled at her intently.

"How far to Black Pit?" she asked, changing the subject as she looked out at the clouds once again.

"Six hundred and eighty-two miles," he said.

Seren looked back at him, eyes wide. Her home village was almost as far from Wroat, and the trip had taken her a month on foot. "How long will we be airborne?" she asked.

"Three days," he said. Seren said nothing for several moments, and Pherris shrugged uncomfortably. "I'm allowing time to take on supplies, of course. I don't see any point in rushing."

Seren looked back down at the clouds. There was no sense of such speed, only a timeless sea of sky. The airship actually felt as if she were moving very slowly. The tiny black shape of Blizzard shot up out of a cloud and dove back down. "I'm going to lie down again," she said.

"Suit yourself."

She climbed down the ladder into the cargo bay. She noticed Omax sitting among the piled crates. She stepped forward carefully, trying not to make any sound, studying the warforged's massive shape. He looked disturbingly human. His head was almost featureless, still capped with the incongruous woolen hat. Flesh and bone were replaced by sculpted adamantine metal and polished dark wood. Yet the creation was not flawless. As she stared at him, she saw a network of dents and scars laced through his body, a history of battle and conflict. Omax's head was bowed. The construct repeated a low chant, almost a whisper, and Seren moved closer to hear. To her surprise she recognized the words. It was a hymn often sung by the monks of Dol Arrah in the fishermen's quarter—the prayer of a warrior seeking redemption.

The song stopped.

"I am sorry, Miss Morisse, I did not notice you," he said. "Did you need something?"

"No," she said. "Sorry to disturb you."

His blue eyes pulsed as he peered over one shoulder.

Seren returned to her cabin, leaving the warforged in peace. The door of Tristam's cabin stood open now, and the hall was filled with acrid, oily smoke. Fearing a fire, Seren looked inside. It was as small as her cabin, but where hers was empty this one was stuffed with clutter. It featured a small pallet and a table, but also contained a narrow bookcase stuffed with leather-bound tomes, loose journals, and yellowing scrolls. A model airship hung from the ceiling, a perfect reproduction of *Karia Naille* with an elemental ring sculpted of silvered steel. The table was covered with vials, crystals, and other pieces of alchemical equipment. The oily smoke rose from a bubbling retort filled with clear fluid. A lumpy clay man the size of a small cat sat on the table nearby, waving the smoke toward the nearby porthole as best it could. Tristam sat on the pallet nearby, reading a book, seemingly unconcerned.

"What is that?" she asked.

"Distillation," Tristam said, peering up at her over his spectacles. "I'm purifying some basilisk humors I picked up in the city. They're useful for potions of leaping, though a lot of people don't like the chalky flavor. If you mix it with a bit of rum, it's fine. I apologize about the smoke; it's sort of a necessary . . ."

"No, that," she said, interrupting him.

He followed her eyes to the clay man. "Oh it's a homunculus," he said. It looked up at Seren briefly and returned to waving away the smoke. "A construct. It helps me in my work."

"Like Omax?" she asked.

"No," Tristam said uncomfortably. "Well, sort of. They're based on the same principles, but a homunculus isn't like a warforged. It's not alive."

"How can you tell Omax is alive and the homunculus isn't?" she asked.

He looked at her silently for a moment. "How can you tell that you're alive?" he said, shrugging. "Listen, Seren, is there anything else? I really am sort of busy."

Seren nodded and turned to leave, but paused in the doorway. "Tristam, why were you so angry when you learned we were going to Black Pit?" she said.

"Because Black Pit is dangerous," he said, not looking up from his book. "I don't think we should risk *Karia Naille* in a place like that."

VOYAGE OF THE MOURNING DAWN

"You were angry about Zed Arthen becoming involved," she said.

"You don't know Arthen," he said. "We don't need him."

"Is he untrustworthy?" she asked.

"It's not that," Tristam answered evasively. "He's good in a crisis. The rest of the time he's only as reliable as he chooses to be."

"Then is it because the lens is the first real clue you've found, and Dalan doesn't trust you with it?"

Tristam's eyes widened. "I don't need your analysis, Seren," he said. "Why don't you go find something to steal?"

Seren glared at Tristam. A dozen scathing replies came to mind, but it wasn't worth the trouble. She stalked out of the room toward her cabin.

"Seren, wait," Tristam said.

She slammed the door of his room, leaving him alone with his homunculus and the smoke.

Chapter Ten

Zed Arthen was not what you might traditionally consider an imposing figure. Short and stocky with bland features, he had a face that did not stand out in memory. Overall, he didn't mind much. Anonymity was a useful tool. Only fools became an inquisitive to be famous.

Arthen walked at an unhurried pace through the dank streets of Black Pit, his cane heavily stumping the cobbles beside him. The village was crowded this late afternoon, as crowded as Black Pit ever got. Most intelligent citizens knew to conclude what business they could before the sun went down. That was simple practicality. In a place like this, you avoided the shadows. The streets were slick with fouled water. A constant stream of sickly gasses roiled up out of Khyber, mixing with the clouds above and producing a chunky, oily black rain that stank like rotting meat. The puddles lingered for days without evaporating, much longer than normal water should. It was disgusting, but relatively harmless.

The people here claimed that you'd get used to the slime after a while, just like they claimed you got used to the shrieks that reverberated from the depths of the pit. It wasn't true. Nobody could ever really get used to this place, not if they were sane. All but the boldest citizens sought shelter when the clouds gathered and said a brief prayer to whatever gods they still believed in when the shrieking began. After all this time, even Zed gave the puddles a wide berth and felt a sense of nausea whenever he heard thunder approaching.

The flow of the crowd parted around a member of the Cleaners Guild. The solitary man knelt near an alleyway, shoveling some of the more offensive leavings of yesterday's storm into a large pail. He wore his guild's traditional apron, mask, and thick leather gloves. The cleaners wore the masks both to protect them from the stench of the rains and to hide their identities, for few citizens would willingly associate with someone who shoveled Khyber's offal for a living. Despite the cleaners' reviled status, there were brass bells on every street corner to summon them. Nobody really knew what the garbage that seeped out of the Black Pit really was, but someone had to deal with it.

Zed did not step aside as the others did, but strode directly toward the man, nodding in respect and dropping a few silver coins on the street. The cleaner looked up with surprise, probably more shocked by Zed's acknowledgment than his donation. The inquisitive couldn't help but respect the cleaners. Living in a forsaken village populated by deserters, murderers, smugglers, and opportunists, they spent their lives trying to make things better. In a few days, the rains would come again and undo all their work, and the cleaners would start over.

In a way, Zed considered them kindred spirits.

Zed turned down a side street, away from the flow of the crowd. He had entered a court lined with small shops. Some bore small signs, advertising themselves as herbalists or apothecaries. Most bore no signs at all, offering wares better left unadvertised. Zed stopped in the shadows of a doorway and propped his cane against the wall. He drew a long pipe, tobacco pouch, and small box of matches from his coat as he studied the streets and windows. Cupping his hand around the pipe to block the wind, he struck a match and inhaled deeply, wincing at the bitter aftertaste. Confident that he was not followed or watched, Zed limped across the court and entered Ein's Apothecary Shop, leaving a thin trail of smoke in his wake. The pungent smell of dried herbs drove away the stink of the rain. Shelves lined the walls, crowded with neatly labeled glass vials or paper packets filled with herbal remedies. A scrawny, nervous-looking little man sat behind a counter, crushing blue flowers with a mortar and pestle. He looked up at Zed suspiciously.

"Arthen," he said. "It has been some time." He looked curiously at Zed's cane.

"It was a strange trip, Neril," Zed said, exhaling a cloud of smoke.

"Did you find what you were looking for?" the apothecary asked.

Zed set a small clay bottle on the counter with a clack. The apothecary looked mildly confused when he saw the label.

"I hired you to remove our problems, not increase them," Neril whispered in a low voice.

"Koathil sap," Zed said in a loud, clear voice. "I understand that your boss is interested in purchasing this?"

"Of course, of course," Neril said with a sigh. The apothecary glanced behind him nervously and reached for the bottle. "Just let me collect this, and I will obtain your payment from Master Ein immediately."

Zed cupped his hand over the bottle and gave a tight smile. "I'd rather deliver it myself," he said. "Just to be sure."

"You'll have your payment, Arthen," Neril said, a hint of anger in his voice. "Master Ein is a man who repays his debts."

"I've heard differently," Zed said, tapping his pipe out on the floor and tucking it back into his coat. "Indulge me, or I take my business elsewhere." He picked up the small bottle, cupping it in one hand.

The apothecary looked at Zed with a disappointed frown. He sadly shook his head at the inquisitive. "Very well," he said. "This way."

The apothecary led Zed through the back room of the shop and up a narrow flight of stairs. The second floor was a narrow hall lined with doors. Zed had the distinct feeling as he followed Neril down the hall that he was being watched from behind more than one door. A large man in black leather armor stood before the door at the end of the hall. He glanced at Neril dismissively, then gave Zed a stern, appraising look.

"Zed Arthen," Neril said. "He has business with . . ."

"We know," the guard said. He gestured impatiently, signaling for Zed to raise his arms. Zed leaned his cane against the wall and complied. The guard patted Zed down thoroughly, pausing to inspect his pipe before returning it to his coat. The guard snatched up the cane with a suspicious frown, inspecting it for any hidden weapons. Satisfied Zed bore none, he handed back the cane and nodded toward the door. Neril shot Zed a final, betrayed scowl and returned to the stairs.

Within was a large office, dominated by a rich mahogany desk. The man who sat behind it might have been handsome once, but his face was pale and slick with sweat. Dark rings hung below his eyes. He looked up from his ledgers with an irritated scowl. Behind him, another guard placed one hand casually on his sword. A pretty young girl sat on an overstuffed chair in the corner, glancing up from the book she was reading with a coy smile.

"Zed Arthen to see you, boss," the first guard said.

Master Ein sneered and snapped his ledger closed. "Sir Arthen," he said.

"Master Arthen," Zed corrected him.

"Of course," Ein said. "Normally I would be quite upset as such an unreasonable demand on my time. My subordinates exist for a reason, to shelter me from annoying distractions. However, if you truly offer what you claim to offer, I am eager to do business."

Zed walked to the edge of the desk, leaning his cane against the side. He set the clay bottle between himself and Ein. He saw the girl look up intently, setting her book aside. Ein reached for the bottle, but Zed nonchalantly plucked it up again.

"Before we trade, let's talk price," Zed said. "Koathil sap is hard to come by."

"Five dragons a bottle. That is my price."

"The tree grows in the Watching Wood, in the heart of Droaam," Zed said. "That's a long walk, Ein, and Droaam makes this place look safer than a lover's arms. Five platinum won't even cover my travel expenses."

"Six."

"It isn't as if this stuff is particularly difficult to sell, either," Zed said, ignoring the offer. "It's in high demand. House Jorasco uses it in anesthetics. A proper assassin's guild would value it as well, I imagine."

"Seven."

"That's not even to speak of its addictive qualities, which I hear are quite considerable if used irresponsibly," Zed said. He began to juggle the bottle between his hands. The girl half-jumped from her seat and approached the table, standing at Ein's side. Ein's eyes widened.

"Eight platinum, no more. And be careful with that!"

"I could get more in Wynarn," Zed said, cupping the bottle in his palm. "The wizards are very eager to get their hands on this stuff."

"Wizards?" Ein asked.

VOYAGE OF THE MOURNING DAWN

Zed opened the bottle. The tiny cap tumbled between his fingers and rolled across the desk toward the girl's hand. "Khyber," he swore, smiling at her. "Could you get that for me?"

She bent and reached for the cap with one hand, then drew back. "Get it yourself," she said, eyes narrowing.

Zed felt something brush over his awareness, like a feather across his mind. He ignored it, looking at the girl evenly. Fear flickered in her eyes.

Ein snatched up the metal cap with a muttered curse and tossed it back to Zed, who caught it in midair. He had missed the exchange between Arthen and the girl.

"Anyway, as I was saying. Wizards," Zed said. "Koathil sap has been discovered to be a powerful naturally occurring conduit for enchantment. It weakens the will, leaves the user open to magical suggestion. It's a relatively recent discovery, but I still have a few friends at the University."

Ein's frown deepened. He glared at Zed with thinly veiled hate. The girl now stood close by Ein's side, eyeing the bottle warily. She placed one hand on Ein's shoulder. "Wizards are of no concern to me," he said, his voice an angry hiss. "I will pay you ten platinum for each bottle."

Zed stopped tossing the bottle. He took the cork out and sniffed its contents curiously. "Now that's a very attractive offer. If I ever actually have any real koathil sap, I'll keep it in mind. In the meantime, how much would you pay for holy water?"

With that, Zed flicked the bottle at the girl standing beside Master Ein, spraying the contents in her face. She shrieked and doubled over in pain. Ein ducked under his desk quickly just as his two guards drew their swords and charged. Zed held his cane with both hands, blocking the first man's sword even as he dodged the second man's blow. He delivered a knee to the first man's groin, followed by a sharp blow to the jaw that left him senseless. He turned and fell back just as the other guard's sword tore through his flowing coat. The guard lifted his blade for another blow, then stopped, jaw dropping open in horror.

The girl who had hovered near Ein had risen to her feet again, but not as she was. Her eyes now shone with an infernal yellow light, and her long fingers curled into claws. A pair of tattered bat wings erupted from her back, and a long tail curled around one long leg. She radiated a bizarre, exquisite sensuality despite her inhuman appearance. She blinked painfully and rubbed at her eyes, still blinded by the holy water.

"What in Khyber is that?" the guard said fearfully.

"A demon," Zed said, recovering the unconscious man's sword. "Now help me kill it."

The guard nodded and charged toward the demon. His sword struck her across the chest. She staggered backward from the force of the blow but took no real injury.

"You don't want to do this, Arthen," she said in a sweet voice. "You want to help me get out of here."

Zed felt a buzzing sensation at the back of his mind, but that was all. Her catlike eyes narrowed when she realized nothing had happened. She turned to the guard instead, who was still staring at his sword in disbelief.

"Kill Zed Arthen," she said.

The guard turned, facing Zed with a dull, confused expression. Zed rammed a heavy shoulder into the guard, knocking him on the floor. He charged past at full speed, keeping his eyes averted from the demon's. He swung the guard's sword, but she caught it in one hand, fingers clenching around the blade.

"Holy water," she sneered, wrenching the sword from his hand. "With a cold iron cap on the bottle. Edgeroot smoke to buffer your will against mine. You came well prepared, Arthen, but it was not enough. I am stronger than you, and you have no weapons."

"You didn't take a good look at the cane," he said. He struck the demon hard across the jaw. Her head snapped back, blood streaming from between her lips. She staggered against the wall, looking up at Zed with a suddenly fearful expression. The cane fell heavily a second time. She shrieked in agony and vanished with a flash of light, leaving behind a smoking plume of brimstone.

"What was that?" Master Ein said in a terrified voice. He peered out from under his desk.

"A succubus," Zed said. "Sometimes they crawl out of the Pit, sometimes they just get drawn here."

"Is it dead?" Ein demanded.

"Unlikely," Zed answered. "They're damned hard to kill. No pun intended. She probably won't be back for a while, though. They usually sulk for a bit when they get caught."

The remaining conscious guard helped Ein to his feet. He looked away from Zed with an embarrassed expression. "Seven months!" Ein shouted. "For seven months Narisa has been beside me! I trusted her with every aspect of my business, all of my secrets!"

"That's what they do," Zed said.

"There's no telling how much damage she's done," Ein said, tearing at his hair with one hand. "How much of what I've done has been really me and how much was that . . . thing?" He gestured vaguely at the smoking floor.

"Hard to say," Zed said. "At the very least, she was the one who made you start drinking koathil. It made it easier for her to control you. My best advice is to get a good night's sleep. And keep a cold iron weapon close at hand; succubi are big on revenge. I'll check in from time to time." He offered his cane to Master Ein, who accepted it with a grateful if harried smile. The inquisitive walked toward the door, no longer moving with a limp.

"Sir Arthen," Ein said. Zed glowered over his shoulder. "Master Arthen," he corrected. "I would appreciate your discretion. If my competitors were to learn about this . . ."

"My discretion for yours," Zed said. "Tell your thugs to stop dealing dreamlily in my city."

"Master Arthen," Ein retorted, feigning insult. "I would not participate in the sale of an illegal substance."

Zed looked back at Master Ein. Zed's face was no longer the bland, easily forgotten face of a random traveler. His eyes were filled with steel. He flipped his sword in one hand, its point directed at Ein's gaze. Master Ein blanched, his former outrage replaced with frightened shame. "Count your blessings, Master Ein," Zed said. "You've won back your soul today. All I want is this favor. Weigh it."

"Of course, of course," Ein said with a deflated sigh. "Whatever you wish. I am in your debt."

"Like I said," Zed said, planting the sword in the wooden floor. "I'll check in from time to time."

The inquisitive made his way out of the tiny shop, pausing to take the small pouch of gold that Neril had left at the edge of the counter. The old apothecary hadn't known what was plaguing his master, but it had twisted what passed for an honest business in Black Pit into something even more reviled. Nobody really knew what the garbage that seeped out of the Black Pit was, but everyone agreed someone had to deal with it. Zed Arthen was one of those people.

"Thank you, Sir Arthen," Neril said, looking up from his work from a grateful smile.

"Master Arthen," he corrected, stepping back out into the streets.

A chill wind blew through the streets of Black Pit. Zed shifted his shoulders, huddling into his coat. His hand found the rip in the fabric left behind by the guard's sword, and he mumbled a quiet curse. This was his favorite coat. He'd have to see about getting it fixed tomorrow. The sun was setting now. That Zed understood the dangers of the Pit better than most only made him more eager to avoid them. The distant shrieks of Khyber grew louder. This was no night to be out unarmed. No doubt all manner of peculiar things would happen tonight, mysteries he'd be called upon to investigate.

Tomorrow would be an interesting day.

Zed walked briskly toward his office. He heard the creak of a shutter as he passed the building next door to his. That was Old Merkin, local spy and information peddler. Arthen pretended not to notice him. So many of the dangers of this world were much less threatening when they thought they weren't noticed.

As he reached the door, Arthen's head cocked suddenly. A strange sound met his ears. Not that Black Pit wasn't a place for strange sounds, but this one was different, a humming counterpoint to the sounds of the Pit. It was familiar. Zed looked to the southern sky and saw a streak of blue moving toward the city. It was the fire of an elemental airship. He recognized the hue of the flame and timbre of the elemental ring at once.

"*Karia Naille*," he mumbled to himself in astonishment, stepping back out into the street for a better look.

It was the simple things that could ruin a man's entire evening.

Chapter
Eleven

Seren wasn't sure what she had expected when Gerith described Black Pit. As the airship circled for a landing, whatever expectations she might have had were wiped clean. She heard the pit before she ever saw it, an eerie harmony of inhuman shrieks echoing from the depths. A tremendous wound split the surface between the jagged Blackcap Mountains and the lush forests to the east. The earth within the pit was a disturbing red, like fresh blood. The surrounding land was black and dead. From above, Seren could see veins of dead soil twisting from the pit into the woodlands. It was as if Khyber were reaching out with long fingers, slowly drawing the life of the forest into itself.

The village perched on a plateau at western edge of the pit. It was no larger than Ringbriar, but while Seren's home consisted of a single road surrounded by houses and businesses, Black Pit was a disorderly sprawl of ill-tended buildings. The setting sun painted the village in a red hue, only deepening the sense that the land was raw and bleeding.

She stood at the rail as the ship circled the noxious coils of smoke rising from the Black Pit. Pherris was busy at the helm, and Dalan had disappeared into his cabin again. Gerith sat by Blizzard's perch, singing a quiet song to calm the nervous glidewing. Tristam and Omax stood at the opposite side of the deck. Seren sensed the artificer casting nervous looks in her direction. He had attempted to confront her a few times since their conversation three days ago, but she avoided him. He had even sent Omax to offer an apology, which she had answered noncommittally. She wasn't ready to forgive him yet.

There was something hypnotic, an odd ghastly beauty to the pit. Seren found it difficult to look away and hoped that *Karia Naille* might fly in for a closer look. The more rational part of her mind was horrified by her own fascination, and she was glad that Pherris kept the ship a good distance away.

"If I woke up and found something like this next to my village, I think I'd move somewhere else," Seren commented.

Pherris chuckled. "The pit was here first, Miss Morisse," he said. "The village came later."

She looked back at him incredulously. "Someone built a village next to that on purpose?"

The captain just shrugged and kept his attention on his course. She noticed that he assiduously avoided looking down.

"I've always wondered about that as well," Tristam said to no one in particular, "What kind of idiot would build a village in a place like this?"

"A certain sort of person just wants to go live where he won't be found," Pherris said. "You should be grateful you don't understand it, Master Xain."

"What's making that noise?" Seren asked.

"Just the wind, or so they say," Tristam said. "Of course, folks here say a lot of things so they can sleep at night. No one's ever gone into the pit and returned, so I guess they can pretend it's whatever they want."

Dalan's cabin door opened and d'Cannith stepped out, wincing at the relative brightness. His expression only soured when he saw the smoking pit beneath them. "Well, at least we are on schedule," he grumbled.

"Two sky towers at the southern end of the village, Master d'Cannith," Pherris reported. "Probably used by local smugglers. If it's all the same, I'd rather just hover in the forest and send Omax in looking for Arthen. As we're not loading cargo, it seems the safest route. No sense attracting attention in a place like this."

"Ordinarily that would be wise advice, but in this case attention is precisely what we want," Dalan said.

Pherris looked back at Dalan incredulously and returned his attention to the wheel. "As you say, Master d'Cannith."

The airship banked, and Seren grasped the rail to steady herself. The pungent smell of the pit grew stronger as the ship circled slowly downward. They swooped over the village, dots below swiftly resolving into people. Some stopped and looked up to watch the airship fly overhead. Others simply trudged onward, too jaded to care or too distracted for it to matter.

A pair of rickety-looking towers stood at the far southern end of the village, bordering the road . Seren thought it strange at first that such a small village would have airship facilities, until she thought about it. If Black Pit really was home to the Brelish black market, the towers would come in handy for the occasional wealthy smuggler. The towers looked shoddy and hastily built. From the clutter that surrounded them, Seren suspected that a few of the locals had made homes inside.

"Prepare to secure the vessel," Pherris said as the ship pulled up alongside the western tower.

"Aye, Captain," Gerith said, gesturing quickly to Seren.

She followed the halfling, leaping from the deck to the tower's docking bridge. A few terrified chickens scampered out of the way, leaving a swirl of downy feathers fluttering to the ground. Seren knelt to tie the rope through one of the iron rings mounted on each side of the bridge but stopped short, looking up cautiously at the four burly men who had emerged from the tower. They looked down at her with smug, dangerous expressions. Their faces shifted to blank looks of terror as a heavy thud sounded on the bridge beside her, followed by another.

"Good evening, gentlemen," Omax said in his even, metallic voice. Tristam stood beside the warforged, letting his coat hang open to display the sword at his hip. Seren tied off the rope and edged behind the warforged, as did Gerith.

"I assume one of you is the tower master?" Dalan asked, stepping forward and greeting the thugs with a disconcertingly pleasant smile.

"Er, yes, that would be me," said the leader of the group. He was the largest of the four, an unkempt man whose wealth of dirt and stubble was broken only by a crisscross white scar on his neck. "Docking fee is two gold per week."

"Omax, please pay these gentlemen," Dalan said.

Omax reached into his pocket and drew out two gold coins. The money looked ridiculously small cupped in his adamantine palm as he offered it to the men. The tower master shouldered one of his henchmen, who nervously stepped forward to snatch the coins. Omax closed his hand over the coins with a clank, nearly snatching the man's fingers. He drew back with a start.

Dalan chuckled and looked embarrassed. "My apologies, but my associate is a stickler for formalities," Dalan said. "I shall need to see the King's Seal, tower master, just to make certain that you are in fact the proper authority."

The tower master chuckled. "This is Black Pit, my friend," he said. "We don't need any official sanction from the King here."

"I see," Dalan answered. "How very interesting. It has long been my personal belief that a man willing to call a total stranger 'my friend' is invariably the least friendly, most untrustworthy sort of person. As pleasing as it is to see that once again I am not wrong, that is no excuse for either your behavior or your odor. If you are not an official authority, then your presence is irrelevant to me. Get away from my ship, or Omax will remove you."

Seren's hand moved to the dagger tucked in the back of her belt as she edged back toward the ship. Dalan glanced back at her, his eyes narrowing, making her stop where she was. Seren caught his meaning—a united front was important. Dalan looked back at the four men and folded his arms across his chest. Standing before the thugs, his face remained calm and unafraid. Omax stepped in front of the guildmaster, calmly tucking the coins back into his pocket. He fell into a relaxed stance, hands curled into fists near his waist, and bowed his head to the four men.

"Bah," the tower master said with a sneer. "Don't let the fat man and his golem intimidate you. I've fought my share of warforged. They die just like men."

Omax lunged forward, seized the man's chest in one hand, and hurled him from the tower bridge. There was a shrill yelp of terror, followed by the soft splat of a man landing heavily in the mud. Omax turned and faced the three remaining men calmly. They backed into the tower, then ran down the stairs as quickly as they were able.

"He survived," Dalan said, looking down as the tower master staggered to his feet and limped hurriedly away.

"What purpose would killing him serve?" Omax asked.

"He may come back," Dalan said, sighing as he strode back onto the ship.

"And if he were to die, others might come seeking vengeance," Omax said, following him.

"If there would be risk whether he lived or died," Dalan said, looking back at the warforged. "Then why let him live? That man is useless scum. Probably a killer."

Omax shrugged at Dalan. "Or just a desperate man," the

warforged said. "Mercy can put a desperate man on a path to redemption."

"Or grant him the opportunity to kill another day," Dalan said.

"Not everyone is a killer, Dalan," Tristam said tersely.

"Tristam, you misunderstand me," Dalan said, looking at the artificer with a smirk. "I trust Omax's judgment and I value his opinions, even if I disagree with them. I was having a philosophical discussion. If you cannot add anything insightful to our discourse, then stay quiet and listen."

Tristam looked away, face darkening. Seren thought she might take some small joy in seeing Tristam humiliated after the way he'd insulted her, but she did not.

"But this is not the time for conversation," Dalan said, heading toward the cabin. "Tristam, get into the village and find Zed Arthen. Take Seren with you to keep you out of trouble."

"I don't really know this village," Seren said to Dalan's back.

"Neither, thankfully, do any of us, save by reputation," Dalan said, pausing at the door. "Nonetheless, if you could survive on the streets of Wroat, I'm certain you'll do well enough here. You'll do far better than Tristam, in any case."

"I will let no harm come to either of you, Seren," Omax said.

"Your loyalty is duly noted, Omax, but I need you to remain here," Dalan said. "I cannot risk leaving *Karia Naille* undefended in case the 'local authorities' return."

"The ship isn't exactly undefended, Dalan," Tristam said.

"Contingencies only retain their strength when they remain in place," Dalan said cryptically. "Omax will remain here as our first line of defense."

The warforged looked at Tristam, waiting for his decision. The artificer looked at Dalan, who peered back with a patient, thoughtful expression.

"Better listen to Dalan, Omax," Tristam said quietly.

Omax bowed to his friend. Dalan closed his cabin door

"Good luck, both of you," Gerith said cheerfully. The halfling climbed back onto the deck, carrying a struggling chicken under one arm. He headed toward the galley.

"Let's go," Seren said, brushing past Tristam and hurrying down the tower stairs.

She exited the tower to find Tristam already waiting at the bottom. She did a double-take, looking from him back at the door behind her.

"Feather fall ring," he said, holding up a hand to display a bronze ring with a smirk. "What good's a little magic if you can't show it off, right?"

"You made that?" she asked.

"I haven't mastered ringcraft, but soon," he said. "My friend Orren Thardis gave it to me after Ashrem suspended my teaching. He was brilliant; probably taught me as much as Ashrem did." Tristam bent low to examine the tower's doorknob. "I think he gave me the ring because he felt sorry for me."

Seren surveyed the area for any signs of danger. A number of locals were still staring at the ship in wonder. The locals all looked generally shady and suspicious, making it difficult to tell if anyone was a relevant danger.

"Wisdom," Tristam said under his breath.

"What?" she asked, looking back.

"That's the password to get through the ward I just put on this door," he said, looking at her earnestly. "Remember it, Seren. Please. I don't want you hurt."

She nodded and gestured for him to follow. She took to the middle of the road, staying as visible as possible to reduce the chance of ambush. Tristam followed, remaining silent for a long time.

"Seren," he finally said, still walking a step behind her. "Did Omax talk to you?"

"I don't like apologies," Seren said. "They're just words."

"Oh," Tristam said. "Well, by that logic, when I stupidly called you a thief, that was just words too. Therefore no harm done and I don't need to offer a worthless apology. Right?"

Seren scowled at Tristam. He offered a crooked grin, and she had a difficult time remembering just why she was so angry at him.

"Fine. Apology accepted," she said, rolling her eyes. They continued walking down the street.

"Boldrei's blood, that's a relief," he said, exhaling. He walked beside her instead of behind, a bit of his cocky self-assurance returning. "I have enough problems without worrying about you stealing something from me in revenge."

She glared at him again, but his quick laugh took the sting off his words. "Joking! If there's one man in all of Khorvaire who has no right to judge you for your past, it's me. All in all, I think if you compared our respective professions yours is more worthy of respect. At least a thief is honest."

"How do you figure that?" she asked. "You're an artificer. You make things that change people's lives."

"We also make weapons, Seren," Tristam said. "For every airship and lightning rail you can name, I can point to the warforged . . . or to Cyre."

"Omax is a warforged," she said. "He seems like a good person. So to speak."

"He is," Tristam said, "but that doesn't change the fact that his people were created to kill. The warforged were supposed to be monsters. The fact that some of them, like Omax, are strong enough to rise above their origins was not intentional."

"If you think so little of magecraft, then why are you helping Dalan find the Legacy?" she asked.

"Because someone has to make sure it's used responsibly," he said. "Whatever it really is, it's powerful, and I don't want to see it misused. That was why I was so suspicious toward you, Seren. I can't stand the thought of anyone exploiting Ashrem's work. You have to admit we didn't meet on very good terms. You had one of Ashrem's journals in your pocket."

"In a bag, actually," she said. "But you think you can trust Dalan d'Cannith with Ashrem's secrets?" She looked at him thoughtfully.

"I do," Tristam said, though he hesitated just a moment. "Dalan wants what I want. He wants to find the truth before someone else does. But that makes me wonder what we're doing here."

"What do you mean?" Seren asked. She looked at him questioningly, then took stock of their surroundings again. A crudely painted sign depicting a full mug of ale hung over a nearby door. A tavern was as good a place to find information as any, so she headed that way.

"We've been looking for the Legacy for a long time now," Tristam said. "Zed Arthen was a member of our original crew, but the search was too much for him. He abandoned us and came here." He looked at her seriously. "I don't trust Zed, Seren. I never liked him, even before he left us. The Knights of Thrane don't cast out one of their own without reason."

Tristam opened the tavern door for her, breaking the tension with an exaggerated, bow. She chuckled and stepped inside. She was surprised to find no one drinking inside. A barkeep in a dirty apron was setting chairs on tables.

"Closed," the man said in a bored voice. "Sundown."

"Sundown?" Seren asked.

"Oh, you're new," he said with an annoyed sneer. His right eye drifted to the right. "Black Pit's no place to be out after dark. Get out quick. Find some place to sleep. Not here."

"We can take care of ourselves," Tristam said.

The bartender scratched his chin, grunted to himself, and

returned to his work, ignoring Tristam. Seren was about to ask the man if he knew Zed Arthen when the door opened behind them. The tower master stepped inside, his clothes stained with jet-black mud. He was followed by the same three thugs as before, as well as two new arrivals. The barkeep quickly flipped the last chair onto the table and hurried out of the room. Seren looked around for any other exit. The only other door was the one the barkeep had just slipped through, and she heard a latch fall heavily in place.

"We saw you lock that tower door, magewright," the tower master said. He advanced as his thugs fanned out to block any path of escape.

Tristam drew his sword and wand, holding them in a ready stance. "Stay back, Seren," he said, stepping between them.

"Put the sword away, boy," the thug said. His comrades drew small crossbows, aiming them at Tristam. "The warforged is the one we want. Just tell us what we need to know and we'll only give you a beating. We'll even let the girl go." He gave Seren a ghastly grin. "Eventually."

"You haven't the faintest idea who you've insulted," Tristam said. "My name is Tristam Xain, and I rank among the most skilled swordsmen in the Lhazaar Principalities."

The man gave Tristam another appraising look and then laughed out loud. Tristam's bold façade faded noticeably.

Seren looked at the man coldly. "Are you an idiot?" she said. "Omax let you live because he could. We aren't worth the pain we'd give you. Leave while you can."

The tower master looked at Seren soberly, then glanced back at Tristam, with a disdainful sneer. He reached for the heavy crossbow at his hip.

A mocking chuckle sounded from the doorway, causing the thug to stay his hand. He turned quickly, aiming his crossbow at the newcomer. A stocky man in a long brown coat stepped into the room. His face was plain and unremarkable except for his sharp blue eyes. A long pipe hung from his lip, leaving a drifting plume of smoke as he entered. The newcomer looked at Seren, Tristam, and each of the men before looking at their leader again.

"This d-doesn't involve you, Arthen," the tower master said, stuttering in fear.

"I'm only trying to help you, Hareld," the man said, tapping out his pipe and tucking it into his coat. "She's right, you know. You are an idiot," He looked at Seren with a sly grin. "You can't even see her hands. Kol Korran knows what sort of weapon she's hiding under that cloak. The boy's no threat. I won't argue that, but look at the girl's eyes. She'll kill the first man that makes a move. Who will be first? Hesitate at all, and at least one of you won't walk away from this. Of course, that's your best-case scenario. That assumes that I don't plan to help them. That shifts the odds considerably."

"Help them?" one of the others said, meekly.

"They are my clients," Arthen said. He plucked a chair from a nearby table and effortlessly wrenched one of its legs free, hefting it as an improvised club. "Shall we begin?"

The tower master lowered his crossbow and gestured for the others to do the same. "No, no, that's not necessary," he said, stumbling over the words. "We'll . . . we'll just go."

Arthen stepped away from the door, pointing the way with his club. The thugs nearly fell over each other in their haste to depart. When they were gone, Zed dropped the table leg on the floor and looked at Tristam with an unpleasant expression.

"So I'm nothing, Sir Arthen?" Tristam asked, snapping his sword into its scabbard. "I am honored to have risen so highly in your estimation."

"Don't start, boy," he said, leveling a dangerous glare at the artificer. "Don't call me, 'Sir.' "

Tristam's face darkened, but he looked away quickly.

Zed looked to Seren, expression softening only marginally. "Zed Arthen, professional inquisitive," he said, flourishing his long coat in a half-bow.

"Seren Morisse," she answered, noticing the many pouches and small tools that hung from Arthen's belt and within his coat. "We've been sent . . ."

"I know who sent you," he interrupted. "Normally I wouldn't mind keeping Dalan waiting, but we should get you back to your ship before dark."

"What happens here at night?" Tristam asked.

"The village is perched on a pit into the deepest hells of Khyber. Do you really need details?" Zed said. "Now let's go."

Seren and Tristam filed back out of the tavern with Zed only a step behind. The streets were empty now, long shadows stretching across the road. The inquisitive hurried past them, his pace brisk as he kept a nervous eye on the setting sun.

"Could be nothing, mind you," Zed said as they jogged to keep up with him. "It's usually nothing. One night in twenty. Of course, that night is well worth worrying about the other nineteen."

"Criminals and demons. Why do you live here, Arthen?" Tristam said, shaking his head as they pressed on.

"Fairly preferable to your own circumstances," Zed said. "Incidentally, Miss Morisse, I know we don't know one another and I hesitate to give advice to strangers, but I'd avoid becoming tangled up with Dalan d'Cannith."

"Arthen," Tristam said in a warning tone.

Zed ignored him. "Whatever reason you have to work with him, whatever reason you think you need him, forget it. He's either lying to you or not telling you everything. Probably both. Leave him behind." He paused for a moment. "Once you reach a port safer than Black Pit, just leave. Don't even say goodbye; just go."

"Like you did?" Tristam asked, leaning close to whisper the password at the tower door.

"I'm serious," Zed said, ignoring Tristam. "Don't give Dalan a chance to talk you out of it." He grasped her shoulder, stopping her at the tower door and looking earnestly into her eyes. "D'Cannith has a way of endearing himself, of making the unreasonable seem reasonable. You do what he wants and you even think it's your idea."

"Zed, stop," Tristam said. He gently took Seren by the arm, pulling her away from the inquisitive. She didn't resist. "Dalan doesn't have any sort of magic. All his dragonmark can do is fix things."

"Magic?" Zed laughed. "I'm not talking about magic. Dalan has never needed magic. The human mind is all he needs. Why do you think he sent you two into a dangerous place like this, unprotected, just before sunset? Because he knew I'd see the ship land. He knew I'd watch whoever came out, and he knew you'd be in danger. He knew I wouldn't leave Tristam to die, and that it was the only way to draw me back to *Karia Naille*. I suppose he told you some nonsense about how he trusted you not to get into trouble." Zed shook his head. "And now here I am, walking right back into his ship. Dalan knows people, Seren." He tapped his temple with two thick fingers. "He gets into their heads. Probably knows me better than I do." The inquisitive sighed as he looked up at the hovering airship. "Just think about what I've said, all right?"

"Seren, ignore him," Tristam said, shoving past Arthen through the tower door. "He's a lunatic."

Seren followed Tristam, only stopping briefly to look back at Zed. The shadows of Black Pit now crept across the streets. Arthen was looking back over one shoulder, into the darkness.

VOYAGE OF THE MOURNING DAWN

It looked almost as if he were considering facing the dangers of being caught in the village at night rather than board *Karia Naille*.

Then, slowly and methodically, Zed Arthen closed the door behind them and made his way up the tower stairs.

Chapter
Twelve

"What are you doing in here?" Tristam asked, pushing open the door of his cabin with an annoyed frown.

Seren looked up with a friendly smile. She sat on Tristam's cot, her feet kicked up on the chair nearby. A thick book lay open beside her, and the homunculus sat in her lap, staring blankly as she petted it on the head. "Just reading," she said. "The door was open."

Tristam looked at her intently.

"What's wrong?" she asked. "Surprised I can read?"

"I didn't say that," Tristam said. "It's just that—"

"I didn't steal anything."

"I never thought you did," he said, looking more amused than annoyed. "I'm just amazed you're still conscious. I left the door open because I was airing out the fumes from my last experiment. It didn't go very well." Tristam hung his jacket on a hook behind the door. Omax stepped into the room as well, ducking to pass through the small threshold.

"What are you reading, Seren?" the warforged asked, squatting in the corner and looking at her book. His blue eyes shone with curiosity as he extended one hand toward her.

"Karrnathi myths and legends," she answered, handing him the book. "Seemed interesting. Pherris didn't have anything for me to do, Gerith is off exploring, and Dalan has locked himself in his chambers again."

"Careful with that book, please; it was my mother's," Tristam said, gently kicking her feet off the chair and sitting down. "So you just invited yourself into my cabin, then?"

"Not the first time a man's been surprised to find me in his room. But surely the first time he's complained."

Tristam looked at her with blank surprise and even Omax glanced up from the book.

"That's a joke," she said, rolling her eyes at them. "My cabin is depressing. It's so empty. When I gathered all my things out of that hole where I lived in Wroat, there was almost nothing. Just some clothes, some tools, some broken furniture I'd taken from someone's garbage. I was actually glad to leave most of it behind. My room is like someone's closet now. It doesn't feel like a home. Sorry I intruded, Tristam"

"Apology accepted," he said. "Now get your dirty shoes off my bed."

She laughed, kicking her heavy shoes onto the floor.

"I hope you didn't touch any of this," Tristam said. He began fidgeting over his table, checking the various vials, crystals, and reagents.

"I know better than to mess with a wizard's experiments," she said.

Tristam peered back at her. For the first time since he caught her in his room, he looked truly annoyed. He returned his attention to his work with a sigh.

"Tristam is not a wizard," Omax said, folding the book closed and handing it carefully back to Seren. "A wizard merely manipulates the forces of magic. An artificer gives magic form, life, and persistence. They are as much different as a poet and a sculptor. Both are masters of their respective art but the results are not comparable."

"I see," Seren said. "So what about Zed Arthen? Is he an artificer as well?"

"Arthen?" Tristam said, giving her an incredulous look. "Khyber, no. Arthen is nothing, just a washed-up exile. A former Knight of Thrane who fancies himself an inquisitive."

"Then why do we need his help?" Seren asked.

"Because Zed knew old Ashrem," Tristam said. "Ashrem had a habit of taking in strays, and 'Sir' Zed was a member of *Karia Naille*'s crew for a while. They shared a weird penchant for riddles and code, the same fascination that makes Ashrem's books nearly impossible to read."

The homunculus took the storybook from Seren, carefully opened it to the page she had been reading before, set it down beside her, and returned to its place on her lap. She stroked the clay creature's head absently and frowned as she turned over Tristam's revelations in her mind. If Zed really knew so much, why hadn't their mysterious rival, Marth, hunted Arthen down as he hunted all of Ashrem's other colleagues?

"If Zed knows so much about Ashrem's codes, why didn't Dalan hire him earlier?" Seren asked.

"Who says he didn't?" Tristam asked.

She thought back to Zed's arrival on the ship. Pherris had seemed to know Arthen, though he only nodded in greeting and returned to his work. She remembered the odd look of reflection, the sense of peace and serenity that she had seen in Arthen's face the instant he stepped aboard. It had only lasted for a moment before Dalan called the inquisitive to his cabin. She only saw him briefly later, hurrying back off the ship early the next morning, returning to his home in the village.

"Four days," Tristam grumbled, setting a glass vial down so hard she heard glass crack. "Four days that traitor's been studying that lens. Dalan even gave him one of Ashrem's encoded journals so he could try to break the cipher. The Host only knows what he's done with them by now, or if he's even still in Black Pit. He could be in Wroat by now for all we know."

"Not without an airship," Seren said.

"Don't underestimate him," Tristam retorted. "I wouldn't put it past Arthen to hit the local speaker's station. The speakers can send a message anywhere. He could arrange for a ship to come pick him up. An airship could sneak in under the cover of the forest, drop a ladder, pick him up, and we'd never know."

"Or he could board that ship across the street," Omax said, nodding toward the porthole.

Seren and Tristam looked through the porthole simultaneously, out at the darkened streets of Black Pit. A sleek red airship, half again the size of *Karia Naille*, now hovered in port at the opposite sky tower. A proud kraken crest was emblazoned upon the hull.

"That's one of House Lyrandar's," Tristam said.

"Another dragonmarked house?" Seren said. "Are the Lyrandar after the Legacy too?"

"I doubt they'd care, if they even knew about it," Tristam said. "The Lyrandar are neutral by nature, merchants and sailors. That's a charter ship."

"Then anyone could be onboard," Seren said. She set the homunculus aside and moved closer to the window for a better look. The little construct closed the book and carefully placed it back on the shelf, sitting down beside it as an improvised bookend.

"It has been docked all evening," Omax said.

"Why didn't you tell me about this before?" Tristam asked.

"It is night," the construct said. "The city is dangerous at night. I feared you might do something rash."

"We'd better go check this out," Tristam said, rising from his seat and reaching for his jacket.

"My point exactly," Omax said dryly. The warforged rose with a weary metal creak.

"What do you plan to do, Tristam?" Seren asked. "Sneak onto the ship?"

"No," he said. "I plan to find Arthen. I'm willing to bet he's meeting with whoever came in on that ship."

"You have no idea where he is," Seren said. "You haven't been in the village since we found him."

"But I can track him," Tristam said. "The same way I tracked you, Seren. If he's carrying that lens, I can find him."

Omax folded his metal arms across his chest and looked down at Tristam. "You truly believe you could put a magical tracking device on Zed Arthen and he would not discover and dispose of it?"

"He'd better not have disposed of it," Tristam said, smirking up at Omax before he pulled his jacket over his shoulders and left the cabin. "It's the damned lens."

"You enchanted the lens?" Omax asked, impressed. "You only had it for a moment."

"And I know Dalan," Tristam said. "I wanted to be able to find it again if I needed to, and knew I might not have another chance. Now let's go find him."

Omax looked at Seren. She imagined she saw a long-suffering look in his mechanical eyes. The construct certainly seemed more human the longer she was around him. "Please help me keep him alive," he said quietly.

Seren nodded and hopped off the bed, kicking her oversized shoes onto her feet. Something about what Tristam said bothered her, though she couldn't quite figure out what it was just yet. The two followed Tristam into the hallway. He was already in the cargo bay, opening the lower bay doors and gathering a rope ladder.

"Shouldn't we wait until morning?" Seren asked.

"What better time to meet secretly with someone in a place like this than when everyone else is hiding in their houses?" Tristam asked. "Besides, remember what Arthen said. One out of twenty days it might be dangerous—and I feel lucky. Besides, Omax can protect us."

"I am flattered, Tristam," Omax said, with perhaps a hint of sarcasm.

"Pardon me, Master Xain," said a stern voice from above. "What is it that you are doing there?"

The trio looked up to see Captain Gerriman standing at the top of the deck ladder. He glared down at them, fists fixed imperiously upon his hips. Though he was half their height, Seren could not help but feel somewhat embarrassed and intimidated by the tiny captain's outrage.

Tristam stuttered for a moment before answering. "We're going into the village, Captain," he said quietly, not meeting Pherris's eyes.

Pherris looked over his shoulder, toward Dalan's cabin, then glared back at them. "Without your captain's permission?"

"We thought you might disapprove," Tristam said.

"Oh, I might!" Pherris said. "And one might think that you should wish to seek my approval or lack thereof, considering that I am in fact the captain of this ship! Now. The reasons for your departure are irrelevant. I can easily guess what they are, and thus your excuses are of no interest to me. Could you answer one question for me, Master Xain?"

Tristam nodded.

"How did you plan to raise that ladder back up after the three of you had climbed down?" he asked. "Or did you plan to leave it dangling there so that any manner of demon or thief could climb onto my ship?"

"I thought maybe Omax would pull it back up and jump down unharmed?" Tristam asked.

Omax laughed.

"I've seen you take worse," Tristam said, "and I can fix you."

"And I can make a fine splint and tourniquet," Pherris said acidly. "By your logic, I'm sure you wouldn't mind Omax breaking your arm."

Tristam looked at Omax. The warforged seemed to grin. Seren had to work very hard to restrain a laugh.

"And this is not even to consider that Master Dalan will be most displeased when he finds you've left without his knowledge," Pherris said.

Tristam looked up at Pherris now, his nervous confusion suddenly gone. "Dalan made a mistake trusting Zed Arthen, Captain," he said. "I have to fix it, or everything we've done will have been for nothing."

Pherris looked at Tristam steadily for a long time, then nodded and stroked his moustache with one hand. "Very well," he said, hopping down into the hold. "Climb on down. I'll pull up the ladder."

Tristam looked at Pherris, confused. "But . . ."

"Do not question the Captain's orders," Omax said, resting a heavy hand on his friend's shoulder.

The gnome cackled and waved them toward the ladder. Tristam climbed down first. By the time Seren landed beside him, he had already drawn his sword and wand. The wand shimmered with white light, illuminating the road around them. She quickly pushed his arm down, covering the wand with his cloak.

"Put that away," she whispered. "The light will just draw anything that's sees us. The starlight is enough to get by."

Tristam looked about to argue.

"Are you going to tell me how to sneak around, Tristam?" she asked.

Tristam shrugged and put the wand away.

"Can you sense the lens?" she asked him, looking up at the Lyrandar airship.

Tristam nodded. "It isn't on that ship, at least." He pointed toward the northern end of town with his sword. "It's that way, somewhere. I can narrow it down if we get closer."

A heavy thud sounded beside them, causing Tristam and Seren both to jump. Omax rose to his full height again, having jumped down without the ladder, and chuckled.

"I thought you said the fall would damage you," Tristam said.

"I said it might," Omax said. "It's your fault for making me curious."

"I thought it was against a monk's vows to frighten people," Tristam said, smoothing his coat over his chest with one hand.

"A soul cannot appreciate the stillness of the pond until it ripples," Omax said. The warforged's head swiveled from one side to the other with a low metallic click, his shining eyes scanning the darkness for any threat. He walked past them, finding his way unerringly in the shadows.

"Is he joking?" Seren asked with a half smile.

"It's always hard to tell," Tristam said, sheathing his sword and following.

Seren moved to Omax's left while Tristam flanked the warforged on his right. She kept her hand on the hilt of her dagger. She was unsure if it would do much good against the creatures of the pit, but it would serve her well if the mortal inhabitants of the village decided to pose a problem. Other than the faint haze of starlight and the shimmering blue radiance of Omax's eyes, the city was in complete darkness. The shrieking sounds of the pit were as loud as she had heard them, growing by the moment. The sound was difficult to describe: a mad, piercing wail underscored by babbling. Seren wanted to go back. When she exchanged looks with Tristam, it seemed he was having second thoughts as well, but Omax's gaze was resolute and fearless. She saw no lights in any of the windows, only the occasional faint crack of radiance behind thick shutters. Though there were a few sconces for everbright lanterns on either side of the street, they did not shine. Seren paused by one and studied the empty bracket atop it. She looked at the others.

"Someone stole the light, I guess," Tristam said, shrugging.

"Or it was removed intentionally," Omax suggested. "I think no one wants to see what happens here at night."

The same thought had occurred to Seren, but she had not wanted to speak it aloud. She gave the sconce a final anxious glance and moved on. Tristam stopped them several times, brow furrowing as he struggled to find the right way. They changed directions several times, until Omax finally sat down in the street and looked up at Tristam patiently.

"Whenever you know where we are going, I am ready," he said.

"Sorry, Omax, but you know this can be tricky to triangulate," Tristam said, scratching his chin as he looked one way, then the next. "Remember how easily we lost Seren?"

Then it struck her, what had bothered her from before. "Tristam, you can track the lens even though you only handled it for a moment," she said. "If Marth is an artificer as well, shouldn't he be able to do the same?"

"Doubtful," Tristam said. "The transfusion I used is very rare. Ashrem taught it to me himself. Even if Marth could do it, he'd have to be an artificer of extraordinary power to sense its location all the way from Wroat."

"And what if he is?" Seren asked. "You saw what he did to the inn. Are we talking impossible or improbable?"

Tristam grimaced. "Improbable," he admitted. "Let's not dwell on that, Seren; we already have enough worries." He pointed. "It's that way."

"Are you sure?" Omax asked, still sitting.

"I think so," Tristam answered, scratching his chin again.

Omax rose with what sounded like a sigh. They continued moving cautiously, if a bit quicker than before. They were almost at the center of town now, and when they emerged at the mouth of an alley Seren thought she heard Omax chuckle.

"How fortunate we are for your magical tracking ability, Tristam," Omax said. "We might never have found this."

A large sign emblazoned with an open eye hung above a door across the street. It read:

INQUISITIVE FOR HIRE
NO QUESTIONS ASKED
ALL QUESTIONS ANSWERED
REASONABLE RATES
INQUIRE WITHIN

"Well, look at that," Tristam said, shoulders slumping as he read the sign.

Seren smiled, but her smile faded as she studied the surrounding buildings. They were uniformly dark and run-down, like the rest of the village. There was no way of telling who might be within, or if Arthen's home was already being watched from one of them. In a place like Black Pit, it was almost impossible to find anything conspicuously suspicious, since everything was already rather shady and threatening.

Then Seren saw the small figure crouching on the rooftop next to Arthen's office. She darted forward, seizing Tristam by the sleeve and pulling him back into the alley. Wordlessly, she pointed up.

"Let's sneak around behind that building to the right," Tristam said. "We should be able to get up on that roof behind him without him noticing."

"We probably don't need to," Seren said. "Whoever that is, they aren't going anywhere unless Arthen does. What if they cry out and Arthen hears?"

"He isn't going to hear anything with the racket out tonight," Tristam answered.

Seren couldn't really argue the point, though the mysterious noise emanating from the Pit made her less eager to stumble through dark alleys. Omax led the way around to the back of the building adjacent to Arthen's. The alley was littered with refuse and heaped with the black filth that fell from the sky. Seren searched the wall for a way up, but saw nothing beyond a few rough handholds in the stone wall. She prepared to climb, but was surprised to find her feet rooted firmly to the ground.

"What are we standing in?" she asked, twisting to look at the ground beneath her.

The shrieking that resounded from the pit erupted much closer. The pile of garbage that littered the alley exploded into movement. A grotesque amorphous shape surged toward them, a greasy pile of gray flesh studded with bloodshot eyes and clicking, fanged mouths. The sound that came from within it drilled into Seren's head, shaking her bones and robbing her of the will to act. She felt the ground suck at her feet. What once was sturdy earth now sucked at her calves. Tristam reached for his wand with a numb, shaking hand. The creature vomited a ball of black spit in the artificer's eyes and he fell back, screaming and clawing at his face.

The thing knocked Tristam down with a fleshy limb and rolled over his helpless form, extending more twisted hideous arms toward Seren. Then Omax was there, charging into the creature headfirst. He hit the thing squarely with a meaty slap and it began to extend fleshy, biting tentacles around the warforged's body. With a heavy grunt and a heave, Omax grasped the beast with both arms and lifted it from the ground, pulling it off Tristam's body. He hurled it to the opposite side of the alley. It struck the wall with the sound of cracking stone and oozed downward, leaving a trail of red ichor in its wake. Omax wrapped one arm around Seren's waist and pulled her free of the quagmire. The shifting ground was swiftly becoming stone again now that the creature was further away.

"Finish it, Tristam," Omax said.

"I can't see!" the artificer said, panicked. He had tilted back his head and was now liberally dousing his face with something out of a vial from his pocket.

The creature pulled itself together with a bubbling noise. Its eyes wobbled unsteadily, then all swiveled in the same direction at once, focusing on Omax. Seren drew her knife, out of habit more than any real belief it would help. With a sudden surge it opened all the mouths on its body at once, screaming with a mad, gibbering cry.

A crossbow bolt shot down from the roof above, leaving a trail of sparks as it flew directly into one of the creature's mouths. The abomination bit down hard. A muffled thud rocked the street just as fire erupted from several of the creature's orifices. A cloud of oily black smoke coughed out a moment later. The monster settled to the earth with a disgusting rasp of released gas.

Tristam looked around, blinking rapidly to clear his eyes. "What happened?" he asked. "Is it dead?"

"That looked like one of your explosive potions," Omax said, peering up at the roof above them.

"That's because it was," said Gerith Snowshale, hopping down from the roof. He tucked his crossbow back into his belt with a scowl. "Are you hurt?"

"Other than accumulating more character, I am fine," Omax said, poking the bite marks on his left forearm with one finger as he assessed the damage.

"Gerith, what are you doing here?" Seren asked, tucking her knife away.

"How did you get one of my potions?" Tristam asked.

Gerith pretended the question did not exist. He looked up at Seren with a charming grin. "I've been spying on Zed Arthen for four days," he said to her. "Didn't you know? I thought Dalan sent you to check on me."

"Not exactly," Tristam said, looking at Omax for support. The warforged was still studying the dents on his arm, ignoring Tristam.

"He doesn't even know you're here, does he?" Gerith said, looking up at Tristam and chuckling with malicious glee.

A sharp reptilian squawk sounded from above, blending easily with the shrieking of the pit, but Gerith stopped speaking and looked up instantly. He replied with a similar cry, and Blizzard landed on the street nearby with a leathery flap.

"Arthen's moving," Tristam said.

"I know," Gerith said, hopping into the saddle. "Keep up if you can, but try to keep your distance. And Seren." The halfling looked at her pointedly. "Keep those two out of trouble."

Omax looked up at Gerith in shock. The halfling gave a final cocky smile and flapped away on his glidewing.

CHAPTER THIRTEEN

Seren's life as a street rat had made her fairly competent at shadowing people, or at least she'd thought as much. She was capable of fading into the background and following a mark for hours without attracting his attention. It was easier with a crowd to act as cover, but nearly as simple on a dark evening like tonight. In a place like Black Pit, it should have been relatively simple. To her surprise, Zed Arthen lost her in less than two minutes. She had only one clear glimpse of his ratty brown coat before he disappeared into another alley, during which she noticed that he had a large sword strapped to his back.

The worst part was that she was fairly certain that he hadn't even noticed her. She had been hanging back farther than usual, with Omax being as conspicuous as he was. The inquisitive ditched them effortlessly, without even knowing they were there. She hadn't seen any sign of Gerith since he had taken off, and could only hope that the little scout was having more luck. It was all in Tristam's hands now.

The artificer stood in the center of a crossroads, brow furrowed as he closed his eyes in concentration. Omax sat on the road in meditation, obviously not expecting Tristam to sort out the answer any time soon.

Seren was not quite so patient. "Well?" she prompted.

She scanned the streets for movement, nervous for any sign of life after the strange creature that attacked them. There was nothing. In fact, the mad shrieking of the Pit was now almost silent.

"This way," Tristam said, pointing to his left. "He's stopped moving. That's good news?"

"Or very bad news, depending on why he's stopped," Seren said.

Tristam laughed.

Omax rose and fell into his usual dauntless stride. They soon found themselves on a path leading out of the village and into the thick forests to the south. The light of a torch shone in the forest ahead. Seren gestured for them to stop. Omax nodded in understanding.

"I will wait here," he said softly, settling into his meditative posture again. "Silence is not my specialty."

Tristam laughed, but it was a nervous laugh. He fell in behind Seren, following closely as she picked her way through the forest. She stopped abruptly, looking back at him patiently. After several seconds, he realized he was literally hanging over her shoulder, one hand clenched tightly on her upper arm. He let her go and stepped back with an embarrassed smile.

"Sorry, Seren," he whispered. "I get nervous sometimes. Omax is the soldier. I'm just a scholar."

"Really?" Seren said, glancing at him in surprise. "So the dashing Lhazaarite swordsman act is just bravado?"

"You're teasing me," he said wryly. "I'm not entirely clueless in a fight, but that's not how I like to handle things. I figure if I can scare the other guy into not fighting at all, then I don't have to worry about getting thrashed."

"Makes sense," she said, moving forward again.

Tristam coughed. "Did you really think I was dashing, Seren?"

She looked back at him, pressing one finger over her lips for him to be silent.

Seren crouched in the underbrush and crawled forward for a closer look at their quarry. Tristam crawled beside her, moving with less grace and drawing a scowl from her. A small clearing lay ahead. Zed Arthen waited there, facing the way they had come. He stood with his back against a tree, one hand tucked in his pocket and the other holding a torch. He was definitely wearing a sword; its elaborate two-handed hilt protruded above his right shoulder. Tristam had mentioned twice before that Zed had been a knight. She wondered if the sword was a souvenir from that previous career.

For a long time, they watched Zed Arthen stand in the forest and do nothing. He occasionally removed his pipe from his mouth, blowing delicate smoke rings into the night breeze.

Tristam shifted restlessly. Seren guessed he had sat down awkwardly and was cramping up. She'd done the same thing the first time she'd spied on someone. She poked him sharply in the side with one finger. He looked at her in surprise. She smiled and laid one finger over her lips again. He frowned miserably and kept still.

After a few seconds, Tristam clasped a hand over hers. She shot him a suspicious look. He pointed to the northern edge of the clearing. Another light was rapidly approaching, and the figure carrying it soon resolved from the darkness. It was a tall, fair-skinned woman with long black hair. She was obviously a warrior, the traditional image of a knight. She wore full armor, carried a short spear in one hand, and wore a shortsword at her hip. Her tabard bore an impressive crest, a monstrous creature with the heads of a lion, ram, and dragon underneath an iron gauntlet, holding a double-bladed sword. Seren did not recognize her but noticed the way Tristam's hand tightened when he saw her.

"Deneith," he whispered. His lips pressed into a grim, lipless line. "Another dragonmarked house."

Zed did not seem at all distressed to see this newcomer, so this was obviously whom he was waiting for. She offered him a formal salute with her spear. He returned the gesture in such a nonchalant, offhand manner that it caused her to frown in disapproval. Seren couldn't hear what they were saying, but saw Zed brush her irritation away with a laughing comment, which only seemed to annoy her more. The two spoke in hushed voices. Eventually the inquisitive reached into his pocket and produced the purple hand lens. Seren felt Tristam tense. She looked down and saw he had drawn his wand. She squeezed Tristam's hand and he looked at her. She shook her head, cautioning him not to do anything foolish. He only fixed his gaze back on Arthen and the woman.

The Deneith warrior reached for the lens, but Zed drew it back with a quiet demurral. Seren wished she could hear what they were saying. She considered moving closer when she saw Zed Arthen suddenly tense and look directly toward their hiding place. Had he seen them? No, Seren quickly realized, he was looking slightly to their left. Arthen dropped his torch and drew his sword with the brilliant hiss of steel.

Then eight of Marth's Cyran soldiers charged into the clearing with weapons drawn.

"Should we help them?" Seren asked, looking at Tristam.

Her reply was the heavy sound of adamantine footsteps charging through the forest behind them. Omax rushed past them and into the clearing with a mechanical howl. A shriek sounded from the tree above and Gerith soared down on his glidewing. Tristam just sighed and lunged to his feet, wobbling as the blood flowed back into his knees. He drew his sword and followed the others. Seren found her dagger and charged as well.

VOYAGE OF THE MOURNING DAWN

Zed Arthen had already taken down the first of his attackers with a heavy cleave of his sword. He whirled with a glare as Seren and the others burst into the clearing, but his fury changed quickly to astonishment when he recognized them.

"These are friends, Eraina!" Zed shouted. The woman only nodded and parried a mercenary's sword with her spear.

"Take the inquisitive alive!" the Cyran leader cried as the attackers shifted formation to address the new threat.

Omax charged that one first, seizing him by his cloak and hurling him into a tree trunk. Tristam pointed his wand into the group, releasing a burst of white lightning that sent two more men flying. A third charged through the blast, putting Tristam down with a brutal slash of his sword. Seren shouted out in anger, lunging while still off-balance from the swing. He looked down at her with a murderous gaze and fell to his knees, his throat bleeding profusely from Seren's knife.

Seren staggered back in horror and watched the man fall face down and lie still. She had been in fights before but had never killed a man. It had happened without thinking. She was so stunned she didn't see the sword cleaving toward her.

"Curse yourself later, girl," Arthen said, knocking the blade aside with his own.

Zed cut the man down with another swing, but left himself open from behind. A soldier clubbed Zed across the back of the skull with the hilt of his blade, driving Arthen to one knee. Seren hurled her dagger at the soldier but it went wide, lodging in a tree. The soldier ignored her, lifting his sword for a final blow. The weapon tumbled out of his hands as Gerith's crossbow bolt bloomed in his eye. Zed staggered back to his feet, paying no mind to the man dying behind him.

"Nice shot, Snowshale," he called out.

Seren turned to find Tristam and was surprised to see him on his feet. The artificer wobbled unsteadily, looking down at his bloody shirt with a sleepy, bewildered expression. A faint trail of white sparkling light streamed from the rip in his shirt to the hand of the woman Zed had called Eraina. Seeing that Tristam was now stable, the dark-haired woman turned and ducked the sword blow of the nearest soldier. She drew her shortsword in a wicked underhand slash, leaving a red gouge across the man's chest.

Some of the injured mercenaries were already retreating, but one charged at Zed Arthen with a frenzied scream, clutching his longsword in both hands. Omax darted in from behind, kicking the mercenary's feet out from under him. He fell face down and immediately rolled to stand again. Omax planted a foot heavily in the man's face and he went limp.

Seren hurried to Tristam's side, pausing only to snatch her dagger from the tree. Tristam tried to push her away as she reached for his bloody shirt but she slapped his hands away. Her fingers brushed against his stomach and she stared at him in astonishment. Though his shirt was soaked with blood, there was no wound.

Zed frowned ruefully as he wiped the blood off his blade with a dead mercenary's cloak and sheathed it. "If they were trying to take me alive," he said, "They weren't trying very hard."

"Whatcha mean, Zed? You look alive to me," Gerith said. He smiled wickedly as he hopped down from a tree.

"Still following me, Snowshale?" the inquisitive asked, sheathing his blade with a clack.

"That's some way to thank us for saving you," Tristam said, still shivering from the effects of Eraina's magic.

"I would have been fine, boy," Zed said.

"Oh, I'm sure," Tristam shot back angrily. "What are you doing showing the lens to a Sentinel Marshal?" He pointed at Eraina accusingly.

Eraina d'Deneith looked at Tristam with a cold expression. Her eyes flicked to the gaping hole in his shirt, then back to his face. "Speaking of questionable thanks . . ." she said simply.

"Time to fight later," Omax said as he heaped the body of a mercenary against a tree. "None of us foresaw the coming of these men, so their presence is our immediate concern. This one is merely unconscious." He lifted the soldier lying under his feet and propped him against a tree, then looked at Eraina. "You are a healer. Can you revive him? Perhaps we can question him."

Eraina nodded, sheathing her shortsword and walking over to the fallen man.

"Belay that, Marshal Eraina," Zed said, cocking his head to one side. Seren could hear it too, now, a steady throbbing hum growing swiftly louder. "We'd best run."

The trees above exploded in a blaze of white light just as a sleek silver airship broke through the canopy. It was larger even than the Lyrandar ship, with the national crest of Cyre emblazoned on the hull. Electricity crackled from a long rod mounted on the hull.

"Khyber," Zed grumbled.

Seren turned and ran with the others at her side; a flurry of crossbow bolts pelted the clearing. She felt a burning pain in her calf and her leg went dead. Just as she stumbled, Zed Arthen wrapped an arm around her waist and kept running, bearing her weight with ease.

"Gerith, we need a distraction and an exit!" Zed shouted as they ran deeper into the woods.

"Working on it!" came the halfling's reply. This was accompanied by a whoosh of air and the flap of broad wings as he swooped overhead and soared up over the trees. The glidewing soared back directly toward the airship, dodging and weaving as missiles rained into the forest. A plume of bright light fired from a tube in Gerith's hand onto the ship's deck, exploding in a cloud of pale gray smoke. Then Blizzard dove again, vanishing into the trees before the Cyran ship could score a lucky hit.

"What else did he take out of my lab?" Tristam shouted, looking back with a scowl.

"Shut up and keep running," Zed shouted.

"Why aren't we running toward the village?" Tristam shouted back.

"Black Pit has enough problems," Zed said. "Those soldiers won't stop shooting if innocent people get in the way."

Under different circumstances, Seren might have argued the existence of innocent people in Black Pit. She kept such comments to herself and just kept hopping along in pain. Each jolt sent waves of agony through her leg. The roaring thrum of the strange airship receded and Zed set her down carefully against a tree. Seren was about to offer thanks, but her words became a confused stutter when she saw the crossbow bolt piercing through her calf.

"A clean wound," Zed said cheerfully. He clapped her on the shoulder and stood, facing the others. "You took it well, Seren. Most men faint the first time they're shot."

Seren only nodded dumbly, fighting the urge to do just that.

"Eraina, please help her," Zed said. "Omax, establish a perimeter. Make sure we don't have any more of those mercenaries chasing us."

The warforged stomped into the woods without a word. The dark-haired marshal knelt by Seren's side, tending her wounded leg with the tender precision of a practiced medic.

"What's your name?" she asked, smiling gently.

"Seren," she said, then stifled a cry as Eraina used the moment of distraction to snap the crossbow bolt and draw both ends cleanly from the leg. Eraina bound a scrap of silk cloth tightly over the wound and whispered a soft prayer. Seren heard

VOYAGE OF THE MOURNING DAWN

the name "Boldrei." Motes of white magic spread from Eraina's fingers to the wound. Her leg felt numb, then cold, and then the pain went away. Her calf twitched uncomfortably and itched a little, but there was no more pain.

"Thank you," Seren said, amazed.

Eraina studied her with an intensely curious expression.

"Can she run?" Zed asked brusquely. "We have to be ready to move."

"Why do you keep giving us orders, Arthen?" Tristam asked.

"This is not the time, Xain," Zed said, watching the sky.

"Yes, Sir," Tristam said. "I guess that's the way it always is. We need your help and you run off to Black Pit, but the instant you're in trouble it's back to giving orders. What's your problem, Zed? Do we all look like squires to you?"

"I will assume that the stress of the moment has overcome your senses and I will let that slide, Xain," Zed answered. "Do not mock me again. Not about that."

"Then tell me what in Khyber is going on here!" Tristam demanded. "Where did that airship come from?"

"Zed was as surprised to see that ship as we were, Tristam," Seren said.

"No," Zed said. "That's not what he's talking about, Seren. Tristam recognized that ship. So did I." Zed looked at Tristam with a sober, pensive expression. "Now is not the time to worry on it. We'll all get our answers."

"We had better," Eraina said, folding her arms across her chest and glaring coldly at Tristam and Zed.

Tristam grimaced at Eraina and quickly looked away, clearly uncertain whether to demand an explanation for her presence or thank her for saving his life. Instead he sat beside Seren with an exhausted sigh. He looked at the bandage on her leg, then at the Deneith Marshal. He shrugged uncomfortably into his heavy coat.

"Shouldn't we be getting back to *Karia Naille*?" Seren asked.

"Gerith went for help," Tristam said. "Pherris is probably on his way to us already."

"How will he find us?" she asked.

"Aeven always finds us," Tristam said.

"Aeven?" Seren asked, but was interrupted by the thrum of an airship overhead.

Seren's heart jumped at the familiar rhythm. Even though she had only been on the ship for a short time, the song of *Karia Naille*'s elemental fire was welcome and familiar. She leapt up just as Tristam did, just as Omax returned from his patrol. She watched the airship pass over the trees and stop, hovering above them. The cargo ladder unrolled and hung in the air with a snap.

"Ladies first, Marshal Eraina," Tristam said with equal parts courtesy and suspicion.

The Marshal did not argue, and quickly began her climb. Seren followed, feeling the strength fully return to her injured leg as she put her weight on it. Gerith and Eraina helped her into the cargo bay, and she turned to help Tristam board behind her.

"Welcome back, Master Xain," Dalan said coldly.

Seren jumped. She had not noticed Dalan d'Cannith standing in the shadows of the cargo bay. He was watching them all with an unpleasant expression.

"How was your evening?" he asked acidly.

"Productive," Tristam answered, facing Dalan with all the confidence he could muster. "More productive than sitting in the airship, doing nothing."

"I missed you, Dalan," Zed said, climbing into the hold.

Dalan ignored Zed's greeting, standing as he was with arms folded across his thick stomach.

Seren looked down to see Omax making his way up the

ladder. The warforged was climbing slowly but surely. Seren thought she heard the wailing hum of the ship's elemental grow suddenly in volume. Omax looked up suddenly.

"Look out!" the warforged cried.

A cacophonous explosion sent a shockwave through the hull, sending her tumbling back into the cargo bay.

The hum had not grown louder at all. The other ship had found them.

"Enemy ship off the port bow!" Pherris shouted, his voice echoing through the bronze tubes.

Seren crawled back to the edge of the bay doors, looking down at Omax helplessly. The warforged was now hugging the rope ladder with both arms and legs, struggling to hold on as the ship heaved dangerously. Sparks flew from his shoulder as a crossbow bolt grazed his armor.

"Draw up the ladder!" Arthen shouted.

"He's too heavy," Tristam said, tugging fruitlessly at the winch.

"Status report, crew!" Pherris demanded from above.

"Omax isn't aboard yet," Tristam shouted.

"Take off now," Dalan said urgently.

Karia Naille banked heavily, pulling higher into the sky. Omax spun helplessly at the end of the ladder.

"Omax!" Tristam shouted. He fell to his knees beside the bay doors, tugging at the ropes. "Someone, help me!"

Gerith and Zed seized each side of the ladder, hauling it up with all their strength. Seren hauled on the ropes too, though she was so exhausted she feared she contributed little. Behind them, she heard Eraina's voice rise in prayer. She felt her exhaustion begin to melt away, and strength surged through her arms. The rope came up, rung by rung. The air thinned as the ship pulled higher into the air. Wind whistled dangerously through the open bay doors. Another explosion resounded as the other ship belched lightning across the sky.

When Omax was only a dozen feet from the hold, the ship turned sharply. The left side of the ladder split with a sickly snap. Seren drew back in pain, the rope burning her fingers as it tore free. Almost immediately the remaining side of the rope began to fray and smoke. Omax looked up at them. The light in his blue eyes dimmed for a brief instant, and he bowed his head against his chest.

"Omax, no!" Tristam howled, hauling on the remaining rope with all his strength. Zed stood by him, trying desperately to at least anchor the slack before Omax dropped further away. Smoke hissed their gloves, but they held firm.

"We need to be away from here," Pherris shouted from the helm. "Is everyone aboard?"

"Damn it, Dalan, do something!" Zed hissed.

Then Dalan was there, pulling the collar of his shirt aside to reveal the swirling tattoo on his right shoulder. Without a word, he called upon his dragonmark. There was no surge of magic, no fantastic display. He merely touched the broken ropes and the ladder was whole again.

"Keep pulling," he said blandly.

Tristam nodded, hauling with all his strength as Zed, Gerith, and Seren did likewise. Omax crawled up through the hull and collapsed in the cargo bay with a metal clang. Gerith fell on the bay door levers, sealing the hull with a heavy thud.

"Aeven, we're clear!" Gerith shouted.

The winds howled around *Karia Naille*, and the elemental ring screamed with burning energy. Seren was thrown back on the deck as a burst of speed surged through the airship.

The sounds of the pursuing ship faded into the distance.

CHAPTER
FOURTEEN

An uneasy silence had fallen over *Karia Naille*. The usual even hum of the ship's elemental fire was now broken by a rattling stutter. The bluish-white fire that orbited the ship was streaked with red. Seren had climbed onto the wooden strut above the deck. It was a precarious position. The elemental ring radiated a fierce heat. Her body would have been soaked with sweat if not for the chill winds that howled over her. Her hair was tied back with a black silk kerchief to prevent it from blowing into the fire.

Seren carefully avoided thinking about what might happen if she fell. She leaned as close to the flame as she dared. The end of the wooden arm was singed black from one of the Cyran airship's lightning blasts. The crystalline hook that secured the elemental to the airship was now webbed with tiny cracks.

"How is it?" Tristam asked. He stood directly below the hook, peering at it from all angles. The others looked up nervously with the exception of the captain, who was intent on the helm.

"It's cracked pretty badly," Seren said. Even as she spoke, the strut rocked, nearly shaking her off. She clung to it with arms and legs. A small shard of crystal splintered off the hook with a musical chime and disappeared on the wind.

"Khyber, the ring is coming loose," Tristam swore. "Pherris, we need to land."

The captain looked up at the ring fearfully. "If I put any more stress on the controls we'll go down quick enough, tinker," he said. "A steady course is all that'll keep us alive now."

"Well, good luck, everybody," Gerith said, climbing on Blizzard's back with a nervous grin. "If anybody wanted to pass on any last words, messages to loved ones, valuable possessions . . ."

Omax looked down at the halfling.

"Just trying to lighten the mood," the halfling said. "Seriously, though. Good luck.

"Seren, try this," Tristam said. He took a small bottle from one of his numerous pouches and tossed it up to her. She snatched it in one hand, looking at it curiously. It was a small, unlabeled black bottle with a long brush clamped to one side.

"It's a bonding agent," Tristam explained. "I use it for ship repairs. Just brush it on the hook!"

Seren nodded. She tried to remove the cap with her teeth, hugging the ship's arm with one arm and both lags.

"Careful, Seren, it bonds in seconds," Tristam said. "Don't get any on yourself."

She quickly took the bottle out of her mouth and decided instead to risk unscrewing it with both hands, clutching the strut with just her legs. The arm shuddered beneath her, nearly shaking her off again. Her heart hammered in her chest, but she held on. Quickly, she held the bottle out and dumped the contents over the hook. The liquid inside was thin and gooey, like syrup. She spread it over the cracks using the brush, or at least did for several seconds until the brush became firmly glued to the hook.

"The brush is stuck," she said, looking down at Tristam.

"Then I guess it's working," Tristam said, his tone somewhat embarrassed. "I'm still working on that formula. As long as you spread it around consistently it should hold."

Seren looked back at the hook. The glue had assumed a shiny, metallic sheen, coating the hairline cracks. The ship's arm still shook, but a great deal less violently than before. Seren tossed the empty bottle over the side and rolled off the hook, hanging by one hand for a moment before dropping to the deck. Omax caught her easily and set her on her feet.

"Well done, Seren," Dalan said, surprising her with his praise.

"Impressive climb," Gerith added, looking up at the thin wooden arm in awe.

"Why didn't we send Snowshale?" Zed asked, looking up from his pipe. "He's lighter."

"Are you kidding?" Gerith asked. "Climbing something like that is insane."

Seren looked at the halfling, then at the flying dinosaur he rode. Gerith shrugged.

"How long will that glue hold, tinker?" Pherris asked, ignoring their discussion.

"Three or four days at most," Tristam said.

"Cragwar isn't too far from here," Pherris said. "We can put in for repairs."

"Can't you use your dragonmark to fix the damage?" Eraina asked.

"I cannot," Dalan said. "I exhausted my rather limited talents fixing the ladder, and even had I not done so, I am wary about mixing magics—especially where the survival of everyone on board is concerned." He glared at Eraina. "Now could someone perhaps explain why a Deneith Sentinel Marshal is on my ship?"

"I might as well ask you why you fly a ship unmarked with any symbols of house or nation," Eraina said.

"A fair question," Dalan said. "But the fact remains this is my ship, and that I have saved your life by allowing you to board it. What are you doing here?"

Seren was surprised that Eraina did not reply that she had

saved Tristam's life and possibly her own as well. The marshal only looked away.

"Marshal d'Deneith is one of my contacts," Zed said, stepping between Dalan and Eraina. "I was meeting her when those Cyran mercenaries attacked. I assure you, we both appreciate the rescue."

"My pleasure," Dalan said graciously, as if it were all his doing. Though his tone was polite, his eyes were shrewd. "A pity we cannot risk returning you to your home in Black Pit. Cragwar will have to do. Of course you are welcome to stay with the crew if you like, Arthen. Your insights are much appreciated, assuming you remember your place. As for you, Marshal, I would be pleased to deposit you in Cragwar as long as you remain locked in one of the lower cabins until then."

"I'm to be imprisoned?" she asked. "Is this the hospitality of House Cannith?"

"As you expertly pointed out, this is not a Cannith ship," Dalan said. "If my proposed arrangement does not interest you," he added, and stepped to his left, gesturing at the deck rail with a flourish, "there is your alternate exit. Feel free to utilize it. Surely your goddess will bear you safely to the ground."

Eraina glared at Dalan in silent hatred but did not rise to his barbs. "I would appreciate a ride to Cragwar," she said. "Thank you."

"Excellent," Dalan said. "Omax, escort the good Marshal to her cabin."

The warforged nodded and stood beside the ladder leading below decks. Eraina offered Dalan a final scathing look and followed him below.

"Tristam, you are excused to your studies," Dalan said. "I would like to discuss what just occurred privately with Zed and Seren." Dalan returned to his cabin and stepped inside, not even offering Tristam a second glance.

Tristam blinked in surprise. "What?" he shot back. "You're just sending me off to my room? Do you even realize that Marth's ship . . ."

"Tristam," Zed interrupted, fixing the artificer with a meaningful look.

Tristam glared at Zed, shrugged, and stormed off below deck. Seren watched the exchange with a curious expression, wondering what had just passed between them.

"What happened down there, Arthen?" Dalan asked as Seren and Zed entered his cabin. The old dog, Gunther, snored noisily on Dalan's bed. Somehow it had managed to sleep through the entire escape from Black Pit.

"When I first saw that lens you gave me, it reminded me of something from Ashrem's work long ago," Zed said. "But I wasn't sure. Eraina is a colleague of mine and has been conducting an investigation on a related matter, so I sent her a speaker post to get her insight. She agreed to meet me privately and booked the first Lyrandar ship, but she refused to meet me in the village. Some people just don't trust me, I guess." He smiled faintly at Seren.

"And you followed him?" Dalan asked, looking at Seren.

"Yes," she answered. "We saw Eraina meet with Zed. The Cyrans attacked only a few moments afterward."

"The soldiers wanted to take me alive," Zed added. "When that didn't work, the whole damned ship came after us. They might have killed Tristam if it wasn't for the Marshal."

"Interesting," Dalan said. "And you saw their ship, Seren? Was there anything notable?"

"Not really," Zed said, interrupting her.

Seren looked at Zed in confusion. "The ship looked like some kind of military vessel," she said, looking back at Dalan. "Large and silver. I saw the Cyran crest, too. Just like the soldiers we fought before."

"That seems rather distinctive," Dalan said, brows rising. "Strange that an inquisitive missed all of that."

"I didn't get a good look at it," Zed said. "I was running."

Dalan grunted, unconvinced. He looked back at Seren. "Is that all you noticed of interest?"

"Other than getting attacked by some monster from the pit, yes," she said. "But why question me about this? Tristam knows more about what's going on than I do. I think he even recognized the . . ."

"Dalan is ignoring Tristam because the boy disobeyed orders," Zed said, interrupting her again. "It was Tristam's idea to follow me, wasn't it? I'm guessing you were just looking out for him." He reached into his pocket, took out the lens and a small book, setting them both on Dalan's desk. "Incidentally, you can have these back, Dalan."

"Thank you, Arthen," Dalan said, plucking up the lens and examining it briefly for any damage. He placed it into one of his desk drawers, then tucked the book into a shelf. "He is precisely right, Seren. Tristam is an intelligent young man, but when he behaves in such a childish way I must treat him accordingly. He is too headstrong for his own good. On a ship like this, responsibilities are clearly delineated. To step outside one's bounds, to disobey orders, is to risk all that we have worked for. If one cannot respect the chain of command, then one must either learn respect or leave." He looked at Zed briefly.

"But if we hadn't followed them, Zed and Eraina would have died," Seren said.

"Wrong on two counts," Dalan countered. "First, their lives are not our concern. No offense intended, Arthen."

"None taken," Zed said with a cynical chuckle.

"Second," Dalan said, "you don't know they were in danger. Any number of things might have occurred differently. The Cyrans did not wish Arthen to die. Perhaps they were only watching, saw you approach, mistakenly believed you intended to attack him and sought to capture him alive. Perhaps the Cyrans followed you—and you led them to Arthen. Perhaps your presence was irrelevant, but Arthen had contingencies in mind. After all," Dalan pointed to the sword hilt protruding above the inquisitive's shoulder, "he did attend the meeting armed."

Seren looked at him. "Did you have a way out of there?"

"I had an escape tunnel prepared in that clearing," Zed admitted. "I could have dashed out and brought it down behind me, but Omax never would have fit inside. I wouldn't leave the big guy behind." He gave a quick smile.

Seren nodded quietly. She suddenly felt very foolish.

"How noble," Dalan said dryly. "Perhaps you retained some of your Thrane honor along with your Thrane steel."

"You're very funny, Dalan," Zed said. "I'm laughing."

"So how did you come to know this Sentinel Marshal?" Dalan asked.

"My contacts are confidential," Zed said.

"As long as she is on my ship, she is *my* business," Dalan said. "If you wish to retain her anonymity, I will gladly deposit her in the woods. On foot it should take her only five days to reach Cragwar, assuming she can forage for her own food and water."

"Fine," Zed said. "She's a colleague, like I said. She's an investigator for the Sentinel Marshals. We've met professionally a time or two and kept in touch through speaker posts. If you want more, just ask her yourself. She won't lie to you. She can't. She's a paladin of the Host, for Khyber's sake. We can trust her."

"Oh, I certainly trust those who blindly place their faith in a higher power," Dalan said. "I trust them to make horrible mistakes, to bring misery to those who disagree with their dogma, and inevitably to die disappointed in the world. I'm surprised you sought a paladin's aid, Arthen. I thought you abandoned your faith."

"This isn't about me, d'Cannith," Zed said. "Don't push me."

"Or you'll silence my uncomfortable truths with your sword?" Dalan asked with a smug grin. "You become more like your old self every moment."

Zed's face darkened. He rose from his chair. Seren took a step back, hoping to look inconspicuous in case Zed drew his weapon.

"Why did I ever agree to help you?" Arthen asked.

"Because we both need the truth, and despite our history we both know we can't find it alone," Dalan said, staring at his desk as he drummed his fingers on its surface. "So did you learn anything useful from the lens and book?"

Zed shook his head. "There are definitely hidden messages in Ashrem's journals that only that lens can read," he said, "but I couldn't break the cipher."

"Are you certain?" Dalan asked peering up at him. "Imagine that. An inquisitive not only fails to find any useful clues but also lets himself be ambushed twice in one evening. I can't imagine what that will do to whatever remains of your reputation."

"Whatever, Dalan," Zed said in a dull voice. He stepped toward the door. "Just put me down in Cragwar, or wherever. I was an idiot to get involved in this again."

"Zed, please," Seren said. "The leader of those mercenaries killed a good friend of mine. This was our only clue to stop him from finding the Legacy. If you discovered anything, anything at all, please help us."

"Ah, the Legacy," Zed said with a dark laugh. "Well, we certainly can't let Ashrem d'Cannith's work fall into irresponsible hands."

VOYAGE OF THE MOURNING DAWN

"I should have a life as easy as yours, Arthen," Dalan said. "So easy to walk away. Hide in a bottle. So easy to be offered a choice and make no choice at all."

Zed stopped in the doorway, his back to Dalan. His hands tightened into fists.

"Did you have something else to add, Arthen?" Dalan asked.

"I didn't break the code," Zed said, "but I recognized it."

"Oh?" Dalan asked, suddenly interested.

"Ashrem didn't create that cipher," Zed said. "Kiris created it for him."

"Kiris Overwood?" Seren asked, remembering the name from Pherris's stories.

Zed and Dalan both looked at Seren with some surprise. "That's right," Zed said. "It's magically encrypted. Without the proper spells to translate the code, it might take a wizard or artificer years to decipher."

"I sense an 'unless,'" Dalan said.

Zed turned around to face Dalan again, extending a hand. "Let me see the lens."

Dalan frowned curiously, then opened the drawer and handed the small chunk of glass back to Zed.

"Look at the frame," Zed said, tracing the white rim around the edge of the glass. "That's petrified dragon bone. And look at the characters."

Dalan bent to study the item. "More illegible rubbish," he said.

"Not quite," Zed said. "That's halfling script. It's a prayer for clarity and wisdom in the name of Balinor, God of the Hunt. It also bears the mark of its creator. These arcane marks are very difficult to forge, and I recognize this one. Kiris Overwood made this herself."

"She signed a piece of glass?" Seren asked dubiously.

"Kiris was a wizard," Zed said, if that explained it.

Seren looked to Dalan, puzzled.

"Wizards are a curious lot," Dalan explained with a wry smile. "They have always been somewhat jealous of the lasting mark artificers leave with each wonder they create. Their arrogance drives them to personalize the few rare things of use that they leave behind. Rare is the wizard who does not sign his work."

"So Marth stole this from Kiris?" Seren asked. "Does that mean he knows how to read Ashrem's cipher?"

"In all likelihood," Dalan said. "A disturbing revelation, but not an altogether surprising one."

"There's more," Zed continued. "The halflings are a people very much in tune with nature. They believe that the gods recreate the world every year on the first day of spring. That belief is reflected in their language. The characters they use to refer to the gods vary by the year, and from the way Kiris wrote Balinor's name I can tell this was made within the last year. Overwood is still alive, Dalan, or at least she was recently."

"Preposterous," Dalan retorted. "Balinor's name? What rubbish is that? You don't even speak the halfling tongue, much know less their customs."

"No, but Gerith does," Zed said. "When I recognized the script two days ago I made him translate it. I figured if he was going to sit on that roof and spy on me all day, he might as well lend a hand."

"Clumsy halfling," Dalan muttered under his breath.

"It wasn't his fault," Zed said. "I knew you'd send someone, so I was looking. Give him credit. It took me two days to catch him."

"Respectable," Dalan admitted.

Seren resisted the urge to laugh. Somehow she wasn't surprised that Gerith hadn't told them he had been caught, or that he'd continued spying on Zed even though the inquisitive knew he was there.

Zed sat down beside Dalan's desk and placed the lens between them. They both studied it intently, and for a time at least Seren could barely tell how much the two men despised one another.

"It makes sense, Dalan," Zed said. "If Kiris wanted to vanish, where better than Talenta? A lot of the land is still wild. The halfling tribes keep to themselves. She could fade away there for years."

"Working to unravel the secrets of the Legacy on her own," Dalan mused.

Zed nodded. "So the man Seren nicked this from either stole it from Kiris within the last few months or commissioned it to be made. Either way, there's a chance that the halflings will know where she is or might at least have some idea of what happened to her."

"How can we be sure this isn't some sort of trap?" Dalan asked. "Overwood has been missing for four years. Might this be some forgery intended to lead us astray?"

"That's ridiculous," Seren said. "Why would Marth bother with something like that? He had no way of knowing I'd steal the lens from him. The times we've run into him so far, he just tries to kill us. Something that contrived seems out of character."

"A good point. I am merely entertaining all possibilities," Dalan said, dismissing his own argument with a wave of his hand. "Pardon my paranoid mind. Perhaps I'm just too wary, but we've found misleading clues before. Of course it isn't as if we have any other leads. Even this one is of dubious usefulness. Any halfling in Khorvaire could have taught Kiris how to write this script. She could be in Xen'drik with a halfling manservant for all we know."

"Granted," Zed answered, "but we can make a decent guess. There's only one place I know of that boasts petrified dragon bone and halfling tribes in close vicinity. It's a place called the Boneyard. We should start there."

"We?" Dalan asked. "I thought you loathed the idea of the Legacy falling into irresponsible hands."

"I guess that's why I'm going," Zed said.

"I hope you've left nothing of value in Black Pit," Dalan said. "We won't be returning there."

"Nothing that matters," Zed said.

"Then it is settled," Dalan said, clapping his hands together. "We'll need Gerith to plot a course. Seren, please fetch the halfling."

Seren nodded and opened the door.

"Oh, and Seren . . ." Dalan continued.

She looked back at him.

"After that, make sure Tristam is well," Dalan said, sounding genuinely concerned. "If I know him, he will be in one of his moods and we shall need him alert and aware when we reach Cragwar."

"Aye," Seren said, exiting the cabin.

She walked out on the deck to find Pherris still at the helm. Gerith sat on the deck nearby, eating a small meal while his glidewing watched with intense interest.

"Gerith," Seren called out.

"The Boneyard, I know," Gerith said. "I was eavesdropping." He threw the last bit of his food in the air; Blizzard snatched it faster than Seren could even see. The halfling stood, wiped his hands on his pants, and walked past her into Dalan's cabin with a strangely morose expression.

Seren walked toward the deck ladder, pausing only briefly to greet the captain. Pherris did not answer. His eyes were intent on the sky ahead as he struggled to control the wounded airship.

VOYAGE OF THE MOURNING DAWN

Not wanting to distract him, she mumbled a quiet greeting and headed to the ladder.

"Thank you, Seren," Pherris said.

Seren looked back at the captain in surprise.

"The ship," Pherris said. "Thank you for saving her."

"Captain, who is Aeven?" Seren asked impulsively. "I've heard you mention the name. Tristam and Gerith mentioned it too."

"Aeven?" Pherris asked with a chuckle. "She's the only member of the crew you haven't met. Don't worry, Seren. She's just shy."

Seren smiled, not sure how to react to the captain's reply. She left him to his work and made her way below deck. Omax was meditating in the cargo bay again. She wondered which of the cabins the paladin was locked in. Seren continued to Tristam's door and knocked lightly. There was no answer. She moved on to her own cabin, leaving him in peace.

"Seren," Tristam said, opening the door and peering out. "I'm sorry. I thought you might be Dalan." He had changed out of his ruined and bloody clothing and was wearing a somewhat somber gray shirt.

"No need to apologize," she said.

He looked back down the hall, beckoned to her, and stepped back inside. With a pensive frown, she followed him. He closed the door and sat at the desk. She sat at the edge of the bed, watching him curiously. The homunculus immediately leapt off the desk into her lap.

"What's wrong?" she asked.

"I have to tell you something, but you can't tell Dalan," Tristam said.

"What is it?" she said.

"I recognized that Cyran ship," he said. He reached into his pocket and took out a small glass sphere. He tapped the side and whispered the words, *"Kenshi Zhann."* The sphere immediately illuminated with swirling blue lights, displaying a model of a tiny airship.

"That's the ship that chased us," Seren said, recognizing it.

Tristam nodded. "I made this model for Ashrem, but I never gave it to him," he said. "It's the *Kenshi Zhann*, the *Seventh Moon*. Dalan didn't see her, but he would have recognized her too."

"Oh?" Seren asked.

"She was Ashrem's flagship."

"The ship he flew into Cyre?" Seren asked.

"Yes," Tristam said. "Ashrem flew her into Cyre just before the Day of Mourning. Orren Thardis flew his other ship, the *Albena Tors*, into Cyre after him. Neither ship was ever seen again."

"But now *Moon* is back," Seren said, "and Kiris Overwood is still alive."

"What?" Tristam asked, surprised. "Kiris is alive?"

"That's what Zed thinks," Seren said.

"Strange," Tristam said. "Zed should have recognized *Moon*."

"Maybe he did," Seren said. "He avoided describing the ship to Dalan. Why would he do that?"

Tristam didn't answer for a long moment. He just looked at her, his eyes lost and afraid. "I don't know," he said. "I don't know who to trust, Dalan or Zed, maybe neither. But I trust you."

"Me?" she said, surprised. "I thought you said you couldn't trust me."

"I say stupid things all the time," Tristam said. "If you hold that against me, we'll never get anywhere. The point is, I trust you now, and I want you to know what's going on here."

She leaned closer to him to listen more intently. "Tell me about *Moon*, then."

"She was Ashrem's oldest ship," Tristam continued. "He commissioned her back when he still designed and sold weapons.

VOYAGE OF THE MOURNING DAWN

The Cannith sometimes sold to both sides of the same conflict, so they weren't always welcome when they showed up. With that in mind, Ashrem outfitted *Moon* as a warship, designed to survive on the harshest battlefields of the Five Kingdoms. If her weapons are still intact, what she unleashed on us back there was only a taste. They'll come after us again, Seren. *Karia Naille* is faster, but we can't run forever."

"What are you getting at, Tristam?" she asked.

"You aren't really a part of this," he said. "I don't mean that as an insult. Cragwar isn't such a bad place. It's much nicer than Wroat and safer than Black Pit. Stay there, Seren. Maybe Eraina will even help you find a safe place to start a new life."

"Why would I want to do that?" she asked stiffly, leaning away from him again.

"Because I'm not so sure we're going to survive this," he said. "I'm not so sure that I'm doing this for the right reasons."

Seren watched him quietly, waiting for him to explain.

"When I first met Dalan, I was Ashrem's apprentice," he said. "I knew Dalan by reputation. He was one of the only people in House Cannith that Ashrem still trusted. Dalan came to me privately. He offered me a work, to create some infusions for House Cannith. Ashrem didn't seem to be interested in helping me join the house, but Dalan was. He offered me contracts on the side, things Ashrem wouldn't accept, so I took them. Ashrem found out about it eventually, of course. He also found out that the camouflage enchantments I thought were being used to help scouts remain undetected in the field were being used by Brelish soldiers to ambush Thrane border patrols. He was outraged that I had used his teachings and his facilities to create weapons. We argued about it, I called him a hypocrite and a few other things. I told him the war would never end if we stood by and did nothing. The old man didn't take that well at all."

"And that's why he ended your apprenticeship?" Seren asked.

"That's right," Tristam said with a sigh. "I never told Ashrem that Dalan was the one to give me the contracts, and Dalan didn't tell him either. When Dalan came back to me, asking me to help him find the Legacy, he said he appreciated my 'discretion,' whatever that means." Tristam laughed bitterly.

"Not that I don't appreciate your sharing something like this," Seren said, "but what does this have to do with my staying or leaving?"

"We're not doing anything noble here, Seren," he said. "Don't stay because you think we're heroes or because you think you're doing some great favor by keeping the Legacy out of Marth's hands. Dalan isn't perfect, and neither am I. I might look like I'm fighting to keep my teacher's work pure, but really that's not it at all. I'm a failure, Seren. Ashrem didn't want me. House Cannith doesn't want me. Now I can tell even Dalan's getting tired of me. Don't stay to help me. I'm not worth helping, and anyone with an ounce of sense sees that."

"Omax doesn't see that," she said. "Neither do I."

Tristam started to voice a reply but found nothing to say. He only lowered his head and clasped his hands over his knees.

"I don't understand why Omax follows me the way he does," he said. "I'm no hero, Seren. I'm here because I have nowhere else to go, and because, really, I want to prove them all wrong. I'm fighting to prove myself to a dead man. That's what you're risking your life for. That's why you should leave us in Cragwar, Seren, and forget any of this ever happened."

Seren set the homunculus on the floor and stood. She looked down at Tristam, arms folded across her breasts. He looked up at her meekly.

"If you want me to pity you," she said, "you'll have to do better than that. If you need me, I'll be in my cabin."

He blinked in surprise. She turned and left, closing the door behind her.

She stopped with a start, finding Omax lurking in the hall outside. The warforged's blue eyes shone in the darkness.

"Thank you, Seren," he said in a quiet voice. "He does not realize what he could be."

She looked at the construct for a long time, then finally nodded and returned to her cabin.

CHAPTER
FIFTEEN

Seren stood at the ship's rail for a long time, looking down at Cragwar as the ship circled for a landing. Gerith walked up beside her after a while, looking over the side and then looking at her in confusion, obviously not seeing what she was so interested in.

"Sorry," she said with a small laugh. "It's just that Wroat is really the only other big city I've ever seen. Cragwar is a lot different, at least from up here."

"Oh, yeah, I can see that," Gerith said, looking back down. "Probably because it's clean. Wroat is too big. Too many people living there. Cragwar's different, probably because it's so close to the Aundairian border. The Brelish army is in command here, and they run a tight ship."

"Why does that make a difference?" Seren asked. "King Boranel lives in Wroat; you'd think he'd command more respect than the army."

"Oh, that's not it at all," Gerith said. "Wroat's pretty far from any enemies, so the Watch is more likely to let things slide. This close to Aundair, any criminal could be an Aundairian spy. Any lapse in discipline could weaken the border. Not that Aundair is ready to challenge Breland, but better safe than sorry, I guess. The military has to be careful—they're on their own here."

"I see," Seren said, looking down at the city again. After a while she realized Gerith was looking up at her with a serious expression.

"What?" she asked.

"Just hoping all that sunk in," he said. "You behave yourself down there, Seren. Not that I'd mind swooping to your rescue and your inevitable gratitude, but I don't want you to get hurt." She looked at him sharply, but he held out a hand to stop her. "I'm not making judgments, Seren. Kol Korran knows every crown I made hasn't been an honest one—but no stealing in Cragwar. Understand?"

She laughed lightly and smiled at him. "I'll keep my hands out of other people's pockets, Gerith," she said.

"Good," he said, his usual bright smile instantly returning. He gave a sharp whistle and vaulted over the rail into the open sky, falling with his arms and legs outstretched. With a shrieking cry and the snap of broad wings, Blizzard swooped past and caught his master.

"One of these days," Pherris said.

The glidewing began its descent, toward a quartet of sky towers at the northern edge of the city. Two of them were already occupied by sleek vessels flying the boar's head banners of Breland. As they drew closer, a group of mounted soldiers emerged from the city and rode toward the towers.

"Hope this goes better than last time," Tristam said.

"Last time went precisely as planned, Tristam," Dalan said. "Merely because you do not know the plan is not an indication that it has failed. Now, someone please let the paladin out of her cell."

Omax disappeared below decks, returning shortly afterward with Eraina in tow. She scowled at Dalan but did not speak a word. The ship pulled smoothly into the sky tower. Dalan strode forward with a pleasant expression, readying his official papers to show the waiting officers. After a few moments' discussion, the soldiers gave the airship a final warning look and returned to the city.

"We should be safe enough here," Dalan said, looking at the other towers. "Even if Marth pursues us, those Brelish ships should be a match for him."

"Always so ready to let someone else fight your battles, d'Cannith?" Eraina said coldly. She brushed past him without another word, disappearing into the tower.

"First time I've seen you let someone else get the last word, Dalan," Zed said.

"What do I care?" Dalan said. "She's off my ship. That's all I wanted. How does it look, Tristam?"

The artificer had brought a ladder from below deck and climbed up to the strut holding the elemental ring in place. He probed at the crystal hook with a delicate silver wand. A broad bandolier holding many of the strange chemical concoctions and focusing crystals from his cabin now hung over his shoulder. Tristam concentrated intently on the hook. "Nothing I can't fix," he said. "I'll need some new lodestones to reseal the enchantments. The crystalline structure is badly fragmented."

"How long?" Dalan asked.

"Three hours, maybe four," he said.

"Excellent," Dalan said. "Time enough to catch a meal and find a copy of *The Chronicle*. I'll leave you to your work." Dalan paused at the door to the tower bridge and threw a small pouch at Seren. She caught it clumsily against her chest and heard the chink of coins inside. "Seren, take care of whatever materials he needs," he said indifferently. "That should be more than enough. Omax, accompany me."

Seren saw the warforged look up at Tristam. Tristam nodded and went back to work. Dalan and Omax entered the tower.

"Just like Dalan to send a green girl into the city alone and keep the warforged bodyguard for himself," Pherris grunted, leaning back against the ship controls. The gnome looked much older and wearier than he had before, or perhaps he had finally allowed himself a moment to rest now that his ship was finally safe.

"I can take care of myself," Seren said.

"See that you do," Pherris said sternly. "I am beginning to like you, Miss Morisse. You bring a dash of common sense that I've sorely missed hereabouts." The gnome's whiskers twitched with a faint grin.

Seren smiled at Pherris, but the old gnome had dozed off where he sat. She looked up at Tristam, still busy with the repairs.

"Lodestones?" she prompted him.

He nodded without looking down. "Natural magnets. They're a reagent for a number of enchantments. I'll need about a dozen," he answered. "I could probably use some more royal water to accelerate the dissolution of this binding agent, too."

"And maybe some frankincense to reinforce the elemental matrix?" she asked.

Tristam looked down at her sharply, almost falling off his ladder. "Yes, that would be useful," he said, impressed. "You've been reading more than my fairy tales, haven't you?"

"I only understand a little," she admitted.

"That's still amazing," he said, his intense expression fading into a smile. "And yes, I could use some frankincense. You should be able to find all of that at any magewright's shop. Be careful, Seren. Don't make any trouble."

"Same to you," she said, returning his smile.

Seren climbed down the tower stairs and surveyed the streets. Cragwar was a busy, happy place. The streets were crowded with people going about their daily lives. Groups of soldiers patrolled the streets and the citizens met them with friendly greetings, obviously content to be under their protection. Though she had already decided to remain on *Karia Naille*, she had to admit that this wouldn't be such a bad place to start a new life. For a city near the border of a potential enemy, it was a peaceful sort of place.

Seren stopped at a corner vendor and used one of Dalan's coins to purchase a delicious-smelling treat on a stick. It looked like a sort of frosted bread filled with cooked meat. It tasted as good as it smelled. She chewed thoughtfully as she watched the traffic and considered her next move.

It was nearly a minute before Seren realized that she had instinctively been casing the local populace, looking for wealthy targets. The instant she realized what she was doing, Seren felt terribly alone. She would never fit in here, not as long as she saw everyone else as targets.

"Once a thief, always a thief," said a voice beside her.

Seren jumped, dropping her food on the ground. Eraina d'Deneith looked down with a sneer. "Best to pick that up, Seren. There are fines for littering in this city."

Seren snatched up her ruined meal and looked at the paladin with a frown. "What do you want?" she asked. "I thought you left."

"Did you kill Jamus Roland?" she asked bluntly.

Eraina's eyes, so dark they were almost black, bored directly into her soul. She sensed anger, pain, and something more, a sense of a power Seren had never felt before. It felt almost as if she were being judged by Boldrei herself.

"How do you know Jamus?" Seren asked, unable to keep a quaver of fear out from her voice.

"Just answer the question. Yes or no."

"No," she said, a hint of outrage in her answer. "Jamus was my teacher. He was my *friend*."

Eraina's brows furrowed quizzically. She looked disappointed by Seren's answer, but she nodded in acquiescence. "Just a thief, then," she said in a sad voice. "You have no idea what you have become involved in."

"Then why don't you explain it to me? How does a Sentinel Marshal know Jamus Roland? He was just a thief too."

"He was not just a thief," Eraina said. "He was my father."

"Oh," Seren said, eyes widening. "I thought you were a member of House Deneith."

"I am," she said. "My mother's husband was disgraced when he learned the truth. If my mother's dragonmark had not bred true, I might have been given to an orphanage. Instead I was raised and educated by the church." She looked at Seren calmly. "Does it truly surprise you that Jamus Roland would have an affair with another man's wife?"

"Not really," Seren answered, "but why are you telling me this? I'm a stranger to you."

"Raised as a Spear of Boldrei, I have taken many vows," Eraina said. "A vow of charity, a vow of mercy, a vow of humility, and a vow of honesty. Do you understand these things?"

Seren nodded.

"Then also understand that our vow of honesty is the most difficult of all, as well as the most important," she said. "For we can neither lie nor promote falsehood. The fact that Jamus never told you who I was is disturbing, for he broke into Dalan d'Cannith's home on my behalf. He died trying to help me, Seren."

"A paladin hiring thieves?" Seren asked.

"I didn't know what he planned, and he knew better than to tell me," Eraina said. "My father has always been a foolish man. For almost a year now I have been hunting the murderer of Bishop Llaine Grove. I was to meet Jamus on the night he died. I traveled all the way from Fairhaven on the promise that he would have the name of the killer I sought. I suppose I should not be surprised that he died. My father was not adept at keeping promises."

"He never told me any of that," she said.

"And now you understand why Boldrei values honesty," Eraina said. "I have wasted a great deal of time chasing you, Seren, thinking that you were responsible for my father's death. Now I know the real killer was on that Cyran ship. Those same mercenaries were probably responsible for Llaine Grove's death as well."

Eraina looked at Seren for a long time, not speaking. Seren had the uneasy sense that the goddess was judging her through those eyes again. She wanted to move away, but could not bring herself to do so.

"The truth, at least, is a relief," Eraina said. "Father spoke highly of you in his letters. I wonder if, in some measure, by caring for you he hoped to atone for my unwanted and neglected existence. My father was a strange man."

"Looks like that bred true, too," Seren said.

"And you have adopted my father's intolerable sense of humor," she retorted. "Jamus obviously saw some value in you, so I give you this final warning. Do not return to *Karia Naille*. I intend to stop Dalan d'Cannith and his allies. It would be best if you did not oppose me."

"Stop them?" Seren asked. "Why? They're hunting the same killer you are."

"No," Eraina said. "They merely seek the same thing he seeks, and their greed will only cloud my path. Dalan d'Cannith is a ruthless, ambitious man. I do not doubt he knows more about the Cyrans than he admits, and I will not abide his dishonesty."

"So you want me to abandon my friends and run away in a strange city?" Seren asked. "What sort of paladin are you?"

"Your faithfulness is admirable, but you do them no favors by letting them pursue petty ambitions," Eraina said. "Do not fear that I would cast you out alone here as Dalan did to me.

I have allies in this city. I can give you gold enough to return to Wroat, or even Ringbriar. I could offer you the protection of the Sovereign Host. You could find a new life in the Church if you wished, Seren. My mercy is a sincere mercy, not a Cannith's false promises."

Seren looked past Eraina, at the crowds of happy citizens living their normal lives. Beyond them, she saw the sky towers standing tall above the skyline. Two rings of green fire burnt with a steady light, holding the Brelish warships aloft. Between them burnt a smaller ring—blue, crackling with red.

"Think about it, Seren," Eraina said.

Seren walked away. She felt the paladin's eyes watch her for a long time afterward.

* * * * * * *

Seren went about her business, picking up Tristam's supplies. She dropped them off on the ship without a word, drawing confused looks from Pherris and Tristam as she went back into the city. For a while, she explored. Would it really be so bad to stay here? Was this such a horrible place?

She looked up at the ring of fire above the walls again, now burning a steady blue. This would be a safe place to live, but no one needed her here. If she were to find a home, it would not be here. After wandering aimlessly for a while, Seren made her way back to the sky tower. She boarded the ship as wordlessly as she had left. Gunther trotted to her feet and rolled over on one side, waiting to be petted. Pherris greeted her with an exhausted smile, which quickly changed to a look of concern as he looked past her toward the tower.

"Are the repairs done, Tristam?" Pherris asked.

"Just touching up the paint now," Tristam said from the ladder. "Why?"

"I've a feeling we'll be leaving soon," the captain said.

Seren looked up from petting the dog. A dozen Brelish soldiers marched out of the tower door, with Eraina at their head. She looked at Seren with a disappointed shake of her head and turned to face Pherris.

"Captain Gerriman," Eraina said in a bold voice. "As a Sentinel Marshal of House Deneith, and with the aid and alliance of the Brelish Crown, I regret that I must impound your vessel and take your crew into custody."

"On what charges?" Pherris asked stiffly.

"You are not being charged with anything," she said, her tone now clipped and formal. "However, I believe that several members of your crew are withholding information pertinent to an international murder investigation. As a Sentinel Marshal, I have invoked my jurisdiction and enlisted these local officials to assist me. Please do not resist."

Seren stood up slowly beside Pherris. Tristam dropped down from his ladder, tucking his tools back into his bandolier. Gerith poked his head up from below deck and quickly disappeared again. Zed, sharpening his sword as he sat on a nearby barrel, set his whetstone aside and sheathed the weapon across his back. Omax stood beside Tristam calmly, waiting for any command.

"Come out, d'Cannith," Eraina shouted.

The cabin door opened and Dalan stepped out. He held a breadstick treat in one hand, chewing absently. He looked at Eraina and her soldiers without concern. "Good afternoon, officers," he said. "May I help you?"

"You heard me," she said. "Order your crew to stand down and surrender."

Dalan bit the last scrap of bread from the stick, tossed it in a pail nearby, wiped his hands on his jacket and took a scroll case from his pocket. He looked past Eraina at the soldiers with a bland expression. "Which of you is the commanding officer?" he asked.

"I am," one said, stepping forward.

Dalan offered the man the scroll. He stepped forward and accepted it, looking at Eraina in confusion. Removing it from its case, he studied the parchment for several moments, rolled it up, and handed it back.

"My apologies, Marshal," the soldier said. "This man has been granted immunity by the King."

"What?" she spat.

Dalan smiled.

"My apologies, Master d'Cannith," the soldier said.

"Not necessary," Dalan said pleasantly. "You're merely doing your duty. You are a tribute to your rank, country, and king." The man smiled proudly. "Now if you would excuse us, we're preparing to depart."

The soldier nodded, saluted, and turned to leave. The others followed in his wake. Eraina remained where she was, scowling at Dalan.

"Let me see those papers," she demanded.

"Why?" he asked, looking at her. "Your jurisdiction extends beyond any diplomatic immunities. You are still perfectly free to find non-Brelish troops to aid you, or arrest us on your own." He looked at Omax and then smiled at her again. "If you believe you are able."

"You know Boldrei grants me power to sense falsehood. You refuse to show me your papers because I will see them as the forgery they are."

"How insulting," Dalan said with a mocking grin. "Is this the diplomacy of House Deneith?"

"This is not over," Eraina said. "You will not escape me. I will find allies and stop you."

"Is that so?" Dalan asked. He looked past her for a moment.

She looked back just as Zed Arthen clubbed her across the temple with the hilt of his sheathed sword. She staggered, attempting to ready her spear.

"Sorry, Eraina," he said, punching her across the jaw.

The paladin struck the deck with a thud. Seren looked at Dalan in shock, as did everyone else but Zed.

"Arthen what in Khyber have you done?" Tristam shouted. "You just assaulted a Sentinel Marshal!"

"She went down a little more easily than I expected, too," Zed said, looking at her limp form with some surprise. "I thought Omax would have to help me for sure."

"That Sentinel Marshal threatened to cause a great deal of trouble for us," Dalan said, turning back toward his cabin. "Get us out of here, Captain. Zed, return the Marshal to her cell."

Zed loaded the unconscious paladin over his shoulder and climbed below deck. As *Karia Naille* swiftly rose above the city of Cragwar, Seren wondered if staying here had been a mistake.

Chapter Sixteen

Old Merkin pushed the battered shutter aside and looked outside again. The street was empty, as it usually was this time of day. Zed Arthen preferred things clean and quiet, so most of the Black Pit citizens avoided doing business here. Everyone feared Arthen, though Old Merkin wasn't really sure why. Arthen had a way of turning up dirt, rooting out secrets, and in Black Pit most folks preferred secrets to stay right where they were. To Merkin, that just meant that Arthen was making waves. People who did that inevitably got put down. No one could stand alone forever.

Until then, of course, there was money to be made.

At the far end of the street, Old Merkin saw the familiar, stocky figure, leaving a trail of pipesmoke in his wake. The coat and clothes were new, but it was definitely Zed Arthen. Merkin waited for the inquisitive to walk down this way, past his window and approach his office. Arthen looked around warily, as he always did. He didn't see Old Merkin, but of course he never did. Merkin chuckled quietly in self-satisfaction.

After Arthen's door closed, Merkin left his home, shrugging into his thick canvas jacket as he walked. He rapped loudly on the door of the inquisitive's office and waited, hands tucked in his pockets as he peered around, alert for any nosey passers-by.

The door opened after a moment. Zed Arthen looked at Merkin with a hawk-eyed gaze and stood quickly to one side. Merkin grinned and sauntered in.

"May I help you?" Arthen asked in a low voice.

"Perhaps you can," Merkin said, voice dripping with sarcasm. "I saw your little trip into the woods the other night, Arthen. Smart money says you were meeting someone from that Lyrandar charter ship. Care to share the secret?"

Zed did not answer immediately. Instead he moved to the window beside his door, looking curiously outside. "You came here alone?" he asked.

"Like I need any protection from you," Merkin said. "I'm the one man in all of Black Pit that knows you're all talk. Now tell me what you're up to, Arthen."

"I have a better idea," Arthen said, locking the door. "Let me offer you a proposition." He turned to face Merkin, but the man who faced Merkin was no longer Zed Arthen. His features were smooth and gray. The left cheek twisted with a swirling burn scar. He looked at Merkin with dead white eyes.

"Khyber," Merkin swore, drawing a dagger from his belt. "Get away from me, faceless!"

"Please," the changeling said. He backed away from the door, holding his hands out to show he held no weapons, only the key to the door pinched between the fingers of his right hand. "The term is 'changeling,' not 'faceless.' If you cannot call my race by a respectful name, then simply address me as Marth."

"What are you doing here?" Merkin demanded. He glanced around for any escape route, but the changeling blocked the only unlocked door. "Did you kill the real Arthen?"

"That is what we do, isn't it?" Marth said with a deep sigh. "Changelings come in the night. They murder the innocent and steal their lives, like parasites. Spies and assassins, all of us. No.

I did not murder Arthen. He is alive and well, as far as I am aware, and far from here."

"Oh," Merkin said, not sure whether he was relieved or disappointed. "Then what are you doing pretending to be him?"

"Zed Arthen is an old associate," Marth said. "I came to him regarding a matter of some discretion. He left abruptly, leaving no clues as to his destination. Rather than dig randomly for information in a place like this, I thought that assuming his identity would lead me to those who knew him. And so it has." Marth gestured broadly at Merkin.

"Arthen and I aren't really friends," Merkin said fearfully. "But it doesn't surprise me that he runs with a diseased faceless."

"I never said I was seeking his friends, nor that I was one of them," Marth said. "I seek only information, and I am willing to pay." Marth opened his left hand, palm out, to reveal a platinum coin.

"Well that's different," Merkin said, sheathing his dagger with a lewd smile. "How can I help you, Master Marth?"

"First of all, tell me who you are," the changeling said. "What common ruffian speaks to Zed Arthen as boldly as you did when you entered?"

"I'm Merkin, a courier for some of the local businesses," Merkin said. "I live next door."

"An informant," Marth corrected. "The local cartels pay you to spy on Arthen, to find out what he's up to, to report which of them he may be investigating next?"

Merkin smiled. "A man has to make an honest living."

"But that's not all," Marth said. "I wager you work for Arthen as well. He pays you to filter the information you pass on to your superiors. You came here hoping to perpetuate your web of blackmail." He looked at Merkin seriously. "Have I hit the mark?"

"Pretty close," Merkin said. "Impressive."

"Arthen and I were friends once," Marth said. He tucked the

coin into his pocket, leaving his hand there. "I know the way the man thinks. I can assure you that any control you believe you maintain over him is an illusion. He is too clever for you by far. You believe you are blackmailing him, but I wonder how much he has learned about your superiors from your churlish thuggery. Look what I have already divined, Merkin, and I am not even trained as an inquisitive."

Merkin's face drooped into a worried frown. He began replaying earlier meetings with Arthen in his mind, trying to remember what he had said, and wondering how much he had accidentally revealed.

"The great irony is this, Merkin," Marth said. He traced the fingers of his right hand along the edge of a nearby table as he paced slowly around it, his eyes on the floor. "You fear me. You distrust me. You call me faceless, for no doubt you have heard the legends. Every village spins the tale of the changeling killer who murders a noble son of the nation and slides effortlessly into his life. We are spies. We are demons. We are monsters unworthy of trust or respect." He looked at Merkin intently. "Yet look at yourself. Every word you use to describe yourself is a lie. 'Courier.' 'Honest living.' At least my face is my only lie, Merkin. You lack the imagination to be truthful."

Merkin shrugged. "Listen, I don't need the lecture. What else do you want to know about Arthen?"

"Nothing," Marth said. "You have already told me all I need to know. If your own relationship with him is any indication, Arthen has covered his tracks with his usual prowess. I doubt you have anything useful to offer me."

"Then what about my money?" Merkin asked irritably.

"Still yours for the price of one question," Marth said. He looked at Merkin intently, empty white eyes staring at his chest. "That coat you wear. It looks familiar. Is it part of a military uniform?"

VOYAGE OF THE MOURNING DAWN

Merkin nodded. "Only good thing the army ever gave me," he said with a laugh.

Marth offered a thin smile. "What nation did you fight for?"

"I don't want to talk about that," Merkin said.

"You are a deserter," Marth said. "A betrayer."

"You said only one question," Merkin snapped. "So pay me and unlock the door."

Marth frowned and drew his hand from his pocket. Instead of a coin, he now held a long amethyst. Merkin swore and dove toward Marth with his dagger, but not quickly enough. There was a brief flash of green light, and then pain so intense that Merkin could not even draw the breath to scream. He curled up on the ground, arms and legs twitching, spittle boiling from his mouth. Marth forced Merkin onto his back with one boot, leaving his foot on the old informant's chest.

"There are few things more reprehensible than a man who would abandon his country," Marth said, looming over the man as he twitched uncontrollably. "A nation that cannot rely upon its sons and daughters has nothing. It is doomed to be crushed under its own weight, consumed by the greed and ambition of its neighbors. You humans call my kind 'diseased' because of our sickly pallor." Marth moved his boot forward, placing it squarely on Merkin's throat. "But it is traitors like you who are a true disease upon all of Eberron."

Marth leaned forward, pressing his weight on Merkin's throat. Marth stared into the man's helpless eyes until he stopped moving. He waited a minute more, just to be sure, then put the wand back in his pocket and stepped away. Assuming Zed Arthen's face once again, Marth exited the inquisitive's office and returned to *Kenshi Zhann* where she hovered in the forest nearby.

As he climbed aboard the airship, two of the soldiers greeted him with nervous smiles.

"Captain Marth," one said, saluting. "We are glad you have returned. Black Pit is no place for any man to be alone."

"Worried, Neimun?" Marth said, returning the salute. "I was in no danger." He felt a scrutinizing presence behind him, and did not even need to look to realize Brother Zamiel had entered the room. He quickly dismissed the soldiers to their duties.

"You seem in high spirits, Captain," Zamiel mused, falling in beside Marth as he began his march to the bridge. A humming pulse ran through the ship as she began to lift into the sky. "Such contentment is very strange for a man who has spent the night alone in an unfriendly village, disguised as one of his deadliest enemies."

"What do you want, prophet?" he asked. "To lecture me for being in a good mood?"

"Quite the contrary," Zamiel said. "Your bravery is an example to the men. I doubt even the murder you just committed would lessen their opinion of you."

Marth prepared a sharp retort, but it died on his lips. The prophet was, as usual, not only remarkably aware of events he had no way of witnessing, but entirely sincere in his macabre praise.

"Unfortunately I learned very little," Marth said instead. "Arthen still keeps others at a distance. He weaves lies to catch the truth like a fisherman. It was a mistake to let him live when he distanced himself from this. I should listen more closely to your advice, Zamiel. Mercy for old friends will be my undoing."

"I never said to set mercy aside entirely," Zamiel said. "I said it was a luxury, and luxury brings harm only when indulged in excess. Kept in its proper place, in moderation, a luxury grants opportunity."

"More riddles, prophet?" Marth asked as they stepped onto *Moon's* large enclosed bridge. The helmsman was already here, working the controls and plotting a course. "You urge me to kill Tristam but show no rancor that I let Arthen slip away so long ago?"

"Arthen is not a threat like Xain is," Zamiel said. "The fallen knight still has a part to play."

"I disagree," Marth said. "Tristam may be useful; he has both ambition and curiosity. Arthen is dangerous. If we find him, we must kill him."

"Then you may soon have your chance," Zamiel said. "My spy has contacted us again, via speaker post."

Marth looked at Zamiel with interest. "What news?"

"*Karia Naille* is bound for the Talenta Plains," the prophet said.

"Overwood," Marth said with a scowl. "So they have found her."

"An unexpected development," Zamiel answered. "I did not expect this to happen so soon. While you deal with this I shall have to return and consult the prophecy, to determine what I may have misread. You will have go to Talenta and deal with them yourself."

Marth was lost for a moment in thought. "If they find her," he mused, "they will tell her what I have done. Do you think she will believe them?"

"A pointless question," Zamiel said, settling into his chair. "If so, I will trust you to deal with it."

Chapter
Seventeen

What amazed Seren the most wasn't how callously Zed Arthen had knocked out Eraina and locked her in her cabin. What disturbed her was that the rest of the crew did not seem surprised or concerned. After the ship left Cragwar, everyone returned to their normal duties. The only differences were that Omax occasionally took a plate of food to the paladin, and every time Seren entered the hold she saw the marshal's spear and shortsword lying atop the food crates. No one even mentioned Eraina, and Seren was not about to bring up the matter.

Tristam spent most of his time in his own cabin, absorbed in research or perhaps depression. Gerith was always busy tending the ship, cooking meals, or scouting the area on his glidewing. Seren felt increasingly alone. She didn't trust Dalan or Zed, and still wasn't sure what to think of Omax. That left her with the mystery that was Aeven.

After all this time, she still had not met the last mysterious member of the crew, only heard her mentioned. Seren began to wonder if there was really an "Aeven" at all. The fishermen and riverboat captains she knew in Wroat were the most superstitious people she had met. It stood to reason that airship sailors were no different. Perhaps Aeven was just some sort of guardian spirit or minor goddess who protected airships?

VOYAGE OF THE MOURNING DAWN

The lush forests of Breland had given way to the broad green plains of Thrane. Having spent the entirety of her life in dreary Ringbriar or overpopulated Wroat, it was fascinating to see so much of the world in so short a time. Seren spent her free moments on the deck, watching the landscape fly by and occasionally commenting on the more interesting things she saw. If Aeven was real, Seren reasoned, it couldn't hurt to talk to her. If she wasn't real, then there was no harm done.

At noon on the second day of their journey, Eraina d'Deneith emerged from the hold, accompanied by Omax. The paladin went directly to Dalan's cabin. Seren heard muffled voices for several minutes before Eraina finally emerged once more, her expression somber. She immediately went to work helping Gerith with the ship's maintenance, not offering any word of explanation. The captain regarded her with suspicious curiosity whenever she was on deck, but otherwise kept his attention on flying the ship.

"Figured that would happen sooner or later," Zed Arthen commented dryly. The inquisitive had been sitting on a barrel nearby, slowly working his way through a chunk of beef jerky he had scavenged from the hold.

"What happened?" Seren asked. "Why did Dalan set her free? Why is she helping us now?"

"Vow of honesty," Zed said, taking another bite. "Makes the Spears do stupid things. That's my best guess."

"Why would her vow of honesty have anything to do with it?"

"You ask a lot of annoying questions," Zed said.

"You're an inquisitive," Seren countered. "Don't you ever ask questions?"

"Sometimes," Zed said, "but they're not always the best ways to get answers. If you want to know why Eraina is here you should probably talk to her yourself. Or just stop bothering me. I really don't care."

Seren grunted noncommittally and headed below deck. Though Eraina's release piqued her curiosity, her real motivation was to get away from Zed. The inquisitive made her uneasy since he had attacked Eraina. She hadn't really put much stock in Tristam's low opinion of the man until that moment. Now she wasn't sure what he would do next. She noticed Eraina was now in the cargo hold, moving the scattered crates into neatly organized stacks. Her polished armor and weapons were set carefully aside in the corner. She wore leather breeches and a sleeveless white blouse that revealed her dragonmark, an exotic pattern of swirling blue and green lines that stretched from her left hand halfway up her bicep. Eraina had obviously been at work for some time, for her hair and clothes were damp from labor. Overall, she looked more like a Wroat dockworker than a Spear of Boldrei.

"Can you give me a hand, Seren?" she asked, pushing a dark lock of hair from her eyes.

"What are you doing?" Seren asked, moving to take up the other side of a heavy box of dried carrots.

"Cleaning up the hold," she said. "I can't understand the halfling's method of organization."

"I don't think he has a method," Seren said, helping her haul the box up on top of another. "I think he likes it random, so that what he finds to make for dinner surprises him as much as the rest of us."

Eraina chuckled as she moved to pick up another box. "That may be fine for him, but not for me," she said. "I like to know where everything is and why it's there."

"Then you're in strange company," Seren said under her breath.

Eraina looked at her seriously. "I don't know what you mean," she said.

"Dalan imprisoned you here," Seren said. "Now you're helping him?"

"Dalan apologized for his behavior and drew a promise from me," Eraina said. "I swore to aid him in his quest in return for his promise that he would help me bring Marth to justice and that he would use the Legacy only for honorable ends."

"And you believed him?" Seren asked, astonished mostly by the answer but also by the accuracy of Zed's guess.

"No," Eraina answered. "I believed in you."

Seren looked at Eraina in utter confusion.

"Tell me, Seren," Eraina said. "What do you have faith in?"

"What do you mean?" Seren asked. "I pray to Kol Korran a little, but I picked that up from Jamus. My parents prayed to the entire Host, but I never did."

"Why not?" Eraina asked. "The gods exist to care for us, just as we exist to serve them."

"I figured that they were busy," Seren said. "I'm just one person. They must have better things to do. Prayer seems too much like begging."

"And Kol Korran?" Eraina asked. "Why is he the exception?"

"He's the god of thieves, so I'm sort of his job, right?" Seren said with a small smile. "I pray to him out of habit. I don't place a lot of faith in things I can't see. I guess that sounds sort of blasphemous to a paladin."

"You'd be surprised," Eraina murmured. "A paladin does not believe blindly, for if we did, our faith would be without worth. A paladin does not hurl herself into battle and beg Boldrei for salvation. A champion who cannot succeed without her favor is no champion at all. A paladin does not close her eyes to the world and wait for Boldrei's voice to fill the emptiness. We see the will of the goddess in all things, but mostly through people. I have faith in the goodness of mankind. Though I may seem cynical, and I have been disappointed frequently, I can assure you that I see miracles every day. When I saw you had returned to *Karia Naille*, I knew Boldrei had spoken."

Seren continued to stare at Eraina in puzzled silence.

"Jamus Roland looked upon you as his daughter, Seren," Eraina said. "He wanted to take you from Wroat, to give you a better life. That was part of his deal with me. My father had his flaws and often failed, but he never ceased to try to make the world a better place. Any person in whom he would place such faith is a person in whom I will believe in as well. You saw something worthy in this crew, something that made you return. I have faith in you, Seren, and that is why I remain."

"No," Seren said. "You remain because Zed Arthen knocked you unconscious."

Eraina laughed quietly and cast a guarded look about them. When she spoke again, it was in a whisper. "What a pitiful Sentinel Marshal I would be if I let one man defeat me in such a clumsy manner. Be honest, Seren, did you not think it a bit foolish of me to threaten Dalan to his face, on his own ship, while so heavily outnumbered. I did not even call upon my dragonmark to protect me. Strange?"

"I did think it strange," Seren admitted.

Eraina smiled enigmatically. "And now I am here," she said.

"But you said . . ." Seren began.

"I said Dalan would not escape me." Eraina finished the sentence for her. "And he has not. I said I would find allies." The paladin placed a hand on Seren's shoulder. "And I have. Honesty in all things. I stand by you, Seren, and as long as Dalan keeps his word I stand by him as well."

"And if he doesn't?" Seren asked.

"Then I hope you will stand by *me*," Eraina said, her voice taking a dangerous edge. "For your own good as well as mine."

Seren nodded dumbly.

Eraina looked satisfied and returned to sorting crates. She chatted idly with Seren as they worked, asking her mostly about her time in Wroat. The paladin was particularly interested in stories of her father. She often interrupted Seren in midstream when she attempted to embellish the tales or gloss over his shadier accomplishments. Eraina had an unerring sense for falsehood that seemed more a natural talent than any form of magic. She wished only to hear the truth about her father's life, as much as Seren would tell her. She accepted all of it, good and bad, with the same sad smile.

Omax entered the hold after they had been working and talking for nearly an hour. The warforged watched them only briefly before joining in their labor. The work went much more quickly after that, with Omax effortlessly lifting crates the two of them could barely budge together. Gerith entered much later, greeting them with a shriek when he discovered his comfortable chaos had become regimented, efficient order. He gave Eraina a scathing glare, whimpered at Seren like a hurt child, and stalked out of the hold with a sack of potatoes over one shoulder. Eraina and Seren looked at each other in silence for several seconds, then burst into laughter. Omax watched them thoughtfully for several moments, then laughed as well.

With the job complete, Seren excused herself and headed back above deck. She leaned out over the rail as far as she dared, letting the unimpeded wind wash over her shoulders and cool her after the hard work. She noticed Zed still sitting on his barrel. He stared off into the distance blankly, watching the land speed past as smoke drifted idly from his pipe.

He looked at her with a scowl. "More questions?" he asked.

"No," she said. "No questions."

"Good," Zed said, looking back out at the Thrane landscape. "Cause I'm in no mood."

Seren continued to look out at the countryside in silence. The sun set behind them, casting the land in a blanket of darkness disturbed only by the light of a rare farmhouse or village. Zed climbed down off his barrel, drawing a look from Seren.

"Because this was my home," he said, answering her unasked question with a strangely grateful smile. "Home is always a part of you, no matter what else changes. I wanted to see it." Without another word, Zed Arthen returned to his cabin.

   ◈ ◈ ◈ ◈ ◈ ◈

The next several days passed fairly uneventfully. One morning she found Gerith and Pherris looking at a pile of large maps as they plotted their course. Gerith traced a thin line across Karrnath with his compass and looked at the captain with a frown. The course they had plotted was an exaggerated curve, cutting north across the Khorvaire continent and then south again toward the eastern edge of the Talenta Plains.

"Still not sure we shouldn't have gone south," Gerith commented. "Would have been quicker than cutting through Thrane and Karrnath, and we could have put into port in Zilargo."

"Whereupon my countrymen would have asked no end of questions that Master d'Cannith would have found most uncomfortable," Pherris said. "After that our mission would be advertised on the front page of *The Korranberg Chronicle*, assuming we survive to see a copy after flying over hobgoblin and Valenar territories unannounced."

"Yeah," Gerith said eagerly. "The interesting way." His little round face drooped when he saw that the Captain did not share his excitement.

Seren studied the map between them. She had never seen a map of the entire continent before, and wondered vaguely why they hadn't merely flown in a straight line. She realized the truth a moment before her eyes found the name of the country to the southeast of them. She looked up quickly in that direction.

That nation was Cyre.

VOYAGE OF THE MOURNING DAWN

It was the first time Seren had ever seen the Mournland. Even from here, she could see churning white clouds boiling over the land. Life itself withdrew from the borders of Cyre. Even beyond the impenetrable mists that marked the Mournland, the ground was bare, vegetation shriveled. The shimmering clouds moved with a peculiar, pulsating rhythm. It was hypnotic and oddly beautiful in its way. A cold sensation spread through Seren as she stared at the white mist. She found it difficult to look away, but something brushed gently against her cheek, breaking the spell. When she looked, there were only Gerith and Pherris, still busy arguing about the ship's course.

They had been airborne for nearly a week and a half when the drab Karrnathi landscape gave way to an endless golden plain. The first morning over the Talenta Plains, Seren awoke and looked over the rail to see a herd of enormous reptilian creatures marching across the plains. Each was easily three times the size of a horse, with thick heads capped with a cropped thorny crest. Their hides were brilliant green, marked with orange stripes. They moved with a ponderous, steady pace, holding their thick tails above the ground for balance. Seren watched them for several minutes in quiet awe before she realized she was being watched herself. She looked to her left and saw Gerith nearby. His tiny chest was puffed out, and his face was flushed.

"Threehorns," he said, pointing to the herd. "My brother leads a threehorn cavalry team. Aren't they incredible animals?"

"They look a little big for a halfling," Seren said.

"Of course," he answered. "That's why we ride them in teams. What do you think of the Plains?" He watched Seren, waiting for her reaction.

"It's beautiful, Gerith," she said, looking back out at the land.

"No place in Eberron like this," he answered. His voice was choked with pride, as if he had crafted the land with his own hands.

"Will we see your home while we're here?"

"Oh, no," Gerith said very quickly. "Not yet. I'm not ready." He met her puzzled look with a wicked grin. "There's a saying among the halflings. *'Kapen hara.'* It means 'family before all else,' and that's what brought me to this crew. My grandfather is the greatest storyteller in all the Plains, but he's too old to go out and gather stories himself anymore. I promised him that the next time we met I'd have a tale that put all his to shame. I've been wandering the world, collecting stories, but I haven't found a better one yet." He sighed deeply. "I've more or less resigned myself to a simple truth."

"And what's that?" she asked.

"Stories are like baking," he said. "A fresh pie is the best pie. So if I can't find a better story, then I'll just have to live through one." He chuckled. "I think I'm on the right track. *Karia Naille* has always been a magnet for trouble. You'll help, of course. A winsome damsel in distress always adds a bit of spice."

"Damsel in distress," she said dryly. "I thought I was the hero."

"No, obviously I'm the hero," Gerith said, "but I can be flexible."

"Thanks," she said dryly.

"Quite welcome," he said. He looked down at the plains again, a beatific smile spreading across his childlike features. "I think you'll like it here, Seren. I hope we're in no hurry to leave. Just be careful around the locals."

"Careful?" she said.

"The halflings are passionate people," he answered. "Their love of beauty knows no bounds. Some of them can be a little rude. They haven't learned any manners, especially around pretty girls like yourself."

"I'm not a halfling," she said.

"Not necessarily a disadvantage," he answered with a wink.

"Eliminates certain parental responsibilities, if you catch my meaning."

Seren smirked at him, holding back a laugh. "I'll be careful," she said.

"Don't worry, Seren," Gerith said. "If all else fails, I'll protect you from those terrible lechers. I'll tell them we're married." He reached up and patted her bottom firmly, then swiftly leapt over the rail before she could react. Blizzard soared off into the clouds a moment later, leaving the mischievous halfling's laughter behind.

"A whole nation of Snowshales," the captain said in a rueful voice. "I think I'd rather go back to Black Pit."

As the ship continued her flight, the landscape of the Talenta Plains only awed her more and more. While what she had seen of Breland, Thrane, and Karrnath had certainly impressed her, the wild beauty of Talenta was inspiring. Seren often found herself drawing away from her duties on the ship just to look out at the landscape, and when Pherris snapped at her to get back to work, there was no real spirit in it. The captain mostly let the ship do the flying and enjoyed the scenery as well, occasionally dozing off in his seat as he stared at the peaceful plains.

She noticed that Tristam had emerged on deck again for the first time since leaving Cragwar. His clothes were stained with soot and chemicals, and he exchanged a nervous smile with Seren as he took a deep breath of fresh air. She began to cross the deck to talk to him when Blizzard dove out of the clouds behind them, flapping toward the ship at a frenzied pace. The glidewing did not slow its approach, and as it drew closer she saw Gerith slumped in the harness on its back. Tristam followed her startled gaze and immediately went pale.

"All hands on deck!" Tristam screamed, startling Pherris from his nap.

Seren and Tristam dove aside just as Blizzard crashed heavily into the deck. The glidewing shrieked in pain and collapsed. Gerith's body hung limp, still secured in the glidewing's harness. Tristam reached for the straps holding Gerith, but Blizzard snapped menacingly at his hand. Tristam backed away quickly, and Eraina took his place. Blizzard regarded the paladin with a suspicious eye but did nothing to prevent her releasing its master from his harness.

"He's alive, just stunned," she said, laying Gerith on the deck.

"What happened?" Seren asked.

The glidewing shrieked uncomfortably and shifted its position, one wing snapping open to reveal a smoking wound on its leathery flesh. Tristam's face went pale when he saw the burn.

"Lightning," Dalan said, looking at the creature with a deadpan expression. "Captain Pherris?"

"I know," the gnome said, busily working the controls. Seren felt the airship accelerate. The blue elemental fire now glowed.

"Damn, too late," Dalan swore, looking out behind them.

Seren looked back as well in time to see a massive shadow emerge from the clouds behind them. It resolved into the sleek, sinister hull of *Kenshi Zhann*, now bearing down on them with methodical, inevitable speed. A bolt of white electricity fired from its bow, missing *Karia Naille* by several yards.

"A warning shot," Dalan said.

"They want us to land," Pherris said grimly. "Awaiting your command, Master d'Cannith."

"We can't outrun them, Dalan," Tristam said.

"I thought our ship was faster than theirs," Seren said.

"Only over short distances," Tristam said. "They'll catch up eventually, and on the plains there's nowhere to hide."

"There's always somewhere to hide," Dalan said. "To Khyber with surrender. Get us out of here, Captain."

Pherris nodded and leaned into the controls. The ship lurched forward with sudden acceleration.

"Shouldn't we return fire?" Eraina shouted.

Omax emerged above the deck, carrying several crossbows and quivers full of bolts. He offered one of the weapons to Eraina.

"*Karia Naille* has no built-in weapons," Omax said. "We must defend ourselves."

"Better yet, wake up the halfling," Zed said. "If anyone knows a place where we can hide an airship in Talenta, it's him."

Eraina nodded, bowing her head in prayer over Gerith's prone body. Omax stepped over her, handing out weapons to the others. Seren weighed her crossbow uncertainly. She had never wielded one before. She looked up to find Zed loading his own weapon, but conspicuously holding it out so she could see how it was done. He gave her a sidelong look, waiting for her to load her own.

When she fumbled with the bolt, he loosed his bolt over the side and reloaded, showing her how to do it again. He never offered his advice or asked if she wanted help. He only showed her the way.

"Save your ammunition, Master Arthen," Dalan chided, hefting his own weapon.

"It just went off, Dalan," Zed said, grinning at Seren.

Moon had drawn closer now, and another bolt of searing lightning exploded from its bow. This time it struck *Karia Naille* squarely in the hull. The ship shuddered violently, throwing Seren to her knees. The ship was so close now Seren could feel the warmth of the elemental fire that held it aloft. A peal of thunder echoed through the sky, and the clouds began to darken.

"Storm coming fast," Zed said. "Magic?"

"Magic," Tristam said. "But not theirs."

"Aeven," Pherris shouted with a triumphant cackle.

Gerith sat up with a start, gasping as Eraina's blessing roused him from unconsciousness. He twisted and struggled frantically, barking incomprehensibly in his native language. Eraina clasped one arm around the scout's shoulders in an effort to calm him, but Gerith only relaxed when he saw Blizzard's head poking out from its hiding place behind a stack of barrels. The creature gave an annoyed squawk and returned to licking his wounds. Gerith laughed in relief when he saw his pet was alive.

"Good to have you back among the living, Master Snowshale," Pherris shouted without looking away from the wheel. "Your counsel would be appreciated!"

Gerith stood up on wobbly legs, looking around at the landscape as he attempted to get his bearings. *Seventh Moon* now soared directly beside them. Seren could see soldiers on the deck readying crossbows. Omax pushed her down behind the ship's rail as he took cover himself. A flurry of bolts thudded into the hull and passed over their heads. The clouds above now churned a dangerous black. A rumble resonated above them as the storm continued to brew. Dalan stood up briefly and loosed a single bolt at the other ship; Seren thought she heard a man cry out on *Moon's* deck.

"There's a small gorge about a half mile east of here," Gerith shouted. "If they lose sight of us we can land there unseen."

Pherris nodded and turned the wheel sharply. The elemental fire now burned pure white as a burst of speed came over the smaller ship. At same instant, the sky exploded in rain and another searing flash of lightning exploded from *Moon*. Seren wrapped one arm around the railing at the savage force of the explosion. A loud crack sounded from deep inside the vessel, followed by the smell of burning wood.

"I think that was the keel," Tristam said in horror. He

staggered clumsily across the shaking deck toward the cargo hold. "Dalan, I might need your dragonmark!"

The fat guildmaster stood and loosed another bolt at *Moon*, then followed Tristam. Omax followed as well, stopping only long enough to pick up a barrel and hurl it at the other vessel. The improvised missile sailed through the void and left a dent in *Moon's* hull, which was answered with another flurry of crossbow bolts. The head of one jutted through the railing just beside Zed's face.

"So tell me about your goddess, Eraina," Zed said with exaggerated calm. "I suddenly find religion interests me."

"Belay your salvation until we are on the ground, Master Arthen," Pherris snapped.

"But if I survive I won't need to be saved!" Zed said with a grin. The battle appeared to have cheered the grim inquisitive's spirits dramatically.

Karia Naille dropped steadily from the sky even as she gained speed. *Moon* dove to intercept them. Another flash of lightning lit the sky, but this time from above and directly in *Moon's* path. The larger ship swerved, losing ground. In the flash of light, Seren thought she saw the silhouette of a slim woman standing protectively over Pherris, arms spread wide against the storm. When the lightning flashed a second time, she saw only the ship's figurehead.

"This is west, Captain, we're headed west!" Gerith shouted, pointing the other way. "The gorge is the other way!"

The captain leaned hard into the wheel to fight the ship's steady decline. Smoke was now rising from between the deck boards. She could hear Tristam and Dalan shouting at one another below. Pherris peered back at *Moon* with a scowl, waiting for something Seren couldn't see.

"Hold fast!" the gnome shouted and turned the wheel sharply.

Seren heard a wooden groan and another snap from deep within the ship as *Karia Naille* spun about in midair. Eraina lost her grip on the rail and tumbled across the deck with a startled cry. Zed snatched her leg before she flew over the side. Their ship hurtled directly toward the larger warship on a suicidal path. *Moon* swerved hurriedly, but their pilot was less skilled than Pherris. The larger ship rolled dangerously as she turned. There was a moment when the black hull passed only a few feet from *Karia Naille*. Two rings of elemental fire passed through one another with the crackling smell of ozone. *Karia Naille* soared off at tremendous speed even as *Moon* struggled to recover from its dive. The rain came down in a furious downpour, covering their escape.

"Captain, we have to land!" Tristam shouted from below.

The gnome continued to fight the controls as the ship shuddered and lost altitude. Seren clung to the rain-slicked rail. She felt terrified and helpless. She saw a flaming board peel itself away from the hull beneath her and tumble into the storm. The gorge yawned in the ground before them, dividing the landscape. The ship wove into the wide stone mouth and everything went dark. Something gripped Seren's arms tightly. A flash of lightning showed that roots had grown from the wooden deck to hold her fast, saving her from falling into the void.

"Don't be afraid, Seren," a woman's voice whispered in her ear.

Then *Karia Naille* struck the unforgiving surface with a crash. Seren's head snapped back against the deck, and then there was nothing.

* * * * * * *

The storm disappeared as quickly as it came. The helm of *Kenshi Zhann* filled with eerie silence. Through the forward panel, Marth could see a vast expanse of nothing. He darted to the window, looking in all directions, milky eyes scouring the sky for any sign of their quarry.

Karia Naille was gone.

Marth spun about in a fury, chest heaving with every breath. His hand tightened about his amethyst wand, though there were no enemies about. He composed himself when he realized that the helmsman was staring at him with open terror.

"I'm sorry, Captain Marth," the man said in a low voice. "I didn't expect them to be so fast, or for the storm to come up so suddenly, or for them to veer at us like that. I take full responsibility for their escape."

The changeling raised a silencing hand, closing his eyes patiently. "You did nothing wrong, Devyn," he said. "Pherris Gerriman is the finest airship pilot this side of House Lyrandar. I am not altogether surprised. His ship, like ours, needs neither magic nor dragonmark to command her—the proper training and an iron will are all that are required." Marth smiled at Devyn. "Next time, Devyn, your will must be stronger than Gerriman's."

The helmsman smiled in relief. "I won't fail you, Captain," he said.

Marth nodded in reply, ignoring the helmsman. Inwardly, the changeling restrained himself from punishing the pilot. He could not afford to do so, not now. Devyn was the best pilot among his crew, other than himself. He would need the fool if *Karia Naille* turned out not to be as damaged as she looked. In the meantime, perhaps his presumed mercy would drive the helmsman to try harder. Anything was possible.

"Land there," Marth said, pointing to a nearby valley. "We will repair the damage to our vessel."

"Captain?" the helmsman said. "We suffered minimal damage, but the *Karia Naille* was crippled. She cannot have run far. If we patrol the area, we may find her."

"There is no need to patrol," Marth said. "I already know where d'Cannith is going . . . even if he does not."

CHAPTER
EIGHTEEN

Seren sat up with a groan, rubbing the knot on the back of her skull. She looked at her fingers and was relieved to see no blood. Rising gingerly, she noticed no other injuries besides several bruises and some soreness where the strange roots had held her during the crash. The plants were gone now, just as quickly as they had appeared. She had survived unscathed.

Zed lay on the deck nearby, looking dazed. Eraina knelt beside him, applying a bandage to the bleeding gash on his forehead. Pherris lay on the deck as well. His right arm had already been splinted.

"Are you injured, Seren?" Eraina asked, looking at her in concern.

"I don't think so," Seren said.

The same, unfortunately, could not be said of *Karia Naille*. The airship had come to rest at the bottom of a narrow gorge, leaving a deep gouge behind her. The lower strut that once held the ring of fire in place now lay cracked and broken nearby. Tristam knelt beside the hook at one end, studying it while Omax hauled debris and sorted it into a pile. Of the elemental fire that once surrounded the ship, all that was visible was a weak blue plume of crackling fire drifting from the upper arm. Sparkling motes of energy periodically separated themselves from the plume and drifted away on the wind. Seren had the impression the fire was slowly dying.

But what truly drew Seren's attention was the woman who now sat cross-legged on the upper strut. She was thin and petite, with long pointed ears and a rounded, childlike face. Long, golden hair hung loose over her bare shoulders. She wore a short dress of pale green that seemed woven of thin leaves. Her eyes were closed in quiet concentration and she kept both hands plunged into the elemental fire. It appeared to do her no harm.

"Don't disturb her, Miss Morisse," Dalan said from the cabin behind her. "She's the ship's only hope of ever flying again."

Seren looked back at Dalan. The fat guildmaster's cabin was a mess. Books and trophies had spilled haphazardly from the shelves. Strangely, Dalan paid the mess no mind. He sat on his bed. His old dog lay limply beside him, whining plaintively and gasping for breath. Dalan sat beside it and petted it with a worried frown. Seren stared for a long time. Dalan showing such concern for his pet was almost more surprising than the strange woman sitting atop the ship's strut. It was more genuine emotion than she had ever seen in the man. Dalan noticed her scrutiny, leaned forward, and gently pushed his cabin door closed. Seren looked back up at the woman on the arm, feeling like an intruder for witnessing Dalan in such a state.

"Who is she?" Seren asked.

"Aeven," Zed said, sitting up a bit, hissing with pain, and quickly lying down again. "She's a dryad."

"Dryad?" Eraina asked. "How is that possible? Such trickster spirits are bound to trees. They cannot leave their forests."

"You know nothing, paladin," Aeven said in a soft voice, never opening her eyes. "The livewood is a tree that never dies unless burned to ashes. Even when cut, it continues to live though it ceases to grow. For a dryad bound to such a tree, this can be both blessing and curse."

Seren's eyes moved to the ship's figurehead. The delicate sculpture remained improbably unharmed by the crash. It was the perfect likeness of Aeven.

"Among my people I was a druid," she said. "The soul of Eberron resonates within me, and I longed to see the world beyond Aerenal. A human sailor offered me a chance to leave my home, cutting and shaping my tree in my image. I was to protect his vessel." Aeven paused, a pained look flickering across her face. "They proved to be wicked men, with savage appetites. Ashrem d'Cannith saved me from their clutches. He gave me a new home on *Karia Naille*. This ship is my forest now." She opened her eyes and looked down at Eraina, her gaze a pure and depthless green.

"Dryads don't like being called tricksters, Eraina," Zed said with a half-smile. "Especially after they save your life."

Eraina's face darkened in shame. "I apologize, Aeven," she said. "I meant no insult."

Aeven only tilted her perfect chin, gave Seren an inscrutable look, and closed her eyes again. Seren had the sensation that the shimmering blue flame was watching her.

"Is there anything I can do?" Seren asked, looking helplessly at the crippled ship.

"Help Tristam," Zed said.

"I don't really know anything about fixing airships," she said.

"No, but you can make him focus," Zed said, drawing a sharp breath as Eraina tightened the bandage around his left leg. "He's been broken up since the crash, but he's more confident when you're around, Seren. If he can't focus, you're going to have to *get* him focused for all our sakes."

"You're beginning to sound as manipulative as Dalan," Seren said.

Zed smirked. "Dalan has nothing on me."

Seren climbed over the rail and dropped lightly to the ground. She stepped back from the ship and examined the damage. The airship looked relatively unharmed save a few patches where the outer hull had been stripped away and the shattered arm. Tristam appeared almost instantly by her side, looking down with a worried expression.

"Seren, are you all right?" he asked, interrupting the question she had been about to ask. "Eraina said you hit your head."

"I'm fine," she answered, offering a soothing smile. "Zed and Pherris look worse than I do, and I think Dalan's dog is hurt."

"You're worried about Gunther?" Tristam asked with a chuckle.

Seren shrugged.

"Compassion is that which separates warriors from heroes," Omax said quietly, dropping another load of debris in the pile.

Tristam gave the warforged a look, then grinned back at Seren. "Don't mind Omax. He gets philosophical."

Seren studied the crippled ship again. "The damage doesn't look as bad as I thought it would," she said.

"Airships are mostly made of soarwood," Tristam said. "It's naturally buoyant in the air, so with a good pilot a crash is usually something you can walk away from. Usually."

"Will it fly again?" Seren asked.

"She, not it, Seren," Tristam said. "Ships are always 'she.' And I don't know. The hull just needs some patching, but the keel arm snapped right off."

"What is Aeven doing up there?" Seren asked, pointing up at the dryad.

Tristam frowned uncomfortably. "Honestly, I'm not sure. She has some sort of connection with the elemental bound to *Karia Naille*. With the damage the ship has taken, the elemental could have become unbound and returned to its home plane—or worse yet, stuck around and killed us all. Aeven has convinced the elemental to remain for a while, but even she can't keep it here forever." Tristam ran one hand through his unkempt hair as he surveyed the wreckage.

"Convinced it?" Seren asked.

"Elementals don't belong in this world," Tristam said. "An airship can bind one and harness its power, but a dead ship can't hold an elemental anymore." He sighed. "That's not even considering that *Karia Naille* will just collapse under her own weight if we leave her lying on her hull too long. She's designed to be buoyed in the air, not lying on rocks. We need to get her up on some sort of hoist or scaffolding so that I can finish the repairs and replace the keel strut. It wouldn't take long to get her airworthy enough to limp to a real city for proper repairs, but we don't have the materials or the manpower to do it." The artificer offered Seren a hopeless look. "I don't know what to do, Seren."

"You kept the ship together long enough for Pherris to land," she said. "That's what's important, Tristam. You saved us. We'll figure out the rest."

He smiled thankfully, but said nothing.

"Something is coming," Omax said, standing up abruptly. The warforged's glowing eyes fixed on the far end of the gorge, along the deep rut the crashing airship had left behind.

Fearing that Marth's soldiers might have found them, Seren reached for her dagger. Tristam's wand was already in his hand. After several moments the sound of heavy footfalls could be heard. Seren thought that they were hoof beats at first, given their speed and volume, but the rhythm was wrong.

A cloud of dust rolled around the corner of the gorge, heralding the arrival of a half dozen large, bipedal lizards. Each was the size of a small horse, their hides a pale gray slashed with brilliant green stripes. Their yellow eyes were catlike and intelligent. Their grinning maws were lined with razor-sharp teeth.

Small forearms hung close to their bodies. Each thickly muscled leg ended with a single sharply curved talon. The creatures wore leather harnesses on their backs, and upon each sat a halfling rider. They dressed in wild outfits of dark leather and bright silk, with thick crystal goggles to protect their eyes from dust. Each carried a quiver of short javelins on his back. The riders fanned out in a half-moon formation as they approached the fallen airship, each rider coming to a halt in perfect unison a hundred feet away. Twelve sets of eyes watched them alertly for any sign of hostility.

"Halfling hunters," Tristam said. He did not make any move toward them, but neither did he put his weapon away.

A loud shriek rang out from above, followed by the leathery flap of wings. Blizzard landed gracefully between the crew and the halflings, his injured wing now healed by Eraina's magic. From the glidewing's back, Gerith greeted them with a broad smile.

"These six fine fellows are elite clawhunters from the Ghost Talon tribe," Gerith said, hopping from his saddle and indicating them with a broad gesture. "This is their leader, Koranth, who will take us to meet Chief Rossa. I believe he's a distant cousin of mine, but it's difficult to be sure. My bloodline is somewhat . . . tangled."

"Color me surprised," Seren said.

Koranth looked at Seren, then at the dagger in her hand. He barked something at Gerith and pointed at her.

"Put your weapons away, please," Dalan said, climbing down the gangplank to join them. "If you antagonize the Ghost Talons, they'll only increase the fee for their aid. I fear they'll already be charging a great deal, given our obvious desperation."

"Sorry," Seren said, bowing her head pertly to Koranth and sheathing her dagger. Tristam put his wand away as well.

The halfling scowled and said something unintelligible.

"Koranth only speaks a little bit of your language, unfortunately," Gerith explained. "The others speak only the halfling tongue."

Dalan spoke to Koranth in the same high-pitched, rapid language, finishing with a formal bow. Koranth gave a small salute and eyed Dalan suspiciously.

"Dalan, I didn't know you spoke my tongue," Gerith said.

"I don't," he said. He tapped the soft black cap he now wore. "Tristam's work. It gives me a rough understanding of their speech. It tends to place words poorly in context, stumbles with regional dialects, and is utterly confounded by slang, but it's better than nothing." He continued speaking to Koranth in the halfling language again.

The two spoke for some time, with Gerith often stepping in to explain when Dalan or Koranth misunderstood each other. Dalan made a loud comment and gestured back each of the crew members in turn. There was obviously some attempt at humor in his introductions, for Koranth's sour face broke into a smile and his fellow hunters laughed out loud. Seren wondered what he had said but was more impressed with how expertly he had said it. In mere seconds and without truly knowing their language, d'Cannith had brightened their hostile mood and earned their respect.

After several minutes of negotiation, Dalan took several folded papers from his coat and handed them to the halfling. Koranth turned in his saddle and whistled shrilly. In reply, an enormous threehorn rumbled around the bend in the gorge. This one wore a complex harness over its broad back. Two halflings sat at the front, each holding a thick rope tied to one of the creature's horns. Two more hung from the back on each side, shortbows slung over their backs.

"Their beast can carry three of us to the Ghost Talon camp, where we can negotiate directly with their chieftain," Dalan explained. "I will go, obviously. Gerith, we will need your knowledge of the culture. Follow us on your glidewing."

"Aye, Dalan," Gerith said.

"Seren, I will require your aid as well."

"Aye," she said, echoing the halfling.

"You should take Omax along," Tristam offered. "You may need his strength."

Dalan looked at the warforged with some surprise. "Are you certain you don't wish him to remain with the ship?" he asked.

"Tristam is correct," Omax said. "You may need me."

"The halfling beast cannot carry you," Dalan said.

"I can keep up," the warforged said, undaunted.

"Very well," Dalan said with a respectful nod. "Probably best we also bring the paladin, if only to keep her away from Aeven for a while."

"Aeven didn't seem angry," Seren said.

"And count us all fortunate," Dalan said. "Aeven's temper is difficult to rouse, but terrible to behold. Gather whatever supplies you will need and bring the marshal, Seren."

Seren murmured her agreement and returned to the airship. She did not see Eraina on the deck, so she went to her cabin. She grabbed a leather satchel filled with extra clothing and, assuming the worst, tucked her belt of assorted thieves' tools inside as well. She slung the bag over her shoulder and turned to see Tristam standing in the hall.

"Seren, take this," he said, in a worried voice. He held out a silver bracelet studded with dark green gems. "Its enchantment is similar to Dalan's hat, so you'll be able to understand the halflings a little, even if you can't talk to them."

"Thank you," she said, slipping the bracelet over her wrist. She gave him a confident smile and walked past him.

"Seren," Tristam called out.

She looked back. His expression was distracted, looking at

the ground rather than directly at her. "Be careful," he said. "Marth has found us twice now with no warning."

"If he finds us again, I'll be ready," she said.

"That's not what I mean," Tristam said. "Doesn't it strike you as odd that he keeps finding us so quickly?"

"Couldn't he be tracking us like you tracked me?" she asked.

"That sort of magic only works at close range," he answered. "It doesn't explain why he keeps finding us half a continent away."

Seren caught the darker meaning behind Tristam's words. Marth's attacks had not been the result of magic or coincidence.

"You think there's a spy," Seren said softly. "Why do you trust me?"

He looked at her earnestly. "Why shouldn't I?" he asked.

Seren was taken aback by the sincerity in his voice. She wasn't used to people trusting her. Impulsively, she leaned forward and kissed him on the lips.

"You be careful too, Tristam," she said.

He blinked at her in silent surprise.

Seren climbed back up on deck to find Pherris still unconscious. Zed had limped off the ship to speak to Dalan. Eraina stood on the deck alone, near the door of Dalan's cabin.

"Eraina," Seren began.

"I heard," the paladin said, walking down the gangplank. "I'm coming."

Seren followed her to the threehorn, wondering how she had missed the paladin on her way below deck. Dalan was already mounted in the center of the threehorn's back. He peered about in obvious discomfort but offered no complaint. One of the halflings watched Dalan carefully, obviously waiting for the fat human to fall out of the saddle. The gigantic dinosaur stamped one foot in boredom but otherwise looked unconcerned as another halfling helped Eraina climb onto the creature's complex harness. A third hunter offered Seren a hand as well, and she took her place just above the creature's right hind leg.

The halfling pointed out a leather loop between her knees and instructed her how to strap herself in using gestures and babbling in his native tongue. In her head, Seren heard another voice superimposed over his words, produced by the bracelet Tristam had given her.

"Hold on there and keep the belt over your left leg secure," the voice said. "If you need to get off quickly, give the slack end a tug. Just don't do that when we're running or you'll fall and bust open your cabbage."

Seren had to cough to cover up her laugh. She wondered whether the "cabbage" was a translating error or just part of the odd halfling sense of humor. Chances were roughly equal that it was either.

With their passengers secured, Koranth gave a sharp cry to his men. The threehorn rumbled into movement, and the clawfoot dinosaurs fell into a trot. While the creature she rode moved with a stolid, powerful inertia, the clawfoots loped along with birdlike grace. Their ease of movement suggested that they were capable of far greater speed. Gerith's glidewing swooped into the sky ahead.

For more than an hour they traveled across the plains. The skies were clear and the land was flat and open. Seren was grateful for that. At least if *Moon* came after them now, they would see the airship coming. As the sun began to set, a small village of brightly painted conical tents and covered wagons came into view. A pair of clawfoot riders rode out to escort them. These creatures were larger than the others, equipped with impressive white leather armor studded with metal spikes. A quartet of glidewings now circled overhead, each bearing another rider.

"How do we know these halflings are not in league with

the men who shot us down?" Eraina asked Dalan, eyeing the halflings with caution.

"Because we are alive," Dalan said, as if that were obvious.

"Perhaps they intend to capture us," Eraina countered.

"An interesting hypothesis," Dalan admitted. "I would argue that even captured we're better off alive than dead, as death offers little opportunity for escape. Now allow me to ignite your paranoia with my own suggestion—how do we really know these halflings don't speak our language?"

Dalan looked back at her with a smirk. One of the halfling drivers glanced at them with an innocent smile and returned to steering the threehorn.

As they made their way through the camp, a small crowd gathered to watch them pass. Men and women, old and young, all emerged from their tents and wagons to see the strangers. Children no taller than a foot peered out shyly from behind their parents. A dozen dogs with low, stocky bodies and fluffy coats danced around them in a barking frenzy. They were led to a large tent at the center of the camp, where they dismounted.

"So now we bargain for their aid?" Eraina asked.

"Already done," Dalan said. "The chief empowered Koranth to bargain on our behalf, so we resolved it back at the ship."

One of Koranth's men was shouting at a group of laborers lounging around a cart heaped high with lumber and tools. At their command, the massive threehorn pulling the cart lumbered off the way they had come.

"So what are we doing here, then?" Seren asked.

"A halfling chief doesn't leave bargaining to underlings," Gerith said. "Nothing is official till the chief approves. It'd be against tradition."

"But the workers already left," Eraina said, pointing at the departing wagons.

"The halflings rarely let tradition impede efficiency," Dalan said. "One of many things I admire about them. In any case, I still have much to discuss with the chieftain."

Koranth looked at them cautiously as they gathered before the tent, eyes resting on Eraina's spear. "Leave the weapons outside," he said to Dalan. "Even that one." He looked directly at Omax.

Omax looked down at the halfling impassively. If he took insult, he gave no sign.

Dalan smiled. "Seren, Eraina, please leave your weapons out here while we meet with the chief," he said. "Omax, it may be best if you remained to guard our possessions, just in case."

The warforged nodded, accepting Eraina's spear and sword and Seren's dagger in grim silence. Koranth removed his boots and set them beside the entrance, glaring and not moving aside so they could enter until they did the same. The interior of the tent was carpeted with thick, soft fur. Six chairs of woven wicker padded with felt stood in a circle. A small table stood before each chair, each featuring several plates of food and a small pitcher of wine.

In the chair directly opposite the entrance sat a halfling who could only be the chief. He was an older halfling a long, white moustache and white hair tied into thick braids. His clothing was outrageous, consisting of a motley suit of green and gray silk, several sparkling beaded necklaces, and a peaked yellow hat capped with a long green plume. A suit of spiked leather armor hung on a stand beside his chair. It was dyed the same riotous color scheme as the chief's outfit.

"Chieftain Rossa," Koranth said in the halfling language. "I present to you Dalan d'Cannith and his associates: Gerith Snowshale, Seren Morisse, and Eraina d'Deneith."

"Greetings, travelers, and welcome," Rossa said, speaking in the Common tongue. He gestured dramatically at the chairs. "I offer you all the hospitality the Ghost Talon tribe has to offer. Sit, eat, and let us talk of friendship."

VOYAGE OF THE MOURNING DAWN

"My thanks, Chieftain," Dalan said. He bowed politely and sat directly across from Rossa. Gerith had already taken one of the other chairs and began chewing a chicken leg noisily. Seren sat between Dalan and the halfling. The plates were heaped with roasted bird meat, steamed vegetables, and crusty black bread. A wave of hunger hit Seren when she saw the food; she hadn't realized how famished she was until this moment. There didn't appear to be any utensils, but that neither concerned nor delayed the halflings from consuming their own meals with their hands, so she did the same. The food reminded her of the bold, spicy meals Gerith prepared on *Karia Naille*. She tore into the offerings with great relish.

"Gerith told us your airship had been badly damaged," Rossa said. "Most unfortunate."

"Yes," Dalan said, "but with the aid of your tribe's carpenters it should be nothing we cannot repair."

Koranth, seated at Rossa's right hand, drew the folded papers from his jacket and dropped them on the chieftain's table. Even from here, Seren could see they were letters of credit, marked with the House Cannith household seal. From her experience with the letters of credit she had encountered in her thieving career, she judged Dalan must have paid the halflings a small fortune.

"I apologize for the price, but it was necessary," Rossa said, though his pleased grin demonstrated he wasn't all that sorry. "Lumber is a prized commodity. We trade with the Valenar for most of our wood, but the elves have been standoffish this year."

"Are the elves preparing for war?" Dalan asked.

"The Valenar are always preparing for war," Rossa said with a shrug, as if it did not concern him. "Invading the Plains or Q'barra, or maybe even readying a fleet to sail Balinor knows where and start a fight with someone new. War is a sport to the elves. If they invade the Plains, they'll get bored and leave eventually. Someone will fight them off. I wish them luck. Meanwhile we're headed as far north as we can get before winter."

Seren found the comment strange. Though the village was built of tents and wagons, none of them seemed to have been uprooted for some time and none of the halflings looked ready to leave.

"I am humbled by your generosity," Dalan said. "It is my honor if the wealth of my House helps purchase the security of your tribe this winter, especially if my charity is forgotten."

The halfling chuckled. "I catch your meaning, d'Cannith," he said. "Have no fear of that. Lumber may be scarce but discretion is our most precious export. As long as your money's good, you were never here."

"Excellent," Dalan said. "Then as our business is concluded, perhaps you would not mind speaking of other matters? I came here seeking someone and hoped that you or one of your tribe might have information."

"Ask, my friend," Rossa said, sipping deeply from his cup.

Dalan was silent for the briefest moment. He gave the chieftain a tight smile and continued. "I am seeking a young woman, a scholar named Kiris Overwood. I believe she was conducting research somewhere in Talenta. Would you know of her?"

"Is this Overwood a friend of yours?" Rossa asked, perhaps a bit more stiffly than was required.

"We are acquainted," Dalan said. "She owes my family a significant debt."

Rossa stroked his moustache with a cackle. "Why am I not surprised?" he said, voice tinged with malicious glee. "Yes, I know her. That girl is the lowest sort of thief. She came to us only a few weeks ago, looking for refuge from the law, no doubt. We gave her a home, and in thanks she stole one of my wife's

VOYAGE OF THE MOURNING DAWN

rings from the very tent where I sleep. My guards pursued her, but she fled into the Boneyard, only a few days' journey from here. A shame and a disgrace it is, that I clasped such a serpent to my breast, but there's little to be done. The Boneyard is taboo to my people. Bad luck will haunt any halfling that enters. My wingriders have watched the area carefully, and she has not emerged."

"So, living or dead, we must seek her there," Dalan said.

"I could not allow you to enter the Boneyard, Master d'Cannith," Rossa said. "My riders are distraught enough at the idea of patrolling such a place. I could not place more friends at risk."

"Most of my associates are not halflings," Dalan said. "We are not bound by the taboos of your people. Perhaps we could aid you as you have aided us, and return what has been taken."

Rossa's eyes lit up as he turned to Seren. "What a clever idea," he said, as if it had only now occurred to him. "Though she is unlikely to be carrying the ring, I am certain I could encourage her to reveal what she has done with it."

"Dalan, there is something you should know," Eraina said in a stern voice.

"Later, Eraina," Dalan said with a warning tone.

"This is important, Dalan," she insisted. "The chieftain . . ."

"I said *later*," Dalan repeated. "Negotiation is my specialty, Eraina. Allow me to handle this."

Eraina rose, her face pale and angry. She strode briskly out of the tent.

"Is there a problem?" Rossa asked, looking after her blankly.

"There is always a problem," Dalan said. "The path of a Spear of Boldrei is beset by obstacles."

"Ah," Rossa said. "Paladins." There was both understanding and odd sympathy in his tone, as if Dalan had informed him that Eraina was afflicted with some incurable disease.

"Seren, Gerith, why don't you make certain she is all right?" Dalan suggested, looking at each of them in turn. "I have much to discuss with the chieftain in private."

Seren looked forlornly at her unfinished meal. She noticed that Gerith took his plate and cup with him without any complaint from the chief, so she did the same. They emerged from the tent to find Eraina pacing back and forth before Omax, who sat on the ground and watched her patiently. She looked up with a cold expression as the tent flap opened, softening when she saw Seren and Gerith.

"Eraina, is something wrong?" Seren asked. "What were you trying to tell Dalan?"

"The chieftain," she said in a low voice, glancing about to make certain none of the villagers were close enough to hear. "He is lying to us."

"Lying?" Seren said. "About what? About helping us?"

"About Overwood," Eraina said. "This tribe has not moved in many months. Why would any chieftain risk the safety of his tribe by lingering so close to a place that is so dangerously taboo, especially in the face of a Valenar invasion? He has lied to us, Seren."

"Chieftains don't lie," Gerith said, absently nibbling the last piece of meat from his chicken bone.

Eraina looked at the halfling scornfully. "Gerith, your trust in your countryman is admirable but misplaced. I am quite adept at detecting falsehood with or without my goddess's blessings."

"No, you don't understand," he said, tossing the bone over one shoulder. "A Talenta chieftain is not a normal halfling. A chieftain is free of all sin and vice. A chieftain cannot lie, and he certainly doesn't have extramarital affairs. And if he did he certainly wouldn't give away family jewelry and then get caught."

He wiped one hand on his shirt. "If such a thing happened, it would shame him and all his tribe, wouldn't it? So it doesn't happen. Ever."

"What are you saying, Gerith?" Eraina demanded.

"What you just saw in there is what we call the *hmael*," Gerith said. "It means the 'golden lie.' The chieftain can't tell the truth because it would harm his pride and put his virtue into question. Instead he tells an obvious lie, and assumes you'll figure out the truth for yourself."

"But a chieftain can't lie," Seren said.

"Exactly right," Gerith said, snapping his fingers. "See? Seren understands. Thus the honor of the tribe is maintained. *Hmael* isn't exclusive to chieftains either. Halflings will often tell an impossible lie instead of the truth, and assume that their friends will be smart enough to figure out the truth and polite enough not to bring it up." He looked from one face to the next. "I can't believe any of you could have been around me for any length of time and not notice me doing that."

"What have you lied about, Gerith?" Seren asked.

The halfling grinned. "If you can't figure it out, you'll get no clues from me."

"I cannot believe your people would embrace such dishonesty," Eraina said.

"The halflings say the truth is like a bathtub," Gerith said, taking no offense. "Dipping in can be quite refreshing at the right time and place, but it's too much trouble to carry along everywhere."

Omax laughed, but Eraina clearly did not find the analogy humorous. She sighed at the halfling and snatched her spear from the ground. "I for one don't appreciate being lied to," she said. "If he'll lie to us about Overwood, how do we know he hasn't lied to us about Marth as well? This could be a trap."

"I know the Ghost Talons," Gerith said. "As long as Dalan's

money is good, we can trust them. And House Cannith letters of credit are very, very good."

"And what if Marth has made them a better offer?" Eraina asked.

Gerith frowned. "We don't really have a choice, Eraina. This was the only settlement I could find that had the resources to help us and was anywhere close by. If we turn to anyone else for help, we may as well just keep walking because *Karia Naille* will never fly again."

"If you fear treachery, Eraina," Omax said, "then all that remains is to be vigilant."

The paladin said nothing.

CHAPTER
NINETEEN

"This is foolish, Dalan," Eraina snapped. "No good will come of this."

"A foreboding prediction," Dalan said. He pushed aside the tent flap and peered outside, probably more out of habit than any real suspicion. Dalan had requested a private tent while he discussed the chieftain's proposition, though he had spent much of his time arguing with Eraina. "If you disapprove so strongly of the course I have chosen, perhaps you might beseech your goddess to provide a reasonable alternative?"

The paladin regarded Dalan coldly. "You know that the Host does not interfere in such a manner," she said. "I do not see why we have agreed to aid a man who cannot even be truthful with us."

Seren almost laughed at that. Was there anyone in the crew other than Eraina who *was* truthful?

"We have agreed to aid him because we are surrounded by his warriors," Dalan said. "I have little doubt that whatever Rossa's interest in Kiris really is, it has nothing to do with a ring. I do not intend to expose her to him while she is still valuable to us—but Rossa need not know that."

Eraina folded her arms across her chest, body tense as she glared at Dalan.

"I see such a statement does not lessen your disapproval, Marshal," he said.

"If you do not intend to honor the agreement you made with Rossa, you should not have made it," Eraina said.

"First you warn me not to trust Rossa because he is a liar, and now you are upset to hear my agreement with him is insincere?" Dalan asked with a smug grin. "Mourn not a ruin built on sand, or so it is said, paladin. Worry not for your honor, d'Deneith, you have made no promises."

"But if I know Rossa cannot trust you," she said, "why should I?"

"Because of your irritating talent for detecting falsehood," Dalan said. "Have I lied to you yet?"

"Not that I can see, but my senses are not absolute."

"Excellent. Then let us cease this bickering and decide how we shall find Kiris Overwood."

"What exactly should we be looking for, Dalan?" Seren asked.

"Overwood herself will suffice," Dalan said. "Tristam will need her spells to break my uncle's ciphers. A pity he is also required to repair the airship. His insight would be useful."

"So we intend to take Kiris with us?" Seren asked. "What if Rossa's men guarding our ship see her?"

"A road to cross when we find her," Dalan said.

"Then what if she does not wish to come with us?" Eraina asked.

"She will come," Dalan said. He took an envelope from his coat and offered it to Seren. It was sealed with blue wax featuring the House Cannith crest. "If all else fails, give her this. Try to reason with her at first, if possible. I would prefer not to fulfill the promises contained therein."

"What if Kiris is not alive?" Omax asked. "If the Boneyard is as dangerous as we have heard, and she has not emerged in weeks, she may be dead."

"Overwood was my uncle's most trusted confidant," Dalan said. "I do not doubt she is resourceful enough to survive in such a place. It would be a simple matter for her to use magic to sustain herself, and I do not doubt she could find a way to protect herself from whatever horrors dwell there."

"Horrors," Gerith said. The halfling laughed bitterly. "What about them? You haven't even talked about the biggest problem, Dalan. Surviving the Boneyard."

Dalan looked keenly at the halfling. "You have known we were bound for the Boneyard since we left Black Pit."

"No," Gerith said. "I knew that we were going *near* the Boneyard. I didn't expect that Kiris would be stupid enough to actually *live* there, or that we'd be stupid enough to *follow* her into the damned place." From the way Gerith spoke the word, "damned" was deliberately chosen.

"Then enlighten us before we continue," Dalan said. "What, precisely, is the nature of the Boneyard and its curse?"

"It's a graveyard," Gerith answered. "It's filled with the bones of dragons as old as the continent itself. Nobody has ever seen a live dragon there. Nobody knows how the bones got there. It's off limits for all halflings. Even the city halflings who ignore the old ways don't take the curse lightly."

"And what is the curse, specifically?" Dalan asked.

"Any halfling who enters will die far from home and be unmourned by his tribe," Gerith said.

"Then nothing prevents you from guiding Seren, Eraina, and Omax there, so long as you remain outside," Dalan said. "After all, they aren't halflings."

Gerith laughed nervously. "You don't understand, Dalan. The curse is there to protect us, to stave off curiosity. With or without the curse, the Boneyard is evil. There are dead things there, things better left undisturbed. That place is dangerous."

"We are already in a great deal of danger, Gerith," Dalan

said. "Or do you not recall our rough landing? Now will you lead us to the Boneyard, or must I rely upon one of Rossa's guides?"

Gerith looked at Omax and Eraina before casting a long, troubled look at Seren. She offered him as encouraging a smile as she could muster.

"I'll help," he said. "But I don't like it."

"And I regret forcing you into such a decision," Dalan said, "but we all must make sacrifices."

"Sacrifice, d'Cannith?" Eraina laughed. "I notice you did not list yourself as one of those entering the Boneyard. What sacrifice do you intend to make, remaining here?"

Dalan met the paladin's mocking gaze levelly. "Do not mistake pragmatism for cowardice, Marshal," he said. "I know my limitations. I do not excel in physical arenas. I would only be a burden in a place like the Boneyard. Here, at least, I can keep a watchful eye on Rossa. I assumed that all those more capable than myself would be willing to participate, but if that assumption was incorrect, please speak up. Do any of you wish to remain here?"

"No," Eraina said.

Omax did not reply. Strangely enough, he looked at Seren.

"Can't turn back once you start," Seren said.

At that, Omax silently nodded his approval.

◉ ◉ ◉ ◉ ◉ ◉ ◉

They set out almost immediately afterward, making their way across the Talenta Plains on foot. Rossa claimed his tribe had no suitable steeds to offer humans, though Seren suspected that he did not wish to send his own animals into the accursed Boneyard. She didn't mind walking. After spending so many days cooped inside the cramped airship, a chance to stretch her legs was welcome. The plains were broad and flat, so they made good time.

Eraina set the pace for the others, moving with tireless energy. Gerith remained mostly airborne and out of sight, returning to adjust their course or prepare a brief meal. With each hour that passed, the halfling's cheerful demeanor grew more subdued. Seren met the change with mixed feelings. While a part of her was relieved that the halfling had ceased his bad jokes and mischievous flirtations, she was saddened to see the cheerful little scout so depressed.

The silence of her companions only added to Seren's sense of foreboding. Eraina was in a sour mood after her confrontation with Dalan. The warforged plodded along just behind her, hardly saying a word. That night, they pitched their tents and slept on the grass in tense silence. Early the next morning, they set out again. Seren had grown so used to the silence that Omax startled her with an unexpected question.

"What do you expect we will find?" he asked.

"I'm not sure," she said, slowing her pace so he walked beside her. "A lot of the world outside Wroat is still new to me. I never know what to expect."

The warforged looked down at her. His metal face radiated concern, or perhaps she just imagined it. "If the halflings fear the Boneyard, we should be extremely cautious."

She laughed. "Whatever frightens halflings can't be all that scary."

"You underestimate them," Omax answered. "If halflings fear this place, we would be wise to do the same. Halflings are tenacious warriors. Have you ever seen Gerith shy away from danger? You have seen the way he leaps to his glidewing, hurling himself into the sky without hesitation."

"That's true," Seren admitted. "Though Gerith is the only halfling I've really known. It's hard for me to imagine him as a tenacious warrior."

"Then you do not truly know him," Omax said. "Gerith has defeated the most difficult foe with ease."

"What foe is that?" she asked.

"Himself," Omax said. "None of the rest of us can claim such mastery. We are all haunted by ghosts, burdened by memories of what we once were, fearful of what we might become, or driven by the impossibly high expectations of others. Most souls look outside themselves for validation. Gerith is one of the few men I have met who knows who he truly is and is at peace with that. He is the strongest of us all, Seren." He looked at her. "And he is afraid."

Seren was silent for a long time. "I never thought about halflings that way, but I never bothered to get to know them. I've never really known a warforged before either. You're more philosophical than I expected."

"Philosophical?" Omax asked with a rattling chuckle. "A philosopher asks the world why he exists, but I already know the answer to that question."

"Oh?" Seren asked. "Why do you exist, Omax?"

"To kill," Omax said sadly. "I am a weapon." The warforged bowed his head and stared at the back of one wide metal hand, a smooth surface of adamantine and darkwood tattooed with an ancient patchwork of battle scars. "I was among the first warforged that were truly alive. Beside a legion of my brethren I led a Cyran assault against the nation of Breland. The soldiers we faced were not prepared for our power. A single platoon escaped, taking refuge in the only fortified structure they could find—a monastery of the Sovereign Host."

"That must have been a long time ago," Seren said.

"To me, the memories are fresh," Omax said. "The monks gave our enemies sanctuary and would not surrender them to us. My orders were clear—those who would not surrender were to be showed no mercy. We battered down the doors and invaded the monastery . . . the monks offered no violence but . . ." The warforged's three-fingered hand closed with a metallic clang. "They would not stand aside."

"Omax," Seren said softly. "You don't have to talk about this if you don't want to."

"It was a slaughter, Seren. They were no match for us, and they knew it." He looked at her again. His blue eyes shone coldly. She did not know what else to say, so she continued to listen.

"One of the last surviving enemy soldiers must have been a wizard or artificer of some sort. As a final show of defiance, he unleashed an explosion that gutted the monastery, burying me and my comrades beneath tons of rubble. The others perished, but I did not. I found myself trapped in silence and shadow. A warforged needs neither food, nor air, nor sleep. So for two decades, I remained there."

"What did you do all that time?" she asked.

"Nothing but think about how I had come to be," he said. "Until at last I saw the light again. Tristam was the one who found me and repaired me. He gave me back my life, and this time I did not make the same mistake."

"To be a warrior?" Seren asked.

Omax shook his head. "No," he said. "To be a warrior is a worthy task, to fight with honor for a cause. That is not what I was. I was created with the power of choice, Seren. Though I am a machine, intended to be a weapon, I was somehow given the potential to become something more. Instead, I chose to obey blindly because it was the easier path. When I looked into the eyes of those monks, I saw the truth too late. Any crude weapon can take life away. When I refused to find a better way, I chose to be less than I could be. I squandered the gift I had been given, and I squandered the lives of those men and the warforged who followed me. Tristam gave me a second chance. I know what I was meant to be, Seren, but I do not wish to be only that."

"You still sound like a philosopher to me," Seren said. "You know the answers, but now you're looking for a new question."

He glanced at her sharply. His blue eyes flickered. "Yes," he said in an amused voice. "That is exactly so. You have a keen mind, Seren. I can see why Tristam admires you."

"Me?" she said. "He's barely spoken to me since we left Black Pit. He's been obsessed with his work."

"Tristam has difficulty allowing others into his life," Omax said. "Yet he cares for you, Seren. Remember that it was only after Dalan commanded you to join him that Tristam volunteered my aid."

Seren blinked at Omax in surprise. She realized that the warforged had not wandered far from her side since leaving *Karia Naille*. Even during their meeting with the halfling chieftain, he had remained as close to the tent as he dared. "Tristam sent you to protect me?" she asked, sounding a bit outraged.

"It seems that way," Omax said. "I think my efforts will be largely wasted. You appear quite capable of protecting yourself."

Seren laughed and smiled up at Omax, but the warforged's blue eyes were locked straight ahead. She followed his gaze to find that Gerith had landed atop a hill. Eraina was already kneeling beside the halfling, shielding her eyes from the sun as she studied the distant horizon. She hurried to join them.

"Well, there it is," Gerith greeted them in a hushed voice. "This is as far as I go."

Beneath them, the grassy plains gradually gave way to a valley of chalky white, nestled just against the mountains. Chasms and gorges crisscrossed the surface, creating a maze of shadowed stone. Large white shapes broke the ground here and there, occasionally curving into a fearsome claw or a narrow skull with empty, staring eyes. The creatures that once owned these bones must have been truly immense if such detail was visible even from here.

"A graveyard for dragons," Eraina said, crouching low as she scanned the area for danger. "Your people were right to be wary of this place, Snowshale. Boldrei warns me that there is evil here."

"You needed Boldrei to tell you that?" Gerith asked, stunned.

The paladin ignored the halfling.

"Are there still dragons here?" Omax asked.

"No," Gerith said. "Nobody's ever seen a live dragon here, though if you ask me that isn't very reassuring. I'd almost rather meet a dragon than whatever frightens the dragons away."

"Or whatever they abandoned here," Eraina said.

"I'll wait in this area," Gerith said, glancing from one of them to the next helplessly. "Are you sure you don't want to turn back? If you want to tell Dalan we didn't find anything . . ." His words died away when he saw Eraina's unflinching glare. "Right then," he said. "I guess lying is out."

"We'll be careful, Gerith," Seren said.

"When you're ready to leave, or if you get in any trouble, fire one of these," Gerith said, offering a half dozen thick, cloth-wrapped tubes to Seren. "Tristam made them. Break them in half and the air will ignite them. They let off a bright light and explode in a cloud of smoke. I'll see them, day or night."

"Thanks, Gerith," Seren said, tucking the tubes into one of her pouches. "We'll be careful."

"See that you do," the halfling said. "My story won't be any good without its heroine." He smiled weakly, then tugged at his glidewing's reins. Blizzard hopped into the air and spread its wings with a crack, soaring away over the plains.

"Where do we start?" Seren asked, staring out at the vast expanse. "It's larger than I thought it would be. Overwood could be anywhere."

"Then it doesn't matter where we start," Eraina said, starting off down the hill.

Seren followed, with Omax bringing up the rear. When they

drew closer, Eraina knelt in the thinning grass. She knelt to pick up a fragment of white stone, then stared out at the bleached expanse with wide eyes. "The ground is bone," she said, gingerly setting the fragment back down. "The entire valley is paved in fossilized bone."

"There is no wind," Omax observed. "This place is undisturbed by the elements. I can see why the halflings would find this place unnatural."

"Let's find Kiris and leave," Seren said.

The others had no argument. They continued onward, the gentle slope of the plains becoming a steep incline. The scattered bone fragments became thicker until they covered the area like loose shale. Combined with the steep incline, the path became treacherous. Seren was forced to kick loose bone away with each step she took, seeking purchase underneath. The sounds of clattering debris resounded into the valley, making Seren wince.

Omax pitched forward as the ground cracked noisily beneath his feet. His right leg sank into the surface up to his thigh, sending a ripple of scattered bone outward. Seren felt the ground pitch beneath her. Knowing there was little she could do, she leapt forward into a roll rather than fight for balance. She tumbled down the valley wall, grunting as the rough surfaces gouged her arms and legs. She finally tumbled to a halt and, finding nothing broken, came to her feet again. She stood in a forest of larger bone fragments. Broken skulls and hipbones lay like fallen boulders. Enormous ribs and claws reached for the sky like spectral trees, crisscrossing in a ghastly canopy. Spires of bare stone erupted from the bone in places, painted with bizarre sienna patterns. The air was still and musty with the faint taste of lime.

Higher up the slope, Eraina helped Omax pull his trapped leg free. The warforged was annoyed but uninjured as he wrenched himself out of the bones. The dragon bones were hollow, like a bird's, and Omax's heavy tread had broken through the surface of one of the larger ones. The Boneyard was covered with layers upon layers of bone. Seren wondered how deep the remains went.

"Seren?" Omax called out, unable to find her amid the broken landscape.

"I'm all right," she said, studying the steep, unstable slope. "I don't think I can get back up to where you are."

"We'll come to you," Eraina said, picking her way gingerly down the slope.

"Be careful," Seren said.

The gigantic skulls of countless long-dead dragons stared silently down at her. Though it had been early morning when they had arrived, the valley was painted in a dusty half-light. She could no longer find the sun. The Boneyard radiated a sense of timelessness. "We have been here for ages," the bones seemed to say, "We will be here when you are gone."

There was something distinctly . . . wrong about the Boneyard. The shadows did not match the light as they should. The colors were not right. The patterns painted upon the stones twisted when Seren looked at them from the corner of her eye. Seren found it both disturbing and somehow familiar. She was an unwelcome intruder in a place where time stood still. She remembered Omax's words; it was obvious why the halflings avoided this place. She retreated into the curve of a fallen jawbone and waited for her friends.

Omax led the way down to Seren, each step cautious and calculated. Eraina followed, spear clutched in both hands as she searched for any sign that the noise had attracted enemies.

Seren saw it first, a furtive movement in the darkness between two towering rib bones. Eraina and Omax did not notice. As they approached, Seren peered out just enough for them to see her. She silently waved them away. A brief look of confusion flickered across Eraina's face, but Omax understood. The warforged marched directly past Seren's hiding place. The paladin followed with an uncomfortable frown. Several seconds after they had moved on, the shadows moved again. Seren saw it more clearly as it moved closer, a young woman in tattered robes, darting through the jagged white forest. The woman didn't offer a second glance in Seren's direction, following Eraina and Omax instead. Seren guessed that she had been drawn by the earlier noise and was investigating the new arrivals but arrived too late to see Seren hide.

Seren crept out from behind the jawbone, falling into step behind the strange woman. Seren could see now that her robes were blue velvet, once obviously of fine quality, now torn and stained with the Boneyard's bleached dust. Her dark hair hung long and unkempt about her shoulders, adding to her savage appearance. Many heavy pouches hung from her belt but she carried no obvious weapons. Seren caught the faint smell of sulfur and jasmine. Seren tucked her dagger carefully away. She moved to the center of the rough path, hands clearly visible and far from her body but ready to spring away instantly if she needed to.

"Kiris Overwood," Seren said, loudly enough so that her friends ahead would hear.

The woman whirled, one hand reaching for her belt, eyes blazing with fear. She stopped when she saw Seren held no weapons, and realized that Eraina and Omax were now standing behind her.

"You aren't Cyran," she said, studying Seren's face intently. A brief look of relief shone on her dirty face, only to be replaced by intense suspicion. "Who are you? How do you know me?"

"My name is Seren Morisse," Seren said, keeping her voice calm and soothing. Kiris moved with the tense energy of a wild animal, as if, finding herself trapped, she would flee or attack at any moment. "I work for Dalan d'Cannith. We need your help."

"Dalan d'Cannith," Kiris said, spitting out the name. "Why am I not surprised?"

"What do you mean?" Seren asked.

The heavy thud of a large and heavy thing falling erupted behind Seren, scattering the bones.

"Khyber," Kiris hissed. "Run!"

Seren looked back in time to see a second shadowy mass distend, like a raindrop, from the end of a twenty-foot claw. It fell somewhere behind the rumpled heaps of broken bone, landing with a thud. Another, third shape struck the ground somewhere to their left, in the darkness. Kiris rushed past them, scrambling over heaps of shattered bone without hesitation.

"What?" Omax said, following the wizard

Then a shrieking, gibbering screech filled the air. Seren screamed as the sound pressed into her mind, driving away all reason. A shapeless mass of flesh covered with fanged mouths and wide eyes launched from the bones and struck Omax in the chest, pinning the warforged to the ground. Another erupted from the path on the other side, lashing at Eraina with fleshy arms covered with countless biting mouths. The paladin parried the blows with her spear, moving to block its path to Seren. The thief knelt among the bones, laughing hysterically as the world melted and swirled before her eyes. In the distance, she saw Kiris unleash a bolt of arcane power into another thrashing beast and continue running without them.

"Seren, focus," Eraina shouted, stabbing at the nearest creature with her spear.

Omax rolled to his feet, still struggling. The creature chewed hungrily at his chest and limbs. Unable to dislodge it, he instead positioned himself over a sharp bone outcropping and fell forward with all his weight. Something snapped noisily and the creature's mad gibbering became a shriek of pain. Its limbs flailed violently, pushing the warforged away. Omax fell to one side, out of its grasp, leaving the thing impaled on the now fractured spike.

Seren's hand found her dagger and clasped the hilt. Her world drew into focus again. She leapt to her feet, holding the weapon in one hand. The weapon would likely do little good against these things, but being armed once again lent her confidence.

"These are the same creatures we fought in Black Pit," Omax said as another rose over a heap of bony debris.

"More are coming," Kiris said as two more dripped from bony overhangs in the distance. "These are aberrations of Xoriat, gibbering creatures that corrupt the earth and spread madness to paralyze their prey. We cannot fight so many. Follow me if you can, but do not expect me to wait for you."

The gibbering sounds became louder again. They pressed in like a wave, clawing at their minds, seeking to tear away reason. Seren's eyes narrowed as she fought for focus. She saw another flash of magic far ahead. Kiris was abandoning them . . . but she was fighting her way toward *something*.

"Omax, grab Eraina's hand," Seren said, sheathing her dagger and digging through her pouches.

The warforged complied, though both he and the paladin looked at her with confusion. Seren drew out two of Gerith's flares, broke the ends, tossed them to the ground, and grasped Omax's other arm. The manic gibbering was broken by a loud shriek, a flash of light, and a choking cloud of smoke.

"Follow me," Seren shouted, charging in the direction Kiris had fled. She hoped they had the presence of mind to follow, because she certainly wasn't strong enough to drag Omax against his will.

They trudged along blindly after her, stumbling out of the smoke. The smell of burning, rotten flesh wafted over them, rising from one of the creatures Kiris had killed. Seren saw a patch of brown movement and ran after it, just in time to see the wizard disappear through a cleft in the bone wall.

Seren hesitated only a moment before darting through after her.

CHAPTER
TWENTY

At first glance, the crack in the wall appeared to extend only a few feet. Kiris had disappeared without a trace. Seren reached out to find the inside wall was actually a dull white curtain, blending seamlessly with the bones. She pushed it aside and stepped into a small natural cavern. A rumpled blanket lay in one corner, surrounded by scattered books. A collection of oddly shaped bone fragments littered the center of the room. The remains of a small fire smoldered in the corner, smoke trickling through a crack in the roof. The chamber smelled of stale sweat and smoke. Kiris Overwood stood in the far corner of the cavern, watching her suspiciously.

"Mind the wards," she said, pointing at Seren's feet with a slender copper wand. "It is safe for you to step over but break their border and the aberrations of Xoriat will swiftly come for us."

The mad shrieking that filled the Boneyard punctuated her warning. Seren looked down and saw a row of shimmering silver runes spanning the threshold. She stepped over with care, as did Eraina. A loud crack sounded as Omax forced his thick bulk through the narrow opening and carefully followed them inside. Kiris darted past them, pulling the curtain over the opening again and offering them a suspicious look.

"You picked a fine time to come here," she said. "Some days the Boneyard is quiet. This is not one of them."

"Are you certain we are safe here?" Eraina asked.

"Quite certain," Kiris said. "The wards both conceal our presence from the beasts and bar their entrance. They cannot even hear us, but I ask that you keep your voices down regardless. While my magic protects against the horrors from beyond this world, sometimes more mundane threats prowl this place. Fortune seekers. Grave robbers. Opportunists." She looked at each of them sharply. "And tell your weapon to keep its distance." She gestured at Omax with her wand.

Omax folded his heavy arms across his chest, neither backing away nor making any aggressive movement.

"Omax means no harm," Seren said.

"So it claims, I am sure," Kiris answered. "Be wary. I saw the damage those abominable things can do in the war, and I know this one well. Tristam was a fool to ever repair it."

"On my honor as a Sentinel Marshal and a Spear of Boldrei, I vouch for the warforged," Eraina said.

"A Sentinel Marshal working for Dalan d'Cannith?" Kiris said. "I thought you mercenaries were more selective."

"There is no need to threaten Omax or insult me," Eraina said, her voice cool.

"I mean no insult, I merely wish to gauge your motivations," Kiris said. "As for threats, that was no threat; it was a warning. If you would ally yourselves with a warforged, you are already in danger. Those beasts have a disturbing propensity for violence and betrayal."

"She is right," Omax said. "Yet I assure you, Lady Overwood, I have set that path behind me. I serve Tristam Xain now."

"Tristam?" Kiris asked, recognition flickering in her eyes. "He is here?"

"He is repairing our damaged airship," Seren said.

Kiris's angry scowl softened in confusion, but only for an instant. "What are you doing here?" she asked. "How did Dalan find me?"

"We found an enchanted hand lens that you created," Seren said. "It was in the possession of a changeling named Marth. We know that it can read certain codes in Ashrem d'Cannith's journals, but we don't know how it works."

Kiris's eyes widened. "You took the lens from Marth?" she asked. "Is he still alive?"

"For now," Seren said.

Kiris frowned. "So Dalan still seeks the Legacy," she said. "I cannot help you, but neither will I offer you harm. You may remain here until the creatures have gone, but then you must leave and forget you saw me here."

"Then while we wait, perhaps you could tell us what you know about this Marth person," Eraina said. "He is responsible for the murder of Jamus Roland and likely Bishop Llaine Grove as well."

"Llaine is dead?" Kiris said, looking up at Eraina with wide eyes. "Llaine's self-righteousness and blind faith in those who supported the war was galling at times, but I can't believe Marth would kill him."

"You are gravely deluded, woman," Eraina said.

"I saw Marth murder Jamus Roland," Seren said. "He has been hunting us in Ashrem's old airship, *Moon*."

"You were aboard that ship on the Day of Mourning," Eraina said. "How did you survive, and why did you allow the world to think you were dead?"

"Why should I care what the world thinks of me?" Kiris said in a hollow voice. "My life ended in every way that matters on the Day of Mourning. Ashrem is gone. My homeland is gone. My entire family perished. Together, Marth and I repaired *Moon* enough to limp out of Cyre. I have been here since we escaped, helping him with his work from afar."

Eraina's stance shifted. The change was slight, but Seren could see that the paladin now held her spear ready. Her eyes were angry, intent. "So you are his ally," she said. "Who is he? Where is his home port? How did he gather his troops?"

"Marth is a visionary," Kiris said after a long silence. "There is no other word for it. He is the sort that others naturally wish to follow. His followers are Cyran soldiers who were fortunate enough to be outside their homeland when Cyre was destroyed." She closed her eyes, as if pained by the recollection. "He is a patriot and a hero, not a killer."

"You are lying," Eraina said. "You lie to us and to yourself. I hear it in your quavering voice. You've suspected what he truly is. What we've told you doesn't surprise you at all, does it?"

"Marth is a good man," Kiris protested, lowering her eyes. "Or he was, once. But you are right, Marshal. I have seen him change since the Day of Mourning, but were it not for him I would be dead or worse. The things we have seen, the horror that Cyre has become, have driven him to desperation. I know he has concealed things from me. His cause is noble, but I have seen the rage that burns inside him. Now, to hear that he might have had a part in these killings . . ."

"What is his plan?" Eraina demanded.

"He only wishes to finish Ashrem d'Cannith's work," Kiris said. "He wishes to complete the Legacy. He returns here from time to time, and I share what I have learned with him. He applies my findings to his work."

"Why here?" Omax asked.

The wizard sighed. "What do you know of the Draconic Prophecy?" she asked.

Eraina removed her left glove and rolled up her sleeve, exposing the dragonmark on her forearm. The twisting pattern closely resembled the marks on the stones outside. "I know some," the paladin said. "The Prophecy appears as a series of arcane symbols, like these. It manifests on the earth, the sky, and some say even the dragonmarks that we bear are part of it. The dragons created it as a guide to what is to come, and what has come to be. The writings often carry magical power."

"Partially right," Kiris said. "Though I do not believe the dragons truly created the Prophecy. I think they were merely the first to discover it and thus it bears their name. After all, if a dragon wishes to name something after itself, who are we to argue?"

"So where does it come from?" Seren asked.

"I do not know," Kiris said. "Such questions cannot be answered. Who created the Sovereign Host? Does the Marshal's inability to answer that question make Boldrei less worthy a goddess?"

"Leave my faith out of this," Eraina warned.

"I meant no offense," Kiris said. "I only mean that there is much about this world that none of us understand. We must take some things on faith as we search for answers, and the origin of the Prophecy is one of those things. We can rely only upon that which we know. The Prophecy is ancient. The Prophecy is powerful. The Prophecy—as far as I know—is never wrong."

"So what do those marks outside say?" Seren asked.

"Many things," Kiris said. "Most of what I have deciphered speaks of a great battle between dragonkind and the demons of Khyber. It says that the dragons would sever the thread that binds the worlds and rend the very essence of their enemies. That battle came to pass before the dawn of mankind. Now the bones and the Prophecy are all that remain."

Eraina's face darkened. "There is more you have not told us," she said with grave certainty. "What does the Legacy have to do with this?"

"Ashrem," Kiris said. "He first found this place many years ago. With help, he deciphered many of the writings outside. He learned how the dragons defeated the demons. They created an . . . anchor, if you will. An artifact that negates magic of all kinds. All arcane energies are forcibly and permanently canceled. All enchantments are destroyed. All gateways to other dimensions permanently closed. The tool the dragons forged to defeat the demons is what inspired the Legacy. Ashrem used the principles he learned here to create it. While Marth searches for Ashrem's lost journals, I labor here to understand the Prophecy as Ashrem understood it. My skill at artifice is nothing compared to Marth or Ashrem, but I have always had a talent for deciphering language and codes. I have learned much."

"And what would the Legacy do to creatures of magic?" Omax asked.

"See the results for yourself," she said, gesturing at the bone samples on the floor. "Magic is a dragon's lifeblood, and it was stripped from them. The other dragons left their brethren where they fell as a tribute to their sacrifice. The dragons who activated the original Legacy knew what would happen, but to ensure the future of our world they were willing to die."

"The Legacy destroys all magic?" Seren asked.

"With how heavily the Five Nations rely on magic," Eraina said, "a thing like that could throw entire cities into chaos."

"It is not a weapon, it is a *tool*," Kiris said. "If used improperly the potential for damage is great; I will not deny that. Why do you think we hide what we do? Marth intends to use the Legacy to tame the wild energies of the Mournland and restore the former grandeur that was our home. He wishes to restore Cyre."

"Marth has deceived you, Kiris," Eraina said. "If he truly wished to help Cyre, he would approach the nations of Khorvaire and ask their aid. King Boranel would gladly aid him if only to remove the Cyran refugees from his borders. Marth need not steal and murder to reach his goal. He chooses a path of evil."

Kiris laughed. "Is that so?" she asked. "Then which nation does your master, Dalan, represent? What good deed will he do when he finds the Legacy?"

"Dalan is not my master," Eraina said. "I seek only justice."

"Regardless, if you believe Dalan is any more honorable than Marth, or that the kings of Khorvaire can be entrusted with the Legacy, you are the one who is deluded. The surviving nations pretend to grieve for Cyre and offer its survivors what scraps they deign to spare, but they do not truly wish to see the Mournland restored. As far as they are concerned, the death of Cyre means one less enemy. If any of them gained the power of the Legacy, they would only use it against one another."

"Better Dalan than Marth," Seren said. "I saw him kill Jamus Roland with my own eyes."

"I don't believe you," Kiris said, though the hesitation before she spoke betrayed her doubt. "I see your disgust. You think I am a fool, but we have come too far. I cannot allow myself to believe Marth is what you claim he is. I cannot turn against him."

"You are blind and pathetic," Eraina said.

"Am I?" Kiris asked, looking at the paladin. "Perhaps I believe he can become the hero he used to be. You embrace a killer who seeks redemption," she pointed at the warforged. "Yet I do so and I am a fool?"

"If he seeks redemption, shooting us down over Talenta is a curious way to start," Omax said.

"Then what if you are right?" Kiris asked. "What if Marth is a madman? If I turn against him it would be one more in a long chain of betrayals heaped upon him. What hope would there be for him then?"

"You are a fool defending a murderer," Eraina said.

VOYAGE OF THE MOURNING DAWN

Kiris looked at the tip of Eraina's spear. "I would think that a paladin of Boldrei would recognize the power of faith. Tell Dalan what I have said. I hope he will understand. I cannot help you, but neither will I tell Marth that you have been here."

"You misunderstand your situation, Overwood," Eraina said. "I am a Sentinel Marshal. You have confessed to aiding a murder suspect. You *will* accompany us. I do not offer you a choice."

"You cannot force me to leave," Kiris said.

"Is that a threat?" Eraina asked, hefting her spear. "I do not fear your magic, wizard."

Seren took a step away from Kiris, moving closer to Omax.

"I will not hurt you," Kiris said. "Neither can you compel me to leave."

Eraina held the wizard's gaze for several moments and then lowered the point of her spear. With a swift, deliberate movement, she scratched a gouge across the wards that protected the door. Outside, the shrieking of the creatures that haunted the Boneyard began to build.

"What have you done, Marshal?" Kiris asked in horror.

"I present a choice," Eraina said, pointing her spear in the wizard's direction. "You can leave the Boneyard with us, or you can remain here and see if these beasts offer you greater mercy than I do. Can you restore your wards before they arrive?"

Kiris's face paled. "I cannot," she said, "but I would rather Marth find me here dead than betray him."

"Idiocy!" Eraina snapped, advancing on the wizard.

"Wait," Seren said, moving between them. "Dalan said you might not wish to help." She took the sealed envelope from her pocket and offered it to Kiris. "He asked me to give you this."

The wizard accepted it with a pensive eye. She broke the seal and hurriedly tore it open, taking out the letter and letting the envelope fall to the floor. Her eyes moved across the page several times, as if she did not believe what she had read.

Her expression grew slowly more troubled. Outside, the beasts drew closer.

"We must leave now," Omax warned, watching the door. "This is a bad place to be trapped."

"Ever the expert negotiator, Dalan," Kiris said in a bitter, subdued voice. "Very well." She creased the letter sharply and dropped it in the fire. She darted for her scattered scrolls, quickly gathering those that were most important and stuffing them into an empty bag. She hoisted the bag over one shoulder and stepped through the curtain. "Stay close. I know the way out."

Omax and Eraina followed. Seren remained a step behind, still stunned by the sudden change in Kiris's demeanor. She glanced back at the discarded envelope, still bearing half a House Cannith seal, and the letter that now burned in the small fire.

She wondered exactly what sort of promise Dalan had made.

Chapter
Twenty-One

Kiris led them through the bone-littered paths to another narrow tunnel in a heap of enormous ribcages. Looking back the way they had come, she gestured nervously at the entrance.

"This passes beneath the valley and will lead back out onto the plains, the way you came," she said.

"Then you go first, wizard," Eraina said, watching Kiris.

Kiris sighed. She reached for her pouch, causing Eraina to heft her spear. Kiris slowly drew a glowing stone from within.

"It's just a light, Marshal," Kiris said.

"Give me your bags and your pouches," Eraina ordered.

"If I meant you any harm with my magic, would I not have attacked you already?" Kiris asked.

"If you mean no harm," Eraina said, "there should be no harm in surrendering them."

Kiris opened her mouth to argue, but the shrieks of the Boneyard beasts drew closer. She quickly took the bag from her shoulder, stuffed her numerous belt pouches inside, and handed it to the paladin. Eraina absently passed it to Seren so that she could keep both hands on her spear. Seren pulled the bag over one shoulder, still stunned by the brusque change that had come over the paladin since they had found Kiris.

"Lead the way," Eraina said stiffly.

Kiris entered the passage, holding her stone high to light the way. Seren entered after Eraina, leaving Omax to bring up the rear. The mad gibbering cries of the creatures drew nearer, passing almost directly overhead. Kiris looked back, the dim light of her stone painting ghastly shadows on her thin features. She placed a finger across her lips, though none truly needed the warning. After several tense moments the creatures continued on their hunt.

The narrow tunnel twisted downward. The air was cold and dry beneath the Boneyard. The faint lime taste was much stronger here. Fine white powder covered the stone walls. Occasionally the light of Kiris's stone would reflect upon a dragonmark scrawled upon the wall. The symbols would sometimes catch the light shine brilliantly in a mosaic of dazzling color, continuing to shimmer in the darkness for some time after they passed on.

"It is just as well that you are forcing me to leave," Kiris whispered. "I think the Prophecy has grown silent here anyway."

"Silent?" Seren asked.

"The Draconic Prophecy is a thing of magic," Kiris said. "Parts of it can be read only under certain conditions. It has taken me some time to understand it as Ashrem did, but one thing is clear. The writings here are incomplete. The tale is continued elsewhere."

"Where?" Eraina asked.

Kiris looked back at Seren with a pained expression. "Why are the three of you working with Dalan on this? Surely you know that he'll only surrender the Legacy to House Cannith. They will use it to amass power, selling it to the highest bidders. Have you thought nothing of the damage that would do?"

"I don't know anything about magic," Seren answered, "but I know Marth murdered my friend."

"Keep walking," Eraina said coldly.

Kiris's gaze flicked to the ground.

"I can see that you hate me, Marshal," Kiris said. "I know how your house and your goddess view the law. I could be no more despicable than if I had killed those men myself. I can respect that, though I regret it. But why do you hate me so, Seren? I did not kill your friend, nor was I even aware that he existed."

"Because you were used," Seren said. "You work for an evil man, yet you refuse to see it."

Kiris laughed. "Then we have much in common," she said.

"What are you talking about?" Seren said.

"You would not believe me," Kiris said. "No more than I believe you."

"All of us already know that Dalan d'Cannith is a manipulative weasel," Eraina said. "Our alliance is one of mutual benefit, not blind subservience. Now be silent."

Kiris continued walking, head bowed. Their trek through the tunnels went on for over an hour, winding underneath the dead earth. At last, a sliver of light shone ahead and Kiris tucked her glowing stone back into her pocket. The tunnel opened on the plains at the foot of a mountain wall. They stepped out onto the soft grass, squinting painfully as their eyes adjusted to the afternoon sun. Kiris slumped against a stone, exhausted. Eraina stood near the wizard, carefully watching her for any attempt to escape. Seren took one of Gerith's cloth tubes from her belt and fired it into the air to signal the halfling.

Several minutes passed, with nothing but soft white clouds marking the sky overhead.

"Something is wrong," Omax said at last. "Gerith should have seen the smoke by now."

"Over here," hissed a voice from behind them.

Gerith crouched amid the uneven terrain at the foot of the

mountain, looking harried and out of breath. He gestured to them impatiently, eyes fixed on the western horizon.

Kiris looked up, eyes wide. "You brought a halfling with you?" she asked.

"Gerith Snowshale, pleased to make your acquaintance," Gerith said, offering a mischievous grin. "Now hurry. We need to get out of sight!"

They climbed the rocky wall to join the scout just as the rapid footfalls of approaching clawfoots sounded across the plains.

"We need to leave, quickly," Kiris said. Over the rolling hills, a half dozen halfling hunters mounted on clawfoot dinosaurs galloped toward them. Seren recognized the one that rode at the head of the pack - Chief Rossa's bodyguard, Koranth.

"Ghost Talons," Kiris whispered. "They've been spying on me for almost a year."

"Dalan made a deal with them for repairs when our ship crashed," Eraina said. "He also offered to help them find you, though he did not intend to fulfill that bargain."

"The Ghost Talons follow me when I leave the Boneyard to trade for supplies," Kiris said. "They even hire nonhalfling travelers to draw me out so they can question me. I was afraid your Gerith was one of them."

"They saw your flare, Seren," Gerith said.

"Sorry. I didn't know they were following us," Seren said.

"I didn't know either," Gerith said. "I didn't notice them following us until you went inside the Boneyard."

"Who are they working for?" Seren asked.

"I do not know," Kiris answered. "As long as I could avoid them, it was never a concern."

"If someone else is interested in what you're doing here, I'm not surprised they hired the locals to keep an eye on you," Gerith said. "The Talons are just the sort to take that job. They're enterprising sorts."

"Enterprising?" Kiris said with a laugh. "You mean scavengers. They hide near the Boneyard because they know that even the Valenar avoid the accursed place. When and if the elves invade, the Ghost Talons can be the first to loot the battlefields. I do not know what interest they have in me. They could be working for anyone."

"Strange that halflings give you so much trouble," Eraina said. "I'd think Marth and his followers could frighten them off for you."

Kiris hesitated. "I have not told Marth about the Ghost Talons," she said. "I was . . . concerned that he might overreact."

"Kill them, you mean," Eraina said. "So much for your faith in your hero."

Below, the Talons had gathered in a small circle just at the tunnel exit. One had dismounted and was studying the grass with a practiced eye. He looked back at Koranth and mumbled something too quiet for them to hear.

"Servants of Dalan d'Cannith," Koranth shouted in a clear voice. "I know that you can hear me; your tracks are fresh. Please reveal yourselves. We do not wish to do you harm. Chief Rossa is eager to see you return. He has dispatched his finest warriors to escort you back to the camp. Do not be afraid."

"More *hmael*?" Seren asked.

Gerith nodded rapidly.

"Should we fight them?" Eraina asked. "Six enemies aren't such terrible odds. I've seen worse."

"I think you miscounted," Gerith said. "I see twelve. Those clawfoots aren't just ponies, Eraina."

Koranth continued to wait in uneasy silence, the last echoes of his voice still returning over the mountains. He gestured to his riders and two of them darted off, one in each direction, searching for them.

"Incidentally, your master sends his greetings," Koranth

shouted. "He is well guarded by my loyal hunters, and will continue to be until you return safely to the Ghost Talons."

"So now it has come to threats," Eraina said in a low growl. "They are holding Dalan."

"What do we do?" Seren asked.

"Honestly, we may as well surrender," Gerith said. "They're all hunters and this is their territory. It's only a matter of time before they find us."

"Can't you escape on Blizzard?" Seren asked.

"Sure," Gerith said. "I can avoid Koranth and his amateurs forever, but Blizzard isn't big enough to carry three humans, a warforged, and me."

Seren knelt and dropped Kiris's bag, hurriedly digging through its contents. She removed the pouches of spell reagents and returned them to Kiris, leaving only the books and scrolls inside.

"What are you doing, Seren?" Eraina asked.

"We came here looking for Kiris because she could help us understand Ashrem's work," Seren said. "Maybe the halflings, or whoever they really work for, just want to get their hands on her work too." She handed the bag to Gerith. "Can you get these back to Tristam without being seen?"

"Of course," Gerith said.

"Those books are mine," Kiris protested.

"And if you let Gerith take them back to our ship, you have a chance of keeping them," Seren said. "Koranth won't give you an offer like that."

Kiris only shrugged in agreement and secured her reagent pouches to her belt.

"You sure you'll be all right?" Gerith asked, looking up at Seren in concern.

"I don't think Koranth wants to hurt us," Seren said. "As long as he thinks he's in control, we'll have time to plan. If they really have taken Dalan prisoner, I'd be surprised if he hasn't already come up with an escape plan."

"Good point," Gerith said. "I hadn't thought of that," The halfling took the satchel and climbed onto Blizzard's back. "Good luck to you, ladies. You too, Omax. Be safe."

Gerith whispered something curtly to his glidewing. The creature made several agile leaps up the rock face, away from the hunters and out of their view. There was only the subtle flap of leather and a blur of motion across the sky to mark his departure. Blizzard's pale blue underbelly perfectly camouflaged it from below.

"Are you lost?" Koranth shouted. "Are the plains so confusing? Shall I send my hunters to guide you to us?"

"No need, we're right here," Seren shouted back.

She stepped out of her hiding place, scaling down the rock wall carefully. Eraina, Kiris, and Omax followed. Koranth scrutinized each of them carefully, especially Omax, who stood at eye level to him even mounted on his steed. The other two roving hunters returned rapidly, their mounts moving with startling speed.

"Dusty and bruised but not wounded," Koranth said. "Rossa will be pleased that you are in good health. Lady Overwood, I presume? We have been looking for you for a long time."

"What do you want with me?" Kiris asked.

"That is Rossa's business, not mine," Koranth answered. He scanned the area briefly. "Where is your scout?"

"He fled," Seren said. "The Boneyard terrified him."

Koranth looked at Eraina. "Is that true, paladin?" he asked, looking at her shrewdly.

"Gerith was quite terrified of the Boneyard's curse," Eraina said. "He left as quickly as he dared."

"That's what they get for trusting a Snowshale," said one of the other halflings. Koranth and the others laughed. Seren realized abruptly that the hunter had spoken in his native tongue, and that Tristam's bracelet had translated the words.

"Truly a pity," Koranth said with a smug grin. "Never fear, we shall guide you back to our camp. You'll have to walk, unfortunately. Our steeds are notoriously intolerant of unfamiliar riders."

Not to mention that if they tried to escape, the clawfoot riders could quickly run them down. Seren smiled at Koranth, trying not to be unnerved by the violence she detected just beneath his veneer of etiquette. Some of the other hunters were less subtle, scowling openly at her. She had the feeling that the Koranth was almost disappointed that they had chosen to surrender peacefully. The halfling gestured with his spear and moved his steed to one side, signaling for them to begin walking.

The hunters rode in a loose circle around them as they traveled back to the Ghost Talon village. In time, the sun set and the hunters struck a rough camp in the shadows of a short cliff. The halflings began cooking the evening meal and pitching tents. Seren stepped forward and offered to help but was ordered to return to the others with a gesture and a curt word that Tristam's bracelet didn't understand. The message was clear. Their status as "guests" was merely a convenient illusion. They were prisoners. Seren returned to sit beside Omax, Eraina, and Kiris. Koranth arrived shortly afterward, depositing a pot of steaming beans, a jug of water, tin plates, and clay cups.

"Thank you," Kiris said in the halfling tongue.

Koranth smiled faintly. "I know that all of you are concerned by our presence here," he said. "Please, do not be. I assure you, we have your best interests at heart. The Ghost Talons have been retained by Baron Zorlan d'Cannith, who has taken a personal interest in your adventures. All of you will be treated as guests of the Ghost Talons until the Baron's emissaries arrive to collect you."

"Politics," Eraina said bitterly. "So that's why your tribe was so interested in this place. I thought your chief just wanted his ring back? Or was that a lie too?"

"A ring?" Koranth asked. "I remember hearing nothing about a ring. Perhaps Rossa misspoke. He is an old man. He says many strange things."

Koranth's smug grin faded as he looked past them, to the west, his eyes narrowing in concern. Seren looked in the same direction. A faint red glow was visible on the far horizon. A plume of gray smoke curled into the night sky.

"Pian, Maern," he said, calling to two of the other hunters. "Wait here and guard our guests. The rest of you come with me. Something is happening in the village."

"It's Marth," Seren warned. "The one who shot down our ship. He's attacking your tribe."

Kiris's face was pale as she looked at the distant fire.

"Then he will rue that he crossed the Ghost Talon tribe," Koranth said.

"We can help," Omax said. "We have fought him before."

Koranth climbed onto his clawfoot with a grimace. "You cannot keep up with us, outsiders. This is not your fight. The Ghost Talons stand and fall on their own."

He kicked his mount into stride and loped off across the plains, three of his hunters following in formation behind him. The other two remained behind with nervous expressions, watching as their brethren departed.

"We should go, Maern," one of the halflings said, his words translated by Tristam's bracelet. "Our families are down there."

"We were told to remain," the other said, though his reply held no conviction. His eyes were on the fire as well, and they were filled with fear. Seren felt as angry and helpless as they did. She wanted to help, or at least convince them to go to their tribe, but what could she say? And then she remembered.

"*Kapen hara*," she said to the hunters. "Family before all else."

They both turned to her, eyes wide, and then looked at each other. Maern bowed his head shamefully. Pian looked back at her with a steady, building resolve. He clapped his comrade on the shoulder and ran to his steed. Maern paused to offer a mumbled thanks and hopped on his steed as well. Together, the two rode off across the plains to defend their village.

Eraina, Omax, Kiris, and Seren stood in the now-abandoned camp, watching as the hunters galloped off across the plains. None said a word for a long moment. They were free now. They could easily escape to *Karia Naille*, assuming Marth had not found it. Tristam might be finished with the repairs. If Gerith had arrived, they might already be preparing to take off.

"Do what you must," Eraina said, hefting her spear as she stared at the distant fire. "I plan to fight. Keep up with me if you can."

The paladin charged off across the plains, not waiting for the others. Omax fell into step behind her. Seren stopped only long enough to look back at Kiris, still sitting beside the fire. If she left the wizard behind, she left behind the first real chance to understand what Tristam and the others had been seeking, and perhaps let an enemy escape to threaten them another day. But as she watched the silhouettes of her friends and the halfling hunters charging to an uncertain fate, she remembered the night that Jamus Roland died. If Tristam and Omax had not stood beside her, she might have died as well. Could she let the Ghost Talons face Marth alone? Could she abandon Dalan to him?

There was really no choice at all.

Chapter
Twenty-Two

Tristam peered up over the side of the ship's railing, removing his spectacles with an exhausted grin. "I think I have it, Aeven," Tristam said. "Try it now."

The dryad's eyes remained closed. Her hands were still clasped in the ball of seething blue fire. Slowly, she extended her fingers. The fire spilled out to each side, extending in two snaking tendrils. They extended around the sides of the ship and met at the newly repaired keel strut beneath. The flame wavered for several seconds, then resolved itself into a steadily burning ring.

Aeven slowly opened her translucent green eyes. She gazed into the fire in wonder. Her childlike face broke into a pleased smile. "Yes, my friend," she whispered to the elemental. "You can stay for a while longer. The tinker has fixed it so we can remain together." She dropped lightly from the upper arm of the ship and kissed Tristam lightly on the lips. "The ship says thank you."

Tristam blinked in surprise. Aeven was already gone, having flitted away to sit on the rail near her figurehead. The young artificer could not help but smile. He put his spectacles back on, dropped down from the rope ladder, and stood back to admire his work. *Karia Naille* had been hoisted on a hastily constructed scaffolding. The ship was not as pretty as she once was. Chunks of the hull were missing and the keel arm was obviously an improvised replacement, but it would do. She was alive again.

"Excellent work, Xain," Zed Arthen said, limping up beside Tristam. The inquisitive had fashioned a crutch out of the halfling lumber and still favored his left leg.

"I couldn't have done it if Aeven hadn't held the elemental here," Tristam said with a sigh. "And if Pherris wasn't such a skilled pilot, the damage would have been a lot worse. We still need to get her to a proper shipwright. She might not even hold together that long."

"I'm not a man who commonly distributes praise, Xain," Zed said, giving Tristam a pointed look. "Best learn to recognize it, or I won't bother next time. I've walked away from more than one airship crash in my time. This the first time I've seen the ship *get back up*. Ash himself couldn't have done a finer job." Zed looked furtively around the canyon. "Especially under the circumstances."

A dozen halfling laborers sat in a circle around a small campfire, laughing and chatting as they prepared their evening meal. The trio of threehorns that had hoisted the airship onto its scaffolding browsed nearby, searching the canyon for sparse foliage.

"How many times is it now, Zed?" Tristam asked quietly.

"Three times," Zed said. "Three times I've caught those halflings trying to sabotage the repairs. They don't know that I know, but I'm sure they're wondering why the scaffolding didn't fall down when it was supposed to."

"Why are they doing it?" Tristam asked. "Do you think they're working for Marth?"

"Doubtful," Zed said. "If that were the case they would probably just kill us, or sabotage the ship so it crashed after takeoff and kill us." Zed looked worried. "Are you sure they didn't do that?"

"No," Tristam said confidently. "The ship is fine. Aeven would know if it had been harmed."

Zed nodded. "Then they're just trying to delay us," the inquisitive said. "They want to keep us here as long as possible."

"Why?" Tristam asked.

"Good question," Zed said. "Toughest part of being an inquisitive is recognizing when not to obsess over the wrong questions. I'm not as interested in learning what their game is as I am in removing us from it."

Zed continued staring at the halflings for a long moment, searching for any clue as to their motives. He gave Tristam a questioning look when he realized the artificer was studying him in turn.

"What?" he said.

"Why didn't you want me to tell Dalan that I recognized *Moon* the first time I saw her?" Tristam asked.

"It would have made things prematurely complicated," Zed answered, looking away again. "Dalan didn't see *Moon* until she attacked us over the plains. Now think about what he's done since then. Why do you think he's spent all his time away from here in Rossa's camp, while you fix the ship? Now that he knows that you know Marth is connected to Ashrem, he's been avoiding you."

"Why?" Tristam asked.

Zed looked at Tristam again, his gray eyes narrowing. "Listen, Tristam. Your employment with Dalan is based upon several important assumptions. There are things that you're better off not knowing, and things that he's better off not knowing that you know. Let's leave it at that."

"For a person dedicated to solving mysteries, you seem pretty intent on concealing the truth, Arthen," Tristam said. "What are you afraid I'll find out?"

"I could answer that question, but I think you'll regret it," Zed said.

"Tell me," Tristam said. "I need to know what's going on here. I need to know how Marth is connected to Ashrem."

"I can't really answer that," Zed said. "But I know how he's connected to Dalan."

"Dalan?" Tristam asked, surprised.

"Zed sighed. "Even back when Ash was alive, Dalan suspected that his uncle was onto some sort of big research. He was always sniffing around, trying to figure out what it was. After Ashrem disappeared, Dalan redoubled his efforts. He figured Ashrem's lost research would be his ticket to the respect he always deserved. Of course, the old man didn't trust his nephew enough to leave him any of his journals. Dalan was a war profiteer, after all, and Ashrem was a pacifist. So Dalan turned to me for help. I owed Dalan a few big favors from back in the war, so I agreed."

"You knew Dalan during the war?" Tristam asked. "Does that have something to do with you being a knight?"

"That happens to be none of your business," Zed said. "Anyway, he hired me to find out who had inherited Ashrem's journals. Seemed a pretty straightforward job. Then some of the journals started disappearing. Then people who owned them started disappearing. I looked into it, and found out that Dalan had been meeting with displaced Cyran soldiers in some of Wroat's shadier inns. I followed them one night after they left; the soldiers boarded *Moon* in the wilderness outside Wroat."

Tristam's frown deepened. "Dalan was working with Marth?" he asked.

Zed nodded. "For a while. I could tell that he didn't like it, though. I think he needed Marth's knowledge of artifice—and that's why he brought you on, Tristam. He needed a skilled, trustworthy artificer so that he could eventually sever his association with Marth."

Tristam absorbed the information.

"When Bishop Grove was murdered, that was the last straw," Zed said. "Dalan stopped meeting with Marth's agents, but by that time they didn't really need him anymore. Marth knew much more about the Legacy than Dalan did. I was disgusted by the entire affair, but I couldn't' expose Dalan. I owe him too much. So I made up a lame excuse to leave and went to live in Black Pit. I didn't want to be involved anymore."

Tristam frowned. "All this time I thought you just abandoned us," he said. "I'm sorry, Zed."

"Eh, you didn't trust me," Zed said with a shrug. "Nothing new to me. If it makes you feel any better, I don't really care what people think of me. No offense."

"So why did you come back to help us?" Tristam asked.

"Because now Dalan's trying to fix what he did," Zed said. "He knows how dangerous the Legacy is. I believe he really does want to stop Marth from unlocking its secrets and see that it's used responsibly. I didn't buy it at first, and that's why I warned you away from him, but I think he's sincere. I'd like to help him, if I can. I'm a big admirer of redemption. The only parts that still confuse me are how Dalan ever came into contact with Marth in the first place and how Marth commandeered *Kenshi Zhann*. Oh, and what in Khyber he's planning to do, of course."

"It worries me more that Marth keeps finding us everywhere we go," Tristam said. "Could Dalan still be working with him?"

"Doubtful," Zed said. "Marth was trying to kill us when he shot us down. My theory is that he has some other way of finding us that has nothing to do with Dalan . . . or anyone else that's been on board *Karia Naille*."

A shrill whistle came from the ship's deck above. Captain Pherris stood at the rail, pointing at the eastern sky with a grim expression. Tristam followed the gesture. At first he saw nothing, so he removed his spectacles. There was a subtle blur of movement in the sky. As it flew closer, it became more recognizable as a familiar glidewing bearing a tiny rider.

"The halfling came back alone?" Zed said, sounding worried. "Best see what's going on, Xain. I'll stay down here and make sure our hosts don't become too curious."

Tristam was already climbing back aboard the ship to wait by Blizzard's perch. With a swoop of leathery wings, the glidewing landed on the ship. The creature's rounded chest heaved with exhaustion. Gerith was nearly unconscious from his frenzied flight. He fell out of the saddle and stumbled toward Tristam. He dropped a heavy bag at the artificer's feet and then collapsed on the deck.

"From Seren," Gerith said, struggling to catch his breath. "Hide it before the Ghost Talons see."

"Where are the others?" Pherris asked.

Gerith explained as much as he could about how the others found Kiris and then were tracked by Rossa's hunters. Tristam felt a wild surge of emotions. He exulted that the clues he had sought for so long might be contained in the books and scrolls Gerith had brought, but he was terrified that Seren and Omax might be in danger.

"What do we do?" Gerith said, looking to Pherris.

"You get to your cabin and get some rest," Pherris ordered. "You're even more useless than normal when you're half dead."

"Aye, captain," Gerith said with a tired laugh.

"Meantime, we wait," Pherris continued. "I wouldn't be surprised if Seren and the others escape before Rossa's hunters can get them back to his village. If they do, we'll need Seren's help to sneak in and rescue Dalan."

Gerith gave a lazy salute and limped away to fall below decks and crawl to his cabin.

VOYAGE OF THE MOURNING DAWN

"Who says we need to rescue Dalan?" Tristam asked once the halfling was gone.

Pherris's fluffy brows lifted in surprise. "Where in Khyber did that come from?" he asked. "Pherris Gerriman does not leave his crew behind."

"Never mind," Tristam said. "I just learned some unsettling truths about Dalan."

"I see," Pherris said. "So I suppose the next time you're trapped on the roof of a building that you and your metal cohort have set aflame, I should pause to weigh the worth of your eternal soul before I come and rescue you?"

Tristam said nothing.

"Right, then," Pherris snapped. "I'll just pretend that you never said what you just said and we shall leave it at that, Master Xain." The captain turned smartly and marched off across the deck.

Aeven knelt nearby, hands folded demurely in her lap. She looked at Tristam with wide green eyes. "The ship is confused," she said. "*Karia Naille* is glad to see her sister again, but wants to know why the *Kenshi Zhann* wounded her so badly."

"I wish I knew, Aeven," Tristam said, shrugging helplessly at the dryad. He picked up the heavy sack of books in one hand and returned to his cabin.

For the next several hours he pored through Kiris Overwood's writings. They were notes on the Boneyard, quotes from the Draconic Prophecy, and copious sketches of magical constructions that Tristam could only assume were part of the Legacy. Unlike Ashrem's own journals, these weren't ciphered. It made little difference. Tristam retained none of it. The words were clear enough, but his mind was too distracted. Each time he sought to understand, his thoughts would trail inevitably to Marth, wondering at his connection to Ashrem, or to Dalan. He wondered how much the guildmaster had lied to him. He thought of Seren, worrying that she might have come to harm.

The sounds of the halfling laborers shouting at one another outside finally gave him the excuse to put aside the books and climb above deck.

"Master Xain, I need a word with you!" Pherris shouted just as Tristam emerged above deck.

He immediately noticed that the Ghost Talon halflings were in a hurry to leave. Some were rapidly packing their remaining supplies onto their mounts. Others were already running in the direction of their village on foot, holding weapons. Gerith and Zed stood at the edge of the deck, watching the halflings silently. Pherris was calibrating the ship's controls, ignoring the spectacle. Aeven sat cross-legged atop her figurehead, watching them all attentively.

"Master Xain, I need your expertise," Pherris said, not looking up from his work.

"What's going on?" Tristam asked.

"A scout just just arrived," Gerith said, looking at Tristam bleakly. "The *Kenshi Zhann* is attacking Ghost Talon village."

"Khyber," Tristam swore.

"Dalan is still there," Zed said, "and possibly the others as well."

"Master Xain, I've a mind to fly to that village and rescue our friends," Pherris said. The gnome captain marched toward Tristam, folding his arms behind his back as he paced across the deck. "I wonder if this ship is in any condition to survive such an adventure. What is your professional opinion?"

"She'll hold together," Tristam said. "As long as we don't push her too hard or take any more direct hits. We won't survive another battle with *Moon*."

"Thank you, Master Xain," Pherris said pertly. "Aeven, can you provide some sort of distraction when we reach the village?"

VOYAGE OF THE MOURNING DAWN

"I have called the storm," Aeven said in her soft, musical voice. "It will fight beside us." Overhead, the sky was already beginning to darken.

"Then let's see about our missing crewmates," Pherris said, stepping up to the ship's controls. "All hands, prepare for takeoff."

CHAPTER
TWENTY-THREE

The Ghost Talon encampment was engulfed in flame. Dozens of halflings ran past Seren as she approached the village, mostly fleeing on foot. Some carried bundles of possessions. Others carried injured friends or relatives. The occasional threehorn trundled past with a bleating cry. Many of the creatures had no riders, having broken free and stampeded away from the doomed settlement.

Hunters mounted on clawfoots either struggled to round up the fleeing dinosaurs or charged into the village to fight. The sleek silver shape of the *Kenshi Zhann* hovered above the spectacle. Plumes of lightning raked down from its bow, ravaging the village. Most of the Ghost Talons were not warriors, and those few who were had been no match for *Moon's* incredible firepower. A dozen charred bodies lay at the outskirts of the village, lying beside their dead steeds. Shrieks echoed through the night, punctuated by the crack of thunder in the distant sky.

Seren caught sight of Omax and Eraina at the edge of the village. Koranth and two of his hunters were surrounded by seven of Marth's heavily armed Cyran soldiers. The riders moved back to back, holding their spears defensively as they prepared to fight to the last.

VOYAGE OF THE MOURNING DAWN

"For Boldrei!" Eraina shouted defiantly and leapt into their midst. She whirled her spear in one hand and her short sword in the other, striking down one of the soldiers before the others even registered her presence.

Omax rumbled up beside her, his massive presence drawing immediate attention. One of the soldiers struck fiercely with his sword, striking the warforged across the chest with a shower of sparks. Omax shrugged off the blow and clapped his hands together heavily on each side of the man's head.

Koranth looked up in surprise. The halfling's anger that his prisoners had escaped was dispelled by a more practical reaction. "Ghost Talon warriors, to me!" he cried. His steed lunged forward, pinning another of the soldiers to the ground with one sharp claw. The other Cyrans a banded together, reappraising the situation now that the odds were not so clearly in their favor.

Seren ran forward to join her friends, dagger in hand, but a flash of lightning revealed an unexpected figure. Kiris Overwood was running into the village, heedless of the danger. Seren scowled. Had the wizard believed nothing that they had said? She'd expected at most that Kiris might simply run away once the others had left her behind, or that she might even help them fight Marth. Was she running back to join her mad hero? Seren hurried after her.

In the center of the village, the *Seventh Moon* had dropped a boarding ladder near Rossa's tent, which remained mostly intact. Cyran soldiers were already hurriedly climbing back up the ladder, back onto the ship. Kiris was headed directly for them when Seren seized her by the shoulder. The wizard whirled around, only to find Seren's dagger held near throat.

"Khyber, Kiris are you insane?" Seren asked. "Are you going back to him?"

"I have to, Seren," she said desperately. "I have to try. I know the prophet is the one doing this, the one twisting him. If I leave him, who will keep him from becoming a monster?"

"He's already a monster," Seren said.

"No, there's still hope," Kiris said. "He hasn't completed the Legacy yet."

Seren's eyes flicked past Kiris, toward the chief's tent. The tent flap opened and Marth and Dalan stepped out. Dalan looked angry but unafraid. Marth held his amethyst wand in one hand and gestured at the boarding ladder. Dalan began to climb.

"They're taking Dalan," Seren said.

"I can stop him," Kiris said, twisting away while Seren was distracted and running toward the tent. "I can reason with him!"

Several of Marth's Cyran soldiers turned with weapons ready as Kiris ran toward them. Seren was a step behind, feeling impotent with only her dagger. Marth turned, staring at them with his ghostly white eyes. Kiris halted in her tracks.

"Hold, do not attack!" he shouted to the soldiers. "Kiris?" he called out.

"Marth, what are you doing?" Kiris cried, eyeing the soldiers warily. "The halflings are no threat to you!"

"They harbored our enemies, Kiris," Marth said. "That makes them enemies."

"Kiris, get away from him," Seren warned as she crouched behind a pile of overturned crates.

"Seren?" Marth said with a faint sneer. "Is that you? You should have remained in Wroat, girl. Kiris, step away from the thief and join us. It is time to leave."

"Is what she said true, Marth?" Kiris asked, voice shaking. "Did you kill Llaine?"

Marth frowned. His smooth face creased in thought, as if weighing his reply.

"I am sorry, Kiris," he said.

A cone of green fire leapt from Marth's wand. Seren leapt away, rolling between two small abandoned wagons. The smell of burning flesh seared the air. Seren looked back to see a twisting, burnt corpse curled in the road where Kiris had stood. Kiris hadn't even had time to scream.

"Kill Seren Morisse," Marth commanded his remaining troops, then turned to board his ship as well.

Seren searched desperately for a better hiding place as three soldiers charged after her. Seren dropped and rolled under a wagon as two crossbow bolts struck the wood with a dull thunk. The storm that had been building during their approach arrived with a fury. The sky exploded in rain. Savage winds tore across the village and Seren thanked the Sovereign Host for whatever coincidence had brought the sudden storm.

Seren rolled to her feet on the other side of the wagon, only to find herself facing four more of the mercenaries. Disoriented by the sudden storm, they turned to face her sluggishly just as a peal of thunder rocked the sky.

No, not thunder, Seren realized as the soldiers looked past her in terror. She felt a looming presence behind her. It was the metallic roar of a warforged. Omax held the other halfling wagon over his head with both hands. With a heave, he hurled it at the soldiers. Eraina, Koranth, and a half dozen mounted Ghost Talon hunters rallied to her side as well. The remaining Cyran soldiers stood in a line, readying their weapons. A bolt of lightning hammered down from *Moon,* blowing the other wagon to splinters and boiling the rain. A second bolt reduced Rossa's tent to ashes.

"Retreat," Eraina called, scowling up at the airship. "We can't fight that airship!"

"Ghost Talons, take cover in the storm!" Koranth echoed, waving his javelin wildly.

Seren fell back, following the others just as the Cyrans withdrew to their ship. She followed the halflings into the shadows beyond the burning village.

"What about Dalan?" Seren shouted over the rain. She looked back over her shoulder to see the bright elemental ring of *Moon* lift into the sky and soar away.

"There is nothing we can do for him now," Omax said.

"What have you done?" Koranth said, staring hopelessly at his village. "What have you brought upon us?"

"Do not blame us for this, Koranth," Eraina said. "Blame Rossa."

"I was speaking to Rossa, curse his ghost," Koranth said. "How can the tribe recover from this loss?"

Just as the halfling's words faded, a second ring appeared in the sky above them, a blazing circle of familiar blue. As she saw the familiar figurehead in the center of the flame, Seren realized that perhaps the storm was no coincidence after all. *Karia Naille* swooped over the village, flying in broad circles as she surveyed the scene below. Seren ran to the center of the village, waving her hands wildly to get the captain's attention. The others followed her as well, including Koranth and his halflings.

The ship's boarding ladder spilled from the hull and Tristam slid down in a flash, sword in hand. Zed dropped beside him, moving a great deal more stiffly with his wounded leg but still holding his weapon with deadly purpose. Seren saw Aeven standing at the rail, her golden hair illuminated by lightning. The winds whirled around her, and she gazed down at the burning village with a strangely cold expression. The look in Aeven's eyes frightened Seren more than any obvious rage or fear ever could. Thunder cracked the sky again. Seren remembered Dalan's warning about Aeven's fierce temper.

"Seren, are you hurt?" Tristam asked.

"I'm fine," she said, running to his side and sheathing her dagger, "but they killed Kiris and took Dalan with them."

"What?" Tristam said, flustered. "Kiris is dead? And why they take Dalan?"

"He probably wants to know how much we know," Zed said. "Dalan's dead, or he will be when Marth is done questioning him. There's no way we can take on *Moon*, especially with our ship in the shape she is."

"Maybe not," Tristam mused. "In this storm, *Moon's* weapons won't be as accurate or affective. If we can catch up quickly enough, we can board and rescue him."

"It's suicide, Tristam," Zed said.

Tristam looked at the inquisitive. "Are you telling me I shouldn't try?"

"No," Zed said. "I'm with you. Just wanted to be clear."

"You know that even if we made it aboard, Marth's soldiers would kill us," Gerith said. "There are too many of them, and only eight of us. That's assuming we all board, of course, which would be stupid, since someone has to fly the ship."

"Koranth," Zed said, turning to the halfling warrior.

"I have heard everything, human," Koranth said. "You have your army, if it means the Ghost Talons have their revenge."

Koranth stepped from his saddle, holding his javelin in both hands. Behind him had gathered a dozen of the tribe's remaining hunters and warriors wielding whatever weapons they had salvaged from the village. Hatred burned in their eyes.

"Everyone aboard," Tristam said.

CHAPTER
Twenty-Four

"That way," Tristam said, pointing south through the raging storm.

Pherris nodded and urged *Karia Naille* to greater speed. Aeven crouched on the rail of the ship near her figurehead, oblivious to the howling wind. Though the rain fell in sheets all around them, the airship and her passengers remained dry. The deck was crowded with Koranth's halfling warriors and their glidewing steeds. The glidewings were agitated by the unfamiliar movement of the airship, so the halflings spent most of their time soothing the creatures. Blizzard glared disdainfully at the other creatures from his perch.

"We're getting closer," Tristam said. "Definitely straight ahead, Pherris."

"Pretty lucky that you happened to enchant something Dalan brought with him so that you could track him," Zed said.

"Nothing lucky about it," Tristam said, still staring into the storm. "I gave Dalan and everyone who went with him something so I could find them if something went wrong."

Seren's hand moved to the silver bracelet the artificer had given her. For a moment, their eyes met and he smiled at her.

Zed chuckled in approval.

"We need to hurry, Pherris," Tristam said. "I can't sense him if he gets too far away and *Moon* already has a lead on us."

"The ship can't give you much more, Tristam," the gnome said.

"I can," Aeven said softly. The dryad lifted her arms to the heavens and tipped her head back. The winds shifted and the storm built behind them, pushing the airship forward.

Tristam turned back to face the assembled crew. "Each of you take one of these," Tristam said. He opened a small pouch at his belt, taking out several glass vials and handing them to Seren, Eraina, Omax, and Zed.

"What are they?" Eraina asked, holding up the bottle and looking at the murky contents suspiciously.

"Leaping potions," Tristam answered. "The halflings have their glidewings, but we'll need these to get aboard *Moon* and back. Save them for now; they don't last long. And for the love of all that's holy, don't miss when you jump onto *Moon*."

"Will the potion work on Omax?" Seren asked, looking at the warforged dubiously.

"We are creatures of magic," Omax said. "We were built so that we could benefit from other such creations. I suspect that the only reason we were given mouths was so that we might drink potions."

"Can you board an airship with your leg, Zed?" Pherris asked.

"My leg is fine," Zed said, nodding briefly at Eraina. "Still a bit sore, but I wouldn't miss the chance to get even with those Cyran bastards for dropping an airship on me."

"All well and good, but do we have a plan beyond 'everyone jump and hope for the best?' " Eraina asked.

"I'm coming to that," Tristam said. "I lived on *Moon* for a while, so I have some idea what we're heading into." He took a roll of vellum from his cloak and unrolled it on the deck, revealing a detailed sketch of the *Kenshi Zhann*'s interior.

"What if Marth has changed the layout since he took the ship?" Eraina asked.

"Old information is better than nothing," Tristam said. "*Moon*'s lightning cannon is its main weapon, but it's front mounted. As long as Pherris keeps *Karia Naille* above and behind her, she won't be able to fire it at us. Our ship is more maneuverable than theirs, so that shouldn't be a problem. The Cyran soldiers will still have crossbows, but with Aeven's storm they'll have trouble hitting anything. We'll use the clouds to approach unseen and, once we get close, Gerith and Koranth will lead the glidewings down *Moon*'s main deck." He pointed at the diagram. "Once they've distracted the crew, the rest of us will leap onto the rear deck. Dalan is probably being held in one of the lower cabins, here." He pointed again. "Omax, Eraina, and Zed will fight their way there and retrieve him. Once you have him, leap back to *Karia Naille* and send off a flare so that the halflings know to break off combat and leave. We'll have the element of surprise and the Ghost Talons to help us, but with a ship as large as *Moon*, Marth's crew likely still outnumbers us. We can't afford to linger long. Wait ten minutes after we jump, Pherris. No longer. If anyone isn't back by then, assume the worst."

"And once we have Dalan back, what's to stop *Moon* from whirling about and firing that cannon at us?" Pherris asked.

"That's where Seren and I come in," Tristam said. He pointed at the map again. "Marth will expect that we've come to rescue Dalan as soon as he's aware of the attack, so Seren will help me sneak through the chaos into this room. This part of the lower cargo bay houses the main elemental containment chamber of *Moon*, the crystal housing that binds their elemental to this plane. While the rest of you do your part, Seren and I will sneak down there and I'll shatter the chamber. *Moon* will bleed out power fast and drift to the ground, crippled. Is all of that clear?"

The others all murmured their assent. Seren did likewise, impressed that Tristam could show such focus and leadership in a crisis.

"What do we do about Marth?" Gerith asked.

"Kill him," Zed said. "Not like he doesn't have it coming."

"Just do what you can, Gerith," Tristam said. "We're not really there to fight. Getting Dalan back and getting out safely is our real priority." He turned back toward the bow of the ship. "Now get ready, everyone. We're getting close."

A blur of light was visible in the distance, the glow of *Moon*'s elemental fire gleaming through the storm. Pherris turned the ship's wheel and *Karia Naille* soared skyward. Churning mist covered the deck as the ship pierced the clouds. It was bitterly cold up here. Seren felt her teeth begin to chatter. The clouds grew thicker, until eventually even *Moon*'s flaming ring could barely be seen.

"She's just below us now," Pherris said, and gestured to Gerith.

The halfling climbed onto his glidewing and shouted to the others. Koranth mounted his own steed and lifted his javelin in one hand. The creatures leapt from the deck, extending their wings with a synchronized snap. They soared down through the clouds, and soon after they vanished she heard Koranth's defiant cry.

"For the honor of the Ghost Talon!"

The sound of crashing steel and startled cries followed. Pherris worked the helm again and *Karia Naille* dipped down from the clouds. *Moon* appeared dangerously close, beneath and just ahead of them. Her forward deck was already covered with Cyran soldiers battling halfling hunters.

"Now!" Tristam said, tossing aside the cork from his potion and throwing back the contents.

Seren drank her potion, as did the others. She winced at the chalky taste, but she immediately felt lighter, more energetic.

"It's better with rum, but we were fresh out," Tristam said with a weak grin. "Just aim yourself at the other ship and jump. It's easier than it looks."

"Unless you miss," Zed said.

"Yeah," Tristam said. "Don't miss." He drew his sword and leapt from the deck.

Seren stood and watched for a brief, awestruck moment. Tristam soared through the air between the two ships, moving with eerie grace. Omax and Zed were next. The massive warforged and the stocky man with his large sword looked almost comical as they soared through the void. Eraina patted Seren's shoulder encouragingly and followed. Not allowing herself any more time to think about what she was about to do, Seren leapt from the ship's deck.

The wind rushed by with a keening howl. She felt weightless as she hung in the air, the distance so great it was difficult to tell she was moving at all. When she looked down, she saw only clouds. Then the moment was past, and she landed lightly on the deck of *Moon*. She looked back the way she had come, at *Karia Naille* hovering high above them.

"Don't worry," Tristam said. "We don't have to jump that. Pherris will move closer when he sees our signal."

"Unless we die," Zed said, hefting his sword with both hands.

"Yeah," Tristam said. "Don't die!"

Zed cackled. "Good luck, Xain."

"Good luck, all of you," Tristam answered as they stormed off across the deck. A Cyran soldier stepped around the corner and opened his mouth in alarm, but fell silent as a backhand slap from Omax sent him crashing limp into the wall.

"I have another sketch of the map if you need to see the way, Seren," Tristam said, reaching for his pocket.

"Memorized it," she said, moving past him and slipping through an open hatch in the deck.

She dropped into a darkened bay stacked with crates and barrels. The sounds of the storm and fighting were greatly muffled, interrupted only by the noisy thud of Tristam landing beside her. She gestured for him to wait and stalked ahead. The bay narrowed to a smaller passage. It was similar to the design of *Karia Naille*, albeit on a larger scale. She pressed herself between a beam and the wall just as one of the cabin doors opened, releasing three startled soldiers who ran past toward the upper deck, oblivious to her. Once they were gone, she gestured to Tristam and they moved down the passage.

A closed door led to the ship's central containment chamber, guarded by a single soldier. The guard held his sword in one hand, looking around nervously as he protected the door. Seren drew her dagger and looked at Tristam.

Tristam shook his head and stepped forward from the shadows. The guard whirled with a start just as Tristam hurled a handful of dust in the man's face. The guard blinked, staggered, and slumped to the floor.

"Only sleeping," Tristam said, examining the door. "These men are just soldiers, Seren. I don't want to kill them if we don't have to. They're only following Marth because they have nothing else left." He looked up at her. "I don't sense any wards on this door. Do you think you can pick the lock?"

Seren studied the lock briefly, then looked back the way they came. She cocked her head slightly, listening to the chaotic melee above. Seeing no one nearby, she stepped back and kicked the door sharply, jarring it off one hinge and shattering the lock. Tristam stared at her blankly.

"Picked," she said.

Tristam didn't argue. He hurried into the room beyond. The large chamber was filled with shining brass runes and shimmering crystals. A large square of the floor was transparent glass, displaying a murky purple cloudscape below them. A cylindrical black column stood in the center of the chamber, radiating heat.

"That's it," Tristam said. "That cylinder contains the crystal that binds the ship's elemental to this plane."

"What are you going to do?" Seren asked.

"Send her home," Tristam said. He took a small tube from his pocket and unfolded it into a four-foot ivory rod, engraved with runes and capped with a square of shimmering jade. He held the staff in both hands and closed his eyes, concentrating as he turned in a slow circle and concentrated on the crystal chamber.

"Why not just blast the housing with your wand?" Seren asked.

"Because that would just release the elemental into this room, not send her back to his home plane," Tristam said. "After years of servitude, they tend to be quite angry—and we don't want to be here for that."

Tristam opened his eyes when the door at the far side of the core chamber opened. Seren quickly darted behind the door, preparing to ambush whoever entered. A tall man in long purple robes stepped inside, long, white hair spilling over his shoulders. Tristam dropped the rod and quickly produced his ivory wand, releasing a bolt of crackling lightning at the changeling. When the smoke cleared, Marth was unharmed. An aura of magical power shimmered around him.

"Impressive but uncalled for, Tristam," the changeling said. "I was prepared for your coming, and I only wish to talk. Had I wanted to kill you, I would have left more soldiers here. After all, crippling the heart of my ship would have been your only real chance of escape."

Tristam's scowl faded, replaced by a look of startled recognition. "Your voice," he said. "Orren?"

"If it pleases you," Marth said. The changeling's features shifted to that of a thin young man with blonde hair tied back in a ponytail. "Orren Thardis is an old name, given by an old friend. I'd hoped to offer you the same thing Ashrem offered me—a new life."

"What are you talking about?" Tristam said, backing away.

"Dalan brought you into his quest only when he realized I would not be his pawn," Marth said. "When he realizes you are worthier than that, he will betray you as he betrayed me. He holds you back, Tristam. He forces you to underestimate your own talent because he fears that you will become something greater than he can control—just as he could never control his uncle. He wants you to waste your life waiting for an opportunity that will never come, and all the while he reaps the fruits of your genius."

"And why should I help you?" Tristam asked. "So I get to be an accessory to murder?"

Marth sighed. "I do not care if you help me, Tristam," he said. "I do not want you to help me. You are my friend, Tristam. I just want you to find your own destiny, and stay out of mine."

"What if I say no?" Tristam asked. "Will you kill me like you killed Kiris?"

Marth's grip tightened on his amethyst wand. "Zamiel was right," he said sadly. "This was a foolish luxury." He pointed the wand at Tristam.

As Seren pounced, she prayed to Kol Korran that Marth's magical shield didn't protect him from steel as well. Her prayers were answered. She felt steel sink into the changeling's back and heard him cry out in pain. Green fire sprayed wildly through the core chamber as Marth staggered into the wall. Seren rolled away, losing her knife.

Tristam darted in front of Marth, seizing and holding his wand ready.

"Your magic doesn't harm me, Tristam," Marth sneered, looking for his own lost weapon.

Without a word, Tristam turned and fired a bolt of energy into the ship's housing chamber. A guttural roar, full of triumph and anger, echoed through the *Kenshi Zhann*. Marth's eyes widened in fear as a creature woven of fire and rage rolled over him. The changeling vanished as the elemental filled the room. Tristam ducked under the blast, shattering the glass floor with his wand.

He leapt into the swirling void with Seren in his arms.

Chapter
Twenty-Five

For several minutes the storm winds howled around them. Tristam held Seren's waist tightly, so she gripped him firmly in return. Though she always thought she wasn't afraid of heights, she discovered she was quite afraid of falling from thousands of feet up. They didn't plummet as they should, but drifted, a feather. Seren didn't open her eyes again until she felt the ground beneath her feet.

Finding herself alive and standing on the soft grass of the Talenta Plains was a most welcome surprise. Seren relaxed her grip on Tristam, though she did not release him yet. She looked around in numb surprise, still shivering from the chill of the storm and the terror of their fall. In the sky far above she could see the twin rings of the two airships. One ring sped away across the sky at extraordinary speed. The other flickered and wavered as she slowly drifted toward the ground. Blue fire also crackled within the ring, as the angry elemental wreaked its vengeance on the *Kenshi Zhann*. The storm was swiftly dwindling to a light drizzle. The eastern sky glowed red with the haze of the coming sun.

"I doubt that when he gave me that ring, Orren intended me to use it like that," Tristam said, looking up sadly at the plummeting corpse of Ashrem's flagship.

"You could have reminded me about it before you jumped," Seren said, finally catching her breath enough to speak. "I didn't realize you could carry two people with it."

"Neither did I," Tristam said.

"What?" she said. She took a step back and glared at him.

"I'm joking!" Tristam said, holding his hands out defensively. "Mostly joking. I mean, theoretically I knew it would support the weight of another light person, but I never really had a chance to test it, and I thought stopping to ask what you weighed wouldn't have been wise."

"What would have happened if you were wrong?" she asked.

"I dunno," he said, tucking his wand back into his coat. "I guess I would have given you the ring and let go." He looked at her seriously.

"So what do we do now?" she asked, folding her arms across her chest.

"I don't know," Tristam said. "It looks like *Karia Naille* escaped." He pointed at the point of flame in the sky. "The others hopefully found Dalan and got back on board. If we can make our way to some sort of civilization and make contact with them, everything should be fine."

"But what about Dalan?" Seren asked. "Marth said that Dalan had been working with him."

"I'm not in the habit of taking lunatics at their word, even if they used to be friends," Tristam said. "Though I will admit it makes a certain amount of sense. If Dalan wanted to crack the secrets of the Legacy, it would make sense for him to turn to one of Ashrem's old partners. I guess when Marth proved to be a little too ambitious, Dalan turned to me instead. Wroat makes a great deal more sense to me now."

"How do you figure?" Seren asked.

"The way I see it is like this," he said. "Dalan was working with Marth, but turned his back on him when he realized

Marth was a killer. Later, he realizes that Marth is a great deal further along in his pursuit of the Legacy than we are. Dalan spreads rumors that he knows a little more about the Legacy than he ever let on, in the hopes that Marth will take the bait and give us a chance to track him. Marth is suspicious, so he hires Jamus to take the fall." Tristam sat down in the grass and smoothed his hair nervously. "Of course that's just a theory, but it looks like we've been lied to from the beginning. I need to talk to Dalan." He sighed. "I'm sorry, Seren. Sorry to have gotten you involved in this."

Seren looked up at the sky. "Do you think Marth is dead?"

"No," Tristam said. "I think he teleported away when the fire came for him. He's still out there, Seren. Still looking for the Legacy." Tristam shook his head slowly. "I have no idea how to stop him."

"We still have Kiris's notes," Seren said. "There has to be something to be learned there. Not to mention Dalan spent a good amount of time on Marth's ship. He must have learned something, especially if any of the soldiers made the mistake of talking to him."

Tristam chuckled. "That's true," he said. "Of course none of this solves our most pressing and immediate problem."

"What's that?" she asked.

"The others probably think we're dead," he said. He looked around at the vast plain, then back at her. "We have no idea where in Talenta we are. All I know is that the Valenar are to the south, the mountains are to the east, and the Mournlands is to the west."

"Then my suggestion," she said, standing up and offering her hand. "Is that we head north."

Tristam smiled, took her hand, and stood. Together, the artificer and the thief began their march across the plains.

Epilogue

Two Weeks Later, the City of Fairhaven

Shaimin loosened the garrote and let the old woman fall on the floor with a wet thud. He leaned back in the elegant mahogany chair where she had been doing her knitting only a moment before. The slim elf rested his chin on one hand as he looked at the corpse. It was almost disappointing. None of the guards had been paying attention. The windows had not been sealed, warded, or locked. He even gave the old woman a chance to see his reflection in the mirror. She didn't yell for help. She didn't have a knife. She only gaped in surprise. Now it would likely be several hours before anyone even found her.

In. Out. Eberron has one fewer duchess. Shaimin's bank account anonymously receives enough gold to feed a poor family for two years.

The gold didn't matter, of course. He had enough to live quite comfortably for the rest of his life. That was all most assassins dreamed of, but then most assassins had no sense of style, no understanding of why they killed. Their greed drove them to prison or to early graves. They had no appreciation for the hunt, no appreciation of the skills required to perform a task well.

Shaimin drummed his fingers impatiently on the arm of the chair. All that time wasted brooding, and still no guards had arrived. Well, he refused to make any more purposeful mistakes merely to make his evening more interesting. He had a reputation to maintain. That didn't make the boredom any less galling. If these assassinations didn't swiftly prove to be more challenging, Shaimin feared that he might well have to enter a more interesting line of work. Perhaps politics? He already had plenty of contacts.

With a heavy sigh, Shaimin d'Thuranni sauntered back to the window and bounded across the rooftops of Fairhaven. He moved with animal grace, traveling with no undue noise or hesitation, drawing no notice from the citizens in the street. When he felt he was sufficiently distant from the duchess's house as to draw little suspicion, he paused and concentrated on the elaborate dragonmark scrawled across his shoulder blades. His senses expanded from his body, giving him a view of the alley below as if he were there. Confident that no undue bystanders were watching, he dropped gracefully to the ground. He smoothed his black silken cloak over his shoulders with a feline fastidiousness, pursing his lips in frustration.

"Do you plan to follow me for the rest of the evening?" Shaimin asked. "Or are you quite satisfied with what you have seen?"

"I am quite satisfied," was the answer. The air rippled. A robed figure appeared from nothing. He was a tall, pale-skinned humanoid with pink burns on one side of his face.

"Hello, Shaimin.".

Shaimin moved his finger off the trigger of the small crossbow he held beneath his cloak. A smile split his pale features. "Thardis," he said with a malevolent grin. "I never believed you were dead. It is good to see you again."

"My name is Marth," the changeling replied. "I am pleased to see you as well, though I fear I am not here to renew old friendships."

"I thought as much," Shaimin said, his interest piqued. "A friend wouldn't spy on me while at work; he'd just meet me at the theater afterward. You wished to ensure that my skills had not deteriorated since last we met."

"And I am not disappointed, Shaimin," Marth said.

"I should hope not," Shaimin said stiffly. "This is regarding Ashrem's legacy?"

The changeling nodded.

"Then walk with me," the elf said, gesturing to the road. "Let us speak of old friends and unfinished business . . ."

ENTER THE NEW WORLD OF

THE DREAMING DARK TRILOGY

By Keith Baker

A hundred years of war...

Kingdoms lie shattered, armies are broken, and an entire country has been laid to waste. Now an uneasy peace settles on the land.

Into Sharn come four battle-hardened soldiers. Tired of blood, weary of killing, they only want a place to call home.

The shadowed City of Towers has other plans...

THE CITY OF TOWERS
Volume One

THE SHATTERED LAND
Volume Two

THE GATES OF NIGHT
Volume Three
DECEMBER 2006

For more information visit **www.wizards.com**

EBERRON, WIZARDS OF THE COAST and their respective logos are trademarks of Wizards of the Coast, Inc. in the U.S.A. and other countries. © 2006 Wizards of the Coast

ENTER THE NEW WORLD OF

THE WAR-TORN

After a hundred years of fighting the war is now over, and the people of Eberron pray it will be the Last War. An uneasy peace settles over the continent of Khorvaire.

But what of the soldiers, warriors, nobles, spies, healers, clerics, and wizards whose lives were forever changed by the decades of war? What does a world without war hold for those who have known nothing but violence? What fate lies for these, the war-torn?

THE CRIMSON TALISMAN

BOOK 1

Adrian Cole

Erethindel, the fabled Crimson Talisman. Long sought by the forces of darkness. Long guarded in secret by one family. Now the secret has been revealed, and only one young man can keep it safe.

THE ORB OF XORIAT

BOOK 2

Edward Bolme

The last time Xoriat, the Realm of Madness, touched the world, years of warfare and death erupted. A new portal to the Realm of Madness has been found — a fabled orb, long thought lost. Now it has been stolen.

IN THE CLAWS OF THE TIGER

BOOK 3

James Wyatt

BLOOD AND HONOR

BOOK 4

Graeme Davis

For more information visit **www.wizards.com**

EBERRON, WIZARDS OF THE COAST and their respective logos are trademarks of Wizards of the Coast, Inc. in the U.S.A. and other countries. © 2006 Wizards of the Coast